To Taste
the Wine

FERN MICHAELS

To Taste the Wine

KENSINGTON BOOKS
www.kensingtonbooks.com

KENSINGTON BOOKS are published by

Kensington Publishing Corp.
119 West 40th Street
New York, NY 10018

All Kensington titles, imprints, and distributed lines are available at special quantity discounts for bulk purchases for sales promotion, premiums, fund-raising, educational, or institutional use.

Special book excerpts or customized printings can also be created to fit specific needs. For details, write or phone the office of the Kensington Special Sales Manager: Kensington Publishing Corp., 119 West 40th Street, New York, NY 10018. Attn. Special Sales Department. Phone: 1-800-221-2647.

Kensington and the K logo Reg. U.S. Pat. & TM Off.

ISBN-13: 978-0-7582-4274-7
ISBN-10: 0-7582-4274-3

First Kensington Trade Paperback Printing: March 2011
10 9 8 7 6 5 4 3 2 1

Printed in the United States of America

Chapter 1

There was a bite of oncoming winter in the air, and a chill wind gusted down the narrow, poorly lit alley. Chelsea Myles shrank from the noisy scurrying of rats and tried to ignore the stench from the open sewer. The brick walls of the adjacent buildings were dripping with green mold and moisture, and she shivered involuntarily, looking down to avoid the sight. One of her shoes, thin-soled and worn, was soaked from a careless step into a puddle.

It had rained again. It always seemed to rain. Chelsea curled her full upper lip and scowled. Rain and dampness only added to the mildew rotting her cheaply made stage costumes. Already there were times on stage when it was almost impossible to say her lines without sneezing or choking. Angrily, she kicked the aged trunk by her side and gasped in dismay when one of the slats split, revealing its contents. She just *knew* Uncle Cosmo had no tools or expertise to repair the trunk. This would be just one more inconvenience to tolerate.

Chelsea crossed her arms over her breasts and stamped her foot. What was she, a respectable, dedicated stage actress, doing with Cosmo's fifth-rate troupe, playing for pennies at local street fairs? Unlike the others, she came by her talent naturally, memorizing lines, with comprehension and ease. Yes, she was too good for this, much too good—and Uncle Cosmo had no right to keep belittling her talent. Chelsea bristled as she remembered how he'd told her she should stop fooling herself and recognize that it was her face and not her ability that made her a favorite with the audience, especially the male audience. "Chelsea, darling child," he would declaim, posturing dramatically whenever she complained about the costumes, "an actress of *real* ability could wear flour sacking and convince the audience that she was Queen Elizabeth herself!"

"And what would *he* know about actresses?" Chelsea grumbled, pushing the various articles back through the hole in the trunk. "All Uncle Cosmo wants is a big street audience so he can have their pockets picked while I mesmerize the poor, dumb fools." She thought again with distaste of the scanty costumes Cosmo demanded she wear, which revealed either too much cleavage or leg. She sniffed, feeling terribly sorry for herself. At twenty-three, she wasn't getting any younger; Uncle Cosmo, who had taken her under his wing at eleven when she was orphaned, had promised that by the age of twenty she'd be a famous actress with all of Europe at her feet. Fool that she was, she'd believed him. She was no smarter than the homely widows Cosmo romanced and cheated out of their money.

Her self-pitying reminiscences were interrupted when Uncle Cosmo's latest protégée ran into the alley. Molly was an urchin, pure and simple. She could barely speak the King's English, but Cosmo had promised to make her an actress. More likely, Chelsea thought with an unladylike snort, he'd make Molly a slick little pickpocket. "Molly, slow down!" she cried sharply. "Watch you don't splash muddy water on my skirts!"

"Yes, miss, but Mr. Perragutt told me to tell you something, and he said to do it right away, like. It's urgent, it is!"

"There's nothing Uncle Cosmo could tell me that's urgent unless it's that the queen herself has come to watch our performance this evening." A sudden jolt of panic stiffened Chelsea's spine. "It's not the law, is it, Molly? I told Uncle Cosmo he'd gone too far when he marked the constable's wife for Swift Billy to snatch her purse!"

"No, no, nothin' like that, Miss Chelsea," Molly assured her importantly. "Mr. Perragutt said there's a real gent in the audience tonight. Worth a few pounds, by the look of him, he is. Mr. Perragutt said he could be very important to all of us."

"Important for the sake of his wallet, he means. And whoever he is, he's no gentleman if he's come slumming to this part of London to watch a sad lot like ourselves."

Molly seemed disappointed in the way Chelsea received her news. "Anyways, Mr. Perragutt said you'd know what to do."

"Uncle Cosmo means that while I'm on stage I should make an effort to capture the man's attention so Swift Billy can do his work, that's the beginning and end of it," Chelsea told her disgustedly. "Wake up, Molly, get your head out of the clouds. You're a nice girl; you don't belong with Uncle Cosmo and the rest of us."

"I don't want my head out of the clouds, Miss Chelsea. I like it up here, and I know if I do everything Mr. Perragutt says, someday I'll be just as grand and important as you are. You're a stage star, miss. I know I'll never be beautiful like you, but Mr. Perragutt said he's goin' to make me into a lady, a *real* lady! Mr. Perragutt said you'll teach me everything he taught you. You will, won't you, Miss Chelsea?"

Chelsea sighed inwardly. What was the point in hurting Molly's feelings? Still, genuine pity and concern prompted her to say kindly, "Molly, Uncle Cosmo is a crooked little weasel, and I hate to admit I'm related to him by blood. He's going to get us all a stay in jail if we don't keep our wits about us. He's right about one thing, though. I'm going to make something of myself one of these days. *If* I can keep two steps ahead of the law, that is."

"Oh, Miss Chelsea, you're such a lady. All nice manners and so refined like. I want to be just like you, putting on airs and walking so dainty. And when some of them men out front get familiar with you, I love the way you stop them dead with just a quirk of your eyebrow. Can you teach me, Miss Chelsea?" Molly asked, looking wistfully at her idol. "Can you?"

"Becoming a lady is a very noble ambition, Molly, and you could do worse, I suppose, than to model yourself after me," Chelsea replied after a moment's deliberation. "The first thing you have to do to be a lady is to tell Uncle Cosmo an emphatic no when he sets up a mark for you tonight. Look him right in the eye and tell him you have too much honor and character to stoop to thievery. You tell him right to his face you'd rather starve than steal."

"But I don't like bein' hungry, Miss Chelsea," Molly whined. "You've got your honor and character already, so I suppose you didn't mind it too much."

Chelsea glanced at Molly, then quickly looked away. She thought about the times she'd been hungry—starving really—but even worse was the loneliness and the fear. And at the tender age of eleven, she hadn't known which was worse. It all seemed so long ago, almost as if it had happened to someone else in another life. But it hadn't. The dirty, ragged child who had hidden in alleyways and cellars was herself.

Her memories were sharp, painful, and there were times, like now, when they returned in a sudden rush, like the sea overcoming the shore, obliterating the present and returning her to the past.

She had lived then in a section of London bordering Knightsbridge. Mum and Da had a little shop just off Candlewick Street where they sold dry goods and notions and Mum's home-baked pastries and freshly preserved jams. If Chelsea closed her eyes, she could smell the wonderful aromas coming from the kitchen behind the shop; she could still hear Da's booming voice as he welcomed a familiar face into the shop.

"Will there be anythin' else?" Da would ask as he licked the tip of his pencil before tallying up the bill. Chelsea liked to sit near him behind the counter, the sun streaming in through the shop window to warm her even on the coldest winter day. Warmer than the sun was Da's smile, and the way he'd wink at her to jump down from her stool and run to open the door for a cash customer.

She was an only child, a rarity in Knightsbridge, where the families numbered nine or ten, often even more. And she was spoiled, or so it was said—nurtured on love and rewarded with candy. Mum was handy with a needle, and Chelsea's dresses were never too short or shabby. The newest dimities and lisle wools hung in her room, and Da saw to it that she had two new pairs of shoes every year. Her coats were the warmest, and Mum always knitted her a new pair of gloves. Chelsea was possibly the best-dressed child in the little academy school at the end of Saul's Lane, except perhaps for the undertaker's daughters, who weren't very pretty in spite of their costly dresses. But even more precious than the security and comfort Mum and Da offered were their love and approval, something she hadn't appreciated until too late. . . .

"You're a good girl, Chelsea." Trudie Myles smiled weakly at her daughter. "I'll be up and about tomorrow for certain. It's just a cold that's got me so low."

"Da says you're to drink this tea, and in a bit he'll come in and bring you a coddled egg." Chelsea placed the cup on the bedside table and began to fuss with her mother's pillows. Mum's eyes were bright with fever, and the little girl could hear the rasping in her mother's chest whenever she tried to take a deep breath. "Da says the doctor will be around this afternoon."

"It's just a cold. He shouldn't fuss so much. I'll be up and about tomorrow, you'll see."

Chelsea accepted her mother's reassuring smile, but she shared her Da's worry. Over the last month several of their neighbors had died, old and young alike. They were blaming it on the night air that rolled in from the outlying marshes at this time of the year; Reverend Lipcott said it was God's way of bringing the faithful back to heaven. Chelsea wasn't so certain Reverend Lipcott was right. Old man Stifel had died of the fever, and everyone knew God would have no use for the likes of him up in heaven.

Mum died of the fever two nights later, the same night Da began coughing and complaining of pains in his chest and head. When the doctor came to make the death pronouncement, he looked at Jonathan Myles and shook his head. Several days later Chelsea realized the doctor had made two death pronouncements that night.

All of London was in a panic because of the epidemic. When Jonathan died, his creditors came to the shop and confiscated stock in payment for outstanding bills. As word spread quickly, the shop shelves were rapidly depleted. A man from Whitehall held court in Da's shop, checking through the ledgers and awarding settlements to the creditors.

Chelsea couldn't begin to understand it all. Engulfed in her grief, she huddled in the room at the back of the shop and listened dully to the transactions. No one paid her the least amount of attention, and even she hadn't given a thought to her future until she heard her name mentioned by the man from Whitehall.

"Chelsea Myles. Do you know of any living relative who might take the child in?" He was speaking to Mrs. Cavendish, the mother of eight children.

"I know Trudie has a brother somewhere," the woman responded thoughtfully. "Some kind of an actor or something. Trudie was quite proud of him, although Johnny wouldn't ha' given a pence for the likes of him. Can't say I'd know where he is. Poor Chelsea, she's a sweet little thing, you know. I'd take her, but we've hardly enough to feed the eight we have, you understand."

"If someone doesn't come forward for the child before tomorrow, she'll be taken to St. Matthew's Home," the man from Whitehall told Mrs. Cavendish. "The landlord wants to take the shop back. He already has another tenant. Can't blame the fellow. An empty shop doesn't bring in the rent, does it?"

"No. But I'd hate to see that little girl go to St. Matthew's. It's hardly an orphanage, is it? More a poorhouse. They'll put her to work God knows where. Perhaps I could take her for a night or two, just until her uncle shows up."

The man shook his head firmly. "I'm sorry, Mrs. Cavendish, but the notice has been put in the newspapers and the man hasn't come forward. I've seen things like this before, and mark my words, it's best to deal with it straight from the beginning. Someone from St. Matthew's will be here in the morning."

"Well, keep your voice down," Mrs. Cavendish warned. "We don't want the poor thing to hear, do we? Bad enough she's lost her mum and da and her life will never be the same. We don't want to put a fright to her when tomorrow's soon enough."

Chelsea huddled against the closed door. She hadn't washed her face for more than a week, and now tears streaked her cheeks, creating rivulets of white against the grime. "A fright," Mrs. Cavendish had said. Nothing could be more frightening than losing the only people in the world who cared about you. The only family, except for Uncle Cosmo, Mum's only brother, whom she hadn't seen in a dog's age. And now they were talking about sending her to St. Matthew's. Chelsea knew exactly what that meant; the children teased one another about it when they wanted to be mean. St. Matthew's, the poorhouse, where people died and never had enough to eat, and where you lived and worked and were sent out to service.

Chelsea pressed her knuckles against her teeth. She didn't want to die! She didn't want to lie in the cold ground like Mum and Da! Where was Uncle Cosmo? Why hadn't he come to his only sister's funeral, and why hadn't he come forward to take her away before St. Matthew's took her?

She crawled away from the door, through Mum's kitchen and back to the alcove where Mum and Da had slept. Beside the window was a trunk where Mum kept her things; "little memories," she liked to call them—all the papers Chelsea brought home from school and the family Bible and letters and newsprint. The thin, yellowed newspaper clippings mostly concerned Cosmo Perragutt, Trudie Myles's brother, an actor with a theater company in London's Cheapside.

Chelsea snuffled as she dug through the trunk looking for the clippings. She wouldn't go to St. Matthew's poorhouse, never in a million years. If Uncle Cosmo didn't come for her, then she'd go to him. He had to be in London somewhere, and she'd find him. She wiped her tears, smearing the grime on her cheeks. Her long black lashes were star points, wet and glistening, and her pink lips moved as she read through the clippings, searching for the latest one.

Even as she searched, Chelsea had the vague feeling she was doing something wrong, something Da wouldn't have liked. He'd never thought much of Uncle Cosmo, and whenever his extravagantly mannered brother-in-law made one of his rare visits to his sister, Da's face would darken and his smiling mouth would grow tense and hard, as though he were biting his tongue. Mum made it a point not to mention her brother in front of Da unless it was necessary.

Yes, all the signals were there. Da hadn't much use for Mr. Cosmo Perragutt and disliked him the same way he disliked some of the salesmen who came to the shop with their courtly manners and cheap wares. But Chelsea was certain that Mum wouldn't have cared for her brother as much as she did or have been so happy to see him whenever he came by if at heart he wasn't a good, kind man. It was that kindness Chelsea depended upon now.

Later that evening Mrs. Cavendish came to the back door with a supper tray for Chelsea. The meat pasty and slab of buttered bread tempted the girl's appetite, and the mug of cider looked cool and refreshing.

"I don't know why you insist on staying down here in the cold," Mrs. Cavendish clucked maternally. "God knows the place is forbidding enough with the shelves stripped and the floor bare. Come upstairs to the flat, Chelsea. You'll have the other children for company, and there's a fire in the grate to warm your bones."

Longingly, Chelsea envisioned herself playing with her friends in front of a cheerful fire. But she knew Mrs. Cavendish would insist on her staying the night, tucking her into bed beside little Anna, and then she'd be trapped until they came to take her to St. Matthew's in the morning. "Thank you, Mrs. Cavendish," she replied after a moment, "but I'm fine where I am."

Mrs. Cavendish frowned, her hands clasped over her round belly. "I wish you would, Chelsea. Your mum would want you to be warm and cozy. She was a good woman, your mum, and your da had the way of a gentleman, I always said." An expression of sorrow crossed the woman's face. "Well then, I've got to be gettin' back to my own brood. If you change your mind, you're welcome."

Chelsea listened for Mrs. Cavendish to close the door

behind her before she bit into the steaming pasty and tore into the bread. She'd had nothing to eat since morning, and she was ravenous. After her supper, she washed her face and hands and smoothed her hair, giving the first thought to her appearance in days. All her clothes, except for what she was wearing and one of her oldest coats, had been confiscated for debts. When she left the shop for the last time, she closed the door firmly behind her, confident that she would soon find her uncle and thus escape the fate of St. Matthew's.

Unfortunately, finding someone in a city the size and scope of London was not as easy as Chelsea's eleven-year-old optimism had led her to believe. It took her nearly three days of wandering city streets before she even reached the Cheapside area. She was so frightened the man from Whitehall might be searching for her that she hesitated to ask the most likely-looking adults for directions, thus limiting her inquiries to beggars and children hardly older than herself. The first night after leaving the shop, she wandered the streets all night long, afraid of the darkness and, worse, of the blackened alleyways, from which came terrifying grunts and hushed voices. The second day, too exhausted to walk any farther, she stopped to rest in the warming sunshine beside a butcher's shop. She fell asleep, but before long a man's boot prodded her awake and a rough voice began yelling about dirty little ragamuffins laying about the doorway of his respectable business.

Hungry, tired, dirty, and cold, Chelsea continued her search on the third day, until by some sort of miracle she found herself standing under the marquee of the Briarside Theatre. It was the middle of the afternoon, and everything was locked up tight; when she knocked timidly upon the great brass-inlaid double doors, there was no answer.

"Whatcha doin' hangin' about here?" asked a voice behind her. "I never seen you here before."

Chelsea turned to find a tall youth squinting down at her. He attempted a smile, a slender wooden pick clamped between his teeth and jutting out of the side of his mouth.

"I asked whatcha doin' around here?" he repeated, stepping in front of her, barring her path when he sensed she was about to run away. Chelsea judged him to be several years older than herself—about fifteen. Long, fine hairs curled softly on his chin in a charade of a beard, and she soon realized his squint was more a part of his overall expression than a sensitivity to the sunlight. His clothes were shabby, too large, and the woolen gloves on his hands only covered his palms; the fingers poking through the knitted wool were ringed with dirt, and his nails badly needed clipping.

"I . . . I was looking for my uncle," she stammered, feeling threatened by the way he blocked her path.

"Just like I'm waitin' for me mum." The youth smiled sarcastically. "And me da is the Queen of England," he added bitterly. 'You're a runaway. I can see it plain as the nose on yer face. Who're you runnin' away from? Maybe I can help. Maybe somebody'll pay to get yer back."

Chelsea backed away. "I am not a runaway! I'm looking for my uncle."

The youth smiled again, and something about it reminded Chelsea of a picture in Mum's Bible, the one in which the serpent is tempting Adam and Eve with the forbidden apple.

"I know a runaway when I sees one. You ain't from Cheapside, cuz I knows everyone from here. Yer clothes ain't clean and they don't fit too good, but they was cut from good wool jus' the same. It was yer shoes that told me you ain't from here and that you're a runaway. Good shoes. Too good for Cheapside."

"Let me go, let me pass!"

"That's another thing, the way you talk. Nah, you're a

runaway fer certain. I'm Jack Hardy." He made the announcement with a certain sense of pride. "I know everything that goes on here in Cheapside, that's how come I know you don't belong here." Quicker than thought, his hand shot out and seized her wrists, pulling her against him and then turning her so her back was to the wall. She could smell the onions on his breath and see the angry red pimples dotting his chin. "How much money have yer got?" he demanded. "Runaways always have a few bob to tide them over."

Chelsea shook her head, frightened half out of her wits. No one had ever treated her this way; no one had ever frightened her like this, not even the man from Whitehall, not even the thought of St. Matthew's. She struggled, trying to wrench free. "I don't have any money, not a penny. Let me go! Let me go!"

From around the corner swaggered a group of youths—a gang, really. When they saw Jack and Chelsea they began to jeer and snicker:

"Hey, boss, catch yer supper, did yer?"

"Whatcha got there, Jack? Caught yerself a pigeon, eh?"

For an instant Chelsea had hoped she'd be rescued; then she realized these were Jack's friends, and they obviously admired him. Their cruel taunts and sneering expressions were directed at her, and they reminded her of a pack of hungry dogs.

"Got myself a little runaway here," Jack announced, his tone now gruff and hard, more of a growl. The little hairs on the back of Chelsea's neck lifted and prickled. She knew she had to save herself; she had to get away from Jack Hardy and his street gang.

"Think we'll get ourselves a reward for turnin' her in, Jack?"

"Nah! Look at her. She ain't worth much as the rags she's wearin'. Who'd pay to get the likes of this pigeon back? My guess is she's run away from service or some-thin'. But I'll bet she's got a penny or two stashed on her somewhere." He pulled viciously on her wrists, enjoying the wince of pain that flashed across her face.

The boys laughed, poking at her, trying to riffle through her coat pockets. "Let me go! Let me go!" Chelsea cried, trying desperately to free herself. There were other people walking the street—vendors, women with market baskets, a man sweeping the sidewalk in front of his shop. Would no one listen? Didn't anyone care? Wouldn't anyone help her?

Jack saw the direction of her glance and looked over his shoulder. Apparently he wasn't completely confident that no one would step forward to help her, because he heaved her away from the wall and pushed her in the direction of a nearby alleyway. For an instant, Chelsea felt him loosen his grip on her wrists. Taking the only chance she might ever have, she kicked him, hard, the toes of her shoes nip-ping his shins and cracking his knee. Jack howled in pain, and Chelsea broke away.

Running, dodging pedestrians, she bolted out into the street almost under the legs of a peddler's horse. She screamed in fright, but to her, at that moment, nothing was more frightening than Jack Hardy and his gang. They were coming after her, shouting for her, hooting and cater-wauling, sounds that made her blood freeze.

Although soon out of breath, she kept running, her legs burning with strain, the muscles exhausted. Ahead of her she saw the dark shadows of an alley between two build-ings that could have been warehouses. Knowing only that she couldn't run another step, Chelsea dodged into the alley, wailing with fright and defeat when she realized there was no access to the next street. She was trapped, and the sounds of thudding feet were close behind her. Wild with terror, she crawled into the shadows and huddled in the recess of a cellar window, her only cover the gloom and a pair of ash cans. Biting back the sobs tearing at her throat, she listened, her eyes squeezed shut in horrible anticipation of being discovered.

"I know she went in here, Jack! I seen 'er when we rounded the corner. She's here, I know it."

"No, I seen 'er dodge around t'other way," someone else insisted. Barrels clattered and cans were tipped over as the youths conducted their search.

"She ain't here, Jack, I tell yer. We're wastin' time while she's gettin' away!"

An eternity later, after the gang had toppled garbage and ash cans and left the blind alley, Chelsea huddled where she was, curling into as small a space as possible. Tears coursed down her cheeks; self-pity and fright and loneliness roiled her innards. And it took her a long, long time to gather enough courage to come out of her hiding place.

If she were ever to find Uncle Cosmo, it would have to be soon. Chelsea was coming to realize that life behind the shop with Mum and Da had not prepared her for this kind of savage existence. When Jack Hardy had had her pinned against the wall and she'd screamed for him to let her go, no one had intervened. People had been walking the street; shopkeepers had been sweeping their walks; women had been walking from market; all had seen what Jack was doing, yet none had stepped forward. And now she was so frightened she even thought about returning to Knightsbridge, considered going to St. Matthew's. Instinctively, however, Chelsea knew no one would save her there, either.

No. Her only hope was Uncle Cosmo.

Life was a muddle of confusion and fear for Chelsea. Several days had passed since the incident with Jack Hardy and his friends. She learned to be careful, traveling the streets in the early morning or late afternoon hours, sleeping in doorways, begging for a crust of bread. She walked all over Cheapside, finding every theater in the area, asking for Cosmo Perragutt at box offices and back doors. She learned to be watchful, wary of groups of people, wary of her own vulnerability. People at the theaters said they'd heard of her uncle, but no one seemed to know where he was at the moment. Someone told her he might have gone to France with a theatrical company. Dispirited, defeated, but having nowhere to go, Chelsea continued her search. Walking the streets and asking after her uncle became her religion, her only hope.

One day, more than two weeks later, Chelsea took a walk down to the wharf, one of her favorite evening haunts. There was a fresh produce market by the docks; after hours, fruit, stale bread, and sometimes hot soup were distributed by a group of uniformed men who called themselves the Salvation Army. Chelsea had found that if she listened to their music and their preaching, they could be counted upon for a scant supper. It was late November now, and flurries of snow had already fallen over the city. The cold was bone-chilling and nothing was more welcome than a cup of hot soup and a slab of bread.

This time, however, she took a new route down to the wharf and came across a dilapidated, ramshackle building bearing a hand-lettered sign: BLEDSOE THEATERHOUSE PRESENTS PERRAGUTT AND COMPANY IN "ROMEO AND JULIET."

Chelsea stopped dead in her tracks, reading the sign over and over again. Could it be? Dare she hope? She'd begun to think that her Uncle Cosmo didn't exist, that he was merely a figment of her imagination.

Hesitantly, Chelsea went around to the stage door and knocked. A man with a long black cigar stuck his head out. "Excuse me, sir," she said weakly, "can I find a Mr. Cosmo Perragutt here?"

The door opened wider, and she could feel the relative warmth touching her face. She stepped in, realizing it was the first time she'd been under a roof in almost a month.

"He's in there, girlie," the man with the cigar said gruffly. "Just bang on the door and go in."

Chelsea approached the closed door. Inwardly she was praying, her lips, blue with cold, moving to her silent plea. Taking a deep breath, she knocked timidly and turned the knob.

Sitting in front of a mirror was a short, portly man. He was applying a false beard to his chin, and the spirit gum vapor filled her nostrils. He glanced up into the mirror, half turning in his chair.

"Uncle . . . Uncle Cosmo?" she asked in an agony of anticipation, a desperate mixture of hope and disbelief. "I'm Chelsea, Chelsea Myles, and I've come such a long way to find you. Please be my Uncle Cosmo, please."

Forcing her thoughts back to the present, Chelsea regarded young Molly in front of her, so like the hungry, defenseless urchin she'd been when Uncle Cosmo had taken her in years ago. The thought of that hunger and just how few coins she contained in her purse made her capitulate. "All right, Molly, one wallet and that's all. You really shouldn't let Uncle Cosmo take advantage of you this way. I suppose it will be all right, as long as you don't keep the money solely for your own benefit. Perhaps you'd better bring it to me." She hated doing this to Molly; her own parents had brought her up for better things than this. Living off ill-gotten gains never sat well with her, but with winter coming there didn't seem to be any other way. Heaven knew the ticket receipts from Uncle Cosmo's productions would hardly keep a bird alive.

"But what about Mr. Perragutt?" Molly asked plaintively. "He said I was to share with him or there wouldn't be enough to get by and everyone would have to do without their wages this month."

Chelsea grimaced. The old rotter, there was enough stashed in his trunk to take them all to the south of France this winter. But getting him to part with it was another matter entirely.

As a child she'd worshiped him as her savior; as a woman she knew far too much about the man to suffer under any false illusions. Gratitude had little to do with reality.

"Molly, you disappoint me. Did you think I wouldn't take care of you? You just bring whatever you have to me, and I'll see it's shared fairly between us." Let Uncle Cosmo starve, as if he would. "Trust me, Molly, trust me. We might even get down to Brighton before winter sets in. You're always talking about never having seen Brighton. And Lord knows I'm due for a rest."

Molly was elated; there actually seemed to be a flush of color in her thin white cheeks. "Oh, Miss Chelsea! You're too kind to me! Too kind! I'll do just what you say, I will. Now if I can just remember my lines for tonight, I'll consider myself lucky." An anxious expression crossed her face. "My stage paint! I know I'll make a mess of meself . . . myself," she corrected when Chelsea raised an eyebrow of admonition.

"I'll help you if you like," Chelsea offered generously, pitying the girl. No amount of makeup would erase the pinched, shriveled look that years of poverty and deprivation had stamped on Molly's face.

Molly preened in happy anticipation. Miss Chelsea herself was going to apply her stage paint! This afternoon she'd washed her hair in rainwater with some lavender soap she'd purloined from Miss Chelsea, but somehow she must have done something wrong. Instead of coming out thick and curly and shiny sable, like Miss Chelsea's, it was straighter and more limp than ever. Oh, well, it wouldn't show beneath the little velvet cap she was to wear in tonight's performance of selections from *The Merchant of Venice* by Mr. William Shakespeare. She would do her best to get the lines right this evening so as not to shame Miss Chelsea. And she would also watch Miss Chelsea carefully—she wanted so much to learn! Learn everything. Her role, that of Portia, was very demanding and exacting, Mr. Perragutt had told her, just slightly less important than Shylock, which he was playing. "The quality of mercy is not strained . . ." Molly mused silently to herself, dreaming of the day she would step into Chelsea's roles. After all, it seemed the natural thing, considering Miss Chelsea was almost eight years older than she was and wouldn't be able to play the parts of young women forever.

Molly and Chelsea struggled with the heavy trunk, dragging it up the steps and into the theater just offstage. The dressing room was even filthier than the alleyway, but at least it was dry—almost. Quickly, knowing exactly what must be done, they lit the lamps and began pulling out their costumes. Molly thought the burgundy velvet gown with its deep, low cleavage and tight bodice one of the prettiest costumes Chelsea owned. From the small jewel box they selected rings and bracelets and other faux stones and golden glitter. Portia was a rich heiress, and when fully costumed Chelsea looked every inch the part.

"Will you be wearing your hair in a braided coronet tonight?" Molly asked.

"No, those tight braids give me a headache; I'll just brush it out and wear it about my shoulders. Now hurry with the mirror, Molly, I can already hear the crowd gathering out front."

"Yes, Miss Chelsea. Mr. Perragutt said he wanted us to be at our best tonight."

"As if I am anything but," Chelsea retorted, offended.

And if it were less than her best, who but Uncle Cosmo would know? The audience for the most part was not familiar with William Shakespeare and wouldn't know the difference if she added her own dialogue to her part. And if Cosmo dared to try to please them by having her sing those bawdy songs he insisted upon, she'd have his head. God, how she hated it when the men in the audience slapped their thighs and leered and made lewd motions with their hands. If she had any spine, she'd have left Cosmo years ago. But what could life possibly offer her except a meager existence as a housemaid or servant—and *that* she would never do. At least this way she was her own person . . . almost.

The object of her righteous indignation appeared in the doorway, his face aglow with excitement and anticipation. Chelsea always wondered what it was Cosmo was expecting—that tonight would be any different from the night before? "Chelsea, dear heart, are you almost ready?"

"You know I'm not! Another half hour at least, Uncle. And do wipe that smile from your face, won't you? You alone seem to take pleasure from this farce."

"Chelsea, dear," he replied, his voice gentle and filled with tolerant understanding, "I will forgive you. Stage fright is the mark of a competent actress."

"It's more afraid of the law bursting in here, I am. Choosing the constable's wife for a mark; how could you be so stupid? I expect to be dragged off at any moment."

"Tut, tut, don't worry that pretty head of yours. Molly, are you prepared in your lines? Jessica is a most demanding role. Get yourself pretty enough now." He winked at the blushing girl. "They're lined up like geese for the slaughter." He rubbed his hands together in anticipation of the box office receipts. "Chelsea, there are some grand gents out there tonight. You play your cards right and you can have them eating out of your hand. I wouldn't be surprised if there wasn't someone important and influential enough to further your career. Someone who might help all of us step up a rung or two on the ladder of success."

"The only ladder you're going to move up on is attached to the gallows. I can feel it in the air tonight, Cosmo; it's making my blood run cold. Can't you call it off for once? Let's just do our little performance and slip away into the night. I can feel a change coming, and I'm not so sure it's a good one. If you want to find yourself at the wrong end of a rope, that's your business. I've got my own neck to worry about."

Cosmo Perragutt was deeply offended and more than a little angry. Talk like this boded ill. It was almost as though Chelsea were wishing something bad upon him. "I don't like your words or your tone, niece, and if you will, please remember to address me as 'Uncle'; I am your own dear, departed mother's brother, and I'll remind you to be grateful that I came to your rescue when she died. I demand your respect."

"When you do something to earn it, you will receive it. Until then, you are merely the manager of this *illustrious*"—she made the word sound like a disease—"theater troupe."

Cosmo's round, cherubic face creased into lines of displeasure. Lamplight glimmered from the top of his balding gray pate, and his blue eyes twinkled with assurance. Just the sight of his gentle expression inspired confidence and trust in the older, wealthy widows he courted. It was difficult to believe that this short, slightly paunchy, innocent-looking man had lived a life of petty crime, profiting from the hard-earned savings of others. Certainly Chelsea had never suspected it until placing herself into his care. If there was a way for Cosmo to exploit someone or something, it never took him long to discover it.

"Don't give me that 'I'm disappointed in you' Uncle

Cosmo. I know exactly what you're thinking—that I've been stepping out of place lately and there must be some way to bring me around."

"Chelsea, dear," he soothed as he always did whenever her blood was up and staining her checks crimson. "We have the troupe to consider, whatever differences there may be between ourselves. The play must go on!" He postured dramatically.

"Don't worry, Uncle, there will be a performance tonight; we all need the coins from the admissions. I suppose the audience will at least be grateful to be out of the rain."

When Cosmo had taken his leave at last, Molly turned to Chelsea, wonder and admiration in her tawny eyes. "Oh, Miss Chelsea, where do you get the courage?"

"It comes with age," Chelsea said sourly. "Now let's hurry and get your stage paint on. I've still a long way to go before I'm ready to meet my public."

When Molly was dressed in the drab, too-often mended costume of Jessica, Shylock's daughter, she assisted Chelsea in donning the burgundy velvet with the indecently low-cut bodice. "I swear, each time I crawl into this thing I'm closer to popping out than I was the time before," Chelsea complained. "I'm glad I decided to leave my hair down; at least it covers some of my shoulders. Quickly, Molly, some powder." She dusted the tinted powder over the tops of her breasts and smoothed the puff over her shoulders. Her paint took no time to apply, she was so expert and efficient. A simple headdress of coronet and veil, a drawstring purse, an incongruous yellow feathered fan, and Chelsea was ready.

"Miss Chelsea, Miss Chelsea, come see," Molly whispered, peeking through the faded and patched stage curtain. "It's a right good crowd Mr. Perragutt brought in tonight."

Joining Molly behind the dust-encrusted curtain, Chelsea peered out, her dark eyes widening in surprise. Cosmo had been telling the truth! This was quite the largest turnout in months. Her practiced eye sought out Cosmo's chosen marks for the evening, coming to rest on several respectably, if not fashionably, dressed gentlemen. Cosmo's pickings would be worthwhile from the look of things.

A movement from the back caught her attention. Swift Billy was snuffing out several house lights so that the footlamps would better illuminate the stage. She saw him glance at a particularly well-dressed woman wearing a becoming hat, replete with violet ribbons and face veil. The hat's crown sat low on the woman's head, its ribbons and laces cascading down the back from the narrow-brimmed front. Chelsea thought of her own sorely outdated wardrobe and wondered how much a hat like that cost. Far too much, she'd wager.

"Welcome, welcome, ladies and gentlemen." Cosmo Perragutt's stage voice boomed articulately. "This evening you are about to enjoy selections from that notable playwright, Mr. William Shakespeare. Sonnets, poetry, selected readings, all performed for your enjoyment. In addition, you will be presented with highlights from the play *The Merchant of Venice*. Now, if I may, I will introduce the players."

At a given signal from Cosmo, Chelsea and Molly stepped out onto the stage. Next came Geoffrey McGowan, their leading man, whose nose was suspiciously red. Already Chelsea could smell the whiskey on his breath, and she sighed inwardly at the thought of the love scenes she had to play with him tonight. Finally Prudence Helmsley, the company soubrette, stepped onstage next to Geoffrey.

"Introducing the cast!" Cosmo announced. "To my left, Mr. Geoffrey McGowan, directly here from a command performance for Queen Victoria herself at the St. James Theatre."

What a lie, Chelsea thought disdainfully as tall, slick-haired McGowan stepped center stage. The nearest Geoffrey had ever been to the St. James was the corner pub.

"And Miss Prudence Helmsley, songstress and actress. Perhaps after the performance Miss Helmsley can be encouraged to reward us with her artistry. Miss Helmsley has performed in palaces and theaters from the Vatican to the Russian court."

Prudence stepped forward and made a deep bowing curtsy, allowing the audience a view of her glandular endowments, which were quite impressive.

"And last but not least, the star of our productions, an actress of unusual ability. And loveliness," Cosmo hastened to add. "The illustrious, the stunningly lovely, Miss Chelsea Myles."

Chelsea stepped forward, dipping into a graceful curtsy. She held her heavy skirts up just a tad, enough to give the men in the front row a quick glimpse of her pointed toe and sweetly arched ankle. Her left hand demurely covered her décolletage, the feather tips of her yellow fan just brushing her smoothly rounded chin. As expected, she was greeted with warm applause, and only one rogue had the ill manners to whistle.

In the audience, Quaid Tanner grinned at Chelsea's introduction. Who would have thought the only escape he could find from the rain would be this firetrap of a theater, featuring a second-rate acting troupe? At first content to see the stage from the back row benches, he'd pushed his way through the crowd for a better view when the actress introduced in such lavish terms as Chelsea Myles had made a particularly alluring curtsy.

Quaid was the kind of man who stood out easily in any crowd. Tall and lean, he moved with an inbred self-assurance, and there was an authority about his sun-tanned face and square jaw, the full upper lip emphasized by a wide, well-trimmed mustache. Lesser men naturally made way for him, and the ladies usually smiled at him with interest, delivering come-hither glances with their eyes.

Chelsea Myles. The name rolled through his brain, and he wondered if it were really hers. Quaid made a point of remembering the names of women who interested him. Chelsea Myles. Her given name was probably Bertha or Mathilda, nothing as unique or fitting as Chelsea. Still, the roly-poly actor who introduced her was correct about her beauty—she was stunning. But could she act? he wondered, then shook his head, smiling. What did it really matter what her talents were? She had the face of an angel and the dark, flashing eyes of a devil—enough to capture any man's imagination without talent. Quaid, who considered himself an expert on women, had missed neither the sudden flash of ankle nor the way she'd demurely covered her bosom as she dipped for her curtsy. Now he took a seat at one of the benches and prepared to watch the show. This evening's escape from the rain just might bring other, more pleasurable escapes—already he was contemplating arranging an introduction after the performance.

Forty minutes later Chelsea Myles had taken center stage, pleading Antonio's case with the crafty Jew, Shylock. As she launched into her crowning piece, Quaid had to put his hand to his mouth to hide his amusement.

"The quality of mercy is not strained. It droppeth as the gentle rain from heaven upon the place beneath. It is twice blessed. . . ."

A sterling performance this was not. She tried, he had to give her that; and an admirable try it was as she clasped one hand to her breast and extended the other in pleading toward Shylock. Antonio seemed decidedly drunk from the way he swayed, unable to gain his balance on both feet.

Glancing around the audience, Quaid noticed that no one else seemed to notice the faulty acting, cheap costumes, and less-than-sober actors. In fact, everyone seemed to be enjoying the show immensely. The décolletage revealed by Chelsea Myles's burgundy gown and the way the lady flipped her hems as she walked had to have something to do with it, Quaid decided. Near the end of the fourth act, he applauded as loudly as the other fools in the audience. And by the time Chelsea made her curtain calls to rousing applause, he had decided it was one of the best performances he had ever attended and that Miss Chelsea Myles was the best actress ever to set foot on a London stage. He had to meet her in person. A late dinner, perhaps, at his motel, in his room.

Quaid was considering which side of the stage he should wait by in order to make her acquaintance after the performance when he heard a woman cry, "My purse! It's gone!"

Backstage, Chelsea winced. Damn that Swift Billy, she thought miserably. Couldn't he have waited until the people were on their way out of the theater instead of relieving them of their pocketbooks while they sat in the house! Wait until she got her hands on him—and Cosmo, too, for that matter.

"We'd better get out of here, Miss Chelsea." Molly was tugging on her sleeve. "There's gonna be trouble, I can smell it."

Chelsea silently agreed and slipped behind the curtain with Molly. "What shall we do, miss?" asked the frightened girl. "We can't just leave our costumes along with everything else we own."

"For once, Molly, you're right. Hurry up, get everything you can." Quickly, in the dying light of the oil lamp, they attempted to stuff the split trunk with their belongings. "Damn Uncle Cosmo," Chelsea muttered. "Nothing works, neither the lamp nor the hinge on the trunk." Overturning it, she instructed Molly to take the opposite end, and together they dragged it back out into the alley. "You start for the rooming house, Molly. I'm going back in there to see what's happened."

"Oh, no, Miss Chelsea, you can't! What if the coppers are in there now?"

"Much as I hate to admit it, I've got to see what's become of Uncle Cosmo. At the very least, the crowd is probably tearing him apart. Get going, Molly, do as I say." Without another word, she bounded back through the stage door, bumping full force into Prudence Helmsley, who looked terrified.

"They've got him!" she cried. "They've got the old man and Swift Billy! Get away from here if you know what's good for you."

"Who's got him?" Chelsea demanded. But Prudence was already halfway up the alley, lifting her skirts above the muddy puddles as she ran.

Chelsea's heart pounded with dread. She had to know what had happened; she had to know if Cosmo was going to implicate the entire troupe. If so, she mustn't return to the rooming house until the furor had died down. Perhaps the woman would be content with having her purse returned to her. Perhaps.

From the wings, stage left, Chelsea peeked through the curtain. The audience was in an uproar, men and woman alike complaining that their wallets or purses were missing. Police whistles blew shrilly, and one of the uniformed men had already collared Uncle Cosmo. He was being dragged away, protesting his innocence above the angry babble of the crowd.

Quaid was watching from the aisle when a flash of burgundy caught his eye. First an impertinent little chin and then a sweetly upturned nose peeked through the dingy stage curtain. A slender hand gripped the base of a long, white throat. He watched Chelsea as she tripped lightly across the stage and approached the plump, protesting actor being held by the police. Tears of denial glistening in her eyes, her throaty voice filled with concern, she bent over him, deliberately displaying her cleavage to the appreciative, burly officer brandishing a nightstick. The yellow feathered fan she'd carried lay discarded near her feet. A pity, Quaid thought in amusement. She might have been able to tickle the old man's way out of his predicament. He grinned, watching. This had to be Miss Chelsea Myles's most impressive performance.

Chelsea worked her magic with the law, using every feminine wile she knew. In the end, Cosmo Perragutt got to his feet and straightened his collar. His voice was eloquent and patient. The police were only doing their duty; mistakes could be made, and he was a forgiving man.

Once the police had released him, Perragutt collapsed against Chelsea, twitching like a puppet on a string. Obviously, he had never come quite this close to being carted off to jail. Quaid choked back his laughter as he listened to the actress rail at the troupe leader.

"No more tricks, Uncle Cosmo. Stand on your own two feet. You nearly did it this time. A hair, Cosmo, a hair from being carted away. No more! I'm sick of this, all of it, the run-down rooming houses and living out of rotting trunks. Do you understand me, you little weasel? No more. Either you make this troupe respectable or I'm quitting!"

"Where would you go?" Cosmo whined, clearly devastated by his near miss with the law. "I told your mother I'd look after you, lass. I promised."

Without answering, Chelsea turned on her heel and stalked across the stage, oblivious to the blowing whistles and the cries of policemen clearing the theater. Cosmo Perragutt followed after her like a sick puppy.

Quaid's interest was fully aroused now. It was clear that Miss Myles was fully aware of her uncle's guilt. He spied the gaudy yellow fan she'd left behind, retrieved it, and followed the pair behind the curtain to return it to her. The door leading out to the alley was wide open, and no one seemed to be behind the curtain. Standing in the doorway, Quaid heard her voice and listened.

"I hope tonight's escapade was well worth your while, Uncle Cosmo. I'd like to pay what's due on my rent instead of skipping out in the middle of the night. How much did you get?"

"I'm not certain, my dear." It sounded as if Cosmo's confidence and arrogance had returned. "More likely there's enough to pay everyone's salary for two weeks. Perhaps even enough to buy you one new costume."

"Now I know you're lying. A new costume is beyond the boundaries of your generosity. Where's the money, Cosmo?"

"Prudence has it. I told her to meet me at the boardinghouse."

"You fool!" Chelsea cried, disgusted. "By now your protégée is on the far side of the Thames, and you'll never see her again." As she spoke, something in Cosmo's face communicated itself to Chelsea. In a flash, her hand whipped out and reached inside his voluminous costume. He struggled, but she held firm and with effort withdrew a woman's drawstring reticule from the folds of fabric. "You're more of a fool than I thought," she told him angrily. "If the police had found this on your person, you'd have incriminated yourself."

"Chelsea, dear niece, those are my life savings. . . ."

"Contained in a woman's purse? Spare me, Cosmo."

"You're so distrusting, child, just like your mother was. Now hand it back like a good girl," he cajoled.

She hefted the purse in her hand, weighing it. "I'd wager

there's enough in here to pay my back rent and see me to several good meals. I'd also say you owe me this, Cosmo, for saving your dirty neck tonight. If I were you, I wouldn't hang about the theater; one never knows when the police will change their minds."

"Chelsea," Cosmo whined as she walked away, lifting the hem of her skirts to avoid the muddy puddles, "you can't do this. Where's your sense of justice? There are others to consider beside yourself."

"As you always say, Uncle, heaven helps those who help themselves."

Quaid stood in the doorway, his tall, broad-shouldered frame almost filling it entirely, the tip of the gaudy yellow feathered fan brushing the underside of his chin as he considered the conviction with which she had spoken those parting words. She'd obviously gotten to where she was now by the hard road and was determined not to give any ground. There had been a note of determination in the way she'd spoken the simple, well-worn phrase, and not a little ambition. If Chelsea Myles had anything to say about the path her life would take, she would see to it she got ahead, regardless of the method. For this, Quaid could hardly blame her. Whenever he'd found himself on the short end of the stick, he had invariably used whatever means available to turn the tables and improve his lot—far too often, in fact, to find fault with someone else in the same position.

Chapter 2

Unaware that her little scenario with Cosmo had been witnessed by anyone else, Chelsea hurried out onto the street in the direction of her rooming house. She had meant every word she'd said. It was impossible for her to continue living this way, without a spare coin in her purse and earning a poor living upon the stage. And it wasn't as though she were without scruples. Cheating and stealing were wrong, and she knew it. True, it was never her hand that reached into someone else's pocket, but living from the proceeds amounted to the same thing. And there was always the threat of being caught, like tonight. Cosmo was getting sloppy, and in his profession that was dangerous. This was the last time, absolutely the last time. There must be a way to free herself—somehow, some way, there had to be more to life than this!

Halfway down the street, Chelsea saw Molly's scrawny little form under a lamppost and her own broken trunk tipped awkwardly on its side. A low moan escaped her as she hurried forward. Now what? Had that silly Molly allowed the contents of the trunk to scatter about London's streets? Practically everything she owned was in that dilapidated container! As she approached, her mind work-

ing on the scolding she would give Molly, she noticed another figure beneath the light, until now obscured from
view by the awkwardly tilted trunk. It was a woman.

"Oh, miss, I'm so glad you've come along!" Molly
gasped gratefully.

"What are you doing here, Molly? You should have
been home by this time, with my trunk!"

"It's this poor woman," Molly hastened to explain.
"She's the one what got her purse stole at your performance tonight. She's real upset and crying and everything,
and she just fell down here, right at my feet."

Chelsea dropped to her knees beside the woman and,
picking up the limp wrist, patted the back of her hand.
"She's fainted, that's all. You say it was her purse that was
stolen?" Chelsea felt the weight of the purse she'd taken
from Cosmo and stuffed it into her bodice.

"Yes, miss. At least that's what she said before she
fainted. She's dressed real nice, and her hat must've cost a
bob or two. She said she didn't want to get involved with
the police."

Chelsea lightly slapped the woman's deathly pale
cheeks. "Molly, see if you can hire a cab to take the lady
home. What was she doing in this part of town, anyway?"

"No, no, no," the woman whispered hoarsely. "Please,
you must help me. My money, it's all gone. All of it." With
surprising strength, she grasped Chelsea's arm, imploring
her help between gulping sobs. "It was everything I had in
this world. It was to pay my passage to the captain of the
Southern Cross."

That at least explained what she'd been doing in this
part of London. The docks were only blocks away.

"Four hundred pounds. Gone. All of it gone! I never
should have gone into that theater, but Captain Winfield
wasn't in his quarters on the *Southern Cross* and it was be-

ginning to rain. . . ." She ended in a shuddering sob. "I thought I'd be safe in there. Safe!" She covered her face with her lace-gloved hands and wept piteously.

Chelsea was truly moved. Twice her hand went to her breast to remove the small purse from her bodice. Twice it fell back into her lap. "Was it your life savings, then?" she asked, her voice tremorous with sympathy.

"No. It was given to me by my sister's husband. For my passage and a bit more besides. Oh, now what am I to do?"

"First of all, I will take you home. Molly, would you call a carriage? Everything will look better once you've had a cup of tea, Miss. Where do you live?"

"In Yorkshire. I've only been in London since the beginning of this week. I've taken a small suite until the ship sails. On Duke's Place, just this side of Bishop's Gate."

Chelsea was impressed with the address. "Molly, haven't you hired that carriage yet? Why are you lagging about? Can't you see that Miss . . . Miss . . ."

"Harris. Mrs. Honoria Harris."

"That Mrs. Harris is in a dreadful state? Now hurry up with it!"

She thought of the probable fare to Duke's Place and decided she could afford it. After all, Mrs. Honoria Harris's four hundred pounds rested snugly between her breasts, and the least she could do was see to it the lady arrived home without further mishap. Molly wanted to turn in early to be fresh for her next performance. Chelsea wasn't pleased at the prospect of traipsing around the city after-hours alone, but she felt responsible for the shaken woman.

Although scarcely ten o'clock, the streets of London seemed deserted as Chelsea and Honoria Harris rumbled along in their hired hack after dropping Molly off at home. From somewhere in the city came the faint peal of church bells marking the hour. Shopfronts and businesses, tightly shuttered for the night, faced the streets with lonely abandonment. Before sunrise, however, those same shops would be thrown open to the public for another day of profit.

As they left the harbor area and drove inward to the city, Chelsea took time to inspect this woman who had been foolish enough to travel the city streets alone and venture onto the docks with four hundred pounds in her purse. Honoria Harris was not as young as she appeared to be at first glance. Her garments and foolish hat were designed for a woman at least ten years her junior. But with her narrow shoulders, full bosom, and trim waist, she gave an illusion of youth—an illusion ultimately belied by her pointy-nosed, long-chinned face.

"You're terribly kind to look after me this way," Mrs. Harris said, but something in her voice hinted that she was accustomed to being looked after and considered it to be her due. Obviously, Mrs. Harris had been carefully sheltered for most of her life, and having her purse snatched right out of her hands was therefore doubly shocking.

When their cab finally came to a halt outside a three-storied, white stone townhouse on Duke's Place, Chelsea scrambled out and turned to assist her charge. "Please, won't you come up?" Mrs. Harris asked. "I could offer you a cup of tea. You've been so kind."

"I'd like to, really," Chelsea replied, "only I'm afraid hiring another cab in this part of town at this hour would be impossible."

"Oh, please, you can ask the driver to wait for you. I'd be so grateful."

Chelsea thought immediately of the expense, then of the small velvet purse nestled between her breasts. Mrs. Harris was obviously overwrought and afraid to be left alone just now. She hesitated another moment and finally succumbed to Honoria's pleading eyes. "Driver, wait for me, I won't be long."

At first the driver seemed reluctant. His eyes slid over Chelsea's costume, and he thought of the less-than-respectable part of town where he'd found his fare. Then he glanced at Honoria, noting her fine clothes and ladylike manner and the impressive house on Duke's Place. "I won't keep her long," Honoria pleaded, her voice thin, almost nasal. "Just for a cup of tea."

Silently the driver agreed, already having considered that it was most unlikely to find another fare at such a late hour in this part of the city. At least if he waited, he would have another paying fare for the return trip.

Honoria seemed unsteady on her feet, and her shoulders were still shaking as Chelsea helped her climb the wide front steps to the door. She had to take the key and turn the lock herself, Honoria's fingers were trembling so. The apartment was at the back of the first floor, and once inside, Chelsea settled the woman into a comfortable chair and propped up her feet on a small stool. "I'll make you some tea if you show me where it is, Mrs. Harris."

"I'm afraid I don't even know your name."

"Chelsea Myles. The tea?"

"Over there, behind the screen. I'm sorry to be such a bother, but no one save that child came to my aid. I thought I could see myself home, but I was too overcome with fright. It was terrible, terrible!"

"Now, don't upset yourself again. It won't bring your purse back."

Behind the woven blind was a small stove and a kettle already filled with water. Although Mrs. Harris's lodgings were poor according to some standards, it was a palace compared to the hovels Cosmo rented for the troupe. Everything here was sparkling and tidy, respectable, some might call it. A small, colorful tray was already fixed with sugar and lemon and two china cups that were almost transparent. Someday, Chelsea told herself, she, too, would have something just as exquisite. While she waited for the water to boil, she watched Honoria remove her hat and gloves. There was no wedding band on the woman's finger, she noticed immediately, which puzzled her, although it seemed in keeping with the surroundings: the sparsely furnished flat described a woman who lived alone.

"You say you've only been here since the beginning of the week?"

The woman nodded. "I've been living with my sister and her family in Maidenhair, just outside London. It was my brother-in-law, Jason, who gave me the money for my passage to New South Wales. He'll be terribly angry when I tell him what happened in the theater. He warned me about London and cautioned me continually to be careful. If my sister, Barbara, were not about to have another child, and if it were not harvesttime on the estate, I never would have had to come to this wicked city alone!"

"Passage to New South Wales, you say?" Chelsea's interest was aroused; she'd never known anyone to make so long a journey. The kettle whistled a warning, and she was distracted from her thoughts to pour the tea as Honoria continued her woeful tale.

"Yes. A terrible, hard journey for a woman like myself, but I suppose there's no help for it, not if I'm ever to find a place for myself in this world." Honoria's tone and expression dripped self-pity, an emotion Chelsea now believed second nature to the woman.

As they sipped their tea, Honoria explained that she was a widow of a naval officer, left with meager means of support. "If it were not for my sister, Barbara, and her husband, Jason," she went on, "I would have had to hire myself out as a governess or nursemaid. As it was, their charity was shortlived. I was hardly more than an unpaid servant in their home, tending their children and overtaking duties in the kitchen."

"Your sister and her husband, they're wealthy, then?"

"Wealthier than I!" Honoria exclaimed resentfully. "Jason is not landed or titled, if that is what you mean. Hardly more than a gentleman farmer, I suppose."

Chelsea watched Honoria over the rim of her teacup as the woman sniffed indignantly and touched her lacy handkerchief to the tip of her nose. She had come across women like this before—bitter, resentful, spoiled women, believing themselves to be so delicate that even the simplest of chores could be accomplished only with whining and complaints. Most likely Honoria's sister, Barbara, was overworked and hard-pressed, and her brother-in-law, Jason, although comfortably fixed, had little money left over to employ servants. Gratitude for being saved from a life in service never occurred to women like Mrs. Harris. "You've never said why you're going to New South Wales," Chelsea prompted.

"To marry, although I must admit I don't care for the prospect. The man is an acquaintance of my brother-in-law, and it was through his solicitations that the arrangement was conducted. It was made quite clear that I was no longer welcome in his house." Once more Honoria brought her handkerchief to her nose and wiped at dry eyes. "The gentleman in question is older than myself and has two children. Or is it three? I can't quite seem to remember. However, they are grown, thank heavens. I imagine it's quite trying to raise one's own children, never mind the Herculean task of attempting to raise someone else's. I can tell you, Miss Myles, those children of my sister's are hardly more than ruffians and spoiled brats! Oh! The things they did to me, the insults and sufferings I've had to bear!" Again the handkerchief found its way to her nose. "I'm not very strong, you know, and I was dreading the sea voyage because of my health. Jason and Barbara never understood, and Jason said that Harlow Kane—that's the man I'm to marry—would send me to the finest doctors. I never looked forward to this marriage, but it would have been a godsend to have someone care for me and look after me. Now, it's all ruined."

"What will you do?" Chelsea asked, pretending sympathy. She was feeling less and less guilty over the small purse in her bodice. In her opinion Honoria Harris was selfish and prideful, qualities that did not make for an admirable woman.

"What can I do?" Honoria replied tearfully. "I'll have to tell Jason what happened. If he wants to be rid of me badly enough, he'll give me more money. I'll be forced to endure his endless lecturing, but in the end he'll abandon his miserly ways and give it to me. As I said, neither he nor Barbara seems content with the services I extend to them."

Chelsea breathed a sigh of relief. Until this moment she'd been undecided what to do with the four hundred pounds. To Honoria Harris, it seemed an important but easily replaceable sum of money; to herself, it meant a chance for a new life.

"I've often thought of traveling to America or to New South Wales," she mused aloud. And it was true, although it had always seemed like an impossible dream. "How much was your passage for the ship?"

"I confess it was only two hundred and eighty pounds. The rest of the fare came out of what was owed me from my husband's estate. Such a shame, to die so young in the service of England."

"He died in a war?"

"No, no, typhoid swept his ship. Still," Honoria argued defensively, "it was in the service of his country that he was there in the first place."

"Of course. Where exactly were you to go in Australia? Melbourne?" Somewhere in Chelsea's travels she had heard that city's name.

"Actually, my destination was Sydney, the heart of New South Wales, and from what Jason's told me, it is quite a city, complete with its own society and culture. I could never abide the rougher aspects of the new colony, and I understand much of it is still quite primitive. Jason tells me a man could very easily lose himself in the territory. Imagine that!" Honoria made it clear that she could never imagine anyone having reason to lose himself anywhere.

What about a woman? Chelsea mused to herself. Is it possible for a woman to lose herself, to begin a new life? A life without Cosmo Perragutt, a life of respectability, chosen through experience and wisdom instead of the panicked ignorance of immaturity. The idea was hypnotizing, intoxicating, and Chelsea suddenly wished she were going to Australia instead of Honoria Harris.

"Have you ever traveled, Miss Myles?" Honoria was asking.

"Hardly. Not out of England, at any rate. My own pocket would never allow it."

"Travel is quite expensive," Honoria agreed complacently. "Of course, I've seen a bit of the world because of my husband's military career. I've been to Ireland and Scotland both, so you see I've some experience with sea travel, and I am definitely not looking forward to almost three months' sailing. I become dreadfully ill, you know."

"No, I didn't."

Oblivious to the gentle jibe, Honoria continued a dialogue concerning her experiences aboard ship, making the prospect of a sea voyage seem close to a sojourn through hell.

"And the food is abominable!" she went on, unaware that as Chelsea bit her lower lip in contemplation, she was considering the idea of starting over in a new life, with new opportunities.

Two hundred and eighty pounds. That would leave only

one hundred and twenty pounds from the four hundred. Hardly enough.

"You weren't thinking of traveling there yourself, were you?" Honoria asked pointedly, interrupting Chelsea's train of thought.

"I didn't know I was until just now," Chelsea replied honestly. "What if we were to travel together, share a cabin? Would the fare be less?"

"Why, er, yes, as a matter of fact it would. Slightly less than two hundred pounds. Miss Myles, are you or are you not considering making this voyage?"

Chelsea bit her lip again, thinking of how narrowly they had all escaped the law this evening. Cosmo was getting sloppy and impulsive. How long would it be before they were all imprisoned, guilty or not? And what chance would she have for making a new life here in London? One needed connections, introductions. No, it was all too impossible. But then, so was traveling halfway across the world to a new country, new people.

"Yes," Chelsea heard herself say adamantly. "I most definitely am considering making the voyage. I wonder, Mrs. Harris, if we might not share a cabin and reduce the cost for both of us. You wouldn't have to say anything about it to your brother-in-law, and the extra money could serve as a neat bit of pin money for yourself. After all, I've heard it said a wise woman always has a bit put by for herself, regardless of the generosity of her husband. And you really have no idea just how generous your intended husband really is, do you?"

Honoria seemed thunderstruck. Travel to New South Wales and share a cabin with a common theater actress. And that was all Miss Myles really was, despite her kindness. She was a common actress.

"I never considered . . . what I mean is, a ship's cabin can be quite close quarters for two strangers. Not that you haven't been extremely kind, Miss Myles, it's just that . . . that I could never deceive Jason this way."

Honoria averted her eyes, unable to face her guest. True, Chelsea Myles had been good enough to help in a moment of need, good enough to escort her home and even come up and make a cup of tea, but after all, the woman was only an actress and therefore socially unacceptable.

"It was only a suggestion," Chelsea said quietly, quickly reading Honoria's reasons for declining her offer. The purse nestled between her breasts was feeling more comfortable all the time. "There will be other ships and another time." Chelsea rose and smoothed the burgundy velvet skirt of her costume. "I'll be going now. I wish you godspeed on your voyage, Mrs. Harris."

"Wait. The idea of traveling together has given me pause. It *would* be nice to have a few extra pounds in my pocket. As I told you, I'm not a very good sailor, and it would be nice to have a female companion. But what would you do in New South Wales? Would you continue acting?"

"I've always wanted to open an emporium. My parents were shopkeepers, and I've inherited a good business head from them. I've made my own way for most of my life, Mrs. Harris, and I intend to continue doing so."

The word "emporium" sounded grandiose to her own ears. She did have big ideas—but it was possible. Anything in the world was possible, if a person worked hard enough. Wasn't she living proof? A few days ago, who would have thought she'd be making plans to go to Australia? Maybe she wouldn't be able to open an emporium right away. But she could start small and perhaps manage a storefront location. If—and it was a big if—it was her ultimate goal, she would manage. Start with a limited amount of stock until she knew what would sell and what wouldn't.

Her markup would have to be reasonable; perhaps she could even undercut the other merchants and draw on her looks and talent. Men loved a pretty face. A cash business, no credit, that would be her number-one rule.

Chelsea chewed thoughtfully on her thumbnail. There were times she bent over backward to break every honest rule there was, but now she had to acknowledge to herself that without Honoria's four hundred pounds she would still be with Cosmo and only half a step ahead of the law. Some way, somehow, she would repay the lady's unknown generosity. She wasn't really a thief; she preferred to think of herself as a victim of circumstances. And victims always needed help. She was helping herself, and if this time it was at Honoria's expense, she would find a way to make it right at some point in time. Now was her chance at a new life, and she had to reach out and take it. She might never get another.

True, she knew as much about Australia as she did about opening an emporium—exactly nothing. And it bothered her to realize she was starting her new life with ill-gotten gains. But she had no other choice if she wanted to survive. From here on in she would regard the entire experience as exciting and challenging. If she failed—but no, she wouldn't fail. One way or another, she'd catch her dream.

A sudden thought struck Chelsea that brought a slow smile to her lips and created a soft gurgle of irony in her throat. If England were still transporting convicts to the colonies in Australia, Cosmo's rashness and greed might have landed her in New South Wales under much different circumstances. This way, with Honoria's money, she would make the same trip in a dramatically different style.

Honoria wasn't so bad, really. She could even be pleasant. Perhaps by the time their journey was finished they would be friends. And if they weren't, Chelsea reflected wryly, she somehow knew in her gut that by the end of their voyage she would have earned every penny of the stolen four hundred pounds.

As Chelsea remained quiet, lost in contemplation of her future, Honoria was struggling with her own unhappy thoughts. She felt almost dizzy with what was going on inside her head—her brother-in-law, the doctor, her terrible experience this evening, and now this young lady offering to sail with her and share a cabin.

Honoria had never been quick and bright like her sister, Barbara, but she had the feeling that something wasn't quite right. Could one really trust an absolute stranger? Honoria shrank back from such unpleasant thoughts. Whatever was eluding her would reveal itself sooner or-later, she knew, and it was just as well, because she was having trouble dealing with the young woman in front of her.

An actress! Daughter of shopkeepers! Surely Miss Myles was on the lowest rung of the social ladder. Still, the idea of having a little extra in her pocket was alluring. "I must speak to my brother-in-law, you understand," she said with an artificial smile. "There's every possibility he will refuse me my passage." It suddenly occurred to Honoria that one hundred and twenty pounds of the stolen money had been her very own from her husband's estate. Since Jason knew exactly how much it cost to book passage aboard the *Southern Cross,* that would be exactly how much he would give her, if he gave at all. Without Miss Myles, she wouldn't have a pence to spare. Traveling *with* Chelsea Myles, she could reclaim almost one hundred pounds for herself after paying for a shared cabin. "I must confess," she added after a moment, "the idea of traveling with another woman is growing more and more appealing. I—well, in short, Miss Myles, I will do everything possible to make passage on the *Southern Cross* with you."

Chelsea stood up abruptly. "I really must be leaving now, Mrs. Harris. It's very late, and the cab is still waiting. I'm glad you're feeling better now and I'll stop by tomorrow. Sleep well."

"I'll try, my dear, although I know I'll dream all night long about Jason and his inevitable lecture. Thank you again for your assistance." Again, the smile she offered was falsely bright and condescending.

Chelsea merely nodded and slipped through the door. Of all the snobbish, self-serving, patronizing . . . She could have slapped that smile from Honoria Harris's face! Chelsea reminded herself how often she'd wished she could escape all the Honoria Harrises of this world, who considered an actress as less than nothing socially.

But at least escape and the chance for a new life were going to be possible at last! In one swift stroke she would rid herself of Cosmo and his band of not so jolly thieves and begin again as a respectable, if not wealthy, woman. Traveling halfway around the world was worth the price, she decided, flushed with excitement at the prospect. Never had she dared to dream of something as grand as this! Her visions of escape and travel had never taken her farther than France, just across the Channel. Australia! New South Wales! And just two hours ago everything had seemed so bleak. Now life was taking an unexpected turn, and although it frightened her more than a little, she was ready for it.

Chapter 3

The following morning, Chelsea's nerves were stretched to the breaking point. She had impulsively decided to embark on a new future, and the thought thrilled and frightened her. Over and over she'd mulled the idea of going to Australia, constantly amazed at her own impetuosity. She'd tossed and turned the night through, contemplating her voyage to New South Wales, resigning herself to the fact that she didn't like Honoria Harris and that spending almost three months in a small, confining ship's cabin would test her patience and her temper, neither of which were strong points in her character.

But when circumstances and options seemed dimmest, she also remembered the four hundred pounds, more than she could have saved in a lifetime! And she knew that Molly, however much she admired and idolized Chelsea, considered herself very much in Cosmo's debt. Obviously the simpering little drudge had immediately informed Cosmo how much was contained in the small velvet purse Chelsea had wrested from his person. Little wonder he'd come banging on her door at the first light of day, demanding his cut. Well, he'd never get it—not if she had anything to say about it!

Chelsea moved about her small, cramped room wishing

the time would pass quickly. The moldy wallpaper, cheap broken furniture, and sagging bed would soon be a part of her past. Taking the chipped porcelain pitcher from the washstand, she filled it from the pump just outside the back door of the rooming house. It would be unthinkable to ask her slatternly landlady, Mrs. Sheridan, to heat the water on the stove. The thought of washing her hair in icy water made her shiver, but having no idea what facilities the *Southern Cross* would offer, she intended to suffer the ordeal. While her hair dried she would inspect her meager wardrobe, stitching and mending where needed. Concentrating on the tasks of preparing for the trip might make her less anxious, she decided; besides, she had to keep busy or she'd start to dwell on her next meeting with Honoria Harris. All kinds of unsettled questions kept creeping into her thoughts. What if Mrs. Harris's brother-in-law refused to replace the stolen money? It would be impossible for her to make the voyage alone. Her passage would take almost all the money, leaving her barely enough to support herself once in New South Wales. Unlike Mrs. Harris, who was to be remarried and would have a husband to look after her, Chelsea would be entirely on her own, responsible for herself. If living with Cosmo had taught her anything, it was that a pence never stretched as far as one hoped.

By midafternoon, she was bathed and dressed in her most respectable gown, a modest fashion of tan linsey-woolsey trimmed with blue that brought out the deep auburn highlights in her freshly washed chestnut hair and emphasized the honey tones of her skin. Thank goodness the extreme circular hooped skirts in fashion a few years ago had been abandoned as overly cumbersome and unmanageable. Now the full skirts were pulled to the rear and supported by a light wire cage, sort of a single-winged farthingale. A snowy-white lace jabot accentuated Chelsea's long slender neck, and the bodice was tight-fitted, as were the long sleeves that puffed near the top. Her hat, a silly confection, was of dark brown straw topped with blue lace and dark veiling and worn at a jaunty angle over her right eye. A short pelisse of the same fabric as her gown completed her costume.

And a costume it was, for Chelsea felt as though she had never embarked upon a more demanding role. She must present just the right note of respectability, just the proper deference, and she must at all costs repress her anger over the woman's patronizing attitude. Last evening, once Mrs. Harris was safe and sound in her own apartment and Chelsea's assistance was no longer required, it had become perfectly clear that Mrs. Harris's opinion of actresses was less than flattering. Now it was up to Chelsea to alter that opinion—and alter it she would. Her cache of coins and notes pinned securely to her petticoat, Chelsea started out for her interview with Honoria Harris.

The smile of welcome on Honoria's face after her quick, sharp eyes had inspected the young woman who had come to her aid the night before was all Chelsea needed to breathe easier. As she sipped tea with the loquacious Honoria, her mind was far away, in the process of purchasing a new dress and a nightgown. She found it impossible to listen to her hostess's unending monologue without taking an occasional mental vacation. After all, in less than an hour, she'd become well acquainted with just about everything in her companion's background and future marriage to the man known as Harlow Kane. Honoria had even pressed her to read three short letters written in Mr. Kane's tight, cramped hand.

"He's a vintner." That is, "he grows grapes and makes wine," Honoria explained as though not expecting Chelsea to know the meaning of the word. Then she wrinkled her nose in distaste. "I can't say I'm fond of the drink myself, and heaven only knows how I detest a man who imbibes too freely. I certainly hope Mr. Kane thinks first of his profits and then of his thirst."

Chelsea suffered Honoria's further ruminations on the evils of drink and dissipation in general before braving the one question she'd been dying to ask. "Have you spoken with your brother-in-law?"

Honoria made a pretense of searching for a handkerchief, pretending not to hear Chelsea's question. The truth was she hadn't spoken to her brother-in-law because she was afraid. She dreaded confrontations, and in one small, deep part of her heart she wasn't at all sure Jason would come forth with the money she needed. If Jason refused to help her, she had no idea what she'd do. And what she dreaded even more than asking for the money was the lack of concern she was sure to see on the faces of her sister and brother-in-law when she told them how she'd been accosted. They simply didn't care about her. Why, she could have been killed. She could almost see her brother-in-law smacking his hands together in a "well, that's over and done with" attitude. Barbara might squeeze out a tear, but she rather doubted it. Honoria could feel a circle of heat work its way around her neck and up to her cheeks. How could she have gotten to this point in her life and have no one care about her?

"Mrs. Harris, are you all right? Is there anything I can do?" Chelsea asked gently, noting the woman's sudden flush.

Honoria had never been quick in her thoughts, but her weary brain raced now. Perhaps, just perhaps . . . "I don't feel all that well, the excitement of everything, I guess," she replied, replacing her teacup in the saucer with a trembling hand. "Might I impose on you and ask you to accompany me to my brother-in-law's house?"

"You might," Chelsea replied cheerfully. So, it was fear that was causing Mrs. Harris to react the way she was. To Chelsea, who could easily identify fear, that much was obvious. Well, if going along with Honoria Harris to her brother-in-law's house was the only way to allay the woman's fears and guarantee the double cabin, she was all for it. But for form's sake, she pretended to ponder the request. "I suppose I could go along with you now if you feel up to it," she said after a moment.

The relief Honoria felt was so great, she was almost lightheaded. This young actress would be perfect to have on hand while dealing with her brother-in-law. Jason would be impressed—not with Chelsea's profession, for she had no intention of mentioning that, but with her lady-like appearance.

"My dear, why don't you see about engaging a coach while I change my dress and powder my nose," Honoria suggested. "It won't take but a minute." She turned in the direction of the small bedroom, then looked over her shoulder. "I am grateful to you, Miss Myles. It seems like you're making my life a bit easier for me right now."

Chelsea waved airily in a "don't mention it" attitude and closed the front door behind her, wondering who was going to pay for the coach. She was going out of her way and giving up a certain amount of her time. Surely Mrs. Harris would see fit to pay—if she had the money, that is. She had the feeling the timid little woman had very little.

Several hours later, a sour-faced servant opened the front door after Honoria pulled the bell chain. "I'd like to see my brother-in-law, please," Honoria said in a quavering voice. Chelsea cupped the woman's elbow to steady her. She couldn't wait to meet this ogre who frightened poor defenseless women into fits of trembling.

The servant was about to close the door and keep them waiting on the stoop when Chelsea stepped forward,

Honoria in hand, and said briskly, "We'll wait inside. Mrs. Harris isn't feeling all that well."

It was a mean-looking, narrow house. There was no furniture in the foyer except a tall coatrack with an attached umbrella stand. There was nothing hanging on the rack and no umbrellas in the stand. The wallpaper was as faded and dusty-looking as the carpet. Chelsea fought the urge to sneeze.

"Does the rest of the house look like this?" Chelsea whispered. Honoria licked her dry lips and nodded.

Jason Munsey strode down the hall and came to an abrupt halt in front of Honoria. He was very tall; Chelsea found herself looking up at him. Honoria, she noted, only came to a little above his belt. She hadn't realized just how delicate the woman was until now.

"What brings you back here?" Munsey rasped. Chelsea decided the man wasn't being particularly unkind, it was just the way he spoke.

"I . . . Jason, you . . ."

Chelsea stepped forward. Honoria would never get the words out, and she looked as though she were going to collapse any moment. "I'm Chelsea Myles," she said briskly, holding out her hand. "Mrs. Harris met with an unfortunate accident last evening. I knew that you and your family would be concerned about her well-being, so I offered to come over here with her because she isn't feeling well. As you can see, she is all right physically, but her nerves are upset. I know you'll want to help. As a matter of fact," she continued, dragging Honoria by the arm through the foyer, "I think Mrs. Harris should be sitting down. Perhaps a cup of tea. Which way is your parlor?"

"Young lady . . . !" Jason Munsey sputtered.

Chelsea turned, her face the picture of innocence. "Yes? Of course you'll want to call your wife. Just show us where the parlor is. I feel a bit faint myself."

In three long strides Munsey was ahead of Chelsea, a look of anger on his face. "I'll call my wife."

"You shouldn't be so bold," Honoria gasped as she sank down into a ratty-looking chair. "Jason doesn't like that in a woman."

"You didn't tell me you were afraid of him, Mrs. Harris," Chelsea said gently.

"I'm not . . . I mean he is over . . . he does intimidate . . . I do hate to ask for charity. . . ."

When Jason Munsey returned with his wife, Chelsea positively stared. She didn't think it was possible for a husband and wife to look so much like one another. Barbara Munsey was as tall as her husband and just as sour-looking. She and Honoria, who was tiny and frail, were nothing alike. Introductions were made, and Chelsea's spine stiffened as she stared haughtily at Honoria's benefactors.

Barbara Munsey stared down at her sister with glittering eyes. "What's this drivel Jason has told me about you being accosted last evening? Speak up, Honoria, tell us what happened."

Chelsea watched Honoria struggle for words. "Mrs. Harris is still in shock, I think," she heard herself say in the woman's defense. "She was brutally accosted last evening and robbed. I just happened to be on my way home from the theater and offered the use of a carriage. It was just brutal," Chelsea repeated, and shuddered for effect, rolling her eyes.

"Robbed? The money I gave you for your trip?" Munsey thundered. Honoria nodded miserably.

"Every cent she had," Chelsea confirmed, giving the frightened woman a pitying look. "I made it my business to stop by Mrs. Harris's lodgings today to see how she was faring. When she told me she had to come here, I could see she wasn't up to making the trip herself. I was only too glad to accommodate her in my carriage. I thought her family should be made aware of what happened. You are concerned, are you not?" Chelsea demanded, but in a gentle tone. She batted her outrageous eyelashes at Jason Munsey, who was trying to look everywhere but at Chelsea.

"They took all your money?" Barbara parroted. "How could you be so careless, Honoria? Jason works very hard for his money. It's not as though we have an unlimited supply. I can't believe how careless you are."

"I wasn't careless, Barbara." Honoria protested feebly. "I didn't want to be killed."

Chelsea smiled coquettishly at Jason Munsey, then gave Barbara Munsey an innocent, "sweet young thing" look. It was clear now that she was going to have to negotiate Honoria's passage because the woman had no intention of asking for herself. "I think, Mr. Munsey, that Honoria needs more money to buy her passage ticket. She seems to have difficulty speaking. She did receive a blow to her throat. I'm sure that's the reason she's being so quiet. It's painful to speak, isn't it, dear?" Obligingly, Honoria nodded.

Barbara Munsey's hand strayed to her hair, fingering the dry crisp curls that were like straw. Suddenly she was aware of her plainness and her dull-looking appearance compared to Chelsea's beauty and elegant dress. She was aware also of her husband's strange behavior. Under normal conditions he would have given Honoria a sharp tongue-lashing and sent her packing. Now he was listening, showing concern, toadying up to Miss Myles. She bit down on her thin lower lip when she saw her husband smile at the pretty young woman.

Honoria left her chair to stand by her sister. "Why is Jason looking at Miss Myles like that?" she whispered.

"He's being civil to your friend," Barbara whispered

back, her blue eyes as angry and narrowed as her pursed lips. "This is unforgivable, just unforgivable, Honoria. I had no idea you were so irresponsible."

Honoria's back stiffened. "I didn't *try* to be accosted, nor did I willingly give up my purse. I had to think of my life. What would you have done, Barbara?"

On the defensive, Barbara drew herself up stiffly. 'I would have fought like the very devil," she hissed. She didn't add that anything was better than having to endure Jason's wrath. Bruises and cuts would be the only things her husband would notice—and even then he'd probably say she hadn't fought hard enough. She tried to feel some sympathy for her sister but failed. All she could think about was how sarcastic Jason would be from now on, reminding her daily how much Honoria had cost the Munsey household.

Once she'd gotten a slight rise out of her sister, Honoria pressed her advantage. Brazenly inching closer, she whispered, "It looks to me like he's flirting with Miss Myles. He's smiling. Jason never smiles."

"Be still! You don't know what you're talking about, Honoria. Jason would never flirt right under my gaze. Besides, women flirt, men leer."

"Call it whatever you like, but he's doing something. Men never leered at me. They never leered at you, either, did they, Barbara?"

Barbara recognized the truth in Honoria's words. Jason was the only man who'd ever looked at her, and only then because his father had prodded him in her direction. But he didn't look at her anymore. Never full face, anyway. He never spoke directly to her, either. When had Honoria become so observant? If the truth were known, she'd been envying her sister of late, knowing she was going off to Australia. A new land, a new husband. It was like an adventure.

Her eyes narrowed as she continued to watch her husband and Chelsea. Jason *was* smiling. Miss Myles *was* flirting—obviously so. Good Lord, what if Jason took it in his head to have a mistress? She'd be a laughingstock among her friends.

In two long strides Barbara was next to her husband. There was authority and a tone of command in her voice as she ordered her husband to go upstairs and get the money for her sister. "Miss Myles will excuse you, won't you, my dear?"

Honoria had never seen her brother-in-law flustered before, and she rather enjoyed the feeling. She almost fainted when he turned to his wife and asked her how much he should get.

Chelsea smiled brightly. "Why, Mr. Munsey, exactly what the thieves took," she replied. "Four hundred pounds. And may I say you are both very generous. Very generous. I'm more than pleased to meet people like you, who are so concerned for their relatives. It's so . . . so refreshing."

Honoria closed her eyes in a silent prayer of thanksgiving. She'd heard Barbara groan at the mentioned amount, but what did it matter? As long as she got it, she didn't really care. And in that moment, she was honest with herself. Without Chelsea's help she'd have been sent packing. Somehow she would have to make it up to the young actress. Though Honoria was certain that Chelsea was not what she appeared to be, it was wonderful to have a friend.

Once outside in the fresh air, Chelsea let her breath out with a loud *swoosh*. Her eyes widened when Honoria laughed, a frail, reedy sound. "We're some pair, aren't we? You really intimidated and shamed my brother-in-law." She bent closer to Chelsea and whispered, "I told Barbara that Jason was flirting with you. I think that's why she was so agreeable to giving me the money—she wanted us out of the house, and *fast.* I do thank you for your help, Miss Myles. All I want to do now is go home and rest. It's been a trying night and day."

"What about your ticket? Have we agreed to sail together?"

"Of course, of course. I'll take care of it in the morning. Stop by tomorrow and we'll talk again. I'll be glad to book your passage, if that's agreeable."

"Of course."

When they reached Honoria's house on Duke's Place, the older woman tripped out of the hackney as though she hadn't a care in the world and blithely bode Chelsea good night—leaving her to pay the fare. Wisely, Chelsea kept quiet. A lady never quibbled over a few coins.

The following day, shortly after the noon hour, Chelsea dressed as carefully as she had the day before for her third meeting with Honoria Harris. The sun shone cheerfully, brightening her mood as she set out on foot for Honoria's lodgings. At last she was going to get away, to make a new life for herself. She felt wonderful.

Honoria welcomed Chelsea with a smile. She fixed tea and set out small cakes she'd purchased that morning.

"I hope you don't mind that I took the liberty of paying for your passage when I bought mine. I didn't want to carry the money one minute longer then necessary. Of course, if you change your mind about sailing, the ticket agent assured me he would refund the money. He would, wouldn't he?" she asked anxiously. "Refund the money, I mean?"

"Certainly," Chelsea assured the older woman. "However, a refund won't be necessary; I have every intention of sailing with you."

"Oh, I'm so glad. I'll just get your receipt, and you can pay me back."

Chelsea's quick mind leapt to unflattering conclusions. It was not unheard-of for a person, once duped, to do a little duping himself; and Mrs. Honoria Harris, despite her seeming respectability, was after all a stranger. "I'm afraid I don't carry that amount of money on me," she said slowly. "As I had no way of knowing you would go ahead and purchase my passage, I didn't bring it." She watched Honoria's face fall in disappointment.

"Oh, yes, I suppose it was foolish of me."

Something was glittering in those bird-black eyes that alerted Chelsea, who'd lived by her wits for too long. Was she just being suspicious, or was Honoria up to a few tricks of her own? "As you say, you've nothing to worry about. Your money will be refunded if I choose not to sail, and then it can be applied to your fare for a single cabin. But I do intend to sail, and I will pay you when I meet you aboard ship."

"Oh, yes, yes, of course." There was a note of doubt in Honoria's voice.

"How much, exactly, is passage for a shared cabin?" Chelsea asked. "You said last night it was slightly under two hundred pounds."

Honoria seemed taken off guard and when she replied, her voice sounded unnecessarily strong. "My passage was exactly one hundred and seventy-five pounds. For sharing a cabin, of course."

Something was amiss, but Chelsea couldn't put her finger on it. Honoria had the look Cosmo always wore when one of his schemes went awry.

"It's settled, then. Where shall I meet you, Mrs. Harris?"

"Dockside, tomorrow evening at seven. We sail on the tide at ten o'clock. And as long as we're going to be cabin-mates for the next three months, won't you call me Honoria? I—I'm sure we're going to become good friends,

Chelsea—I may call you Chelsea, mayn't I?" She smiled
nervously and chattered on without waiting for Chelsea to
reply. "Anyway, I just wanted to thank you again,
Chelsea, for being so helpful yesterday. It's fortunate that
we met."

"Yes, it is. You look so pale, Mrs.—Honoria. Are you
feeling ill?"

"No, not really. I—I suppose it's all the excitement,"
Honoria said wanly, waving an immaculate white handkerchief near her face.

Chelsea's suspicions were once again aroused. Honoria
was visibly upset and seemed to find the need to grope for
explanations and ingratiate herself, as if to cover up some
wrongdoing. But what could it possibly be? No money
had changed hands. What then was her problem?

In New Queen Street's Gentleman's Club, a fanciful
name for a pub, Quaid Tanner sat near the window and
stretched his long legs out before him. A fragrant cigar,
one of the few he allowed himself, was clenched between
his teeth, and a glass of ruby claret rested near his elbow.
As he gazed with unseeing eyes out onto the thoroughfare
at the scurrying shoppers gripping their purchases, he reflected upon his actions earlier that day when he'd waited
his turn in line to pay his passage home. His raven's-wing
black eyes had scrutinized his prospective fellow passengers for the voyage on the *Southern Cross* and finally come
to rest on a wan, frail-looking woman who'd been speaking with the ticket agent.

"And your servant's name, Mrs. Harris?" the ticket
agent had asked.

"Miss Chelsea Myles!" the woman had pronounced
with authority.

Quaid had inched forward when he'd heard Chelsea's
name mentioned. He'd immediately recognized "Mrs.

Harris" as the woman whose purse had been stolen two days before. How, then, had she come to acquaint herself with Chelsea Myles? A slow smile had softened his features as he'd recalled the scene between Chelsea and her uncle when she'd wrested the woman's purse from the folds of his garments. It was obvious this woman had not the slightest idea Chelsea had taken possession of the purloined purse; otherwise Miss Myles would be in the bowels of Newgate Prison instead of sailing as maid to her victim.

But before he'd had a chance to muse over the possibilities, it had been his turn at the window. Prior to leaving, Mrs. Harris had stepped aside and placed the tickets in her reticule. Soft brown eyes tinged with anxiety had locked for an instant with his inquiring gaze. She'd smiled briefly, then tucked her reticule under her arm and left.

Quaid had paid for his first-class passage, sticking the ticket in the breast pocket of his Chesterfield, intending to follow Mrs. Harris. Was it possible that the engaging actress was going along on the voyage as a maid, a common servant? The idea was suddenly so ridiculous that he had stopped in his tracks. Was he so eager to know the answer that he would track Mrs. Harris like a dog on the scent of a bitch in her first season? That was when he'd found his way into the Gentleman's Club.

The grimace on Quaid's face was almost comical as he sipped his wine. He shuddered and pushed the glass across the small table. It was a sin to serve such brew and worse yet to have to pay for it. In its worst year his vineyard had produced a finer vintage.

Clonmerra. Even the name was music to his ears. Clonmerra. If he hadn't had to come to England to search out new markets for Clonmerra's wines, he never could have made himself leave. Named for the Tanner ancestral estate in Ireland, it was his home and his fortune. Since leaving it, the weather conditions in his fertile valley had been his prime concern. How were his vines faring? His hands itched for a knife to trim back the runners. His mouth watered for the luscious fruit, rich with nature's sugar, which would ferment the crushed grapes into claret and port and sweet sauterne.

Soon it would all be his again. He would walk among his vines sampling, tasting, hovering, picking at the leaves, and watching over them as though they were his children. But his voyage to England had proved less than successful. Few wine merchants seemed interested in importing wines from Australian vineyards, those upstart enterprises that, however fine their product, sought to intrude on an established European market. Quaid was already anticipating another trip within the next three years. Perhaps the greedy American market would be more amenable to the risks of importing from "down under." Until then, he would hoard his vintage in aged wooden casks, improving the flavor, aging the wine, and hoping for the best.

His less-than-successful trip was more than discouraging since Clonmerra needed capital to continue operation. Only a handful of merchants had signed contracts with him; hardly enough to meet his needs, especially since England had discontinued the practice of sending the surplus of her convicts to New South Wales. Convict labor was cheap and provided much of the necessary manpower.

Quaid's eyes dropped to the ring he wore on the little finger of his left hand. The black opal was magnificent, he knew, flashed and shot through with color—the blues of the Australian sky, the greens of her lands during the wet season, the golds of the sunsets, the crimsons of the dawn upon the red earth. It was a perfect stone, flawless, and he had mined beneath the hard brown earth of Coober Pedy to find it himself. He had received many offers for it, outrageous offers of money, yet he could not part with it. To him it represented Australia itself, the land to which he was born, the land he loved.

Perhaps it was time to return again to that godforsaken mine to try his luck again. Some instinct told him that this particular stone had a mate somewhere. Together they could command a princely sum, enough to put Clonmerra back on its feet again.

It was a matter of principle, and of integrity, not to draw on the inheritance his father had left him. He had accepted the vineyards and title to the opal mine; if he wasn't man enough to make a success of them by sweat alone, then he wasn't entitled to the rest. More often than not he believed he was acting foolishly. Technically the inheritance was his, to do with as he pleased. Yet he was determined to prove—to himself, if not to the world—that he was a man, capable of designing his own future without depending upon money made by the sweat of another man's brow. It was a strength his father had admired in him, and it was something he intended to live by all the rest of his life.

The Clonmerra account in the Sydney bank was precariously low, but Quaid now had enough to replenish it from the sale of three white opals. He could last another two years, tending to his greedy, insatiable Clonmerra, at which time he would either find himself a success or destitute.

He was shaken from his sobering thoughts when he noticed a flurry of commotion across the street. Miss Chelsea Myles was exiting a shop, her arms laden with parcels. Two young men were competing for her attention, both offering to relieve her of her burdens. A smile tugged at the corner of Quaid's mouth. He wouldn't have recognized her dressed in such a modish fashion, had it not been for the proud carriage of her head and the haughty set of her shoulders, which threw her softly rounded breasts into prominence above her narrow waist. Was Miss Myles completing some last-minute shopping in preparation for her sea voyage? The urge to laugh aloud was so overwhelming he clapped his hand to his mouth and pretended an oncoming sneeze. He'd almost be tempted to wager the opal on his little finger that Miss Chelsea Myles had no idea she was going aboard the *Southern Cross* as a hiring woman to Mrs. Harris.

As Chelsea tripped along ahead of the two young men carrying her parcels, her trilling laughter grated on Quaid's nerves. Not that he wanted to be one of the fools waiting upon the lady. In fact, he wasn't certain exactly what it was that irritated him; he had enough problems without adding a thieving actress to his list. She passed quite close to the window, and he could see clearly the smooth fair brow, the gleaming chestnut hair, the tawny eyes that flashed with merriment or outrage. Beautiful. His eyes followed her out of sight; he was mesmerized by the easy grace with which she walked, the peculiar tilt of her head when she turned to speak to one of her young swains. She looked for all the world like a lady, and if he hadn't already known what she really was, he'd have been fooled. But a maid?

Quaid laughed all the way back to his lodgings, thinking of Chelsea Myles as a servant to one of her former marks. And the laugh erupted again when he entered his room and saw her tattered yellow feathered fan, now mounted in the frame of his mirror. He'd have to take that with him back to Clonmerra. Miss Chelsea Myles's rendition of Portia had left much to be desired, but when pleading her uncle's innocence to the police or strolling down the street as haughty as Queen Victoria herself, she was magnificent.

Yes, he would definitely take the fan with him. And he hoped he wasn't mistaken about her sailing aboard the

Southern Cross. A satisfied and eager smile worked the corners of his mouth. All birds had more than one feather to pluck.

Chelsea steeled herself for her farewell scene with Cosmo. She'd been rehearsing her lines all night long in her sleep and all day long as she packed her trunk, a new one purchased on Threadneedle Street. Now it was just after five in the afternoon, two hours away from meeting Honoria Harris at the Baynard's Castle wharf. Cosmo had hired a dray to convey his small troupe and their props to a theater on Fish Street, a notoriously disreputable part of the city.

While the others were loading the dray, she drew her uncle aside, determined to break the news to him in private. "Chelsea, just because you fancy yourself the star performer of this production company," he said with great authority, whilst leaning on his cane, "is no reason for you not to pitch in and help load with the rest of us. We must all do our share—"

"I'd like to talk to you, Uncle Cosmo," Chelsea interrupted softly. "Come with me to my room so we can enjoy some privacy."

Cosmo sucked in his ruddy cheeks. Trouble. Whenever Chelsea called him "Uncle Cosmo," it meant trouble. Any other time she behaved as though he were something kicked out of the gutter. His queasy stomach churned. He didn't want to engage in an argument with her, at least not before he'd managed somehow to get a share of her four hundred pounds. "Can't we talk later? After we load the wagon?"

"No, I'd like to speak to you now. Just a few minutes, I promise. Come along, Uncle, we haven't had a family chat for some time."

Family chat! Now he *knew* there was going to be trou-

ble! "Are you packed?" he asked, his Adam's apple bobbing nervously.

"Oh, yes, I've been packed since this morning. Come
along, Uncle, this won't take long."

Cosmo stood inside Chelsea's room while she closed the
door. Not such a bad place, really, but the way Chelsea
complained one would think it was an East End slum. Well,
he was getting sick and tired of her high-handed ways. She
was his niece and he was her protector; she should exhibit
more respect for him, and he intended to tell her as much.
And as for the four hundred pounds she'd taken from him,
she had better hand it over. If he'd known there was more
than three pounds in that little purse, he would have
fought to the death before letting Chelsea get her hands on
it. All manner of mean, grasping thoughts raced through
Cosmo's•head as he formed the words that would intimidate his niece into handing over his hard-earned money.

"Uncle Cosmo," Chelsea began, "I'm afraid I've some
news for you, and I don't believe you're going to like it.
We have, you and I, come to a parting of the ways."

At her words, all color drained from Cosmo's face. His
quick eye took in the packed trunk—a new trunk! No
doubt paid for with a part of the money she owed him.
Bile rose in his throat. Where would he find a replacement
at this late hour? Chelsea's fair features and womanly figure were more of a box office draw than he'd ever admitted to her.

"I want to better myself, Uncle," she went on. "We are
going nowhere with this shoddy little production, except
perhaps to Newgate, and I want no more of it. I'm leaving."

"You ungrateful little guttersnipe!" he roared in his best
"wounded patriarch" voice. "Where would you have been
if I hadn't come along and taken you under my wing when
your parents died? I've always done my best for you,

Chelsea, and this is the way you repay me. I won't have it!"

"Your best isn't good enough, Uncle Cosmo." She pretended a coolness she didn't feel. "I possibly would have been better off today if I'd gone into service—or even let myself be taken to St. Matthew's."

"How can you be so ungrateful? I won't have it! I'm warning you! I won't have it!"

Cosmo's eyes glittered, and something in his tone filled her with apprehension. "What will you do?" she asked, forcing a bravado she didn't feel. Now she regretted this confrontation; she should simply have left, giving her uncle no opportunity for his tricks.

Cosmo smiled nastily. "I could have Swift Billy in here to force you into the dray. He and Prudence would tear you apart if they knew about the four hundred pounds. Speaking of which, where is it, Chelsea? I want it now!"

"I don't have it," she lied. "I used it to pay for my passage out of London. As I told you, I'm leaving."

Cosmo peered deeply into her tawny eyes. "If what you say is true, we'll just go down to the wharf and obtain a refund. You see, Chelsea, dear niece, you're not going anywhere, not without me, at least."

"You! You're the reason I'm leaving—to get away from you! I'm sick of this life, of the shabby costumes and men leering and living a hairsbreadth away from the law. I don't want to waste my life rotting in prison, and as long as I stay with you and your merry band of thieves, that prospect looms closer every day."

"So it's the law that frightens you? What would you say if I told you I would have no compunction about turning you over to the authorities? Perhaps I cannot force you to stay with me, but I assure you the police have a place for ungrateful girls like yourself."

For an instant, Chelsea was taken aback. But only for

an instant. "Uncle," she said smoothly, "if you were to put me in the company of a policeman for one minute, I would tell him how you managed to acquire that pocketwatch you're so fond of sporting. Let me see"—she tapped her tooth with a fingernail—"that was a gift from a certain Mrs. Hodges, wasn't it? And I believe there was also an unsuspecting widow by the name of Mrs. Smythe. And aren't there one or two Mrs. Perragutts floating around near Portsmouth? Both of whom belong to you, am I correct? Do you know the penalty for bigamy, Uncle?"

A fine sheen of perspiration formed on Cosmo's upper lip. Everything Chelsea said was true, but he was not about to give up so easily; perhaps there was still a way to get some of that money after all. "May I ask, my dear, just where you are going?"

"To America," she lied smoothly.

His eyebrows shot upward. "America! Even first class to America doesn't require four hundred pounds! Hand the rest of it over, Chelsea, or I'll call Swift Billy in here, and you know what a nasty little rotter he can be."

"Call him, then," Chelsea challenged. "Call him and tell him how there were four hundred pounds in the purse he snatched and explain to him how you gave it to me for safekeeping. I did get the purse from you, didn't I? If you think that little Neanderthal will listen to reason, you've another think coming, Cosmo."

"You're an ungrateful witch, Chelsea," Cosmo growled, recognizing the truth in her words, "and if your poor mother could only hear the way you've repaid my kindness . . ."

"Save your breath, Uncle. My poor mother has been dead for over ten years. Ten years slaving for you, doing your bidding, living off your crimes. It was easy to take an eleven-year-old child and train her to your ways, but the child is now a woman and more difficult to handle."

Chelsea drew herself up to her full height. "I believe we've said all there is to say, Cosmo. I've already sent the costumes and other property belonging to the troupe out to the dray."

She turned her back on Cosmo, squeezing her eyes shut, almost expecting him to attack her from behind and throttle her within an inch of her life. He felt betrayed, and perhaps he had every right, but she had her rights, also, and she was making full use of them. A long, long moment later, the door closed behind her.

So this was the way it was to end, she thought, almost ten years of her life. Several minutes later, when the dray pulled away from the doorstep, Chelsea sank down onto the edge of her bed. Already she missed the small security of the troupe. Security. She was on her own now, responsible for herself. Say what she might about Cosmo and his preferred way of life, he had always managed to put food in her belly and keep a roof over her head. Was it wrong to want so much more?

A small, slow tear formed in the corner of her eye. Not only was she leaving the troupe, she was leaving England, her birthplace, and everything and everyone she knew. Quickly she brushed her tears away. It was silly to cry over nothing. She had a chance for herself, and she was going to take it! She didn't know what life held in store for her, but it had to be better than this. In fact, she would see to it!

Chapter 4

Honoria Harris glanced around her tiny quarters to see if she had inadvertently left anything behind. Penurious by nature, she believed there was no sense leaving anything of value for the landlady. Now, as she prepared to leave her apartment, she felt no regret at leaving England, no aching sense of loss. Later, she knew, when the last sight of England was left behind, she would cry torrents. Not even when she'd received news of her husband's death in the service of the queen had she felt so desolate, so completely alone.

Jason, who had not given her an argument when she'd said he needn't come to see her off, had at least offered to make arrangements for a carriage to pick her up at her lodgings promptly at six-thirty. The remainder of her money was carefully pinned to her chemise, and another packet, a small one containing coins, was tucked into the waistband of her petticoat. She decided the arrangement she'd made with Chelsea Myles was definitely to her liking, as it left her with a little extra, a bit of a nest egg to— as Miss Myles had put it—make her feel less at the mercy of her husband. This way she wouldn't have to beg if she wanted a ribbon or a bit of lace. It would be a new beginning, and a wiser one this time, she hoped.

As yet, her life hadn't been idyllic. The youngest of two daughters and not favored with good looks, she'd been pressured into an arranged marriage to the third son of a respectable but hardly wealthy family. Then, when Andrew had died, she'd quickly become the poor relation and found herself at her sister's mercy. Still, Jason and Barbara had been kind enough, in their way. And Jason had paid for her passage and trousseau. He'd seen to it that she would be married in style. She would not shame him, he had decided, but neither would he allow her to forget that she would always be in his debt.

At first the penurious Honoria had been appalled by the number of new garments Jason had insisted she order, thinking he meant her to pay for them out of her small inheritance. But when she'd learned he was accepting the bill himself, she'd allowed herself the pleasure of delighting in her wardrobe, admiring all the fashionable dresses and fondling the delicate, lacy nightdresses. Her new shoes were of the softest leather, and the gloves displayed infinitely delicate stitching. Jason was sending her off fully equipped to entice a new husband. Secretly, she believed he'd given her the trousseau to compensate for his exaggerations concerning her womanly charms in his letters to Mr. Kane. She knew for certain that he had never revealed her age. As though thirty-three were so old!

Honoria checked the tiny timepiece pinned to her bodice. The carriage should be arriving at any minute. She hoped Chelsea would be prompt; it wouldn't do to make an unflattering impression on the captain, would it? Her conscience pricked her for a moment when she remembered that she'd registered for the sailing as Mrs. Honoria Harris and maid. Since servants were never invited to take meals in the dining room, their fare was greatly reduced. She hoped Chelsea wouldn't be too upset when she discovered the little ploy; she could always say it was a misunderstanding and profess innocence. Perhaps it wasn't quite honest, but then was Chelsea Myles being honest with her? As unpleasant as it was to think about it, some nagging suspicions concerning her travel partner persisted.

A furious pumping in her chest forced Honoria to sit down. Every time something went wrong, she had one of these attacks. Without looking in the mirror, she knew that her lips had a bluish tinge and her face was ashen. Too much excitement. Once she was out on the open sea her health would improve, she was certain of it. Most physicians recommended a sea voyage to restore the constitution; why had her doctor objected? Just because she'd been having these episodes more frequently lately? It was probably just nerves, no matter what that quack said.

Honoria took a deep breath and relaxed. It was over, anyway, and what was done was done. She felt weak but eager to get on with her trip. Rising slowly, she grasped the arm of the chair to steady herself, then tugged at her gray linsey woolsey traveling dress and patted the white ruffle near her neck. When she spied her reflection in the mirror, she had to admit that she was the one who looked like the maid. No doubt Chelsea would arrive at the harbor with twelve trunks in tow, all of them crammed with the most luxurious costumes and accessories, and all of them flamboyantly colorful and dramatic. Just once she wished she had the courage to see herself flamboyantly dressed, wearing low-cut bodices and figure-defining undergarments. Her bosom was every bit as generous as Chelsea's; in fact, they were very close in size. Perhaps, in the privacy of their cabin, Chelsea would allow her to try on Portia's costume, just to see what she looked like.

A knock sounded at the door; the carriage had arrived. After instructing the driver about the baggage, she left the flat without a backward glance. There were no memories to leave behind.

When the carriage arrived at the wharf at exactly seven o'clock, Honoria was almost giddy with relief. It was true, it was happening, she was really leaving to begin a new life. The giddiness stayed with her, and when she alighted from the carriage weakness overcame her again. A portly, elderly gentleman came to her assistance and was escorting her up the gang rail when Chelsea arrived on the scene. Instantly she rushed to Honoria's aid, managing to get her aboard ship and settled into their assigned cabin.

"Truly, I don't know what's come over me," Honoria said apologetically. "I suppose it's all the excitement."

Chelsea frowned; she didn't need a sickly companion. A vision of Honoria retching into a chamber pot set her teeth on edge. "Are you ill, Honoria?"

"Not really," Honoria replied, averting her eyes. "I believe it's simply the excitement. Please, don't concern yourself with me. I'll lie down and rest for a while."

But Chelsea wasn't satisfied with the explanation. "If you feel ill now, how are you going to feel once we set sail? Seasickness can be a terrible affliction, I'm told. If it isn't too late, we could change our cabin arrangements. You might not want me here if you're ill."

The surge of panic at the thought of being left alone did terrible things to Honoria's heart. "Please," she gasped, holding her hand out to Chelsea, "don't even consider such a thing. Think of the difference in the passage fare. I'll be fine. You did say you would help me. Leave me to rest. I'll be fine, I promise."

Chelsea wondered if she'd jumped from the frying pan into the fire. A sickly companion in close quarters was more than she'd bargained for. And speaking of close quarters, the cabin they were to share certainly fell far short. Perhaps there had been a mistake; surely a double cabin should be larger than this one—and shouldn't there be two beds instead of a built-in bunk and a trundle?

Honoria lay back, her hand on her forehead. She felt awful, worse than before. If only she had some tea and brandy . . . Dare she ask Chelsea to get it for her? A queasy feeling erupted in her stomach as she felt her chest tighten again. This time she didn't even think twice. "Chelsea, could I impose on you to see about some tea with a tad of brandy?"

When Chelsea returned, Honoria sucked greedily at the rim of the cup, traces of the tea dribbling down her chin. "It's not hot," she whined. "It won't help me if it's not hot."

The pity welling in Chelsea's breast died. "I'm sorry, it was the best I could do. I was lucky to get it at all," she said defensively, remembering the cook's reluctance to open his kitchen before breakfast in the morning. It had been a mistake to share her cabin with Honoria. She could feel it in her bones.

"Chelsea, as long as you're unpacking your trunks, do you think you could do some of mine? At least a night-dress and my slippers. A fresh gown for tomorrow. There really isn't anything else for either of us to do at the moment, and since I'm confined to my bed, we can chat while you unpack."

Chelsea's mouth quirked. Well, that settled the question of who was to sleep on the trundle. "Honoria, you have seven trunks. I have only two. I'll be here all night. You can't possibly wear everything you own, and at any rate, where do you suppose I would put it all? This cabin is hardly large enough for one woman, much less two. I intend to speak to the purser about this. Surely a double cabin is larger than this."

"No . . . no, don't," Honoria protested. When she saw the question in Chelsea's eyes, she added, "No, don't leave me! I couldn't possibly stand being left alone. The cabin really isn't so small, once the trundle is tucked under this bed." She leaned back into Chelsea's supporting arms, willing her to stay. Then, the whine back in her voice, she added, "Chelsea, everything will be so wrinkled and we'll look quite disheveled when we go above on deck. The gowns need to be hung so they smooth themselves. I think it would be best if they were hung *now.*"

"Cosmo, I think I will live to regret my hasty decision," Chelsea muttered beneath her breath.

"Did you say something, Chelsea?"

"No, just talking to myself." She grimaced when she saw Honoria inch closer to the wall, her hands clutching the coverlet on the bunk. Dear old Cosmo would laugh his silly head off if he could see what she'd gotten herself into. Three months of being a nursemaid.

By the time she'd finished unpacking her own trunk, Honoria was sound asleep. Chelsea tiptoed over to the bunk and stood looking down at the sleeping woman. Carefully, gently, she undid the buttons at the top of Honoria's dun-gray gown and then removed her shoes. At least she would be comparatively comfortable while she slept. What was she going to do if Honoria became really ill? Who would care for her? Not liking the answer, Chelsea opened Honoria's trunks and began removing the contents.

From time to time, as she pulled out various garments, Chelsea marveled at the quality of the fabrics and the fine stitching. In her entire life Chelsea had never owned anything half as grand. Her eyes narrowed as she looked at the sleeping woman. This was a trousseau fit for a princess. And Honoria, in Chelsea's opinion, was not a princess. Everything was new, except for a few serviceable gowns, and everything was beautiful. Lace-edged petticoats, satin-embroidered chemises, ingeniously boned corsets, and delicate pantaloons. She itched to try on one gown in particular, a lavender silk brocade. It was a gown for dancing, for tantalizing a man, a gown for bewitching. Delving into the bottom of the trunk, she found a pair of matching satin slippers.

Stunned by the luxuriousness of Honoria's possessions, Chelsea sank down onto the narrow trundle. How was it somebody like Honoria could have all these fine things while she herself wore what amounted to tatters? It wasn't fair. Someday, she promised herself fiercely, she, too, would have things as fine, even finer, and a husband to give them to her.

But what upset her more than anything else was the knowledge that Honoria was a lady of class and breeding, attributes she, Chelsea, could never possess. Never, that is, unless she married into them. Now *that* was something she hadn't considered, a rich husband. A wealthy *gentleman* for a husband, someone to lend his own class and breeding and elevate her in this world. A giggle erupted and she choked it down. Why in the world had she thought she had to make her own way in this world? She had something Honoria would never have—beauty. Wasn't it Helen of Troy whose face had launched a thousand ships? Chelsea's fingers grazed her delicate chin and the soft curve of her nose. Well, perhaps she couldn't launch a thousand ships, but certainly there was one little square rigger out there looking for a home port.

It wasn't until she'd hung the last of Honoria's gowns that Chelsea noticed the movement of the ship and the creaking of the timbers. Or was it Honoria's low moans of discomfort? Glancing over at the bunk, she saw her companion lying with eyes fixed on the ceiling. "Honoria, I'm going up on deck. We're under way, and I want to take a last look at London."

Honoria nodded, unable to speak. If she unclamped her teeth, she knew she would retch. The last time she had felt so terrible was when she was a young girl with rheumatic fever, the illness that had left her in such a delicate condition. She clamped a hand over her mouth and rolled toward the wall. There was no need for Chelsea to see how ghastly she looked. She envied Chelsea's vitality. The actress literally bubbled with good health and nothing seemed to bother her. She would probably spend three months at sea without any ill effects, eating and drinking at her own pleasure, completely free of seasickness.

"Dear God," she prayed aloud after Chelsea had left the cabin, "don't let this entire voyage be like these past hours." But she knew her prayers were not destined to be answered. She just knew. Tears gathered in her eyes as she fought to control her queasiness. Why, when she was embarking on a fresh beginning, did life have to be so miserable?

Chelsea followed the glowing lanterns along the companionway to the stairs leading abovedeck. She found a spot to lean against the rail looking out over the stern for her last glimpse of London. It seemed twenty-odd other passengers had had the same idea. The city dockside was glowing with gaslight, magical nimbuses of brightness softened by the evening fog. She could still hear the shouts and calls of the stevedores as they loaded or unloaded cargo. Far up the Thames loomed the towering structure of London Bridge, and behind her she could hear the muted bells of St. Paul's striking the half hour.

So she was leaving the only home she had ever known, London, one of the oldest cities in the world, traveling to ports unknown, to a raw and exotic land. Would she ever see home again? Ever again hear the chimes of St. Bride's or smell the delicious aromas from the bakers of Whitechapel Street? Suddenly tears sprang to her eyes, and a lump formed in her throat. This had been her city, her place, the shops on Cheapside, the peddlers outside the East India House, the lawns and gardens of St. James Park. She was leaving it, all of it, perhaps for good. A woman's deep, choking sob tore through the silence. Everyone aboard ship seemed moved and melancholy, all thinking the same thoughts, all experiencing the same sudden homesickness.

"She's a beauty by starlight," said a deep voice behind her, so unexpectedly close that when Chelsea turned she found herself pressed against a broad masculine chest.

"Excuse me . . ." she began apologetically, instantly drawing backward.

"I said, she's a beauty," he repeated. "London, I mean."

"Yes. I was just wondering if I shall ever see her again."

"If you like it here so well, why are you voyaging to Australia?"

Was she mistaken, or was there a barely disguised challenge in his tone? The lantern shed its light behind him, making it impossible to see his face clearly. She was impressed with his height and the width of his shoulders and somewhat intimidated by his approach. "Why does one travel to New South Wales?" she answered vaguely.

"A number of reasons come to mind. To seek one's fortune, to begin a new life, to marry, to join family, even to explore the gold fields. Which is your reason?"

Chelsea turned back to the rail, leveling her gaze on the city lights, which were becoming fewer and fewer as they sailed down the Thames. She didn't care for this man's impertinence. And he was standing much too close, improperly so. Pressing against the rail and pretending great interest in the scene over the stern, she hoped he wouldn't realize she hadn't answered.

"I suppose we can eliminate the gold fields." He laughed softly. "That proves to be too strenuous for most men and is hardly a fitting occupation for a lady like yourself."

Chelsea's annoyance increased. Now he sounded as though he were mocking her.

"Ah, perhaps there is a suitor waiting impatiently for your arrival. Where is your destination once we land in New South Wales?"

"I hardly believe that's any of your business," Chelsea answered, trying to keep the annoyance from her voice. "I don't know you, and I'm not in the habit of speaking with strangers."

"That tells me something, at least," he remarked dryly. "This must be your first voyage, else you would already know what a tight little group passengers aboard ship make. Three months at sea hardly leaves room for distance or, in most cases, even proper demeanor. You will find, I'm certain, that acquaintance is made rather quickly here."

Chelsea's instincts were aroused. Something about this man alarmed her, made her feel as though he knew far more about her than he revealed. As she turned and peered through the darkness, searching for recognition, they were approached by a ship's officer, the gold insignia on his dark jacket illuminated by the lantern's light. He tugged at the visor of his cap and introduced himself. "Nelson Rollins, ship's purser. Cabin number, please?"

"P-seven," Chelsea volunteered, grateful for the interruption.

"That's portside seven," the purser informed her, checking his log for the name of the cabin's occupant. "Mrs. Honoria Harris," he intoned formally, "the captain would be pleased to have you join his table for dinner tomorrow night. Will you accept? Oh, pardon, Mr. Tanner, I see you've already made Mrs. Harris's acquaintance. Mr. Tanner will also be joining the captain tomorrow evening."

For a moment Chelsea was confused. Then she realized the purser thought she was Honoria. "Who else will be joining the captain?" she asked lightly.

"Mr. Tanner, of course, Mr. and Mrs. Crane, and myself. Captain Winfield would be delighted for your company, Mrs. Harris."

Chelsea felt deflated. Obviously she wasn't good enough to be asked to sit at the captain's table.

"Will you join the captain then, Mrs. Harris?" the purser persisted.

"Where will Miss Myles be sitting? " she asked curiously.

Once again the purser checked his list. "I don't see any . . . oh, yes, Miss Myles, your servant. Naturally, Miss Myles will take her supper either in the kitchen, or she will be permitted to carry a tray back to your cabin."

Even in the darkness Quaid could see the flush that stained Chelsea's cheeks, making him think of a smoldering fire ready to burst skyward.

"Mrs. Harris? Dinner?"

"Naturally, Mrs. Harris couldn't refuse the captain," Quaid assured the purser. "Could you, Mrs. Harris?"

At a loss, Chelsea found she could only shake her head and murmur, "Of course not." Servant! Maid! Damn that Honoria with all her high-handed delicacy and manners.

"May I walk you to your cabin, Mrs. Harris?" Quaid asked gallantly when the purser had left.

"I'm quite capable of finding my way back alone," she assured him. "Thank you anyway."

"No, please. Often the lanterns are unpredictable in the companionways. I insist." He stepped back, allowing her to pass in front of him. "You really shouldn't have come on deck alone, Mrs. Harris," he told her as they strolled toward the stern and the hatch leading below. "It's quite dangerous. I advise you to come above in the company of your maid; it's much safer."

Chelsea stopped in her tracks. "Are you suggesting I be

concerned about the integrity of crew aboard this ship or the passengers, Mr. Tanner, or are you warning me of some other danger?" Her eyes flinted sparks of indignation. How dare this man treat her so familiarly? Twice she'd had to shrug her elbow out of his grip.

"Neither the passengers nor the crew need alarm you." He laughed, a deep, masculine rumble of amusement. "But the sea is another matter entirely. It's quite easy to fall overboard, did you know?"

"No, I didn't," she replied tartly. The sooner she got to her cabin, the better; she wanted to be rid of this impertinent pest.

"Yes, well, it's true all the same. I insist you keep your maid at your side. What did the purser say her name was?"

"Why is everyone so interested in my maid?" Chelsea demanded.

"Interested?" he queried innocently, but to Chelsea it sounded like a barb. "I'm only interested in your safety. Oh, Mrs. Harris, remember to make arrangements with the galley for her meals. The poor woman does have to eat, and since she is traveling on your ticket at a reduced rate, you must see to the arrangements yourself."

"Why don't you let me worry about how my maid is going to eat. Trust me, she won't starve. Right now she's indisposed." Chelsea's brain was reeling with the force of her angry thoughts. Reduced fare! Traveling on her ticket! That tricky, deceiving Honoria Harris! No wonder she had to sleep on a trundle bed instead of a proper bunk. Even Cosmo wouldn't have had the nerve to pull a stunt like this.

Chelsea led the way down the hatch, stepping carefully down the stairs that had been installed for the passengers' convenience. Mr. Tanner followed close on her heels.

"Honoria," she heard him murmur. "I had an aunt by that name, a dour-faced spinster. Somehow, it doesn't seem to fit you."

Chelsea was becoming more rattled by the moment, but she was determined not to let it show. "Actually, Honoria is an old family name, but I prefer to use my mother's name, Chelsea."

Quaid's brows shot upward. "Two unusual names? No doubt another family tradition."

"No doubt," Chelsea snapped. "Here is my cabin, Mr. Tannert. Thank you for escorting me." In the bright light of the companionway, she was able to get a closer look at him. Tall, dark, lean, with a complexion that bespoke long days in the sun. He certainly was handsome, but why did he constantly wear that mocking grin?

"The name is Tanner, not Tannert. Quaid Tanner. Since this is your first voyage, Mrs. Harris, I put myself at your disposal. If I can be of any assistance, I will be happy to oblige."

"I hardly think that will be necessary," Chelsea demured sweetly. "Good night, Mr. Tanner."

Quickly, before he could say anything more, she opened the door and slipped inside, closing the door behind her and leaning against it. Her heart was beating as though she'd just escaped with her life.

Something about Quaid Tanner disturbed her. She hadn't liked the way he'd kept on speaking about her maid and calling her Mrs. Harris. And there'd been a light in his eyes, a merriment, that had made her feel as though he knew the answer to some great riddle or was party to a joke. Why, oh, why had she allowed the pretense to continue? Behind her, startling her so that she almost jumped out of her skin, came a sharp rap.

"Mrs. Harris," Quaid called through the door. "I thought you'd like to know that we're neighbors, so to speak. My cabin is just across the companionway, portside eight."

Chelsea's jaw dropped, and the most she could manage was a tart, "Good night, Mr. Tanner!" She listened to the soft thud of his door as it closed.

Only one gimbaled lantern glowed softly, and in the dimness Chelsea was aware of Honoria's movements. She turned in time to see the other woman hang her head over a slop pail and retch with painful, dry heaves. At the moment, Chelsea was hard-pressed to keep from adding to the woman's agony. Maid indeed!

For a few brief moments Chelsea gloried in Honoria's retching. She was paying for her deceit right now. The question was, when would she, Chelsea, be called on to pay for *her* deceit? She waited determinedly until Honoria had leaned back against her pillow. Better to get all of this out into the open right now.

"I'm sorry, Chelsea," Honoria murmured before Chelsea could speak. "I did so want to start off this trip feeling fit and hale. I don't want to spoil it for you."

"That's very kind of you, Honoria, but aren't you a little late with your concern for me? I just found out, by accident, that you signed me on as your servant. For shame, Honoria! How could you do such a thing? I thought we were friends. Just now the purser came up to me, called me Mrs. Harris, and invited me to the captain's table for dinner. In front of another passenger! I was so dumbfounded that you could play such a trick on me that I was left with nothing to say. Now everyone is going to think I am you and you are me. And I'm not going to be the one to undeceive them. How much did you save by doing this?" Chelsea demanded suddenly.

Honoria waved her hand as if to say it didn't matter. Well, Chelsea thought, it matters to me! She watched as Honoria leaned over the slop pail a second time. "I don't know why I did it, really I don't," Honoria said weakly. "Something came over me and I just did it. I was wrong and I apologize. Please forgive me."

"You've made a fool of me," Chelsea said tightly. "I was so nice to you, helping you home that night and then going to your brother-in-law's house with you, and this is how you repay me. I don't even have a decent bunk to sleep in! How would you feel if I'd done this to you?"

Honoria groaned. Couldn't she ever do anything right? All her life she'd bollixed things up. This time she'd really done a job of it. Whatever would she do if Chelsea moved out of the cabin?

"When I asked the purser about what Miss Myles was to do in regard to her meals, he said 'the maid' would be permitted to eat in the kitchen or have a tray in the cabin. Ohhh," Chelsea said, throwing her hands in the air dramatically.

"Take my place," Honoria suggested suddenly. "Pretend to be me. I'm ill, and I have a feeling I'm going to remain in this condition for the remainder of the trip. It's the least I can do to make up to you for what I've done."

"Take your place?" Chelsea echoed as though the thought hadn't occurred to her the moment the purser had called her Mrs. Harris.

"It's not so unthinkable. No one on board knows either of us. We won't be hurting anyone. For your part all you'll have to do is see to it that my meals are brought to the cabin. I think that's fair, Chelsea."

"I don't have the proper clothes to pretend to be you, Honoria. My wardrobe is meager, at best."

Honoria leaned over the bed again, and this time Chelsea pitied the white-faced, retching woman. When she leaned back against the pillows again, Chelsea could see that she was exhausted and thoroughly drained.

"You can wear my things," Honoria offered wearily. "I

know you'll take care of them. You can tell me about the dinners and the get-togethers when you return to the cabin. We could even keep a journal to remind us of this trip."

Chelsea's conscience pricked her. The woman did look ill, was in fact ill.

The outlook of having to suffer through the night—let alone the next three months—with Honoria's illness was not a pleasant one, but she was committed now. Chelsea knew she was being selfish in thinking of herself at a time like this, but she was disappointed that her "fresh start" had such a tarnished beginning.

In the end it was Chelsea who, through the night, whispered calm reassurances to Honoria and pressed cool cloths to her brow. When the first light of day finally peeped through the porthole, she was nearly as exhausted as her bunk mate. Her first night aboard the *Southern Cross* had proved a dismal portent for her grand new future.

Chapter 5

Most of the day had passed before Chelsea was able to struggle from her trundle bed. Honoria had been asleep since sunrise, allowing Chelsea her much-needed rest. As she sat on the trundle, face turned toward her sleeping companion, she contemplated three more months of inconvenience with a sinking heart. Surely there was *something* that could be done; perhaps a doctor would know. Honoria was certainly not the first victim of seasickness—perhaps one of the ship's officers would know what should be done.

Rising quietly so as not to disturb Honoria, Chelsea washed quickly and dressed, her stomach rumbling ominously all the while. It was too late for breakfast, but perhaps it was close to lunchtime. Quickly, she brushed her glossy chestnut hair with long strokes, piling the heaviness atop her head and securing it with tortoiseshell combs. Pinching her cheeks and dabbing a bit of powder on her nose, she left the cabin, closing the door softly behind her.

"Yes, Mrs. Harris," said Nelson Rollins, the purser. "A terrible affliction, terrible. I've seen cases of seasickness that have confined strong men to their beds for an entire voyage. Why don't you come to my office after lunch and

I'll give you some laudanum for your maid. Give it to her when she's at her worst; it will help her sleep through the rigors. Be careful, however: laudanum can be addictive."

"I'll be careful, Mr. Rollins," Chelsea assured him. "I'll keep it on my person at all times and administer it to her only when she absolutely needs it."

Rollins found himself smiling at this lovely, sweetly solicitous young woman who expressed such deep concern for her servant. Captain Winfield was certainly going to enjoy his dinner this night in the company of Mrs. Harris.

When Chelsea stepped into the dining room to help herself to the cold buffet laid out for the passengers, she spied Quaid Tanner deeply involved in conversation with a gentleman. He didn't appear to notice her, and she was glad for it. Another pall had settled over her bright expectations for this voyage, and it's name was Quaid Tanner. She didn't like the man; he was impertinent and forward, and his slightly derisive yet altogether respectful treatment of her the night before still rankled. It was almost as though he realized the little deception in which she'd become involved.

Hastily choosing a luncheon of cold sliced meat, bread and butter, and several pickled eggs, Chelsea poured herself a brimming cup of hot coffee and took the meal out on deck, where she could enjoy the sea breezes and avoid Mr. Tanner at the same time.

"A pity you didn't awaken earlier," a woman's voice said behind her, interrupting her solitude. "You've just missed seeing us round out of Portsmouth into the English Channel. You really should make it a practice to rise early; otherwise you'll not be sleepy at bedtime, and aboard ship everyone turns in early." This advice came from a portly woman tucked into a heavy velvet cape that covered her from neck to toe. "Forgive me for not introducing myself. I'm Mrs. Porter Crain. I've made this voyage several times before, and I surely hope this will be the last. And you're Mrs. Honoria Harris. Porter calls me a busybody, but I got your name from the purser."

The woman's vigor was overwhelming. She talked knowledgeably and enthusiastically about everything, giving advice for life at sea, instructing Chelsea to walk twenty times around the deck morning and night, and urging her to partake lightly of the galley's fare before sleeping. "My father was a doctor of unsullied reputation as well as an experienced traveler, and his advice has always been excellent."

Chelsea's ears pricked up at that. "Then perhaps you can tell me a remedy for seasickness?" she asked.

"There's little one can do," Mrs. Crain replied. "A terrible affliction to be sure. You're not suffering, are you, my dear?" The woman's eyes flicked over Chelsea's generously laden plate. "If you are, I would suggest a plain diet and cool tea and not forcing yourself to eat so heartily."

"Oh, no, I'm fine. It's my companion who's ill. She suffered the night through, and the purser, Mr. Rollins, said he would give me some laudanum for her after I've had my lunch."

"Good! You looked to me like a young woman of healthy constitution. I'm glad to hear you're not in any discomfort. Laudanum is fine, given sparingly. At least it will allow the poor woman to regain her strength, somewhat. I fear you're in for a dreadful voyage if your companion is already ill at this stage of the voyage. Why, we haven't even hit open sea yet. Perhaps you should see about other accommodations, Mrs. Harris, else you'll be as enervated as your companion before the voyage is over. There's an empty first-class cabin next to ours. I should speak to the purser if I were you."

Chelsea thought of the additional money a first-class cabin would require. "No, I couldn't possibly leave her," she declared firmly. "It would hardly be Christian, considering the circumstances."

"Religion has little to do with one's health, Mrs. Harris." Mrs. Crain chastised. "You don't want to arrive in New South Wales depleted of your strength and energy. Australia is a hard country, especially for women."

"You've lived there, then?"

"Yes, for more than twenty years. I remember when Sydney was a refuge for the convicts who landed in Botany Bay. Freed men, of course," she explained. "Those still in penalty were used in work crews, cutting roads and working farms. There's little I don't know about Australia, Mrs. Harris, and I speak with the voice of experience. Are you traveling to family?"

Chelsea was momentarily at a loss for words. Was everyone aboard this ship so blatantly curious? Living in London among strangers, for the most part, had not prepared her for this kind of interested scrutiny. First Quaid Tanner and now the prying and authoritative Mrs. Crain. "In a manner of speaking," Chelsea said at last, not wanting to reveal more than was necessary.

Mrs. Crain seemed not to notice her evasive answer. "It's wise for a young woman to have family or contacts in Australia. It's not a place for a woman on her own, no indeed. I know you're traveling with your maid. I hope you plan to keep her in your employ. Labor is so available and so inexpensive in New South Wales, doubtless she'll find herself on the streets otherwise."

The taste of the cold beef turned sour in Chelsea's mouth, and it was almost impossible to swallow. After sipping some coffee, she managed to say, "Surely you exaggerate, Mrs. Crain. I should think there would be many opportunities for women in a burgeoning new city."

"Not unless that woman is firmly attached to a man," Mrs. Crain declared vehemently, her ash-gray curls bobbing with each shake of her head. "I confess, it's a situation I deplore, but one that exists nevertheless. It's far worse than London even when it comes to seeking employment, and almost impossible for a decent woman. It's the population, you know. Too many hands for the same job. Although perhaps a well-trained English lady's maid would find an easier time of it. I could understand how those talents might be in demand. However, she would be competing for wages, and believe me, the cheaper bid would win out."

Again the food seemed to lodge in Chelsea's throat. And she had thought making her fortune and bettering herself would be easy in a new colony. A new beginning! Yes, if she was willing to hire herself out as a servant, a blow her pride would never withstand.

"So, if you've any fondness for your maid, you'll keep her in your employ."

"Yes, yes, I intend to do so. You'll have to excuse me, Mrs. Crain; I must meet Mr. Rollins for the laudanum."

"You might try giving her a few drops of peppermint to settle her stomach. And I believe I'll be seeing you again at dinner. Good day, Mrs. Harris." And as abruptly as she'd come upon her, Mrs. Crain dismissed her.

When Chelsea returned to the cabin with the laudanum and specific instructions for its use, she found Honoria still sleeping, finding at last some escape from her misery. Chelsea almost envied her the oblivion; her own recent interview with Mrs. Crain had left her depleted of energy and filled with worry. If what the woman said was true, then Chelsea had jumped out of the frying pan and into the fire. Lying down on her narrow trundle, she forced herself to close her eyes and clear her mind. What was done was done; there was nothing to do about it now. She was on her way to Australia, and she would find something, some way to make a better life for herself.

Later, she was awakened by the sound of Honoria retching into the slop pail. She was glad she had closed the curtain surrounding Honoria's bed. It was bad enough to hear the choking and gagging, worse still to observe at firsthand what the woman was going through.

When the episode was over, Chelsea softly lifted back the curtain. "You aren't feeling any better, are you, Honoria? I've brought you something to help you rest, but the purser said it shouldn't be taken on an empty stomach. Would you like me to bring you something from the galley? Tea, a light bread roll?"

Honoria shook her head, her pale hand going to her damp brow, standing out in stark relief against her greenish complexion. "No, nothing just now. I'm feeling better, really I am," she reassured Chelsea, but she didn't sound convincing.

"Then at least let me put a cool cloth on your head." She moved to the washstand to drench a cloth and wring it out. It occurred to her that she was acting the part of Honoria's maid as though in fulfillment of the way she had been registered on the passenger list.

Leaving Honoria with the cooling cloth, Chelsea picked up the slop pail and left the room. She hadn't even closed the door to their cabin when she bumped into Quaid Tanner in the companionway.

"Mrs. Harris, where are you going? Is something wrong? The stewards carry the slop pails; you shouldn't be doing that."

"Yes, I should, the stench is unbearable. My companion is ill."

"How kind you are, to care for a servant with such diligence." That slow, knowing smile was back, irritating Chelsea to distraction. "Even to the degree of emptying her slop pail."

"Mr. Tanner," Chelsea said through clenched teeth,

"I've come to the conclusion that you're a busybody, and I don't like the way you constantly refer to my relationship with my maid. I'd hate to think you're one of those men who enjoy vexing unprotected women. Now, if you'll excuse me, I must dispose of this."

But much to her annoyance, he followed her up on deck, watching as she hoisted the pail with a single effort. "You did that very well. Almost as if you were quite practiced in housework." His voice made her clatter the pail against the rail, and she almost lost it into the salty waters of the Channel.

"Out of necessity one learns to do many things, Mr. Tanner. Now, do you know where I can rinse this, and where I can get a few drops of peppermint? Mrs. Crain tells me it will sweeten the stomach."

"Leave it, I'll see to it. I'll find you your peppermint and bring them both back to your cabin."

"I appreciate it, Mr. Tanner," Chelsea acquiesced reluctantly. "Thank you."

"My pleasure. I always like to help a lady in distress. I suppose it makes me feel more manly."

Chelsea stopped for a moment and looked up into his face. This was really the first opportunity she'd had to get a really good daylight look at this man who seemed to take such pleasure in annoying her. Her initial impression of broad shoulders and powerful chest had been correct, but she hadn't noticed his flashing dark eyes and strong jaw. Dark hair, almost jet, cut into soft, waving ruffles, blew gently in the sea breezes, falling over his ears and drifting onto his sun-polished brow. But that knowing amusement was there, in the crinkle of his black-lashed eyes and the tilt of his lip, which drew a shallow cleft in his chin. It was as though he knew a secret, a very amusing secret, and Chelsea's stomach tightened with dread as she imagined it was *her* secret he knew. In rebuttal to his patronizing attitude, she spoke more sharply than she intended.

"Mr. Tanner this may surprise you, but I was not in distress, and I care nothing for your opinion of your manhood. I would be grateful for the peppermint; just leave it and the slop pail outside my cabin." Stiffening her shoulders and lifting her chin regally, she passed by him with an air of distant coolness.

As Chelsea prepared to dress for dinner that evening, she considered her choice of gowns. In her wardrobe there was really little choice; she'd have to wear the same tan gown trimmed with blue that she'd used to impress Honoria at her apartment. All the others were common street dresses, barely fashionable and shamingly drab compared to Honoria's wardrobe. Chelsea looked longingly at Honoria's trousseau gowns. It wasn't as though her companion would mind; in fact, she'd given her permission. Hungrily her eyes perused the hanging gowns, already choosing a deep wine-colored silk banded with a deeper shade of velvet around the hem and sleeves and delineating the neckline of the bodice. Tiny rhinestone buttons marched from the bodice down to the waistline, and from beneath the open, elbow-length sleeves peeked a close-fitting inner sleeve of écru lavalier lace. The dress would be perfect against her fair skin and deep chestnut hair.

"Honoria, did you bring any jewelry aboard?" She asked as she held the gown against her body and looked at herself in the mirror.

"Just . . . just my mother's diamond ear studs. They're pinned to my petticoat. Yes, you take them, Chelsea, for safekeeping."

"I'll see to it," Chelsea said happily, moving behind the curtain to retrieve the ear studs from Honoria's petticoat. They would provide just the right touch, complementing the rhinestone buttons on the gown. "Are you certain you don't want me to bring you some tea and biscuits? You should have something in your stomach, Honoria. You can't keep retching this way."

"No, nothing now," Honoria replied weakly. The very thought of eating anything made her stomach churn. "I promise you, this is only temporary; in a few days I'll be myself."

Chelsea thought of Mrs. Crain's warning that the *Southern Cross* hadn't even broached open sea yet. "Honoria, perhaps this trip is too much for you. Perhaps we should ask the captain to drop you off before we leave the coast altogether."

"No! Oh, no." Honoria's eyes widened in horror. "I couldn't, I simply couldn't. I must go to Australia. I must, there's nothing for me here any longer."

"Shhh!" Chelsea soothed. "It was just a notion; I was only thinking of your health. Look, I'll be leaving in a few minutes, and I've sent for something that might help you."

The small bottle of peppermint was sitting in a cup outside the cabin door just as Quaid Tanner had promised. Chelsea added a few drops to the slop pail near Honoria's bed, grateful for the way it sweetened the air. Unstoppering the vial of laudanum, she added a few drops to a cup of water. "Here, drink this, Honoria, it will help you rest." When Honoria's nose wrinkled at the bitter taste, Chelsea encouraged her to take a few drops of peppermint on her tongue. "Open up, dear, this will hide the taste and help your stomach. Wider, Honoria, you aren't a bird. There now, you'll begin to feel better soon."

"You're so kind to me," Honoria said hoarsely. "I'm sorry to be such trouble."

Thirty minutes later, Honoria was asleep again and Chelsea was ready to go up for dinner. The wine-colored silk fit her like a glove; if anything, it was a tiny bit tight in the waist. Her looking glass told her the ear bobs were perfect in her tiny lobes and the tendrils of hair she'd curled with a heated iron wisped against her cheeks. She frowned as she peered into the mirror. Would the damp sea air frizz the curls, making her look like Honoria? Assuming Honoria's identity for a short while was one thing; looking like her was quite another.

Guilty feelings washed over Chelsea. How could she be so uncharitable? True, it rankled that Honoria had put her in a subservient position, but even so . . . Her confused feelings stayed with her as she wended her way down the narrow companionway to the dining room at the ship's stern. Before entering, she reminded herself that she was Chelsea Myles, actress, and she could carry off any role. Taking a deep breath and holding it for an instant, she opened the door and stepped into the candlelit room, pleased to note that every head turned in her direction as the steward led her to the captain's table. Resentment and guilt were left behind in the companionway.

A tall, silver-haired man in a striking blue-and-gold braid uniform rose from the chair when he noticed her approach, as did Mr. Tanner and a stout, pleasant-faced man whom she assumed to be Mr. Porter Crain. "Mrs. Harris, I am Captain Evan Winfield, and I'm delighted to have you at my table," declared the distinguished-looking officer. "Have you met our other dinner companions? Mr. and Mrs. Porter Crain, Mr. Quaid Tanner."

Chelsea smiled in greeting and allowed the captain to hold her chair for her. Gracefully she arranged her skirts and sat down, pleased to have been placed at the captain's right elbow and somewhat annoyed to find the impertinent Mr. Tanner on her other side.

The meal was simple fare but expertly served. Obviously Captain Winfield was a stickler for propriety. Several wines were served with the various courses, and Chelsea noticed Quaid Tanner roll the liquid on his tongue, savoring its flavor. So, the man had a weakness for spirits. That would account for his easy familiarity and his lack of manners.

"You seem to be quite familiar with wines, Mr. Tanner," she remarked, arching a critical eyebrow.

"Yes, I am," he replied easily. "I've worked the vineyards in New South Wales since I was a boy." Then, turning to the captain, "May I compliment you, sir, on your choice of a fine claret. French, isn't it?"

"Yes, I find the French wines more subtle than the Spanish, do you agree?"

"I quite agree," Mrs. Crain interjected. "Although I am prejudiced against the Spanish. Such earthy people, far too emotional for my liking. Don't you agree, Porter?" She turned to her husband, who appeared far more interested in his plate than in his wife's opinion.

"Are you familiar with Australian wines, Captain Winfield?" Tanner was asking. "There's a port we produce in the Hunter Valley that is remarkably close to the color of Mrs. Harris's gown. Rich and full-bodied."

Chelsea's eyes flew to Quaid. What had he meant by that remark? The grin he bestowed upon her made her want to tug at the bodice of her gown to cover her white skin and generous bosom. "Full-bodied" indeed! Who was this man, anyway? No gentleman would admit to working in farm fields; that was left to hired help. Yet here he was sitting at the captain's table as though he were an honored guest. Suddenly the memory of her own duplicity, the maintenance of which had secured her a seat at the captain's table, brought a blush to her cheeks. If as much could be said for Quaid Tanner, his first-class cabin and fancy accouterments notwithstanding, then he was a charlatan.

As if he could read her thoughts, he glanced at her, his dark, impenetrable gaze sending her mixed signals: interest, speculation, knowledge. Finding him impossible to tolerate, Chelsea turned to Mrs. Crain, reassured that one simple question would set the woman off on a dissertation of any subject she chose.

After dinner, when everyone had left the dining room, Mrs. Crain suggested a sociable game of whist. Although it was a drawing-room pastime of which Chelsea had no knowledge, she realized with a surge of panic that almost every gentlebred lady in England would have played the game at some point. So she demurred politely, turning to Mrs. Crain, "I'm so sorry, it will have to be another time. My companion is really quite ill, and I must get back to her. Captain, do you suppose I might bother your cook for a pot of tea and some biscuits?"

"I'll see to it myself and have a steward place it in the cabin," he offered generously.

Issuing her good nights to her dinner companions, Chelsea stepped out on deck rather than go below to the stuffy cabin and Honoria's retching. She was leaning against the rail and looking up at the stars when she heard a movement behind her. Without even turning, she knew who it was.

"These are not the same stars that shine in the Australian sky. You'll find that Orion and the Great Dipper are upside down, and there will be some constellations you've never seen."

"I'm not familiar with constellations, Mr. Tanner. I simply enjoy starlight for what it is." She heard the quaver in her voice—he was standing much too close!

"Did anyone ever tell you that when you blush it's like roses in the snow? Pink roses." His voice was low, intimate, keeping her from turning to face him. As Chelsea Myles, actress, she'd had enough experience with men to know how to handle them, but as Chelsea Harris, gentle woman, she couldn't possibly be familiar with the necessary language. She would have to discourage Quaid Tanner some other way; it would simply take a little longer.

"Did I ever tell you you look very familiar to me?" he said, and his words made Chelsea's skin prickle. "I know I've seen you, but I also know we were never properly introduced. I would remember if we had been. No, it has to be that I've noticed you somewhere, although it seems to me that the circumstances must have been unusual."

"Unusual?"

"Yes. You must have been dressed differently. I don't seem to place you walking the Strand or shopping near the East India House. No, it was something quite different. Perhaps it was at the theater, come to think of it," he mused aloud.

Chelsea thought the deck was going to rise and hit her in the face. The theater! How many theaters had she performed in? Who could know every face in the audience? She felt herself trembling. For twenty-four hours she had posed as Honaria, eaten at the captain's table, made acquaintances. If Tanner recalled where he'd seen her and revealed her, she would spend three months abroad this ship as an outcast. It would be unbearable. What did he want? What would it take to keep him quiet?

"Yes, perhaps it *was* at the theater. I admit to being a devotee," she braved, holding her breath, waiting for his next statement. When it came, it rocked her to the core.

"No, no, it couldn't be. I've only been in London for a short time and never attended the theater. . . . Just a minute, yes, I did. It was a rather disreputable production of *The Merchant of Venice,* I think. I remember a woman had had her purse stolen and made quite a scene about it. I tell you, Mrs. Harris, I will never forget the expression on that poor woman's face!"

Chelsea's heart began to pound, but her quick mind warned her not to admit to anything. This was exactly what she didn't want! To be known as an actress, to be labeled once again, to be forced beneath the standards of respectable society. It had been her intention to ask Honoria not to mention that she knew Chelsea was an actress, but here was someone who owed her nothing, nothing at all. With a sense of deep foreboding she turned to face him; he was so near she caught the scent of the dinner's wine on his breath. "What do you want?" she asked him, her tone cold and dead.

There was a flash of white teeth in the darkness; she felt him move closer, and just when she thought he was going to put his arms around her, he pressed his hands against the rail on either side of her, trapping her between them. "What do you think I want?" he asked softly, dangerously.

Alarm swept through Chelsea; she hadn't expected him to be so cavalier. In fact, she had hoped he would do the gentlemanly thing and take pity on her. She had gone too far, she could tell by the dark look in his eyes. This was not some schoolboy who could be twirled around her little finger. This was a man with no trace of the boy left in him. She was frightened, yet excited. Raising her head slightly, she locked her gaze with his, matching insolence with insolence. "You haven't answered me, Mr. Tanner."

Quaid's lips tightened into a thin line. He hadn't counted on having her stand her ground with him, almost mocking him. He had expected her to demur, pretend not to understand his double entendre. Now it seemed it was Chelsea who was enjoying herself—and at his expense. It wasn't that he'd meant any harm, and truth to tell, he wasn't a man who went about ruining a woman's reputation. It was just that she was so damned amusing when he deviled her. But now it had gone too far. Or had it? Quaid found himself wondering just how far she would go to keep her secret. "You haven't told me what you're offering, Mrs. Harris."

A slow flush crept up Chelsea's neck and stained her cheeks. No doubt he was contemplating how and where he could get her alone without anyone learning about it. The look in his eyes told her he wanted more than just a daring kiss in the shadows. Oh, yes—this man would demand much, much more.

The flush on Chelsea's face faintly surprised Quaid. That she was lovely was unmistakable. He looked down at her hand, which was clasped near her bosom. The skin was smooth and white, but the nails were clipped short. It was a graceful hand, but not that of a pampered lady; this young woman was obviously used to working, something Quaid had to respect. Her chestnut hair shone with red-gold highlights under the light of the lantern, and her fair skin, freshened by the sea breezes, was smooth and flawless. He knew she was an actress, and not a very good one at that, and he also knew that her occupation alone cast doubt upon her breeding and character. But there was also an undeniable air of quality about her. It was easy to believe she was well-placed and finely bred. Her voice was soft and naturally musical, her movements confident and graceful, her actions and carriage very much those of a lady.

But when he looked into her face, as he did now, he saw something far more exciting. Her mouth seemed to be made for kissing, prettily pouted, inviting. Her eyes were deep and tawny, lighting with merriment when the mood struck her, as during dinner, and flashing with fury when she grew angry.

His bold, speculative glance strayed to her bodice and the revealing cut of her wine-colored gown. Ripe, full breasts jutted provocatively, inviting a man's hand to caress them.

Chelsea could feel Quaid's eyes devouring her in the dark, and a sense of panic gripped her. What would he demand for his silence? What price would she pay? She could hate him for what he was doing to her, but she had learned early in life that everything she ever wanted had to be paid for—and at the same time she had also been taught that life was a series of bargains and compromises.

"You haven't answered me, Mrs. Harris. What are you offering?"

Her hand crept up to her throat and then to her ears, fingering one of Honoria's diamond ear studs. Somehow, some way, she would repay Honoria, she swore to herself.

"Jewels, Mrs. Harris? Oh, no, I want something much more precious." He moved closer, aware of the fragrance of her lemon-scented soap, and of something else, something more elusive.

The movement of the ship bracing through the waves seemed to rock Chelsea as she stood, captured between his arms, glaring up at him brazenly. She was unaware of the glittering stars and the orange sliver of moon that lit the forecastle deck. His nearness, his intimate demand, the danger she saw flashing in his eyes—these swamped her senses and filled her soul. He was playing with her, she knew, a cat-and-mouse game she had no chance of winning. One way or another Quaid Tanner would strike the bargain, and she would keep it.

Chelsea's eyes blazed and seemed to spew hatred with such an intensity that Quaid was taken aback, causing him to remove his hands from the rail. He hadn't expected such wrath in bargaining for a kiss! Braving the emotion that flowed from her eyes like lava from a volcano, he pulled her against his chest, pressing her tightly to him. At first she struggled, forcing her arms between them, arching backward. But he held her fast, insisting, urging. Those lips that so invited, the smooth fair skin that tempted a man's hand, the gentle curves, generous yet not over-blown, all were there in his arms.

For a moment she went lifeless in his arms; all struggles ceased, and tawny eyes stared up at him, smoldering with indignation and flashing with rage. But the rejection he was looking for was nowhere to be found.

Chelsea tensed herself for what was to come. His arms tightened around her despite her struggles. Then he was forcing her closer, crushing her, his body hard and muscular. She felt herself caught in the intensity of his gaze, aware of his power, knowing beyond doubt that he meant to have his way and would have it. In spite of herself and her outrage, she was drawn into the depths of that dark gaze, aware that under different circumstances, in another time, she could drown in those dark liquid pools and yield to his demands with a fevered pleasure. He was devilishly handsome, sensual, awakening the woman in her.

When he lowered his head she braced herself for his kiss, tightening her mouth against his onslaught. Instead, she felt his lips gentle against her brow, slipping into her hairline and descending in a path to the sensitive skin at her ear. She was aware of the spicy scent of his cologne, of the close stubble of beard on his chin, of the softness of his lips as they traced patterns across her cheeks.

Chelsea's knees weakened, and the arms she held so rigidly between them in protest were losing their force, relaxing, yielding. Whoever this Quaid Tanner was, whatever he was, he was no clod, no blunderer who fumbled with a woman's clothing and handled her roughly. This was a man who knew how to be tender, to wait for a woman's response, and artfully bring her to full awareness of herself as a woman and of him as a man.

Her arms dropped to her sides, useless. Gently, his hand cupped her face, lifting her chin, raising her lips to his own. Then, just when she thought he would release her, his kiss deepened, the moist tip of his tongue smoothing the satiny underside of her lips and penetrating ever so softly, ever so slowly, into the recesses of her mouth.

A riot of confused emotions railed within Chelsea's breast. She acknowledged her attraction for this enigmatic, impertinent man and realized that had she not been always on the defensive, she would have been tremendously drawn to him. Without reason or logic, her arms came up from her sides and encircled his back, fingers smoothing over his coat jacket, feeling the smooth plane of muscle that bespoke energy, vitality, and hard work. Prolonging the contact between them, she offered herself to his kiss, knowing that despite herself and his veiled threats of blackmail, he had kindled a spark of womanhood within her and she wanted him to bring it to flame.

Feeling her moist lips soften and part, offering themselves to him, Quaid groaned softly and moved his mouth hungrily over hers, tasting the sweetness within. This was what he'd wanted—a kiss willingly given, a kiss that was gentle yet spoke of passion.

When he released her his fathomless ebony eyes searched hers for an instant, and time seemed to roll eternal for Chelsea. From somewhere inside her came a desire to linger in his arms, to feel again the touch of his mouth upon hers; and the desire began to build and crescendo. He meant to exact a price for his silence, and it was a payment she suddenly found herself far too willing to pay. Long, thick lashes closed, and she heard her breath coming in ragged little gasps of surprise and wonder. Boldly she brought her mouth to his once again, offering herself, kissing him deeply, searchingly. He was chasing away her reservations, blotting out the knowledge that he had forced her into this position. Nothing mattered but this man and the feelings he had awakened in her.

She kissed him as she had never kissed another man.

There had been other kisses, other caresses, but none that elicited this response in her. Not even when she was six-teen and thought herself to be wildly in love with a much older, very experienced man, an actor in Cosmo's troupe, had she felt this way. Then, she had been a girl exploring the frontiers of her womanhood, fumbling hurriedly through the love act in the dank shadows of a theater, be-lieving herself to be so much in love that she had bitten back restraint and disappointment. She had been so young, so afraid, but still she had given. When she'd discovered her lover was a married man seeking only a few nights' distraction, she'd become bitter and resentful, deciding never again to allow herself to be exploited by a man. Something inside her had died at that betrayal, but now, here in the arms of Quaid Tanner, she felt a renewal of the feelings she had so long resisted.

His gentle fingers caressed her cheek, and when he spoke, his voice was husky with emotion, little more than a whisper wafting through the night.

"Come with me, Chelsea." It was a demand; it was a question.

Chelsea felt intoxicated by the moment; she knew Quaid Tanner was a man who could make her senses reel and ig-nite her passions beyond anything she'd ever experienced.

A tiny voice resounded in her head, telling her she should pull away and run, run as far away as she could. Explanations could be made, excuses pleaded as to her mistaken identity and as to why she had perpetuated the misunderstanding. She had never meant things to go so far, and Honoria was not so sick that she couldn't set things right. She shouldn't allow this to happen, however much her senses and body cried out for it. She should hate him for the price he was exacting, the sweet, sweet price.

He seemed to find his answer in her kiss, in the pressure of her body against his own. His hand cupped her throat, and he could feel the abandoned rhythm of her pulses, which sent a streak of fire through his loins. He had bargained for a simple kiss, but she could offer so much more! He had wanted her from the first moment he had seen her walk on stage, and he knew he wanted her even more now, more even than his next breath. The way she clung to him and opened her mouth to the pressure of his told him she was not a coquette playing out a flirtation. Chelsea was a warm-blooded woman hungry for the touch of a man.

Chelsea forced herself backward, bracing herself, denying him access to her lips. "No, no, there must be something else you want, anything else. I can't, I can't!"

"You can, you can," he murmured. "I want you, Chelsea. I want you and you want me. Don't deny it. Don't deny us." Again his words were spoken so softly that she might only have imagined them. "There's nothing I want so much, only you."

He took her hand in his and led her along the deck; only the scattered gimballed lanterns lighted their way. Chelsea was dimly aware of voices in the distance and the sluicing of water beneath the ship's hull. She had no idea where he was taking her, and she didn't care.

Chapter 6

As he walked beside Chelsea along the decks of the *Southern Cross*, Quaid found himself admiring her profile and appreciating her nose, which lent her an arrogant air. It was upturned slightly, in perfect balance with her clear, intelligent brow and softly rounded chin. The fair oval of her face was offset by a wealth of gleaming dark hair, which glowed chestnut in the light of day and took on the deeper hues of sable by night.

Chelsea moved beside him, knowing he was studying her and liking what he saw. She felt herself bloom beneath his quiet gaze and held herself proudly. She was not a girl any longer but a woman, and she would pretend no coquettishness or false modesty; she knew he would not allow it. This man would demand she yield to her passion and delight in the pleasure he gave her. She knew, somehow, that this night would not end with her wanting and needing so much more than she received, as it had when she was sixteen. Tonight she would not cry for her lost innocence, burning all the while with frustration and guilt.

When he led her down the companionway to his cabin, she did not even turn her eyes in the direction of her own quarters; there was nothing in there she wanted. What she wanted, regardless of the reason or the method, was to find herself once again in Quaid Tanner's arms, living the fulfillment and promise she had found in his eyes. She was inexplicably drawn to the danger of it all like a moth to a flame, and she would not allow herself to consider the consequences. There was only the here and now—everything else could be faced some other time, when her brain worked clearly and no mysterious little fires hungered to be quenched.

Behind the closed door of his cabin, Quaid took her once again into his arms, hungry for the touch of her, the feel of her. Hidden from the eyes of the world, his lips claimed hers once again in sweet possession.

It seemed then to Chelsea that his mouth became part of her own, and she engaged upon a hesitant exploration of it with the tip of her tongue. White teeth, large and square; full, sensuous lips; a clean mouth, tasting vaguely of her own and of the port wine from dinner. She clung to him, unwilling to allow even the narrowest space between them. His kisses were intoxicating, making her light-headed, heightening her craving for more, ever more. It seemed to them as though the *Southern Cross* had entered the path of a tidal wave; they were inexorably thrown and tossed upon a stormy sea, which rocked their senses. They strained toward each other, captured by the designs of sensuality, caught in a yearning that penetrated the barriers of the flesh and drove them to join breath and body, spirit and soul.

When at last they could bear to part, he led her over to his bed and placed her upon it. Quickly, nimbly, he lit the lantern on the far wall and lowered the wick until the cabin was lit with a dim golden glow. He turned to look at her, those dark eyes conveying exciting messages from beneath thick black brows. As though hypnotized, Chelsea began to work the tiny rhinestone buttons on the front of her gown, never taking her gaze from his, feeling the power of his will as her fingers fumbled and shook.

"No, let me do that for you," he said. "I want to unwrap you, as though you were a Boxing Day present meant for me alone."

At that moment she felt as though she were indeed meant for him alone—that it was fated his eyes should be looking at her as they were now, filled with desire, brimming with expectation, fated that his voice should be so soft, so gentle, yet could vibrate through her like the deep, rumbling note of a violin, plucking at her senses, casting a spell over her. If at first the actress in her had set out to play a part by succumbing to his wants and striking his bargain, now she had fallen prey to the role, and the woman in her responded and welcomed his touch.

He moved beside her, deftly replacing her hands with his, undoing the tiny buttons and slipping the wine-red silk from her shoulders, exposing her skin to his touch, to his kiss. As layer after layer of concealing fabric fell away, her passion grew, smoldering within her ready to burst into flame.

In the cabin's golden glow, he laid her back against the pillows, following her body, leaning over her to nuzzle her neck and inhale her fragrance. He blazed a trail from her throat to her bare breasts, and she trembled with exquisite anticipation. All things moved to the distance, nothing and no one existed beyond this moment and place. The only reality was the way her body reacted to this man. Pleasure radiated upward from some hidden well, and she allowed herself to be carried with it, unable to hinder the forward thrust of her own desire, lifting out of space and time into the turbulent waters of her aroused sensuality.

Chelsea's perceptions thrummed and heightened wherever he touched her; her emotions hurled and spun, wreaking havoc upon her senses. He left her then to divest himself of his own restraining garments, and when he returned it was to be greeted by her eager hands and greedy fingers as she held him to her as closely as a secret.

She had watched as he had undressed, had seen the hard, rippling muscles that lay beneath his broad chest and the planes of his back. He was sun-bronzed to the waist; curling patterns of chest hair narrowed to a thin, fine furring over the flatness of his belly and invoked Chelsea's gaze to his nether region, which stood proud and erect with pulsing anticipation. The sudden paleness of his lean haunches delineated the dark patch of hair surrounding his manhood, and his tapered hips flared into thighs thick with muscle and hard with strength.

She had never seen a man this way, undisguised by clothing and immodestly bathed with light; yet she knew somehow that he was above most men in his magnificence. The secrets of the male body, which had only been hinted at in her hurried and limited experience, were now revealed, and she found them beautiful.

As her hands moved over him, Quaid was filled with a sense of his own power and exulted in her undisguised passion for him. He had been held in the spell of her gaze as she'd watched him undress. She was so beautiful with her moist, kiss-reddened lips parted seductively, and her languorous, heavy-lidded gaze hinted at a depth of passion that excited him unbearably. Damn, but he was hungry for her; he would have liked to spread her beneath him and plunge into her fiery depths, to feel himself become a part of her. Each curve of her body was eloquent, the roundness of her breasts with their pink pouting crests, the slender arc of her hips that narrowed into long, lean legs, the golden hue of her skin gleaming softly with a sheen of desire. But he would take her slowly, savoring every inch of her, delighting in the pleasure they would share.

When he moved to cover her with his body, it was her turn to protest, just as he had when she'd begun to undress herself. "No, let me," she whispered, rolling over on top of him and leaning on one elbow.

As she bent over him, her cloud of dark hair tumbled around her face, grazing his shoulder and tickling his chest. She smoothed his chest with her fingertips, trailing through the patch of dark curls, exploring the regions that were smooth and hairless, then moving to the flat hardness of his belly. He heard himself gasp as her hand wandered dangerously close to his groin and then flew upward again to his chest. He wanted to applaud her daring, yet he almost laughed when he saw her eyes widen at her own boldness. "Touch me," he encouraged, taking her hand in his, moving it downward again. When she hesitated, he asked, "Do you like it when I touch you? Here?" He caressed her breast, feeling its weight in the palm of his hand, relishing the softness of it and the hard little crest that jutted into his palm. "And here?" he asked, sliding downward to the softness of her belly. "Here?" His fingers grazed the satiny flesh of her inner thighs, whispering past the fleecy curls between her legs.

She allowed her hand to follow his, adventuring into uncharted territory, combing past the thicket that surrounded his eager shaft. Hesitantly, her fingers explored him, moving upward to touch the velvet-smooth tip, upon which poised a drop of moisture, like a glistening tear. As she turned her head to watch the progress of her fingers, her hair hung like a curtain, shielding her face from his view. His member was incredibly sensitive to her touch, and it pleased her to hear his sharp, indrawn breath as she traveled the length of it downward to the surprising vulnerability between his hard-muscled thighs. She felt desire ripple through him and realized with a curious proud excitement that she was in command of his passions.

When she lifted her head to look back at him, her tawny eyes heavy with desire, he was reminded of a feline who has just discovered the cream crock; the little smile she bestowed upon him was rife with a cat's self-satisfaction. And she was feline, he found himself thinking, sleek and smooth and silent, like a jungle cat, a black panther who has just given chase and is now anticipating the feast. She reached out to touch him again, this time watching him, aware of his every reaction, relishing the masculine hardness of him and feeling it pulsate in anticipation of her touch. When she closed her hand over him, a deep throbbing sounded in his chest and rumbled from his lips. Unable to withstand her sensuous onslaught a moment longer, he reached up and pulled her beside him, and this time it was he who took the superior position. Only having her, losing himself within her, would satisfy.

A golden warmth flooded through Chelsea as he brought his mouth to hers once again. His movements were smoothly executed as he drew a path from one breast to the other, covering each first with his hands and then with his lips. She clung to the strength of his arms, holding fast as though she were fearful of falling in on herself, never to be found again.

His hands spanned her waist and rounded to her buttocks, lifting her slightly from the bed. Tortuous, teasing explorations of his tongue made her shudder with heightening passion. Her fingers clutched and pulled at his dark, ruffled hair as though begging him to stop, while her body arched into his, feverishly exposing herself to his maddening mouth. He searched for and found the secret places that pushed her to the brink of release, only to have his worshiping kiss follow another path before returning again to the first.

A yawning ache spread through Chelsea, demanding satisfaction, settling at her core and forcing her to seek relief by writhing and thrashing about restlessly. Quaid held her there, forcing her to him, adoring her with his hands and lips until she could deny herself no longer. Her body flamed, her back arched, and her world divided in two parts: her need and his lips. And when the tremors ceased and his mouth covered hers once again, she tasted herself there. She was satisfied, yet discontent; had feasted, yet was famished. There was more she wanted—much, much more. She wanted to share with him the release of his own passion, to participate in bringing him to that same wonder.

She urged him onward, assuring him she was ready. Grasping her hips, he lifted her and wound her parted thighs around him. She guided him into her, pulling him forward, driving him downward, knowing that same need within her, a desire of a different, cooler color than before. It was as though once having slaked her thirst, she could now enjoy the flavor. Moving with him, becoming part of him, Chelsea fueled his passion and renewed her own. Together they were flung upward; together they found the sun.

Afterward, they lay together, dozing in one another's arms. And even in their sleep their lips sought and their hands soothed.

When Chelsea awakened it was to find his face inches away from hers, his dark, fathomless eyes watching her. When she returned his stare, he grinned.

"What are you forever smiling about?" she asked, stretching her arms above her head as she wrested herself from sleep.

Just like a cat, he thought, his grin widening. "I'm smiling about you. You're so predictable at times, and at others you're an enchanting surprise."

"That's hardly a compliment, Mr. Tanner," she chided.

"You're already deviling me again. No woman likes to think of herself as predictable."

"But you are."

"May I have an example?"

"Whenever I mention your maid, you flush and become angry. You were quite funny, and I couldn't resist deviling you, as you so charmingly put it."

"I don't think it was charming of *you*," she countered. "You knew all along who I was, and you took pure delight in making me squirm."

"As I said, you were predictable."

Chelsea stretched again and then laid her head on his shoulder, her fingers winding through his chest hairs. "Now tell me when I'm the enchanting surprise," she fished brazenly.

"Can there be any doubt? Tonight. I had meant to extract a kiss, and instead I'm transported by the entire woman. You are delightful, dear Chelsea."

She stiffened, the fingers that grazed tenderly along his chest becoming the claws of a cat as she swiped her nails over tender skin.

"Ouch!" he exclaimed, sitting up abruptly. "Why in hell did you do that?"

She pounced on him, intending to rake hell with her nails, spitting and spewing sudden fury. "A *kiss*! A kiss is all you wanted? When I offered you my ear bobs you said you wanted more, much more! I thought . . . I thought . . . Ooooh!" She came at him again, face flaming, claws reaching.

He subdued her by rolling on top of her, holding her hands firmly over her head. "I knew you were a cat, but I foolishly forgot about your claws. Is that what you think of me? That I force myself on women? That it is impossible to have a woman lay with me unless I trick her?"

"You said it, not me!" Chelsea spat.

"Take it back!"

"No! You're a bounder, Quaid Tanner, and I'd like to tear your eyes from your head. You knew who I was from the moment you saw me aboard ship, didn't you?"

"Even before, madam. I knew you were sailing on the *Cross* because I recognized Mrs. Harris as the woman in the theater who'd had her purse snatched, and I heard her give your name to the ticket agent and tell him you were sailing as her maid."

"It was never true. We were to share a cabin at a reduced rate. I was never to go along as her maid. When I'd learned what she'd done, she was too sick to make amends, and . . . and . . . I was insulted that she should be asked to sit at the captain's table, while I, as her servant, was to take my meals in the galley or in the cabin. She gave me permission to use her identity. It's all a misunderstanding!"

"A misunderstanding like forcing your thieving uncle to give you Mrs. Harris's purse that night at the theater?" He laughed, knowing the sound infuriated her. "Oh, yes, I was witness to that little scene. And isn't it Mrs. Harris's own money you used to pay your passage? The truth, Chelsea; there's too much between us now to lie."

"I don't owe you any explanation. Not one! So you knew all along who I was?" She had slipped down in the bed, sheets modestly covering her breasts. Her hair was tousled from lovemaking and raged about her head, her eyes flamed with accusations, and all in all she presented a very pretty picture.

Quaid nodded affirmation. "Look over there," he told her, gesturing. The gaudy yellow feathered fan he'd retrieved from the stage the first time he'd seen Chelsea was stuck behind his shaving mirror, its bright plumed tip hanging at an odd angle. Chelsea instantly recognized it.

"That's mine!" she hissed. "Where did you get it?"

"The night you met Honoria Harris. You dropped it."

"You sneak! You bounder!"

He sensed her intention to climb out of the sheets and continue her attack. Before she could move he had seized her again, holding her back with the weight of his body and the strength of his hands. "Look who's calling whom a sneak! For shame. Every time I had to call you Mrs. Harris I almost choked."

"More's the pity you didn't," Chelsea snapped. "A man like you can't be trusted. How do I know you won't expose me to the captain before I can get Honoria to straighten out this mess? It's all her fault, presuming to sign me on as her maid and then making herself a profit on my fare! And I don't want you telling anyone I'm an actress; I'll have enough to live down once Honoria sets thing right. Or do you intend to keep on blackmailing me?"

"God forbid!" He recoiled in pretended horror. "What you do is your own business. We all have to make a living one way or another. If you choose to do it dishonestly, that's no concern of mine."

"You wretched lout!" Chelsea cried, trying to convince him she was wounded to the quick. "I had no other choice."

"Of course you did; you just didn't like the other choice. You took the one that was easiest and most beneficial to you."

Gone was the little innocent throwing herself on the wolf's mercy. The leopard resumed in full force, claws glinting, teeth bared. "You're despicable!"

"I find you rather endearing, too." Quaid grinned. "Come here, I think I want to love you again."

"Let go of me. I'm through striking bargains with you."

She wrestled out of his grasp, panting from the exertion. Oh, how she wanted to scratch that all-knowing grin from his too handsome face!

"But I'm not through with you," he told her, his voice heavy with meaning, his eyes glowing with a victory about to be won. His arms were wrapped around her, holding her close, stilling her rebellious actions. Her feet were kicking, her fingers curled to scratch, but he flew in the face of danger to press her beneath him, trailing incredibly slow kisses along the line of her jaw and down to the base of her throat, where he could feel her pulse throb.

"We're good together, Chelsea, you and I," he murmured. "You know it, and I want to hear you say it."

"Never." But even to her own ears the word sounded less than convincing. His mouth had taken a patternless path to her breasts, nipping and teasing the sensitive flesh. "Never," she repeated, feeling the resistance leave her arms, feeling her legs falling still beneath his.

"Tell me, Chelsea," he urged, the tip of his tongue grazing the soft underside of her breast. He released her hands and lowered himself over her, his lips tracing a warm, moist trail across her torso and lingering in the downy triangle below. "Say it, Chelsea, say it."

An involuntary shudder rippled through her, and she felt herself growing limp and yielding beneath his touch. As her back arched and she brought herself to meet his lips, she heard the words come of their own volition, breathless and urgent. "Yes, yes, we're good together. So good."

Chelsea moved about her cabin the next morning attempting to straighten and set things to rights. The small porthole remained open to allow a minimum of air, but it seemed to do little good without any cross ventilation.

Thanks to the laudanum, Honoria seemed to have spent

a peaceful night, but since awakening that morning she'd done poorly; the dark circles beneath her eyes and her sickly complexion showed Chelsea just how exhausted she really was. After a meager breakfast of warm tea and a few nibbles of toast, the malady had struck her anew and she'd just finished retching into the slop pail.

"Please, Chelsea, give me more of the medicine," Honoria begged. "It's the only thing that brings me any peace."

"You know what the purser said, Honoria. Try to endure it, just for a few hours. You can't spend the next three months drugged into oblivion."

"But I'm so ill."

"Yes, and that's why I think I should ask the captain to put you off the ship. Mrs. Crain told me at breakfast that we'll soon be rounding Plymouth before heading south along the French coast. Honoria, please, you're obviously in no condition to withstand this journey."

"No! Please no. Don't you understand, there's nothing here for me in England, nothing." She turned her face to the wall, tears streaming down her cheeks.

"Then at least let me help you bathe and change your nightdress. You'll feel better," Chelsea promised. She was truly worried for Honoria. At breakfast that morning the captain had predicted foul weather. If Honoria couldn't bear the gentle sway and roll of the ship under the best circumstances, how was she to withstand a storm? Still, Chelsea was extremely sympathetic to her plight; she understood what the woman meant when she said there was nothing left for her in England. Nothing.

After Honoria's quick bath and change of nightdress, Chelsea's chores were almost completed. Only emptying the slop pail remained. As she left the cabin, she found herself facing portside 8, Quaid Tanner's quarters. He had not appeared for breakfast that morning, and she supposed he was still sleeping. She would have liked to pound on his door and awaken him, but she dreaded seeing the slow grin on his insolent face. It wasn't until the wee hours of dawn that she'd crept from his bed across the companionway into her own. And it wasn't until then that she realized he'd never given her his promise never to reveal that he knew her to be an actress. Damn him! He'd tricked her last night—not once but twice!

Later in the afternoon, when Chelsea went on deck for a breath of fresh air, she met Mrs. Crain once again.

"How is your maid?" asked the woman. "Mr. Crain said he saw you tending to the facilities earlier. You really should leave that to the steward," she admonished.

"If you were in my cabin, you'd advise otherwise, Mrs. Crain," she replied testily, resenting the woman's intrusion. "And it serves to make my companion more comfortable."

"Still, you mustn't forget your station, my dear. Although I think it quite admirable the way you tend your servant. She is no better, then?"

"Hardly. I was forced to give her another dose of laudanum an hour ago. Since the weather began blowing up, her misery increased."

"Have you thought it might be a mistake to force the poor thing to endure this journey? The other passengers seem to be doing quite nicely," Mrs. Crain observed approvingly as though she herself had something to do with everyone's good health. "It would be a shame to mar our journey with an invalid. It casts a pall over everyone, I assure you, Mrs. Harris. And there's something else to consider—you wouldn't want to be a nursemaid for the next three months, would you? If you would like, I can have Mr. Crain speak to the captain for you before we turn south. Leaving your companion at Plymouth might be the kindest gesture."

"I said as much to her myself, but she pleaded with me," Chelsea admitted.

"And are you in the habit of allowing your servants to contradict you? If you are worrying about traveling alone, dear, let me assure you that Mr. Crain and myself will take you under our protection. Servants are easy to find in New South Wales. Surely you can't be thinking of the inconvenience of tending to yourself for the time being. Isn't that what you're doing now, not to mention tending to your patient as well?"

Mrs. Crain was making good sense and Chelsea knew it, but it was more her concern for Honoria that made her feel the journey was unwise. "Mrs. Crain, would you come and have a look at her? I'd feel so much better if you would."

A few minutes later Chelsea stepped out of her cabin into the companionway behind Mrs. Crain's portly figure. Even before she spoke, the woman was shaking her head.

"That's a sick woman in there. It's simply inadvisable to take her on to Australia. She'll never make it, and it's my guess there's more wrong with her than simple seasickness. I declare I've never seen such a ghastly complexion! I insist you speak to the captain about putting her off in Plymouth, Mrs. Harris, or I will be forced to speak with him myself."

Just then Quaid's cabin door opened. He had heard Mrs. Crain and saw the effect her words had had on Chelsea. "What's the trouble, Mrs. Crain?"

"Oh, Mr. Tanner, I've just been in to see Mrs. Harris's maid, and I tell you the poor woman will never make it to Australia. If you ask me, there's something more amiss here than seasickness, as I was just telling Mrs. Harris."

Quaid glanced at Chelsea, looking for her reaction. "She has no one left here in England," Chelsea explained.

"When I suggested she leave the ship she became so upset I'm afraid to mention it again. But I do want to do what's best for her." He saw Chelsea's genuine alarm and believed her to be sincere.

"No matter what a servant wants, Mrs. Harris, you must think of the rest of us," Mrs. Crain interjected. "Something like this can affect the entire ship, don't you agree, Mr. Tanner? There is also Mrs. Harris's convenience to consider."

Chelsea glanced at Quaid, then looked away quickly. There had been speculation in his dark eyes that perhaps she *would* find it more convenient to dispose of Honoria after all. Then she would be spared the embarrassment of explaining about the mistaken identities.

"I'm certain Mrs. Harris will do what's best, Mrs. Crain. Now, if you'll excuse me, I believe it's time for lunch."

"Oh, yes, it is, isn't it? Never skip a meal, I always say, especially at sea. Don't you agree, Mr. Tanner? I didn't see you at breakfast. I hope you weren't indisposed. So often a sea voyage can deplete one's energy, don't you think?"

"I only expend my energies in the most worthy endeavors, Mrs. Crain." When his dark eyes smiled at Chelsea, she could feel herself flush.

"I'll see you in the dining room, then. I must meet Porter and see to it he takes his elixir before eating. Helps the digestion, you know."

Mrs. Crain braced herself along the walls of the companionway to return above deck in search of her husband. The *Southern Cross* was heaving and pitching with greater force than before, and Chelsea looked toward her cabin door, thinking of poor Honoria.

"What will you do, Chelsea?" Quaid asked. "Will you have her put off before we leave the coast? If so, you must act quickly. Very soon now the captain will turn the *Cross* southward, and England will be far behind."

"What do you think I should do? I hate to see her suffer this way, and yet I've no power to set her ashore if she refuses."

"I'm certain you've considered the benefits of setting her ashore," he said dryly. "It will relieve . . . let us call it a 'compromising situation.'"

"I knew you'd be thinking that!" Chelsea cried angrily. "Is that how little you think of me?"

"No, Chelsea dear, it's how much I think of you that bedevils me." His voice had grown soft, intimate, reminding her of the night before when he'd persuaded her to say things she never meant to say. His arms came around her, pulling her close to him, crushing her breasts against his powerful chest. "All morning I thought of nothing else but you," he whispered before his mouth came crashing down over hers.

Chelsea turned her face away and struggled to break free of his embrace. "That was last night, Mr. Tanner, and this is today!" she told him coldly. "And as every actress knows, repeat performances can be boring."

He held her for an instant, then released her. "And as any actress can tell you, Chelsea, there's nothing so rewarding as a part well rehearsed."

Chapter 7

Quaid stretched his long, lean frame on the too short bed, careful not to disturb Chelsea, who was sleeping beside him. She needed her rest; tending to Honoria Harris nearly sixteen hours out of twenty-four was taking its toll on her. The past two nights she had slipped across the companionway and through his cabin door, which he now kept unlocked for her. This she only did once her patient was sleeping heavily under the sparing doses of laudanum and the stench of their cabin became unbearable.

Because of the rough weather, it had been impossible after all to insist that Honoria go ashore at Plymouth. The passage to Plymouth's inlet was hazardous at all times, but the concealed rocks and sandbars made it almost impossible to navigate during a storm. The next port on the *Southern Cross*'s itinerary would be Lisbon, Portugal, nearly eight days away. Quaid doubted Honoria Harris would live to see it.

His arm tightened gently around Chelsea. Whatever charade she had started out to play, her devotion and attention to Honoria now was admirable. Lips caressing her cool brow, he inhaled the rosewater scent of her softly waved hair. There was something about this woman that stirred a tenderness within him, something that excited him at the same time. When she made love with him she was a goddess, and when enraged she was an imp. He liked the way she could see to the unpleasant tasks of nursing a sick woman and then appear at dinner refreshed and lovely, complete with impeccable manners and an air of good breeding; in fact, she was a better actress offstage than on.

Chelsea's eyes opened sleepily to find him looking at her. "Do you always watch me when I sleep?" she asked, annoyed.

"And are you always angry even before your eyes are opened?"

In reply she turned her back to him, the sheets slipping down from her shoulder to reveal a graceful length of smooth back and the barest hint of full hip, which invited the caress of his hand.

"And are you always randy in the morning?" she countered then. "Have you nothing else to do or think about?"

"I'm always thinking about you, Chelsea." To prove his point he pushed against her, making her aware of his arousal as he slid his hand around her to cup her warm full breast.

"It's too early," she groaned. "I can barely feel my toes wiggle and you want to tumble."

"It's not the wiggle of your toes that intrigues me," he whispered close to her ear, nipping lightly at her earlobe.

"You rascal, where did you learn such bad manners? It's not gentlemanly to awaken a lady." Pushing her face into her pillow, she pulled farther away from him.

"Did I ever say I was a gentleman?" he asked, moving closer, his lips beginning an exploration of her neck and shoulder.

Chelsea's eyes widened and she rolled over onto her back,

clutching the sheets around her breasts. "Aren't you? A gentleman? You seem to dress well enough, and you are traveling first class."

"And is that all that's required to make a gentleman?"

"Well, it's obvious you're not the village idiot. Just who are you, Mr. Tanner?"

"Does it matter?"

"Yes, it matters! You seem to know enough about me!" Now her curiosity was piqued, and a worried frown creased her brow. "Just what is it you do in Australia?"

"I grow grapes to make wine. In essence, Chelsea dear, I suppose you could say I'm a farmer."

"A farmer! You mean with chickens and a cow and . . . and . . ."

"Sheep," he added for her. "I keep sheep to tide the farm over when the grapes fail." He tried to keep from smiling over her disappointment. Chelsea was at her best like this when she was directly honest. It was obvious the idea of his being a common farmer was abhorrent to her, and more likely she would have liked it better if he'd told her he was a grifter, one of those confidence men who picked pockets and separated country bumpkins from their seed money by playing shell games on city street corners. "You're not prejudiced against working men, are you, sweet?"

"Somebody has to do it—farm, I mean." She scowled. "Only I never thought you . . . what I mean is, I'm not surprised. Not at all. Your complexion gives you away, you know. Tanned and ruddy. You've the look of a man who spends long hours out of doors. Are you rich?" she asked bluntly. "Your wardrobe is quite good, and you are traveling first class. I know for a fact that costs a pretty pence."

"Rich? Hardly. I've told you, I'm a farmer. A working man. Clonmerra, that's my farm, requires my labors, and I give them. I've a few hands who work for me, but I keep myself close to the land."

Chelsea was truly alarmed now, and she looked it.

"Chelsea, sweet," Quaid said wryly, "I'm thinking you're a snob."

Now she was incensed. A snob! She jumped to her knees, still clutching the sheet, glaring down at him. "Quaid Tanner, I'm no such thing and you know it. I come from humble beginnings myself. But I can't help wondering what else you haven't told me. I suppose you've a wife and seven children stashed away on that place you call Clonmerra." The idea of his being married settled like a stone in the pit of her stomach. Fool that she was, she'd allowed herself to turn down another blind alley. When would she ever learn?

"Would it make a difference?" he asked, taunting her deliberately. He wanted her answer, he wanted to hear her say it would make a difference because she wanted him for herself. He wanted a commitment, and then he would tell her the truth.

"Do you?" she demanded.

"Have seven children? No, Chelsea, I don't have seven."

She struggled from the bed, feet becoming tangled in the sheets, almost throwing herself onto the cabin floor to escape his touch. "Once before I called you a bounder, and you've said nothing this morning to make me revise my opinion!" Gathering together every shred of dignity she could muster, she grabbed up her nightdress and robe and hobbled to the door. "Good day, Mr. Tanner! I suggest you keep your cabin door locked from now on, because if you have any midnight visitors, they won't be friendly." She flung open the door and paused only for an instant to make certain the companionway was empty before stalking across to her own cabin.

Quaid rolled over onto his stomach, fist beating into the pillow, which carried the scent of her hair and was still warm from her body. Now why in hell had he done that? So much for his aptitude at pillow talk. He wanted her, yet he'd driven her away. There wasn't much he actually knew about Chelsea, but one thing about her was undeniable— her ambition. Perhaps that was why he had led her to believe he was an itinerant farmer scratching a living from the land. He wanted her to want him for himself.

Quaid's fist beat into the pillow again. He was a fool and he knew it, just as he knew he wanted Chelsea for himself under any circumstances—even if he had to appeal to her ambition and greed to get her.

Chelsea moved her stool closer to Honoria's bed. She was waiting for Mrs. Crain and the captain. Since returning to the cabin earlier that morning, she'd found Honoria doing much worse than before. It wasn't just the seasickness; there was something more. Honoria was dangerously ill. Chelsea grasped the woman's hand, hoping to impart some of her own strength.

It seemed that everything had gone wrong since she'd first heard Honoria scream that her purse had been stolen. And certainly this morning had done nothing to cheer her. She knew Quaid must think her a fortune hunter, and nothing could be farther from the truth. The whole purpose of this voyage was to give herself a new beginning, to allow her to make something of herself, to better her life. Why did she have to meet this man, this farmer? Why hadn't she set the record straight from the start, told him she wasn't Mrs. Harris directly? Why, why, why? If she'd been truthful, she wouldn't be in this mess now. Wouldn't have flagrantly given herself to a man in exchange for his silence. Wouldn't have allowed herself to fall in love with him.

The thought caught Chelsea unawares, and she winced.

No, it couldn't be love. After all, what did she know about him? Only that he kept sheep and grew grapes. Not enough to love, surely. But the touch of his hand did desperate things to her pulse, as did the expression in his eyes when he made love to her, telling her all the things every woman wanted to hear. He meant them; even now, she believed he had meant every word. Only why did he have to be a farmer? A man with no fortune, except endless prayers for good weather and high market prices. It wasn't the future she wanted.

There was something more waiting for her in Australia; she could feel it in her bones. She wouldn't lose sight of her goals now. Especially not now.

"Am I going to die?" Honoria raised herself weakly on the narrow bunk. She tried to focus, but the laudanum made everything look fuzzy and disjointed, and just this small effort of raising herself exhausted her. She called Chelsea's name weakly, but there was no response.

Wearily she closed her eyes, knowing she would sleep if she gave in. She wanted to fight this seasickness, but she knew it was a losing battle. And it wasn't just the seasickness. Her heart had been fluttering wildly all day, just the way it had when she'd made her last visit to Dr. Chaters in London. He'd been crotchety and cranky when she'd refused the medicine he'd tried to force on her. He'd gotten even crankier when she'd told him about her scheduled trip to Australia. Actually, he'd exploded in rage, threatening to notify her brother-in-law about her condition. She'd begged him not to get in touch with Jason and had accepted the medicine. She didn't want to be a burden, she'd explained, and this trip and the man waiting for her meant a new life. She'd seen the pity in his eyes and had ignored it. But the last thing the good doctor had said to her was if she stepped on board ship, she'd never step off.

She'd gone home that day to her cramped apartment and finished sewing the lace on one of her nightdresses, a frilly bit of nonsense far too grand for someone like her. But Jason had insisted on paying for her beautiful trousseau, and in the end she'd accepted his generosity. Now it was hers, every exquisite item. All hers, for all the good it was going to do her now. She'd been a fool to attempt this voyage, and she knew in her heart that she would have changed her mind at the last minute if Chelsea hadn't agreed to accompany her. One could hardly die alone. God was being merciful to her when he'd allowed Chelsea Myles to enter her life.

Yet Chelsea hadn't just entered her life, she'd catapulted into it. Almost as if it had been arranged. Honoria leaned back against the pillows and sighed. She might be a sick woman, but she wasn't as stupid as some people thought. She'd been suspicious of Chelsea from the beginning, and now she was certain that the money Chelsea had used to pay her way to New South Wales had been taken from her, Honoria, that night at the theater. The thief who had picked her pocket had given the purse to Chelsea, who was using its contents to buy herself a new life. The newspapers would call it a scam. Well, she didn't feel too guilty now about using Chelsea because she was sure Chelsea had used her.

Chelsea ought to take care of her. Honoria had to admit, however, to being more than a little surprised and comforted by the way Chelsea waited on her, almost as if she really cared what happened to her.

The wild flutterings in her chest increased, making her cry out.

Chelsea opened the door and raced across the small cabin, the slop pail banging against her knee. "What is it, Honoria? Tell me."

Chelsea's cool hand on her forehead seemed to ease the fright Honoria felt. Her heart seemed to quiet, too, at Chelsea's touch. Panic, that's all it was. Honoria sighed deeply and reached out for Chelsea's hand.

Chelsea clasped the frail, dry hand in both of hers. "I wish there was something I could do for you, Honoria."

"You're doing more than I had any right to expect. I want to talk to you, Chelsea. I have things I must say to you, and I want you to be honest with me. I don't know what I would have done without you."

"Honoria, you're so weak. Why don't you wait till later to talk when you feel stronger. It's such an effort for you. I can tell."

"Of course you can tell, you're no fool. I'm the one who's the fool. There isn't going to be a later. I know how ill I am. So do you. I want you to tell me truthfully what you plan to do once you get off this ship. I don't want any lies; I want the truth."

For Chelsea it was a relief to share her story. When she got to the part about Honoria's purse, she took a deep breath, trying to find just the right words, when Honoria interrupted gently.

"I know all about it. I *wanted* to believe you, the way I wanted to believe I was going to live to marry Harlow Kane. I couldn't prove you were involved, and I didn't want to have the police making trouble for Jason or myself. I just wasn't up to handling something like that. It was so nice of you to have tea with me and to intervene for me with Jason. He really wouldn't have given me the money if you hadn't shamed him into it. Barbara was so jealous." A dry little laugh accompanied her words. Chelsea smiled. "So, what are your plans now?"

"I have no idea. The little money, your money, that's left will tide me over unless you want it back. I'll have to get a job, I suppose. I was looking to put my past behind me.

I'm young and healthy; I can find work of some kind." She lowered her voice. "I met this man aboard ship, and he seems very interested in me. He lives at a place called Clonmerra. Something might develop with him. That's the best answer I can give you, Honoria."

"Tell me," Honoria asked, wistfully blunt, "have you been taking care of me because you felt guilty?" Without giving Chelsea a chance to answer, she continued, calmly and purposefully. "I don't blame you for being angry because I signed you on as my servant, but I was angry and it was my way of not letting you get away with my money. None of that's important anymore. What is important is I don't want to die alone. That's the main reason I made this trip. I was hoping against hope that I would be strong enough to weather the voyage, but I'm not."

"Don't say that, Honoria. The weather will improve and so will you. You have to try to eat something. Toast and tea will help. I just wish there was something I could do to make you feel better." As she said them, Chelsea realized she meant the words. How terrible for Honoria that she had no one but herself.

"You've bathed me, combed my hair, emptied my pails, changed my bedding, and given me the medicine. I couldn't ask or expect more from you. I don't think a sister could have done more."

Tears gathered in Chelsea's eyes. "Honoria, you're making me feel so guilty."

"I think we both feel guilty. That's what I want to talk to you about. We've established that I'm going to die. Don't shake your head, Chelsea, it's a fact. I went to the doctor before I left. He said I would never set foot off this ship if I was foolish enough to go against his advice. We have to think about you now and my last days. I'm being generous and selfish at the same time. If you take care of me, see that I'm dressed properly for burial, whatever I have is yours and that includes my identity. You can even have Harlow Kane. Think about that, Chelsea."

She was thinking about it, fast and furiously. It was a possible answer to her future. After all, wasn't she an actress? She could pull it off. But if she did what Honoria suggested, where was her "fresh start"? It wasn't that she'd suddenly developed an honest streak. There could be so many problems. She looked up to find Honoria staring at her, waiting for her to say something. "It's a grand thing you want to do for me, especially after the way I duped you," she said, surprising even herself as the words tumbled out. "As you said, we're even, with you signing me on as your servant and all. You don't have to be so generous. I'll take care of you just as I have been doing. What kind of person would I be if I refused to help out with you being so sick? I might be a thief," Chelsea said virtuously, "but I'm not callous."

Honoria felt as though her life were draining from her. Here she was, being forgiving and trying to do something nice for Chelsea, and she didn't want to accept. It was important to Honoria that Chelsea agree. Someone had to carry on. "The clothes, my diamond earrings, the money I have left, they'll all be yours, Chelsea. Think about it. What if that scoundrel uncle of yours takes it into his head to go to Australia for a "fresh start" just like you? What will happen to you then? I'm giving you a chance for a new life."

"Honoria, you don't have to do this. I said I'll take care of you. I owe you that much for what I've done. You're getting upset, and I can see you're feverish. Let me give a cool cloth for your head."

"Not until you agree. Everything, Chelsea, everything will be yours. It's what I want."

"Why? Why would you want to give me all your things and your most precious possession, your good name?"

"I gave my word that I would marry Harlow Kane. If he finds out now that I duped him the way you duped me, what will he think? I know that's not really important, but word will get back to Jason and Barbara, and they'll die laughing at what a fool I was. They don't even know I'm sick. Jason will feel like a fool. He'll never go to Australia, and Mr. Kane won't communicate. I'm sure of it. You'd be safe, Chelsea. As Mrs. Kane you can do as you please. It's important to me. Call it granting a dying woman's last wish. Why is it so impossible for you to accept what I'm offering?"

"I don't know. You don't have to do this. I will take care of you. But if it will make you happy, I'll agree to everything you want." For now, Chelsea added to herself. Later, she would decide what to do. Honoria was the important thing right now. If agreeing to what she wanted made her feel better, so be it.

Honoria nodded weakly. "It's settled, then. Get pen and paper and write what I tell you. This way no one can ever accuse you of doing away with me and stealing my good name. Quickly, Chelsea, before I nod off again."

Chelsea's heart hammered as she sat, pen in hand, scribbling furiously. She had to prop Honoria up while she signed her name in delicate little letters.

It was done. Chelsea didn't know if she should laugh or cry. She sat for a long time holding Honoria's hand, listening to her uneven breathing. Although she tried to think about the woman's generosity, all she could think about was Quaid Tanner. If he asked her to marry him, she wouldn't have to make use of Honoria's generosity.

A long time later, Chelsea got up and rubbed the back of her neck. She felt terrible, as if she'd been through a bout with Cosmo. Her eyes were drawn to the beautiful dresses hanging in the cabin. They were hers now. So were the diamond earrings. Everything in the cabin was hers, even Honoria's soul . . . for the moment

She cried. For Honoria.

Honoria slept fitfully for the next few hours. From time to time she cried out. A short while later she rallied, her eyes bright and sparkling. She stared at Chelsea for a few moments, and her voice was strong when she spoke. "You've been so good to me, taking care of me the way you have. I want to thank you before it's too late."

"Don't talk like that. We're waiting for Mrs. Crain and the captain. I know he'll put into port as soon as possible once he sees you."

A look of consternation crossed Honoria's plain, narrow face. "I don't want anyone to see me this way," she wailed. "Please, Chelsea, don't let anyone come in here."

"Hush, hush, it's for your own good, I promise. You can't stand any more of this journey, and you must go ashore. We're sailing the French coast now; it shouldn't be long. Lisbon is still days away, and I don't want to see you suffer any longer than you must."

"France? I don't know anyone in France," Honoria gasped fearfully. "Where will I go? What will I do?"

Chelsea bit her lip. Honoria had echoed her thoughts exactly. It was a question she'd been pondering since returning to the cabin.

"You won't be alone. I intend to stay with you." Even as she said the words and made the promise, her heart sank. Good-bye, Australia; good-bye, new beginning. Good-bye, Quaid Tanner.

"I can't let you do that for me." Honoria turned her face to the wall, but not before Chelsea saw the grateful tears.

"I can and I will. I promise. But first we've got to get off this ship!"

"It will be such a relief to leave this cabin," Honoria confessed. "I can see the sun is shining. Chelsea, I want to feel the sun on my face."

Chelsea thought of the confining atmosphere of the small cabin and agreed. It was so little to ask, and perhaps the fresh air would work a miracle. "Would you like to go up on deck?"

"Oh, Chelsea, do you think I could? A breath of fresh air, sunshine."

"Here, let me prop you up so I can brush your hair. I have a clean nightdress all laid out for you, and you can cover up with your cape. Careful now, let me do everything; don't exert yourself."

By the time Chelsea had tended to Honoria, even that small effort had left her exhausted and she was falling asleep again. Alarmed, Chelsea picked up the tiny gold watch on the bedstand and counted the hours since the last dose of laudanum. Nearly six hours. Surely Honoria wasn't still under its effects.

Now more frightened than concerned, she rushed from the cabin and banged on Quaid's door, praying he'd be there. The door swung open abruptly, and she nearly toppled into his arms.

"Madam, I didn't know I was in such demand," he said lightly, grinning.

"If there was time, I'd slap you for that," Chelsea flared. "I need you to do something for me. It's Honoria; she wants to be taken up on deck for some air. Please, Quaid. It seems very important to her. Will you carry her?"

Quaid's brows lifted. Chelsea's alarm was genuine, and she didn't seem to care that once Honoria was on deck her own little charade would undoubtedly be revealed. Count on Mrs. Crain to extract information, even from the dying. "Of course, I'll do it," he said, his tone serious, "but do you think it wise if she's so ill?"

"It's what she wants. Please come, you be the judge."

Stepping across the narrow companionway into Chelsea's cabin, Quaid was immediately taken aback by the pathetic creature in the bed. Only the day before yesterday he'd peeked in and seen Chelsea sitting beside Honoria, tending patiently to her. Was it possible for someone's condition to deteriorate so rapidly? At the time he'd been more interested in Chelsea, whose compassion and sensitivity had greatly impressed him.

Against the rough white bed linens and dark teak walls of the cabin's interior bulkheads, Honoria was even paler. Huge, dark smudges circled her eyes, and her lips were tinged a curious blue. Chelsea moved to his side, touching Honoria gently on the hand. "This is Mr. Quaid Tanner, Honoria. He's come to carry you above. Do you still want to go on deck?"

Grateful eyes peered up at Quaid, humbling him. "I'll be very careful," he said softly, assuring her. "You'll be light as a feather in my arms, and I believe the sun is shining today just for you."

Honoria smiled weakly, lifting her arms to hug his neck as he lifted her. Chelsea grabbed a blanket from the bed and followed behind as he carried his fragile burden.

Myriad thoughts struck Quaid as he brought Honoria onto the deck, the bright sun falling mercilessly on her face. With a timid action, she turned into the shadow of his neck to shield herself from the intrusive light. He wished he were on Clonmerra walking through his vineyard, or in the pub in London where he'd watched Chelsea lead her lovestruck entourage down the street. He'd even be glad to drink that poor excuse for wine; anything not to have to witness what he felt was the inevitable.

Honoria turned her head once again, this time to look out over the expanse of green sea. Then it was as though Quaid could feel the last breath leave her body; he heard a sigh, and she sank in his arms. He braced his legs for footing against the gentle pitch and roll of the deck, and when he turned to face Chelsea, all that needed to be said was there in his eyes. The white linen handkerchief in Chelsea's hands had been knotted and unknotted into a limp string. Her head dropped, and tears rolled down her cheeks. Her prayer was a silent one.

"I'll take her back to the cabin," Quaid told her, not attempting to keep emotion from his voice. He had never known this woman, yet he mourned her.

"No! No, don't! She wanted to be up here, in the sunshine!"

Chelsea's cry brought the attention of several other passengers who were strolling the deck of the *Southern Cross*.

"What's wrong, Mr. Tanner?" The purser approached, but when he saw Honoria lying limp in Quaid's embrace there was no need for explanations. "Please, sir, take her below; we've the other passengers to consider."

Chelsea's eyes flew to Quaid. "No. Not yet," he replied. "She wanted to feel the sun and catch the breeze." Although it was spoken quietly, something in his tone forbade contradiction; the purser stepped aside. Quaid's reward was seeing the gratitude in Chelsea's eyes.

Later that afternoon Honoria Harris was given to the sea. The ceremony was mercifully brief, and no one shed a tear for this unknown woman except Chelsea. Mrs. Crain had come into the cabin and prepared the body for burial, and exhibiting her innate aptitude for organization had even suggested which prayer the captain should read from the ship's Bible.

"And now we lay this good woman to rest, O Lord! Take her into your everlasting fold and keep her," Captain Winfield intoned. The sailors tilted the board, and as Honoria's shrouded body fell beneath the greedy waves,

Chelsea heard the captain say, "Receive your child, Chelsea Myles, O Lord, and deliver her to heaven."

Chelsea nearly choked, and she felt physically ill. Dear God, now she'd never set the record straight! Honoria was being buried under the wrong name! Her name! It was as though she were witnessing her own funeral. She opened her mouth to protest, but no sound came out; she was mesmerized by the sight of the shroud falling over the deck into the sea.

Quaid, who was standing beside her, nudged her elbow. "Leave it be," he said quietly. "There's nothing to be done for it now."

Chelsea's brain spun wildly. It was done, then. It would be entered in the captain's log that Chelsea Myles, maid-servant, had died at sea. But that was her name! Everyone knew that was her name! No, that was wrong; to everyone aboard ship she was Mrs. Harris, Mrs. Honoria Harris. Only Quaid called her Chelsea.

As soon as the brief ceremony had been completed, Mrs. Porter Crain barreled over to Chelsea and Quaid. "There's been a mistake, a terrible mistake!" she jabbered. "Am I or am I not correct in thinking that poor woman was buried under the wrong name?"

The deck seemed to heave, and Chelsea's knees began to buckle beneath her. This wasn't the way she wanted the truth to come out, not here in front of all these people. She'd wanted to speak to the captain and purser privately first; this was all going to be too humiliating.

Quaid's hand reached out and grasped Chelsea's arm. He could feel her tremble beneath his touch. "Whatever do you mean, Mrs. Crain?" he asked, disarming the woman with an admiring glance.

"Didn't you hear what the captain said? Chelsea Myles. Chelsea! Isn't that your own name, dear?"

Before she could answer, Quaid replied, "Yes, it is, as a matter of fact." He allowed a frown to crease his brow. "How astute of you, Mrs. Crain." Then, turning to Chelsea, "Wasn't your maid's name Ellie, Mrs. Harris? Eleanor Myles, wasn't it? There must be a mistake in the passenger list, Mrs. Crain. Would you be so good as to set the matter straight before the captain enters it in his log? I'd like to take Mrs. Harris below; she's had quite a shock today."

Mrs. Crain puffed with importance. "Yes, of course I will," she assured them. Then to Chelsea, "Don't feel too terrible, my dear. As I told you, there are servants aplenty in New South Wales. Eleanor, you say, Mr. Tanner? My dear, would you like me to write to the poor girl's family? I'd be more than happy to spare you from that unpleasant chore."

Chelsea sat on her trundle bed and looked at the bed Honoria had so recently vacated. She'd really only known the woman for little more than a week, and yet she mourned her. Or was it guilt over her little charade that lay so heavily on her heart? She had never meant it to be this way, never. Who would have thought Honoria would die? Mrs. Crain had said it wasn't only the seasickness, that it must have been her heart. Still, she should have stepped forward and seen to it that Honoria was laid to rest under her own name! But as Quaid had said, what purpose was there to it now? Confused, angry, Chelsea erupted into a flurry of activity. Her own sense of decency had been offended, and she had to admit to herself that rarely had she ever had difficulty with her scruples.

Unable to sit still a moment longer, she stripped the bed of its coarse linens and, wrinkling her nose, dumped them in an untidy heap by the door. She wanted the offending linens out of the cabin entirely; they smelled of sickness and death. She fought with the door to open it and kicked the bed linens out into the companionway.

Heart beating like a drum, she then dragged Honoria's trunks into the center of the cabin. At first she had every intention of packing each and every article belonging to Honoria and having the lot returned to her sister in England. Then she decided against it. Jason and Barbara Munsey had effectively renounced all claim to and responsibility for Honoria. From what Honoria had said about them, and from what Chelsea herself had seen, they probably considered themselves well rid of their poor relation and would want nothing to remind them of her. Instead, she'd see the trousseau and personal effects were delivered to Honoria's intended. Let him take care of the matter. Surely Honoria had his letters somewhere; there would be a name and an address.

She began to sort through the wardrobe, laying aside piles of dainty chemises, lavishly ruffled petticoats, and delicately sewn nightdresses Honoria had never worn. What a shame to pack them away and deliver them to a man who would have no use for them, she thought wistfully, looking at the impressive array of gowns, each one rich in silk trimmings and expensively made. How sad her own wardrobe was compared to Honoria's.

Not liking the turn her thoughts were taking, Chelsea began to fold and place all the articles in Honoria's trunks. The tiny diamond ear bobs were tucked inside a little velvet pouch and dropped into one of the drawers. That was where she found a packet of letters written in a bold, masculine hand. She put it aside, deciding to read them later in order to locate this Mr. Kane Honoria was to have married. Ribbons, laces, and scents were gathered up from the dresser and placed beside the ear bobs. In another drawer Chelsea found Honoria's purse, and in it was a fold of bills. Remembering what Honoria had saved by listing

Chelsea as her maid, she sat down to count it out and claim her rightful share, replacing the remainder back inside the purse.

Chelsea looked down at the amount in her hand and mentally added it to the remainder of her money. This was ridiculous, she told herself. What use would Mr. Kane or Honoria's sister have for the money left in the purse? Honoria had told her to take the rest for herself. Quickly, before she could change her mind, Chelsea retrieved the purse and placed it among her own things, a frown still creasing her fair brow. For that matter, what use would a man have for a dead woman's belongings? What would Mr. Kane do with undergarments and silk hose? They, too, were retrieved from the trunk.

In short order everything Chelsea had meticulously packed was once again strewn across the bed. It would be sinful to let these things go to waste in a dry, stuffy attic somewhere. It was what Honoria wanted, Chelsea reminded herself yet again. It wasn't as though she were robbing the dead, heaven forbid. It was more that she was granting Honoria's last wish. And that thought put her mind at ease.

In the end it was Chelsea's own meager wardrobe that rested inside Honoria's trunks.

Unable to explain her feelings even to herself, Chelsea remained in the cabin over the next two days, taking her meals alone. Despite the logic that had prompted her to keep Honoria's belongings, a deep wave of grief seemed to have settled over her. Several times there'd been a quiet knocking on the door and Quaid's voice had sounded through the panel. Yes, she was all right; yes, she wanted to be alone. In the end it was Mrs. Crain who insisted Chelsea open the door and speak to her.

"We're all extremely worried about you, my dear. You

mustn't carry on this way or you'll make yourself ill. However fond of her you were, it's all behind you now. Get yourself dressed and come to dinner. I've already told a steward to bring you hot water for your wash. If you don't think you're able to use it by yourself, I'd be happy to assist." This last held a threat.

"I'm not really hungry, Mrs. Crain. . . ."

"Nonsense! Everyone is hungry! I never took you for a shrinking violet, my girl, and if you don't get some spirit about you, Australia will eat you up. I've already told you it's a country particularly hard on women. Now move! I'll expect you in the dining room in half an hour." And as quickly as she had arrived, Mrs. Crain left, bustling through the narrow door.

When Chelsea entered the dining room later that evening, Mrs. Crain immediately waved to her from across the room. Turning her head neither to the left or right, effectively restraining herself from looking for Quaid, Chelsea tilted up her chin and crossed the room to Mrs. Crain.

"Now, that's the way I want to see you," the woman said approvingly. "You're much too young to shut yourself up in your cabin. Porter"—she turned to the pink-cheeked gentleman beside her—"you remember Mrs. Harris, don't you?"

"Of course." Porter stood, as did the other gentlemen at the table. "I'm so glad to see you're feeling better, Mrs. Harris," he said as he moved to help her with her chair.

Introductions were remade and condolences issued, but Chelsea was aware only of a distinct feeling that she was being watched. She could feel Quaid's eyes upon her as though in intimate caress. Smoothing the white linen napkin over her lap, she directed her attention to Mrs. Crain, who was regaling their dinner companions with a story of a shopping spree in London. But it was Quaid's voice she listened for, straining to hear the deep timbre of it as it reached her from where he was dining on the other side of the room.

"You look perfectly charming this evening," Mrs. Crain commented. "Doesn't she look charming, Porter? That shade of lime green is most becoming on you, isn't it, Porter?"

All through dinner Chelsea was aware of Quaid, even though she never turned her head to look at him. Not even when she heard his laughter immediately followed by a feminine titter. Another notch in his belt, no doubt, she found herself thinking nastily. Despite his services on the day Honoria had died, Chelsea still harbored a grudge against him. What he'd done to her wasn't fair, tricking her and making her believe he was a gentleman of substance. Instead, he'd turned out to be a farmer—and worse still, she'd realized over the past two days that he had never denied having a wife and children. And if all that wasn't bad enough, there were the feelings he had aroused in her, emotions she was wise enough not to put a name to.

"Will you stay for a game of cards?" Porter asked Chelsea as the last of the dinner dishes were being cleared away. "Merriam would be so delighted to have you join us."

"Merriam?"

"Yes, my wife."

"I'd like to, sincerely, but I seem to be getting a headache. Will you excuse me if I return to my cabin?" With that, Chelsea bade them all good night, promising to appear for lunch the following day. She couldn't get out of the dining room fast enough, away from the sound of Quaid's laughter.

The hour was late, the moon riding high in the heavens, when a white slip of paper slid under Chelsea's door accompanied by a gentle tapping. She was lying propped up in bed when the sound caught her attention. Even without looking, she knew who had put the note under the door and wouldn't have been surprised to see the handle turn. Quaid Tanner was not a man to take no for an answer, just as she knew she would never be able to sleep without getting up to see what his note said.

The crisp white paper fluttered in her hand. "Chelsea, I want to talk with you. Anytime, anywhere. Q."

Chelsea gave an unladylike snort. Anytime, anywhere. Right now in his cabin was closer to the truth. Obviously he hadn't been able to persuade the owner of that female titter to help wile away the long night hours.

She grabbed up Honoria's heavy woolen robe—no, it was *her* robe now—and pulled it on, roping the belt tightly around her waist. She'd be damned if she went to him now. The future lay before her, and falling in love with a farmer who most likely had a wife and children was not in her best interests. She hadn't pulled herself away from her homeland and gone sailing halfway around the world just to end up used and discarded. If Quaid Tanner was looking for diversion on this journey, he'd have to find it elsewhere.

Not wanting to make herself available to further notes and tappings on her door, she stole quietly out of her cabin to go up on deck. It was late, everyone would be settled down for the night; she could be alone except for the seaman keeping watch. Besides, the fresh, cold sea air might clear her head and bring some much needed order to her thoughts.

She slipped down the companionway and up the stairs, and had barely set her foot on deck when a hand reached out and seized her arm. "Let me go!" she cried, alarmed.

"Shhh. Do you want to waken the entire ship?"

She stopped struggling long enough to peer at the shadowed figure holding her. "Quaid Tanner, what are you doing here? Why don't you leave me alone?"

"I saw you pull the note out from under the door and knew you would try to avoid me by coming on deck. I waited for you."

"More likely you were spying on me. If I'm correct, you've already confessed to sneaking around and watching me, even back in London." She felt close to tears and heard the telltale tremor in her voice. Everything was becoming intolerable . . . but she knew there was no one to blame but herself.

Quaid grinned, a flash of white teeth in the moonlight, and led her across the deck to the rail. White crests foamed beneath the ship's hull as the *Southern Cross* sailed the black Atlantic waters. "I suppose I *was* spying, but I wanted to see you. You've been hiding out for the past two days, and I was worried about you."

"You didn't seem particularly worried at dinner. And I have not been hiding out, I simply wanted to be alone."

"And that's exactly what I want, sweet," he murmured, pulling her into his embrace. "I want to be alone, with you."

He bent his head, his lips nearly touching hers, and she was mesmerized by the overwhelming hunger she saw in his eyes. She almost succumbed, almost fell into that strong, warm embrace, but then she struggled and wrested herself free. No, she couldn't allow this, couldn't torture herself this way. He didn't care about her; he'd only used her and wanted to continue until he was through with her.

"Don't turn away from me, Chelsea." He was angry, and his eyes glinted dangerously—or was it the moonlight? "You've been through a bad time, and I only meant to comfort you. I know you find this hard to believe, but I care about what happens to you."

"You care!" she replied with a sneer. "That's why you used me, tricked me! I should hate you for that."

"But you don't, do you?" He reached for her again, moving closer.

Quickly she stepped backward, avoiding his touch. "Don't count on it, Quaid." There was danger in her voice, which sounded harsh and brittle even to her own ears.

"Feisty tonight, aren't we?" he asked lightly.

His attitude infuriated her. She wanted to claw that grin from his handsome face. Why did he always seem to find her amusing; why was he always laughing at her? "You're despicable."

"I find you rather endearing, too." His grin widened. "Come here, let's make love and put this fighting aside."

"If that's an invitation to your bed, you can forget it." She turned away from him. "I'm going back to my cabin, and if I've any luck at all, you'll fall over the rail, and I'll never have to see that silly grin again."

"Oh, no, you don't." He reached out and seized her by the shoulder, his fingers biting into soft flesh. "You're going below, but it's to my cabin, and if you utter one sound, I'll wring that pretty neck. The time for playacting is over, Chelsea. This is real life we're living." He lifted her easily, holding her against him. Although she struggled, she thought better of screaming for help. Being caught in this particular compromising situation would do nothing for her reputation.

"Put me down!" she hissed. "I don't want to go with you; I don't want to be with you!"

"Yes, you do, you just won't admit it. And quit struggling, for God's sake; you'd think I was trying to kill you instead of make love to you."

"You take too much upon yourself. Why would I want

you to make love to me? I can't even stand to have you touch me!"

"We'll see about that, won't we?" He squeezed through the narrow doorway leading below. In the companionway, when she nearly grappled out of his arms, he took the more drastic measure of throwing her over his shoulder and carrying her into his cabin.

"Let me out of here!" she cried, beating at him with her fists. "I don't want to be here!"

"Shut that mouth, you're enough to wake the dead. And I wouldn't be so quick to be discovered nearly naked in my cabin, Chelsea love. Mrs. Crain can be quite inventive when it comes to repeating a story. And then, to protect my own reputation, I'd be forced to reveal exactly who you are. You wouldn't like that, would you?"

"I've told you before you're a bounder, but I was wrong. You're a full-blooded bastard, Quaid Tanner, and I hate you!"

He dumped her unceremoniously onto the bed, falling on top of her, pressing her into the hard mattress. "You don't hate me, Chelsea. But you do feel something for me, you've already admitted that. And you like to have me touch you," he told her, leaning forward to nibble at the base of her throat, his hands working beneath the opening of her robe. "You like it when I touch you here." His fingers skimmed lightly over the smooth skin of her inner thigh. "And here." His lips blazed a trail to the satin-smooth valley between her breasts.

Chelsea writhed beneath him, wriggling away to escape his insolent touches, afraid to feel the fire that threatened to engulf her in the passion she had come to know in his arms.

He nuzzled the pulse spot at the base of her white throat, feeling it race beneath his lips. He wanted her, wanted to feel her skin warm beneath his hands. He could already feel the fight leaving her, could anticipate the return of passion she would show him. Against the dark wool of her robe, her skin was pink and fresh. Each curve and hollow of her body beckoned to his lips and hands. Her long sable-dark hair twined through his fingers as he turned her face to his. When his mouth claimed hers she fought him still, twisting and turning to escape. He deepened his kiss, searching for an answering response. It came when he whispered her name, when his fingers gentled on her flesh, when he breathed his need for her. Then, with a little moan, like the sound of a stricken child, she turned into his embrace, offering her mouth to his, yielding beneath his touch.

Discarding her robe and finally removing her nightdress, the last obstacle between his hands and her body, he took her hands in his and placed them on his belt, invoking her without words. His garments fell away beneath her ministering fingers; she left his newly exposed flesh warm from her kisses, continuing until he was naked beside her. Their passions rose like the wildness of a winter storm, hungry mouths searching, feverish hands touching.

They tore at each other, each seeking what only the other could give. There was no yesterday, no tomorrow, only the here and now. And when their passion had abated, lips swollen from loving and bodies glistening with the sheen of desire, they lay in one another's arms glorying in the journey they had shared. Kiss-softened mouths, tender exploring caresses, bodies still warm from passion's fever, they basked in the afterglow of a moment only two could share.

Chelsea lay with her head in the crook of his shoulder and found herself thinking it was her favorite place in the whole world. Once he had overcome her resistance he had been gentle, so gentle, and even now a golden warmth spread throughout her body, touching her in places that had become familiar to his hands and open to his lips.

Quaid cradled Chelsea in his arms, his lips grazing her smooth, fair brow. Once he had thought of her as a jungle cat, a sleek, black panther, but now she purred in his embrace like a kitten, soft and yielding, tempting to the touch. A strange expression crept into his eyes. How was it that only this woman could bring him such fulfillment? It was as though they were a matched pair, the two of them, dark-haired and dark-souled, finding in each other a release and response that had to have been preordained. From the first he had known she was inexperienced in the ways of love, despite the fact that she had offered herself to him so casually in order to buy his silence. He was sorry for that. In truth he had only been seeking a kiss, but when it had become clear that she thought he expected much more than that, he had allowed the deceit to continue. Again, it was something he regretted.

Chelsea sighed deeply, snuggling into Quaid's embrace. If only time could stop here. She never wanted to leave this bed and Quaid's arms. His sleek, manly body molded perfectly against hers; it was so comforting here, so safe. Was it possible she loved him? Could she throw away her dream and ambitions to stay with this man forever?

"There's something I must ask you," Quaid said softly, his voice a deep rumble in his chest.

"Hmmm?" came the sleepy murmur as a languorous contentment stole over her. "Don't ask me anything that will break this spell you've woven over me." She closed her eyes and snuggled deep into his embrace, fingers playing aimless little games through the fine furring on his chest. In a moment her eyes opened, lit with curiosity. "Well, aren't you going to ask me?"

"No, I'll break the spell." His lips touched the top of

her head, and he breathed in the fragrance of her hair. There was still the freshness of the salt air in it and something else, something vaguely reminiscent of the bougainvillea vine that grew outside his house on Clonmerra.

From his serious tone she knew whatever he had to ask was probably not pleasant. Now her curiosity was fully aroused. Rising from his arms and perching beside him on her knees, she stared down into his face. There were shadows and questions in his eyes that triggered an alarm.

"All right, then," he said at last, "I want you to tell me what you plan to do once you land in Australia."

"Oh, is that all?" She was relieved. She'd thought he might ask her something about her past and Uncle Cosmo, something that might make her ashamed. "I really haven't formulated any plans, not exactly. But I do know that I've left the theater behind in London. I want something more for myself, money, position, a place of importance."

"And how do you plan to achieve this?"

"Oh, I don't know. Something will come along, something always does."

He found himself laughing in spite of himself. "Live by the seat of your pants, do you?"

"More by the slip of a petticoat." She assumed a dramatic pose, one hand behind her head, sheet dropping to reveal her lovely breasts. "My face is my fortune, sir, and I intend to trade on it before the years rob me of opportunity."

"Be serious. " He slapped her lightly on the rump. "I want to know what you've planned for yourself once you get to Australia."

"I'm telling you I really don't know. But I do know I won't go into service to some grand lady or raise her brats for her as a governess. No, I want to be the grand lady, and if there are any servants about, they'll owe me for their employ."

"So you've grand ideas, have you?"

"And why not? Do you think I left everything I ever knew or everyone who ever knew me behind in England just to take up the same sort of life? Cheap clothing, poor lodgings, living off ill-gotten goods, that's all part of the past, and I don't want to think about it. There's something better for me in Australia, I can feel it. I seemed to have known it the instant Honoria told me that's where she was going. Perhaps that's what's waiting for me, a husband. Honoria was going to get married, you know, and from what she told me he was quite well-to-do. Although he did have children somewhere, and as I said, I don't relish the idea of raising some other woman's brats."

"Do you ever plan to have brats of your own someday?"

"Children," she corrected. "Other women have brats." And laughed, letting him know she wasn't completely serious.

"You still haven't told me what you'll do," he persisted, ear turned for every nuance of her answer.

"But I have told you." She tickled him under the ribs, making him squawk in laughter and protest. "I plan to be a grand lady, and once I set my mind to something, I always get it in the end. Somewhere out there is a man who has everything I want: money, title or position, more money."

"You don't want much, do you?" Quaid laughed.

Chelsea bristled. "No, not much at all. And why shouldn't I have it? Other women do, some of them at least, and not all of them got it by working their fingers to the bone and slaving, I can tell you that. If a woman wants to make her way in this world, it doesn't hurt to have a man lay the path for her. Better still, is a man who already has everything and wants to share it. I ask you, did the queen herself come by her throne through her own labors and good conscience? Indeed not." She laughed. "It was handed to her because she happened to be born into it. For those of us not fortunate enough to be *born* into a life of luxury, it's a simple matter of using our heads and choosing correctly, don't you think?"

Quaid was silent; he was looking at her, measuring her, and she didn't like it. She could feel the heat in her cheeks beneath his appraising stare. "Don't look at me that way. I've worked hard; I deserve the finer things life has to offer, and I'll appreciate them, I can tell you. A man won't find me ungrateful, at least not the right man who has everything I want."

"You're a candid little beast, aren't you? Most women would never admit to being fortune hunters, to themselves or anyone else, for that matter, and especially not to a man."

"I feel quite safe in telling you this," Chelsea said as she lay back in his arms, head nestled on his shoulder. "After all, you've nothing to worry about, have you? You keep sheep and grow grapes, and you never did tell me whether or not there was a wife and babies waiting for you in Australia. You've nothing to offer me, so you're also safe from my greedy clutches." She yawned sleepily, nestling down once again.

"What if I told you there was no wife, no children?" His tone was serious again.

Chelsea's eyes opened, and she was very still for a moment. "*Are* you telling me?"

"I said what if?"

"Then I would like you better; I wouldn't think you such a faithless bounder."

"As if you'd had nothing to do with my so-called faithlessness, you little witch! Chelsea, you amaze me. Your virtue and scruples are always perfectly suited to your logic. And vice versa."

"You still haven't answered me. Do you have a wife and children?"

"No, I don't. There never seemed to be time to take on a family. I'm only just now getting Clonmerra established, and I've little energy left for the nicer things in life." He smiled down at her. "I'd like you to see it someday."

"So I can feed your chickens and shear your sheep? No, thank you. I've told you, I want something better out of life. Uncle Cosmo only uttered one truth in his entire life, and do you know what it was? 'Life is not a dress rehearsal.' I believe that."

Something in Quaid died a little at Chelsea's words. He was incapable of giving her all the things she wanted, and it might be years before Clonmerra was self-supporting. If it weren't for the months he spent living below ground like a wombat in Coober Pedy, digging for opals to feed Clonmerra's greedy coffers, he might have gone under before this. He'd had offers for his land and his vineyard, offers that would have permitted him to live a life of ease, but he was attached to the land, and bringing Clonmerra to the glory it deserved was an obsession with him. He wasn't starving and he had more than enough, but not enough for Chelsea. Not yet. God save all men who love ambitious women!

"I'm leaving the ship tomorrow when we make port in Lisbon," he said abruptly. "There's business I must take care of, and I don't know if it will be done in time to continue the voyage on the *Southern Cross*. I may have to take another ship."

Chelsea didn't know whether to laugh or cry. It had crossed her mind many times that three months spent aboard the *Southern Cross* with Quaid would be her undoing. She felt far too much for him, emotions that were dangerous to her long-range plans, emotions she refused even to name. And now he was telling her that he might

TO TASTE THE WINE 149

not be sailing the rest of the journey with her. From the way he'd said it, it was almost a certainty—a decision, perhaps, that had already been made . . . not by circumstances, but by Quaid. "What will you be doing in Portugal?" she asked.

"There's a winery with which I've contracted for a shipment of vines, which I'll bring back to Clonmerra. They may do very well in our hot climate."

Chelsea noticed that when he said, "Clonmerra," it could have been a woman's name, a woman he loved. An emotion she refused to recognize as jealousy exploded in her chest. She didn't want to think about this now, not when he was so close and his arms so warm around her. "I suppose that leaves me to the mercy of Mrs. Crain." She tried for levity but suddenly found the effort too much for her.

He tried to read her thoughts, half hoping, half dreading she would ask to come with him. When she spoke again, her words startled him into momentary silence.

"I suppose this is good-bye, then?" She waited for his response, every moment an eternity. Part of her wanted to run as far away from him as possible, yet she needed more than life itself to remain in his arms. She almost blurted that she wanted to go to Lisbon and continue the journey with him, but she bit back the words. Where had everything gone wrong? This wasn't the way she'd planned it. She would not fall in love with Quaid Tanner! There was more to life than wasting away on a farm somewhere and growing old before her time. There had to be more! A feeling of dread overcame her, and an echoing voice whispered that it was already too late.

"No, it's not good-bye," he murmured, turning to press himself against her. "There's still tonight."

Quaid's mouth claimed hers in a deep, searching kiss that reverberated through her soul. For a moment, just for a moment, she had believed he would ask her to come with him. Instead, he was doing tender things to her body and evoking her answering response. Chelsea threw herself into Quaid's arms, moist lips parted and welcoming. It tonight were all she would have, then she would make it a night to remember.

Chelsea stood straight and still, a white-knuckled grip on the starboard rail as she watched Quaid wend his way through the dockside havoc at Lisbon port. The scape of the city perched on the rolling hills went unnoticed. The sun glinting off the charming red-tiled roofs and white-washed building façades, the intriguing sound of a foreign language, all meant nothing. Only the sight of Quaid's dark head and the proud set of his shoulders were real. Her eyes followed him until he was out of sight, and even then she stared in that direction. Her eyes dropped to the magnificent opal on her finger, Quaid's gift to her last evening. Why wasn't it bringing her some kind of comfort? It had to mean something. Payment for services rendered; farmer or not, Quaid was a gentleman. Well, he was gone, out of her life, and now she was free. There were no choices to be made, and the danger of giving her heart had passed. Why then, did she feel this emptiness inside, this hollow anxiety as though she had somehow missed a very important cue?

Chapter 8

Quaid never returned to the *Southern Cross*. Chelsea had watched until the last possible moment, then had stood at the rail long after the sight of land had vanished beyond the horizon.

The remainder of her journey aboard ship was long and tedious. She came to know every board and nail that comprised her cabin, and she was able to be entertaining and charming in the dining room with her fellow passengers. Mrs. Crain loaned her several books on the flora and fauna of Australia, and Chelsea became well versed in the names of various flowers and birds as Mrs. Crain schooled her lessons. Once she'd picked up the basic rules, polite games of whist and cribbage whiled away the quiet evenings. Chelsea, a natural mimic, was soon at ease with her new style of living. Choosing the correct fork at dinner was no longer a problem, and neither was the meaningless chatter at which ladies of good breeding were expert.

To replenish supplies, the *Southern Cross* had put in at strange and exotic ports of call whose names had been meaningless to Chelsea before this: Morocco, Cape Verde, Cape Town, and Madagascar. When the *Southern Cross* sailed across the equator, she longed for the cool, damp climate of England, and when they traversed the Tropic of

Capricorn, they were becalmed for nearly eight days before a God-blessed wind rolled around the earth to puff gently into the sails. As they traveled southward, people became darker skinned and finally black, and she listened incredulously to natives whose tongues were capable of making almost incredible patterns of speech.

Once, while docked in Madagascar, Mrs. Crain learned from the captain that there was a Chinese trader on the next quay. Seizing Chelsea's elbow, she said eagerly, "Come along, girl, and bring your purse. I smell a bargain in the air!"

And bargains there were. Yards of silks for dresses and lace for trimmings. Uncountable ribbons and fragrant oils and perfumes. Sandalwood boxes and lacquered chests. Tortoiseshell combs and pearl-handled brushes. Their purchases were carried back to the *Southern Cross by* porters whose heads barely showed over the intimidating pile of goods, yet Chelsea was able to heft her barely touched coin purse with satisfaction. The pale lilac silk she had bought would make a beautiful gown, as would the printed dimity and featherweight linen, which Mrs. Crain had advised would be cool and practical in Australia's heat.

Like children beneath a Christmas tree, Chelsea and Merriam unfolded, unrolled, and inspected their purchases. Chelsea's cabin overflowed with silks and fine muslins for petticoats and yards and yards of laces. Merriam Crain had stockpiled Chinese teas and various spices from the Orient, and tins of sweetmeats and dried fruits had been bought with social gatherings in mind. Over and over she reminded Chelsea that everything they had bought would cost ten times as much in Sydney, and both felt as though they had stumbled upon a king's treasure.

The *Southern Cross* approached Australia from the southwest, crossing the frontier town of Melbourne and traveling up the eastern coast to Sydney. Here the waters were blue and foaming, schools of whales sounded the depths, and a playground of porpoises frolicked in their wake. The captain had ordered food scraps to be stowed and not dumped overboard because of numerous sharks in these waters, and the cacophonous clatter of pots and pans accompanied the vociferous complaints of the ship's cook.

Chelsea strained for her first sight of Sydney. Over the headwaters she could see ribbons of white sandy beaches hemmed by low jagged sandstone ledges. And beyond the spit of land she could just make out the tall masts of hundreds of other ships that had docked in Port Jackson. Farther south of them was Botany Bay, the notorious harbor that until recently had welcomed thousands of England's convicts; when the community of rejects had been declared unhealthful, the colony had been forced to move north to the magnificent anchorage of Sydney Cove.

Once entering the harbor, signs of civilization immediately made themselves known. Houses and businesses lined the wharf, and in the distance loomed the stunted ridges of the Blue Mountains. It was mid-January and the beginning of Australia's summer when the *Southern Cross* made portage. Women paraded the dock areas, their colorful parasols bobbing like a garden of flowers in the gentle sea breezes. A flurry of activity could be seen, and the sound of men's voices, their harshness softened by distance, wafted over the water. Merriam Crain stood by Chelsea's side and pointed out various places of interest: the Common House, the Hall of Records, the courts of justice, the governor's mansion. Stevedores hauled ropes thrown from the decks of the *Southern Cross* and pulled the ship into dock. When she heard the thunder of the gangplank dropping onto the wharf, Chelsea's heart beat frantically. She was here, she had arrived, and the future spread out before her like a blank piece of paper; it was up to her to write her own destiny. It was an exciting thought, and one that thrilled, yet frightened her.

It wasn't until she saw his face that she realized she'd been looking for him. Before this moment it had been a ridiculous hope that she would see him again, find him waiting for her. Ever since he had left the *Southern Cross* there had been an emptiness, a deep hollow core, that had brought her eyes more than a few times to his cabin door. He had told her before leaving the ship that, in all likelihood, he would reach New South Wales before she did, since the *Southern Cross* put in at so many ports of call. It had been a formless hope, yet here he was, his dark eyes searching the rail of the ship, looking for her. And when he at last saw her, he raised his hand in welcome.

Chelsea tried to slow the beat of her heart as she watched him climb the gangplank. He hadn't forgotten her, no more than she'd been able to forget him. Over and over she had considered what she would make of her life in Australia, and she had never come up with a satisfactory answer. Now the answer was walking across the deck toward her, sun-bronzed and tall, broad-shouldered and lean, with a light in his eyes meant only for her. In the weeks since Quaid had left her, she had learned that ambition and dreams were cold companions on lonely nights. Being a farmer's wife wasn't the worst fate in the world; there were always the long winter nights under downy quilts.

Walking toward her, Quaid knew why he had been so impatient for the *Southern Cross* to make Sydney Cove. It wasn't the remainder of his baggage in the ship's hold nor the oaken casks in which French grape vines had been carefully stowed. It was clear now; his only reason for being here was standing at the rail with her dark eyes fixed on him and a welcoming smile touching those adored lips. Chelsea. Only propriety prevented him from taking her in his arms and pressing his hungry mouth to those sweetly curved lips.

"Mr. Tanner!" exclaimed Merriam Crain, intercepting his direct path to Chelsea. "How in the world did you manage to arrive in Sydney before us?"

"We only stopped in Cape Town for supplies," he told the voluminous woman. "I managed to book passage on a cargo ship heading directly for Sydney and arrived only three days ago." He was looking over the top of Merriam's head directly at Chelsea, whose tawny eyes held him in a fragile embrace.

"You remember Chelsea Harris, of course," Mrs. Crain was saying. "Things weren't as lively after you left us, Mr. Tanner. Porter, for one, missed playing cards with you, didn't you, Porter? Porter?" She turned around to look for her husband, who had gone off in another direction. "Now where is that man? Excuse me, won't you? Porter!" she called, and walked away, leaving Chelsea and Quaid alone at last.

"You're beautiful," he told her, "even more beautiful than I remembered."

"Is that why you've come here?" she challenged, her tone light, her voice deliberately casual.

He hesitated, his eyes narrowing slightly. "You won't give an inch, will you?"

"And should I?"

"What do you want from me, Chelsea?" Why couldn't she say something that would tell him how she felt? Time hadn't changed him; he'd been miserable all these months without her. He wanted her; he loved her.

"What is this, Quaid, an inquisition?" Why was he standing just beyond the reach of her hand? She wanted him to catch her up and carry her away.

Her demeanor was so cold, the fury in her eyes burned through him. He wanted to sweep her into his arms and take her away with him. Instead, he matched her tone and replied, "I was wondering if you still harbored the same ambitions we spoke about just before I left the *Southern Cross*. You remember, about waiting for the man who has everything and will hand it to you on a silver platter. Didn't I hear Mrs. Crain introduce you as Chelsea Harris? Still haven't confessed have you?"

Chelsea turned away, sudden tears stinging her eyes. "Leave me alone. If you've come here to humiliate me and hold threats over my head, it won't work."

"Dammit, Chelsea, that's a low blow. I thought you knew me better than that. I thought we were . . ."

"What, Quaid? Thought we were what?" She spun around to face him, choking back a sob. "You thought we were lovers? Companions? Shipmates? Friends?" Say it, Quaid, she silently begged. Say you want me with you. Say you'll marry me.

"All those things," he told her quietly. "Even more. Chelsea, would you come to Clonmerra with me?"

"Need someone to feed your chickens and clean your house?" Even before the words were out of her mouth, she regretted them.

"It wasn't what I had in mind, but I'll take you on your own terms," Quaid said bitterly. He never saw Chelsea's arm strike out. The slap resounded as sparks shot through his head, and her next words made him want to throw himself overboard.

"You bastard! I'm good enough to feed your chickens and shear your sheep and warm your bed, but not good enough to marry? No, thank you. I wouldn't go to that farm of yours if you got down on your hands and knees and begged!" When her arm swung out again, he caught it, holding her wrist painfully in his grasp. He pulled her forward until she was tight against him, her head snapped backward from the force of his action.

"I want you, Chelsea. I want you so much I can't think of anything or anyone else but you. I can give you a life at Clonmerra, but I can't marry you." His voice was deep; there was misery in his eyes.

"Can't or won't! In the end it's all the same, isn't it? You're not the man for me; you never were. At least, not the right man. Oh, get out of my sight! Go back to your precious Clonmerra. I thought I was free of you when you left the ship in Lisbon. You make me sick, Quaid Tanner, physically sick!"

Without waiting to hear any more, Chelsea turned and ran. Her flight away from Quaid was intercepted by Captain Winfield himself. "Mrs. Harris, is something wrong?" he asked solicitously. "Don't tell me now that you're here in Australia you've changed your mind."

"No, Captain." She dabbed at her eyes. "I suppose I'm only a little homesick for London."

"This is your home now," he said kindly. "Come along with me, I know someone who'll dry your tears."

He led her along the busy deck, helping her skirt the seamen and stevedores who were unloading the holds of the *Southern Cross*, to his quarters behind the helm. He held the door for her, and she stepped out of the bright sunshine into the cool dim interior of his cabin. Someone was standing just inside the doorway, a tall, dignified man wearing an impeccably tailored white suit and pale gray waistcoat. He held his wide-brimmed white hat in his hands, and there was a speculative expression in his light eyes. "You know I take a paternal interest in all my passengers, Mrs. Harris," Captain Winfield was saying, "and I am proud to be able to introduce you to your intended, Mr. Harlow Kane. Mr. Kane, Mrs. Honoria Chelsea Harris. Mr. Kane approached me with a letter of introduction and explained the situation. I'm surprised you never mentioned you were coming to Australia to be married, Mrs. Harris."

Harlow Kane stepped forward, taking Chelsea's hand and pressing it to his lips in a perfunctory gesture of gallantry. Now that her eyes had adjusted to the dimness of the cabin, she could see that her first impression of a distinguished gentleman had been correct. In fact, Harlow Kane was impressively dressed as a man of some means, and the sprinkling of gray at his temples contrasted favorably against the deep tan of his skin. When he bowed over her hand, she caught the flash of a jeweled stick pin in his cravat and the aroma of Bay Rum cologne.

She remembered the letters stashed away in Honoria's trunk, all of which she had read. Mr. Kane's stiffly written platitudes, and his penchant for making arrangements for Honoria with her brother-in-law and her sister, had left her unimpressed with the man. If ever she was to make her confession, now was the moment.

"Captain Winfield," said a voice from the doorway. "I need your signature to recover my goods from your hold. Excuse me, I didn't realize you were busy."

"Come in, Mr. Tanner. I was just about to pour sherry in celebration of Mrs. Harris's marriage to—"

"Harlow Kane!" Quaid exclaimed.

"Er . . . I see you know each other." The captain was clearly unnerved by Quaid's intrusion and reaction, but hospitality forced him to include his unexpected visitor in the celebration.

Chelsea looked from one man to the other, feeling the hatred that sparked between them.

"I see you've imported some cuttings, then. From France, I assume," Harlow was saying smoothly to Quaid. "I hope they made the voyage successfully, unlike last year when everything was lost."

"I packed them myself and gave specific orders for their care. If what I've just seen is any indication, I should think I was quite lucky. This year," Quaid said soberly. "So if you've come to witness my ruin, Kane, I'm sorry to disappoint you."

"Not your ruin, Tanner, your destruction. You really should accept my offer for Clonmerra while I'm still willing to pay an attractive price. Next year, when your vintage fails . . ." Harlow shrugged.

"I'd burn Clonmerra and salt the ground before I'd sell it to you, Kane."

"You say that now." Harlow accepted the glass of amber sherry from the captain. "Next year will be different. I always get what I want, Tanner, remember that. And I'm a very patient man. Bellefleur is growing, and I want your land. It's only a question of time."

"Gentlemen, gentlemen!" the captain interjected. "This is hardly the time to air your differences; we must think of the lady." He offered Chelsea a glass and watched her take it with trembling hands. "Can't you see you're upsetting her?"

"I'm terribly sorry, my dear." Harlow moved to her side protectively. "If you didn't hear the captain when you so rudely intruded, Tanner, this is my wife-to-be, Honoria Chelsea Harris."

For a long moment Quaid stared into Chelsea's eyes, not believing what he had just heard, waiting for her to announce that she was not Mrs. Harris, willing her to discard the charade and come into his arms. His ebony gaze held hers, waiting, waiting.

"To the happy couple!" Captain Winfield toasted cheerfully.

Unable to tear his eyes from hers, Quaid watched as Chelsea put the glass to her lips, sealing his fate and accepting her future. In response, his glass sailed across the cabin and shattered into a million fragments. Like his heart.

He turned and thundered out of the captain's cabin, a bitter taste in his mouth. How could she do this? He knew she was ambitious and even greedy, but how could she agree to marry Harlow Kane? She was a liar, an imposter, he told himself. If ever there was the time to confess her duplicity, it had been at that moment in the captain's cabin.

Quaid's shoulders slumped. His heart lay like a stone, heavy and lifeless, in his chest. Who was he to condemn Chelsea for being ambitious and greedy, for being a liar and an impostor, when those same sins were his own? He'd told the truth when he'd said he couldn't marry her. His love for Clonmerra had exacted yet another price from him. In the past he'd been more than willing to do or say anything to keep Clonmerra, and always in the past it had been a price worth paying. But not this time, not today. Losing Chelsea had proved to be far too costly. How had he fooled himself into believing that she would want him under any circumstances? Her reaction today had proven that she, too, had a price, one he couldn't afford to pay. She wanted a prosperous marriage, security, and a life of ease, the very things he couldn't give her. He'd hoped he could trust her, hoped she'd understand.

But now it was too late.

When Quaid stormed out of the captain's cabin, the sweet sherry turned to vinegar on Chelsea's tongue. What had she done? She wanted to run after him, explain that at the moment he'd come into Captain Winfield's cabin she had been about to confess that Honoria Harris was dead. Now it was she who was dying, inch by inch, betrayal by betrayal! Damn him, anyway. He'd added insult to injury inviting her to live with him on his precious Clonmerra with no assurances for the future and not even the cloak of respectability. Harlow Kane at least asked a woman to marry him before he expected her to live with him.

Until this very second she'd had no intention of retaining Honoria's identity in front of Kane. But she was frightened enough, and enraged enough, to want to lash out against Quaid's rejection. If he didn't want her, there was one man who'd already spoken for her. Peering over the rim of her glass, Chelsea scrutinized this tall, debonair Australian. Close-cropped graying hair revealed a well-shaped head and proud, intelligent brow. His skin was dark, darker even than Quaid's, and held the mellow bronze of long days in the sun. She guessed him to be somewhere past fifty, but he held his age gracefully. Slim, with only a slight thickening at the waist, he seemed to be youthful and active. He didn't have Quaid's broad shoulders and powerful thighs, but he was a handsome man, she decided. And from what she heard him telling Captain Winfield about his estate, he was rather well-to-do, with a certain position in society.

"When will the wedding take place?" Captain Winfield asked, breaking through her daze. "I wouldn't allow too much time to pass, Mr. Kane. A man doesn't find himself promised to a lady of Mrs. Harris's charms every day. Don't let her get away."

"I don't intend to, Captain." In a slightly possessive move, Harlow stepped closer to Chelsea and smiled down at her. "As soon as it can be arranged, I think. When will it be, Honoria?"

Hearing herself called by that name stirred something inside Chelsea. "Please, I prefer to be called Chelsea. It's a family name of sorts." Had she really said that? Was she actually going to go through with this marriage? Her glance fell on the glistening shards of glass and the wet stain of spilled sherry.

"But your brother-in-law referred to you—"

"I know. But I prefer the name Chelsea."

"Yes, of course." He was momentarily disarmed, and she judged it a position in which he rarely found himself. "When shall the wedding take place, my dear?"

When Chelsea couldn't bring herself to answer, he bent toward her solicitously. "That cretin has upset you, hasn't he? You're not to worry about him. Clonmerra may border on my Bellefleur, but that is all we have in common, and you've seen the last of him, I promise you. If I have my way, and I believe I will, Clonmerra will be mine one day soon and Quaid Tanner will be gone entirely."

"He's a neighbor of yours?" Chelsea asked in disbelief.

Harlow nodded. "But not a neighbor as you know in England. The house on Clonmerra is nearly five miles away from Bellefleur, and you're not to give him a second thought. We rarely socialize, although I must admit there is a section of society here in Sydney that finds him not only acceptable but charming. But that opinion is quite limited, my dear, and I don't share it. Mr. Tanner's interest in Clonmerra is quite recent. He and his brother were hardly more than boys when they were sent to England to be educated."

"A brother?"

"Didn't you know? Of course, how could you? A brother, Luke, younger by a year or so, if I recall," Harlow told her. "A rascal, running about like a wild animal, consorting with the Aboriginals, hardly civilized. Not that Quaid was much better. A disreputable family, I assure you. At every turn some sort of gossip or scandal was attached to Clonmerra. Although I must say Mr. Tanner's interest in Clonmerra has never ceased to amaze me. When he was a boy I wouldn't have thought he'd ever return from England to take up the reins. Now, about our wedding," he said, throwing Chelsea off guard with the abrupt change in subject.

"Surely, Mr. Kane," she murmured, lowering her dark lashes coyly, "you will allow me time to recover from my voyage and to become acquainted with my intended."

Harlow frowned. "A delay would make things . . . inconvenient," he replied, clearly in no mood for maidenly reluctance. "There's your reputation to consider. You couldn't possibly reside in my house until after the wedding."

"Is there nowhere else to stay?" she asked sweetly. "I'm simply not prepared to marry while—while in this state of exhaustion."

"There is a summer cottage," Harlow conceded, "and you could take your meals at the house. But it's hardly fit accommodations."

"Nonsense, it will do perfectly. And I do appreciate your understanding." She lifted her eyes, holding him with her gaze, flirting outrageously. "You are so sensitive to realize a woman needs to be courted."

"Courted—hardly, Hon . . . Chelsea. There's no time. The vineyards demand my attention. This is summer, and soon it will be harvest. Grapes to be picked, wine to be bottled."

"There will have to be time, Mr. Kane." She lowered her eyes and drooped her shoulders in an attitude of disappointment. "I cannot wed a stranger. It would be impossible." She allowed a tremor to enter her voice, evoking sympathy.

"Perhaps she's right Mr. Kane," Captain Winfield interceded. "After all, she's never seen you until today, and I know Mrs. Harris to be a woman of delicate sensibilities." He paused thoughtfully, and Chelsea knew he was recalling her enduring attendance to Honoria. "It's been a difficult voyage for her in many ways, among them the tragic loss of her maidservant, who was a lifelong companion."

"I'm sorry, I didn't know," Harlow apologized benefi- cently, but there was something in his eyes that told Chelsea he was not a man who easily gave in to a woman. This was simply a concession. "We'll postpone the wed- ding for the time being, until just before harvest."

Glad for the respite, however grudgingly given, Chelsea smiled . . . and curtsied. "You won't be sorry, Mr. Kane." Simple words, yet she was able to communicate to him that his patience would be amply rewarded.

Chelsea admired the way Harlow issued orders to a sea- man to have her trunks brought to his buggy, which was waiting on the wharf. She noticed that several business- men checking cargo on the quay tipped their hats respect- fully. Obviously Harlow was well-known in the city, and he confirmed this by telling her he had had lunch with the governor earlier that day.

"Do you come into the city often, Mr. Kane?"

"Quite often, but rarely at this time of year. As a vig- neron I have my responsibilities to Bellefleur. I've more free time during the winter months, and I keep a town- house here. Inns and rooming houses are not sufficient for my needs."

"Who takes care of your townhouse when you're at Bellefleur?"

"I've a housekeeper and her husband."

"And at Bellefleur?"

He turned to look at her, brows raised. "At Bellefleur I've two daughters to keep house. That will be one of your responsibilities, Chelsea, taking those girls in hand and making a home for my son, Franklin, and myself. Martha and Emma seem to have little talent for anything, and housekeeping the least."

"You brought me all the way from England to keep

house and train your daughters in domestic chores?" she asked boldly.

"Your brother-in-law, Jason, told me you were quite helpful in his household."

This Chelsea could not believe about Honoria and supposed it was just another boast on Jason's part to entice Harlow and rid himself of a burden. "Helpful, yes, Mr. Kane, but I was hardly a drudge." She slipped off one of her wrist-length gloves and extended her smooth white hands for his inspection. "These hands do not scrub or garden or prepare meals, Mr. Kane. If you wanted a housekeeper, you could have secured one without a promise of marriage."

Harlow was clearly taken aback. He was unused to having women speak their minds so directly. "Your brother-in-law misled me, Mrs. Harris. I asked for a woman to tend my house and train my children."

"No, no, Mr. Kane, you asked for a slave, which I am not. Either you employ servants to bring to Bellefleur, or I will find myself other arrangements."

Harlow didn't answer, merely occupied himself with maneuvering the buggy onto the busy thoroughfare. This was becoming complicated, he thought to himself. He'd asked for a lady to share his bed, and that seemed to be exactly what he'd gotten. Chelsea Harris wasn't amenable to having a hand in Bellefleur's growth and prosperity. In fact, she wasn't at all like his first wife, Irmaline, who had died just a year before last.

"You will stay the night at the Red Lion Inn," he told Chelsea coldly, showing his irritation. "We will leave for Bellefleur at first light. I will make arrangements for dinner to be served in your room."

"And what will you do this evening?" she asked innocently, ignoring his coolness.

"I, Mrs. Harris, will be busy securing servants to come

to Bellefleur. I take it since you've learned to do without a personal maid, you will continue to do so."

"I'll be happy to make the concession, Mr. Kane. For the time being, at least. A housekeeper, scullery maid, and laundress will do nicely—to start."

Harlow's pale gray eyes bespoke his displeasure, but Chelsea didn't notice; she was too busy contemplating the distance between Clonmerra and Bellefleur. The buggy wheels seemed to be clicking the same words over and over as they rode the cobblestones on Queen Street: *"Five miles down the road. Five miles down the road. Five miles down the road."*

Chelsea's first morning in Australia seemed to be a celebration of radiant sunshine over the clear blue waters of the harbor and heralded by the screech and warble of strange, exotic birds. Chattering parakeets sat in the tree outside her window at the Red Lion Inn. Crimson and yellow-crested finches busily tended their nests, and the bright musical notes of a black bird she recognized from Mrs. Crain's books as a currawong welcomed her arrival. From somewhere nearby came the pugnacious, aggressive cacophony of a flock of kookaburras.

The morning was still, but heat would follow, and she had dressed appropriately in a cool muslin dress, eliminating two of her three petticoats. Her window faced Oxford Street and gave her a view of the far hills. Sydney, as she had noticed during the buggy ride to the inn, was very much reminiscent of an English village bulging at the seams and more than ready to burst out as a full-fledged city. The buildings' façades were brick and painted clapboard, and most of the streets were paved with cobbles or laid with quarry stone. Only the side thoroughfares retained evidence of a frontier colony, red-packed clay worn into grooves by wagon wheels and treading feet. Used to the age-worn look of London, Chelsea found everything in Sydney new and sparkling, although the town itself was over one hundred years old.

She watched out her window, enjoying the sights, while she waited for Harlow, who had cautioned her to be ready at first light. It was now several hours past dawn, and still he had not arrived. She almost hoped he wouldn't come at all, that she'd offended him beyond endurance with her protests and demands.

A sprite black buggy rolled up Oxford Street, followed by a common dray with a blue-shirted man at the reins. Chelsea recognized Harlow driving the buggy, and she saw the dray was filled with boxes and cartons and three women perched among the cargo. Chelsea smiled to herself as she descended to meet him; it would seem her intended was willing to honor her wishes—for the time being, at least.

Harlow drove the buggy at a brisk trot, the well-oiled springs providing a comfortable ride. "It's going to be a scorcher today. Keep your parasol slanted against the sun," he warned. "No reason to ruin that lovely English complexion. We'll make Bellefleur by dusk," he told her, "providing we keep to a good pace. We'll stop twice to change horses at way stations where I've made arrangements."

"You're so well organized, Harlow," she commented sweetly, hoping to flatter a smile to his face. She had no desire to ride a full day with a scowling, ill-tempered man.

"It pays to be organized, and I've an eye for detail. You will approve of my choices for the servants I've employed. Mrs. Russell comes recommended as a fine cook and the other two, I don't remember their names, should serve adequately as scullery maid and laundress." His voice held no emotion, but his pale gray eyes glowered in the shade of his wide-brimmed hat.

"I'm certain to be pleased with your choices, Harlow. I know you're not a man to tolerate less than the best." How long must she keep flattering him until he was in a more pleasant mood? She suspected Harlow Kane could be a very tiresome man.

"Your assumptions are correct, Chelsea. I consider myself a very discerning man, although my children might consider me a taskmaster. I believe in building character; unfortunately, my—their mother spoiled them intolerably."

"From your letters I received the impression that your children are nearly grown."

"They are grown. Franklin is twenty-six, and Martha, the oldest girl, is twenty-four. Emma, the youngest, is already eighteen."

She pretended surprise. "Harlow, you must have been only a boy when you married!"

"Hardly. I arrived in Australia when I was twenty and assumed the duties of Bellefleur from my father's brother, who left no heir. I married Irmaline at twenty-five."

"Then you weren't responsible for founding Bellefleur; it was your uncle."

His sidelong glance was stern and forbidding. "I, madam, made Bellefleur what it is today with no assistance from anyone or anything. My uncle perceived himself a gentleman vigneron and was on the edge of ruin when I arrived and took things in rein. Bellefleur is mine, it belongs to me; it is my right!"

"Of course it's yours, Harlow, I didn't mean to indicate otherwise." Hastily she smoothed his feathers. What had she said to make him so angry? This man with all his pride, Chelsea immediately realized, could be enraged with a careless word, and the thought was unsettling.

"Forgive me. I didn't mean to become so emotional," he said easily, giving her the impression that Harlow Kane made apologies only when the occasion suited him. "I am a jealous man, Chelsea," he warned. "What is mine is always mine. There are those who would stop at nothing to take what belongs to another. I've fought men like that before in my life, and I've always won."

Chelsea remembered another warning he'd issued just the day before, when he'd warned Quaid that one day he would take possession of Clonmerra. The sound of Harlow's voice and the corresponding glint in his eyes made Chelsea uneasy. She was beginning to understand that Harlow was a self-righteous, jealous man who could be more than a little dangerous in his methods. Still, there was a quality of power about him that was magnetically attractive. He, at least, was a man who knew what he wanted and, more, how to go about getting it. He was not one to be easily managed, however acquiescent he had been about securing servants to appease her. There would be a price to pay for that demand, she knew, and hoped that when the time came it would not be too high.

Chapter 9

For more than an hour Harlow had been silent, intent on driving the bay mare over a rough patch of track, giving Chelsea time to peruse the landscape. This was the land Quaid loved, she thought, this rich, rugged land scrubbed bare by winds and parched by summer sun. A strong land, unyielding and unforgiving. Low, sloping hills were littered with dry brush, and the arid soil grew little but thornbushes and pungent eucalyptus trees. The wide-brimmed hat Harlow had suggested she wear was a blessing against the blazing sun, but even the fine net veil could not keep the powdery red dust from smudging her face and crusting on her eyelashes. The light muslin gown she wore would require careful laundering and sun-bleaching, and she wished she could take down her hair and brush away the offending silt.

Crows circled overhead crying to one another, and small gatherings of raucous kookaburras shrieked their maniacal laughter. In the distance, she heard the bark of a dingo, and once during the day-long journey a small, bearlike creature lumbered across the road in lazy disregard of their oncoming buggy. A hairy-nosed wombat, Harlow had explained, telling her she would come to know many strange creatures in this land of upside down. When he discovered her fascination for native wildlife, he began pointing out various species of birds and trees and promised there was every likelihood they would come across a herd of red-necked wallaby.

Twisted, forbidding gum trees stood sentinel along the roadside and reminded Chelsea of old men, prompting her to recite, "There was a crooked man who walked a crooked mile." Galah birds and gray cockatoos with blushing-pink breasts swooped skyward, delighting Chelsea with the spectacle of their colorful feathers against the stark landscape.

"You appear to approve of Australia." Harlow seemed pleased.

"Most heartily," Chelsea agreed, "although I find my eyes are hungry for the sight of green. So many months sailing blue waters, and now to come to this raw umber color. Do you still miss England's green lawns and hazy mornings, Harlow?"

"No. Not from the first. This is my land, where I belong, and it belongs to me. You'll have your fill of green once we get to Bellefleur. From the front porch you can look over the vineyards, acres and acres of green, rolling off into the distance. The leaves of the Madeira vines are almost black, and they seem to ease the eye from the rest of this gaudy landscape." As he spoke his voice became gentle, almost caressing.

Just like when Quaid told me about Clonmerra, Chelsea thought. These two men, hating one another, yet having more in common than most friends. Or was it the effect this wild, untamed land had on those who sought to claim it and bring it under control?

When the sun was sinking behind the far ridge of hills in the west, Harlow prodded the horse to quicken its pace. Chelsea saw now the need to change horses at way stations. The distances and the pace would kill a good animal in less than a year.

"I want to make Bellefleur before dark," Harlow explained. "Just as suddenly as the sun rises, it sets. Twilight and dusk are almost unknown here most of the year. In a few minutes you'll be hard-pressed to see your hand before your eyes."

Shortly, he turned off onto a secondary road, more narrow than the first, if possible. As they drove there seemed to be a semblance of order; someone had trimmed the shrubs and bushes back from the road and had taken care to fill in potholes and remove the larger stones. "We're on Bellefleur now, and soon you'll see the first of my vineyards."

Another turn and they passed through a wooden gate, and then as far as her eye could see over the rolling terrain were the grapes of Bellefleur. Even the air seemed sweeter, heavy with the scent of ripening fruit. No taller than a man, the vines grew upward from a single trunk, spreading outward at their tops and falling toward the ground again in long, graceful boughs. Row upon neat row, soil cultivated and bare of weeds between, stood the vines.

"These will make sauterne," Harlow told her. "I imported them myself from France, and if the weather holds, we'll have a magnificent harvest. At one time Australia was populated with military people and convicts. I'm happy to say that sad state of affairs has been changing over the past years, and along with it the people's penchant for stronger drink like rum and whiskey. World markets are opening to Australian wines, and I intend to be the forerunning supplier. I've already secured markets in Germany and British colonies in the Far East, which really isn't that far from this part of the world. One day Queen Victoria herself will serve a Bellefleur wine at a state dinner, and my reputation as a vigneron will be established. My next market will be America, and my dream is to penetrate the French monopoly."

It was the most he'd spoken all day, Chelsea noticed, and it was not about his family or about their impending marriage, but about his conquering the world wine market. "How much of this is Bellefleur land?"

"All of it!" Harlow waved his arm. "In that direction, to the north, is Tanner's land. Someday soon, that, too, will be known as Bellefleur."

Chelsea looked off in the direction of Clonmerra, a stab of longing in her heart. She wanted to be with Quaid, hearing him tell her about his land, his dreams. She had no idea what she was doing here with Harlow, continuing a charade that had caused her nothing but grief and allowing herself to be manipulated into a marriage she didn't want. Perhaps in time, she told herself. Harlow was a wealthy man, and Bellefleur was certainly impressive. And Harlow would marry her; Quaid wouldn't.

Over the next hill she could see the house, tall and wide, light coming through the long, narrow windows in welcome. A steepled roof like a witch's hat sat atop the two-storied bay, and around the lower floor ran a trellised veranda. Green eucalyptus hemmed the edges of the wide, sprawling lawn, and willows lent a graceful softness to the sharp corners of the house. At the end of the drive, cobbles had been laid and curved gracefully in a semicircle to the front door.

"It's lovely," Chelsea heard herself say, and Harlow seemed pleased.

"It's mine," he answered as though anything he claimed for his own could never be less than perfect.

When they clattered up the drive, however, Chelsea saw she'd been mistaken. Here the hedges and bushes were overgrown and in need of attention, and what she had thought was a lawn was merely a weed-filled rectangle, brown and parched and unsightly. The veranda railing surrounding the lower floor was sorely in need of paint and repair, as were the dismally gray shutters and window frames. How was it that the vineyards were kept so meticulously while the house had been left to go to ruin?

Harlow retrieved Chelsea's bag, which contained all her immediate necessities until the dray arrived, and dropped the rest of her things onto the drive. A cloud of red dust shot upward, causing her to sneeze three times in rapid succession. He handed her down from the buggy and led her up the walk and across the porch and through the front door.

"Emma! Martha!" Harlow bellowed from the wide central hall. "Come down here!"

The corners were gritty with dust, and the faded carpet had long ago outlived its usefulness. The dark stained wood floors were scratched and dying for a broom. Beyond, in the drawing room, she noticed that white sheets covered most of the furniture, but the heavy velvet draperies were thick with more of the red dust. Spartan. Shabby. Dirty. The stairs leading upward were covered with more of the worn carpeting, and the balustrades needed painting.

Two primly dressed young women appeared at the top of the stairs. "This is my oldest daughter, Martha," Harlow said, gesturing toward the taller, more angular girl, her straight brown hair parted unflatteringly in the center and pulled to a matronly bun at the nape of her neck. "And Emma, my youngest." Emma proved to be just the opposite of Martha, a mellow-faced, plumpish young woman with frizzy hair a dull shade of blond. "This is Chelsea Harris, my intended," Harlow told them.

"Pleased to make your acquaintance," Martha said tightly, insolence and defiance rampant in her demeanor.

When Martha made no move to either embrace her or even hold out her hand in welcome, Chelsea turned her attention to the younger girl, Emma, who held a vague smile on her plump face and a dreamy expression in her eyes. Ignoring her father's introduction, she said, "I thought your name was Honoria. At least that's what you wrote."

"I prefer using Chelsea."

"I like Honoria much better. I looked it up in one of Mama's books, and it means honor and virtue."

"Perhaps she's neither honorable nor virtuous and feels Chelsea fits her better," Martha snapped.

"Martha!" Harlow barked. "Make your apology instantly!"

She's ugly, Chelsea thought, ugly inside. A little primping on the outside wouldn't hurt, either.

"I always thought stepmothers were old and mean, like witches," Emma said, apparently pleased to find that Chelsea was neither. "You mustn't listen to Martha. She enjoys saying terrible things. Don't you, Martha?"

"Idiot," Martha muttered, reaching for Chelsea's valise and heading for the stairs.

"Girls, that's enough," Harlow interjected, silencing them at once. "You'll have Chelsea thinking you've no manners at all. Your mother taught you better than this, and I want both of you to give my bride-to-be a proper welcome." Turning to Chelsea: "Emma will show you to the sewing room for tonight, and the garden house can be prepared for you in the morning. It's hardly livable as it is now."

"That will be fine," Chelsea agreed.

"Yes, and I hope you've prepared a generous dinner, daughters," Harlow added. "I employed three female servants while in Sydney, and they'll want to eat before they retire for the night."

Emma and Martha looked from their father to one another and then at Chelsea. Servants! Father had always said there was no need for servants with two able-bodied females about the house. Their own mother had died slaving for her husband, who'd enjoyed being waited upon hand and foot. They knew their father for what he was—a selfish man, caring only for his own comforts. Why, then, had he suddenly changed his attitude? As one, they turned again to stare at Chelsea, realizing with mixed emotions that she was responsible for this unprecedented phenomenon. And while on the one hand they resented the fact that Harlow was considering his bride's comfort when he had ignored their mother's, they were also grateful. Servants would make life much more pleasant.

"We had planned cold mutton for dinner, since we didn't know when to expect you. There should be enough for . . . for everyone," Martha told him, still a little stunned. "Perhaps Chelsea would prefer something brought up to her room. She must be tired from the long buggy ride."

"That would be most kind," Chelsea replied gratefully. She was tired, and in truth, she'd seen enough of Harlow for one day. Following Emma up the staircase, she turned to look down at Harlow. "Good night, Harlow. Sleep well." She allowed a certain tenderness to enter her voice and struck a dramatic pose with her chin lifted high and her hand resting delicately on the banister.

"Until tomorrow, Chelsea," he murmured, transfixed by the sight of her loveliness in the lamplight and by the sound of her soft, feminine voice. He had already decided she was quite an elegant creature and would be an asset to Bellefleur and his social position. But now there was something else stirring within him, something very close to desire.

Harlow's hungry eyes followed Chelsea's ascent. The desire he felt flickered and burst into flames. He found his feet taking him to the stairway. His eyes narrowed in determination as he made his way up the stairs. He'd been without a woman for a long time. The feelings he was experiencing would suffocate him if he didn't find release.

There was no need to deprive himself, and she was, after all, a widow—wise to the ways of the marriage bed.

There were no locks in Bellefleur. Harlow's hand went first to the knob, but then he changed his mind. He rapped lightly and waited a moment before turning the knob. The sight of Chelsea's frightened face drove him across the room. Standing in her petticoats, she presented an alluring picture, one he had no time to study. All he wanted was to devour her youthful body and satisfy his needs.

"Harlow!" Chelsea spun around looking for her dress to cover the cleavage exposed by her petticoat. "What . . . do you . . . We aren't married yet!" she cried, reading the intent in his eyes.

"You aren't a virgin," Harlow said intensely as if that explained everything.

"That doesn't give you the right to burst in here and assume that you can . . . It isn't proper! What will your daughters think? Don't you care what I think?"

"I need you. I've been counting the days, waiting for you. I can't wait any longer. It would be cruel of you to make me wait," Harlow said as he started to undo the buttons on his shirt.

Chelsea's mind raced. She was trapped and she knew it, but still she tried. "I've been without a man a long time myself," she lied. "But I can wait. Waiting and anticipation will make our union all the sweeter." God, was that groggy voice hers? Of course it was.

She watched in horror as Harlow's shoes and then his socks were kicked aside. She sucked in her breath, holding her dress tightly in front of her. When Harlow's trousers dropped to the floor, she gasped, half in awe and half in fright. He was a monstrously big man and very well-endowed. She gasped again as he stepped toward her, his eyes narrowed and his mouth a grim, determined line.

Even if she struggled, she would be no match for him. Of all the damnable rotten luck. She backed off a step and then two. Harlow reached for her, and the dress slipped to the floor. The sound of her petticoat ripping was so loud, she thought she would scream. Within seconds she was exposed to his avid gaze. Shame ran through her like a river, and tears that went unheeded streamed down her cheeks. Her arms, outstretched to ward him off, were suddenly held in a viselike grip. She felt herself being pushed until her back was against the wall.

Chelsea whimpered as Harlow's large hands cupped her breasts. His touch was rough, brutal, and she knew the soft, white flesh would carry his mark for days. She waited, clenching her teeth. Without a sound, he drove into her, jerking her head backward. Chelsea opened her eyes and found him watching her, pumping furiously and oblivious—or indifferent—to the pain he was causing her. When it was all over, she slumped in his hold. But he drove into her again, crushing her breasts and muttering obscenities that he ordered her to repeat after him. She cried out, a sick kitten cry that went unheeded.

Harlow shook himself as though trying to get his bearings. His hand settled on the top of Chelsea's head, pushing her down till she was on her knees. Both hands gripped her shoulders, forcing her to do what he wanted. She made her mind a blank and obliged her intended husband. Minutes later he gave a loud grunt of satisfaction and released Chelsea, who fell back and immediately crawled away like a wounded animal.

Harlow took his time getting dressed, all the while watching Chelsea cower against the wall. "That was splendid, my dear, just splendid. The next time we will use the bed. You do like making love in bed, don't you?"

"Yes," Chelsea whispered. He bestowed a lurid smile

upon her as he made his exit. Love! He called what he had just done making love! She'd been raped, physically as well as mentally. But she'd survive; she had no other choice. Oh, God, what had she gotten herself into?

While Chelsea lay in her bed quivering with fright, Harlow Kane dropped to his knees in his room. And prayed. Not for forgiveness, but to be made a stronger man in the face of temptation. His prayers finished, he undressed, hanging each garment carefully in the wardrobe, his thoughts on his work schedule for the following day.

Chelsea wakened early, the nightmare of the past hours still with her. If she could put Harlow out of her mind, she might be able to accomplish something. She'd barely slept at all, dozing off just before dawn. The mirror told her she looked tired, but only half as tired as she felt. She should have fought, struggled, screamed, done something to ward off Harlow's advances. But instinct had told her then as well as now that if she had, she'd be carrying some pretty ugly bruises.

While she stared in the mirror, Chelsea talked to herself. Perhaps last night was just . . . something that happened because he hadn't had a woman for a long time. Now that he was satisfied he might wait until they were married. Married. Dear God, what if last night was truly an indication of what married life with Harlow would be like?

How was she to act today? As if nothing had happened? As if last night were just an ordinary night in the life of Harlow Kane? She'd have to take her cue from the others. If she didn't want to do that, the other alternative was to leave. Her head pounded as she dressed. What was it she was supposed to do? Something about the girls and the garden house. The cold water she splashed on her face did little to clear her muddled head. It didn't make her feel better, either. Her eyes were ringed with dark smudges, her skin was too pale, and her hands trembled as she dusted powder and rouge on her cheeks—for all the good it did.

The garden house, yes, that's what she had to do. It was going to be a busy day, and she decided to wake Emma and Martha early. If the little house was to be made ready before evening, they'd need an early start. There was no way she was going to spend another night in this house.

Emma and Martha both grunted their displeasure at the prospect of working all day at the summer house, but Chelsea's stubborn determination won in the end. When she walked downstairs, the middle-aged woman Harlow had employed was already in the kitchen, a sour expression on her weather-lined face as she clattered pots and pans and issued stern orders to a very young pink-faced girl of about fifteen.

"Jenny, look in the larder and see if there's enough flour to make bread today. If we ever get the ovens clean, we might have a decent meal tonight! I've never seen such a filthy kitchen, and as for the rest of the place . . ." She threw up her hands in disgust. Then, having just noticed Chelsea enter the kitchen, she dropped her arms in embarrassment. "I'm sorry, miss, I didn't mean to be overheard."

"Mrs. Harris," Chelsea corrected her. "Mr. Kane's two daughters will be down shortly. And don't apologize, I quite agree with you."

"I'm Mrs. Russell. Mr. Kane hired me as cook and housekeeper, and this here is Jenny, scullery maid, and she's a good hand in the dairy. Do you know there's not a drop of butter in the house? Nor fresh milk, either. Jenny says the poor cows are near to dying for want of milking. If it wasn't for one of them having had a calf, they would have, but he keeps them comfortable enough, I suppose. There's Bette, and she's out in the dining room, trying to make order of the place so a body can take a proper meal."

"We won't worry about the dining room, Mrs. Russell; the kitchen is our first priority." Quickly Chelsea appraised the situation. "You seem to be a fastidious woman, and Martha, Miss Emma, and myself will do what we can to help put this place in order."

"Yes, Mrs. Harris." Mrs. Russell approved of this young woman who, unlike so many of her class, wasn't afraid to dirty her hands. "Mr. Kane went out about an hour ago, before sunup. I can brew a fresh cup of tea for your breakfast, and there's an egg or two in the pantry."

"Just tea, Mrs. Russell, and the same for Miss Martha and Miss Emma. Have you and your helpers eaten?"

"Aye, what there was, and it wasn't much, I'll tell you that. Jenny, run out to the dairy, and skim off some cream for Mrs. Harris's tea." Then turning back to Chelsea, "The way I see it, we should tackle this stove first off, and then the pantry. Seems like every dish and crock in the cupboards needs a good scrubbin', and if I could find the lye, I'd bleach this old wooden floor to the color it should be. How in the world did a grand house like this come to this condition?"

"Mr. Kane lost his wife some time ago, and Martha and Emma don't seem to be interested in housework. Mr. Kane didn't think that he should hire help with two daughters having so little to do. He was wrong, it appears."

A thin young woman with straight blond hair entered the kitchen. "This here is Bette, and once we get this house in shape she'll be your laundress. She's also handy with a needle. Bette, meet Mrs. Harris; it's her you'll take your orders from."

Bette gave a curt bob and smiled. "Pleased to meet you, ma'am. I've made some headway in the dining room, but it'll take the rest of the day before it's done."

"I just told Mrs. Russell we'll concentrate on the kitchen

for now and then the garden house. I've decided to stay out there until my marriage to Mr. Kane."

If either Mrs. Russell or Bette thought her sleeping arrangement strange, they said nothing but quietly went about boiling water for tea and pulling crockery and dinnerware down from the cupboards for a bath of hot water and suds.

"What is all this clatter down here?" Martha called; entering the kitchen with Emma not far behind.

"Martha, Emma, this is Mrs. Russell and Bette. Jenny is out in the dairy. Have some tea with me, and then we can get started on our chores."

"Chores?" Emma squeaked, and looked at Martha accusingly. "You said now that we have servants we wouldn't have any more chores."

"For the time being, Emma, we all have to pitch in and get this house in order," Chelsea said in a no-nonsense voice. Not for anything were these two going to escape remedying the havoc their laziness had created. "We'll start in the kitchen first. There'll be time enough later to enjoy the benefit of servants. For now, we'll all work together."

Chelsea was as good as her word. She worked relentlessly, trying to wash and scrub the night's events from her mind. Nothing escaped her notice, there was no corner dark enough to hide in and no place far enough away to avoid her scrupulous inspection. Her single-minded concentration on getting the house in order was the only thing that kept her from going mad. She hadn't come so far from England to live in conditions worse than she had known, she told herself. Later, she would think about what she was to do in regard to Harlow. For now, all she had to do was keep a clear head and stay as far away from him as possible until she'd made a decision.

In the end, both girls succumbed to Chelsea's driving determination for cleanliness and worked as hard as she did. Along about noon they stopped to munch on some hard-boiled eggs and cool tea that Mrs. Russell had prepared, along with a tin of biscuits found in the recesses of the pantry. The kitchen had been miraculously transformed; and only the floor remained to be done. Mrs. Russell assured Chelsea she would see to it with the help of Bette. Young Jenny, who was Mrs. Russell's granddaughter, would work in the dairy, scrubbing milk pails and butter vats.

"We'll put things aright yet," Mrs. Russell announced with confidence. "Give us a week, two at the most, and it'll be a house we can all be proud of. Tonight I'll see to having one of the men come over to fix that back step. I nearly broke my neck on it."

Chelsea nibbled thoughtfully on her lower lip. "I . . . I'll speak to Mr. Kane about assigning us a handyman." Us. Did that mean she was going to stay? Why was she acting as if what she was doing were the most important thing in the world? As if she were going to stay. What did she care about the back step or the six or seven other jobs in need of a good hammer? One step at a time, one day at a time, she thought tiredly.

"Father will never allow one of his field hands to work near the house," Martha announced with authority. "He says they're much too valuable in the vineyard, and after all, isn't that the purpose of Bellefleur, to produce wine?"

"Your father never wanted to hire servants, either," Chelsea reminded her, forcing herself to remain pleasant. Martha had been a bone of contention all morning, and she was becoming sick of her haughty attitude. "I intend to ask him, anyway. Now, if you're finished eating, I want you to take me out to the garden house so we can get started. Emma, you bring along the buckets and scrub brushes; Martha, you carry the brooms and mops if Mrs. Russell won't be needing them."

"Take them," the housekeeper said without hesitation. "I'll send one of the girls out to help just as soon as they're done here."

"Thank you, Mrs. Russell. And perhaps you can find something simple to prepare for dinner tonight. We're all going to be exhausted before this day is over, and I don't want you to go to any more trouble than necessary."

"No, ma'am. I found a rasher of bacon in the cold pantry and a bag of beans in the larder along with a crock of molasses. Would baked beans and brown bread suit your fancy?"

"Sounds delicious. Come along, girls, get your pails and your brooms, we've still got work to do."

Emma made a disagreeable face and pouted. "Can't I stay here with Mrs. Russell? I'm tired!"

"We're all tired, Emma. March!"

Chelsea followed Martha down the path leading away from the back of the house. Through a copse of gum trees in a tiny clearing stood the garden house. On first sight Chelsea thought it charming. It had once been painted a mellow sand color the same as the main house, and its trim was a delicate shade of federal blue. A trellis that held wild roses climbed one wall, and the roof was tiled in umber brown. It appeared larger than she had expected, although in reality it constituted just one large room with several windows and a rough-hewn door. A small black kettle stove stood in one corner, and there was already a bed in another.

"Franklin used to live out here sometimes when he brought friends home from school," Emma offered, "and long before that Father's Aunt Paula used it to paint pictures. I don't know why you want to be out here; we've plenty of room at the house."

Because your father raped me last night, that's why! Chelsea wanted to scream. "Until I . . . until I *decide* if I'm going to marry your father, it wouldn't be proper. There's no older woman here aside from Mrs. Russell, and a housekeeper doesn't suffice as a chaperone." She couldn't believe she was saying these stupid words or that the girls were listening to her. She couldn't tell them about last night or the fear that there might be other nights just like it. Here she would be comfortable and have a semblance of freedom to come and go without questions. She would be able to think here. Until the hour when she said "I do," she would still be free.

If that time ever arrived.

"How old are you?" Martha asked bluntly.

"Twenty-two. And yourself?"

Color stained Martha's sallow cheeks, and Chelsea knew it was because the young woman was already two years older than herself and without prospect of marriage. Picking up the hem of her skirts and tucking them into her waistband, Chelsea went about opening the windows. With the broom she chased cobwebs from the corners and issued instructions for the mattress to be beaten. "I'll be needing more furniture than this," she told Emma. "A table near my bed and a lamp and a rug on this floor wouldn't hurt."

"Franklin could carry it, if he's in the mood, that is. We never know what Franklin is going to do until he does it. He makes Father very angry at times."

"Most times," Martha interjected.

"Most times," Emma repeated. "That's because Franklin doesn't like living here on Bellefleur. He likes the city, and he says someday he's going to go all the way to England and never ever come back."

Chelsea stopped work to look at Emma, who was idling near the rose trellis sniffing the faded blooms. She wished she knew whether or not Emma was addle-witted. At times she behaved like a very young child, but there were moments when her insight was almost startling.

"Doesn't Franklin want to become a vintner like your father? It seems Bellefleur would have much to offer a young man. His future could be secured."

"Franklin doesn't care about his future," Emma said. "Father says he's good for nothing and will never develop the tongue or nose you need to make really fine wine. If Franklin doesn't want to carry your furniture down here, perhaps Father will do it himself. He's very strong, did you notice that?"

"I noticed," Chelsea said coolly.

"I don't like to scrub and clean and do chores. I like to cook sometimes, but never when it's my turn. Isn't that right, Martha?"

"What do you like to do?" Chelsea asked, ignoring Martha's mutters of annoyance.

"I like to read, and sometimes I paint a little. Father used to let me take out the buggy, but since I became lost one day down by the lake he doesn't let me take it anymore. I wandered and wandered, and I was so frightened. It was already dark when they found me near Mr. Tanner's house. He was very nice to me, and since then we've been friends. . . ." She clapped her hand over her mouth and widened her eyes in alarm.

"You've become what?" Martha demanded. "You know Father would be angry if he knew you even spoke to the man, and I quite agree with him."

"You only say that," Emma argued. "You told me once that you think he's very handsome, and I think you're smitten with him, aren't you, Martha?"

"I say he's a devil!" Martha cried, a frown drawing her thin face into a scowl. "Don't let Father hear you mention his name, and don't say I didn't warn you."

"Father doesn't like him," Emma chattered on, apparently oblivious to Martha's admonitions. "Martha swoons over him. Franklin likes him very much. I think he's very handsome. No one knows why he hasn't taken a wife. Some people say he has a wife back in England. I don't know if that's true or not. I don't care, either, but Martha cares. Every chance she gets she talks about him, and once I met her out walking and she was coming from the direction of Mr. Tanner's house. She had a funny look on her face. I think she kissed him."

Chelsea kicked the bucket and was instantly sorry when her toe started to throb. "Does he ever come here?"

"Only if we have a party or something like that. He hasn't been here since Mama died. We haven't had any parties since Mama died. That's the reason. I think that's the reason. Ask Father, he can tell you more about it."

"Which is the direction to Mr. Tanner's house?"

Emma walked over to the long, narrow window and pointed to the right. "Over that hill and then you'll come to a dirt road. Follow it all the way and you'll see his house. He had lots and lots of flowers all over the place. Father says he wastes water on flowers."

"If you two think I'm going to do all this scrubbing while you jaw at each other, you have another thought coming," Martha snapped as she splashed soapy water on one of the walls.

"Stop being so hateful, Martha. Chelsea is our guest and should be treated as one until she becomes our new mother."

Martha turned to Chelsea in a flash, her blue eyes dark and narrowed. "You'll never take my mother's place. You're too young for my father—I'm older than you are. Don't ever call yourself my mother. I know why you're here. Your own family didn't want you, and you think you can come here and take what is rightly Franklin's and Emma's and mine."

"And what would that be?" Chelsea demanded.

"His money," Emma volunteered. "Father has a lot of money. He'll have even more after vintage if the weather holds. Don't pay attention to Martha; she's angry because Father sent her one and only suitor packing because he said all William wanted was her inheritance. Now William lives in England, and I know that he's written her several letters."

"Shut up, Emma, that's family business, and she's an outsider. Besides, it isn't true, so stop telling lies and start scrubbing."

"It is so true!" Emma whispered to Chelsea as she dipped her rag into the sudsy water.

After that they worked in silence, scrubbing, sweeping, and polishing until the interior of the garden house sparkled. When it was all done, Chelsea wiped her brow and thanked them both for their help. Martha ignored her little speech and started back for the house.

"Don't pay attention to her," Emma said comfortingly. "She said you were marrying my father for his money and that we wouldn't get any. She told Franklin you were too young and you'd have a baby and that would be even less for all of us. Martha wants to go back to England. Our mother was from England, and we still have family there. She used to tell us what it was like. Martha hates Father sometimes, especially since he sent William packing. Since then, no other man has come to call on her."

Emma certainly was a wealth of information. Fey? Witless? Whatever suited her purposes, Chelsea decided.

"Let's get back to the house," she said, taking one last look around at her new home. "There's nothing I'd like better than a bath. I think I'm going to be stiff for weeks to come."

* * *

Harlow Kane directed the individual watering of his vines. A fine lay in of claret wine was promised this year; conditions had been perfect throughout the spring when the blossoms set. But it was difficult to concentrate on the coming harvest when his thoughts were so chaotic. He liked being in control, and it was unlike him to be so indecisive; nevertheless Honoria Chelsea Harris had proven to be a great distraction since he had met her at the ship two days before.

He searched for an apt description of his bride-to-be, and his mind kept coming back to the word "ripe." She was a lady in her prime. There was something very sensuous about her and, although he disliked the implications, also something very practiced. She was a far cry from the description Jason had given in his letters. He'd been led to expect a small brown wren, and what he'd received was a glossy dark swan. It wasn't that he was displeased to have a beautiful wife; in fact, he was delighted. But her very beauty, her lusciousness, was undeniably disconcerting. There was a certain comfort to be had in a plain wife who practiced the virtues of housekeeping instead of vanity, and in his opinion every lovely woman was vain.

Servants. She'd demanded servants when every available penny should go into improving the vineyards. Only in Sydney, where appearances counted, were servants necessary. Yet he had secured them for her, and he knew from that point on that she would continue to demand a life of luxury and opulence. Until last night he had been undecided whether or not she was worth this kind of disruption in his life. But seeing her naked, cowering against the wall, had almost driven him insane. He'd taken her like an animal, and she'd allowed it. Now he knew he must have her at any price.

Last night he'd caught her off guard and seduced her; the only thing he'd felt was relief. The next time he'd teach her what he liked. Chelsea Harris would be an apt pupil. He was sure of it. A small brown wren could never stir a man's desires like a single scorching glance from a dark-feathered swan.

At the noon hour when the men broke for their midday meal, Harlow had even been tempted to return to the house to see her. Irmaline had been the perfect wife for a man struggling toward success, patient and enduring and steadfast. Chelsea was the kind of woman a man needed once he'd achieved his goals and was moving on to take his rightful place in society. Beautiful, poised, witty, a natural lady—qualities he might have searched the world over and been unable to find in one woman. He would be the envy of his business associates, and she would belong to him. A suitable treasure to add to the glory of Bellefleur. She would grace his table and decorate his house, and she would follow him with those deep, tawny eyes. Other men, richer and more influential, would toast her with Bellefleur wine and want to drown their envy.

Harlow's attention was captured by the sight of his son, Franklin, riding into his line of vision. Bare-chested and browned by the sun, he was an imposing sight. Young. So young. At that moment Harlow felt old. Chelsea was younger than Martha; she was of a more fitting age to marry Franklin than himself. Then Harlow laughed, a lusty sound. Franklin might be half his age, but he was also only half the man. No, Harlow assured himself, he would have no trouble satisfying Chelsea, regardless of her desires. These young men like Franklin with their sullen mouths and self-indulging natures could never be a threat to someone like himself.

When Franklin came abreast of him, Harlow's tone was sharper than he had intended, colder than he wanted. Why did this son of his always bring out the worst in him? "I told you to trim back the sauternes and keep a watch for mold since that rain last week. What are you doing on horseback? There's work to be done."

Franklin screwed his face into a tight grimace. Dammit, why did it always have to be like this: Father giving orders and he being subservient? Did he give him no credit at all for using his head? Why couldn't he ask a civil question and wait for a civil answer? With an effort he swallowed his wrath, but his voice betrayed the intensity of his emotions. "I checked the sauternes, and they don't need trimming. This blasted sun is so hot they need every bit of cover the leaves provide. I saw to the watering, and now the men are working among the muscatels. If we're not careful, we'll harvest a crop of raisins instead of wine grapes. I was just going to the cook's shed for something to eat."

"I said the sauternes needed trimming. We've got to lighten the boughs or the fruit will be hanging in the mud and go to rot. Now see to it!"

Franklin's hazy gray eyes, so like his father's, darkened with sudden hatred. Regardless of the fact that he'd been raised among the vines, Father still refused to trust his judgment. Now he would have to cart the men back to the sauternes and see that they carefully cut a leaf here and a leaf there, just to satisfy the old man's pride and feelings of proprietorship. "Why can't you trust my judgment for once?" he said abruptly. "The men are near dead on their feet in this damnable heat, and I tell you the sauternes are holding up better than we are."

"Watch the way you speak to me, Franklin. I will not tolerate disrespect from any of my children."

It was on the tip of Franklin's tongue to tell his father that in order to gain respect one had to give it. Instead, he flicked the reins and rode off defiantly toward the shed, his initial destination.

Harlow wasted no time watching his son. He walked to

the end of the row and hefted himself onto his own mount, digging his heels ruthlessly into the animal's sides, spurring the horse forward. He would see for himself whether Franklin had spoken the truth.

At dinner that evening, Chelsea took her place at the table and forced herself to look directly at Harlow. She was stunned to see him smile at her. There was nothing in his eyes to indicate what had transpired the evening before. As he continued to act as though nothing had happened, anger replaced Chelsea's nervousness. How dare he! She wanted to scream out what had happened to the entire table. Instead she pasted a smile on her face and sat quietly, adding to the conversation only when directly spoken to. Once she pleaded tiredness, and Harlow smiled fondly in her direction. She almost choked on the food in her mouth.

After Mrs. Russell's plain but excellently prepared dinner, Harlow apologized to Chelsea for his family's lack of graciousness. "We've all eaten like gluttons," he told her. "We've been without a woman's hand in this household for too long. Your insistence that I hire servants for Belle-fleur was advice well taken. Neither Martha nor Emma have much talent for housekeeping."

"Chelsea nearly worked us to death today, Father," Emma complained. "Look at my hands, just look!"

Chelsea was taken by surprise at Emma's complaints. Of the two Kane daughters, she'd expected only Martha to tattle.

"I see them," Harlow said smoothly, "just as I saw the kitchen looking as a kitchen should look, and as I see this dining room cleared of a month's red dust. I take it your time was well spent, Emma."

Chelsea felt herself breathe a sigh of relief. And then

Emma continued her complaint. "But did you know that she insisted we scrub the garden house for her, and now she wants *our* furniture to be put there?"

"*She* is the cat's mother, Emma. You will please restrain yourself from referring to your future stepmother in such a disrespectful manner. And stop whining. I approve of a good day's work, and I've already had two workmen bring the furniture down to the garden house. Chelsea prefers to stay there until we are married, and I respect that decision."

Both Martha and Emma were astonished at their father's easy acquiescence to this young woman. Even Franklin, who had been silent and sullen throughout dinner, seemed to show a glint of respect in his heavy-lidded eyes. Chelsea felt giddy with relief.

"Harlow, I promised Mrs. Russell I would ask you for a handyman to repair the back step," she said—pressing her advantage. "It's quite a hazard, and we wouldn't want an accident, would we? There is also other repair work to be done, as well as some painting. Bellefleur could use a face lift, don't you agree? Especially with our wedding in the not-too-distant future."

The words were out, and now she couldn't take them back. Our wedding. Hers and Harlow's. Subconsciously she must have made the decision to stay while she worked. She'd known in the back of her mind that there was no place for her to go. Or was she playing a game, waiting to see what would happen? She was dangling herself in front of Harlow the way a cat dangles cheese for the mouse. His attitude today, his generosity, was making it easy for her to do a turnabout. Maybe last night had never happened; maybe she'd dreamed it. There was every possibility it would never happen again. If she did decide to go through with the wedding, she'd make sure she had a voice in what went on as far as her own welfare was concerned.

And now her intended was about to refuse her request; Chelsea could read it in his eyes. She stared at him intensely, willing him to agree, and felt more than satisfied when she saw a flush stain his cheeks.

Harlow cleared his throat. He never allowed useful labor to be wasted on the house when it could be put to better use in the vineyards. His children, knowing this, suppressed conspiring smiles and waited to hear his refusal. Harlow, meanwhile, was remembering his decision to take his rightful place in society. Chelsea was right, the house was a disgrace, and he would be shamed before his peers.

"I'll send several men, use them as you will," he told Chelsea. "There's still several weeks till harvest, and their labors in the field are not quite so necessary."

Martha gasped audibly. How easily Father offered luxuries to this interloper, the same luxuries he had denied her mother, who had worked like a slave.

Harlow, aware of Martha's reaction, added, "And do whatever you think best for the house. We'll have a prenuptial party such as Bellefleur has never seen." He turned abruptly to his son, who had been very quiet all evening and was now reaching yet again for the privately labeled wine bottle. "Franklin, you've had more than enough. Get to bed or you'll be useless in the fields tomorrow."

Harlow's voice and manner were harsh, as though his son were a small boy in constant need of reprimanding. Chelsea saw an emotion very close to hatred spawn in the young man's eyes, and bitterness draw his full, sullen mouth into a thin line. Without a word, he pulled himself to his feet, nearly upsetting his chair, and stalked out of the dining room toward the front hall, shoulders square, head high.

Suddenly she felt very bad for Franklin. Harlow should

never have humiliated him that way in front of his sisters, and especially not in front of her. But she'd noticed throughout dinner that Harlow was not kind to his children, and she worried that his display of deference to her would cause irreparable jealousy.

"I'm very tired myself," she announced, placing her napkin on the table and rising. "I'll be going to bed if you'll excuse me." Heart hammering in her chest, she held Harlow's gaze with hers, eyes unwavering, almost daring him to even consider a repeat performance.

"I'll walk you to the garden house," he offered, ignoring the look in her eyes. All during dinner he'd done nothing but think of her naked in his arms. Right now, he wanted to reach out and touch her to prove to himself that she was real and that what he'd experienced last night hadn't been some kind of dream.

"No, thank you, Harlow," Chelsea said firmly. "I prefer to say good night here. I'm very tired, and tomorrow promises to be equally exhausting. Good night, Martha, Emma." If he made one move, gave any indication that he was going to follow her, she'd walk out of his life right now. She would suffer his conjugal rights once they were married, but not until then. She could feel Harlow's eyes burning through her as she swept out of the room. She didn't care. Let him take his outrage to bed, anything, as long as she was able to avoid being with him herself. There was only one man whose touch she wanted, one man whose body could evoke her response. And he would only come to her in her dreams.

Chapter 10

The long days ahead were filled with work, but also with a sense of accomplishment. Chelsea had taken the unpolished gem of Bellefleur's house and made it gleam. If all this was to be hers, she reasoned, she would turn it into something worth having. Somewhere in the past week or so she had begun to think of herself as already married to Harlow Kane, and of his house and its surroundings as hers. Once things were restored to their former elegance and order, she would live the life she'd always dreamed. It was all so simple, really. Marry Harlow and all of it would be hers. If only she could drive Quaid Tanner out of her mind the way she cleared dust out of corners. But each night she dreamed about him, all day her thoughts were with him, and the knowledge that he was just over the hill at Clonmerra offered little comfort. She wanted to be with him, to touch him. And when her need for him grew too great, she plunged herself into restoring the house on Bellefleur with a vengeance. She would prove her worth to Mr. Quaid Tanner, show him that her past didn't matter and that she merited the respectability of marriage.

Soap and water were used by the vat. Bedding was brought outside to air in the bright sunshine. Carpets—

Turkish carpets, Martha explained—were beaten and brushed and scrubbed clean of years of dirt and neglect. Furniture was polished till it gleamed, and every dish, crock, pot, and pan was scoured spotless. Emma was put to polishing the silverware and serving trays in the wood ashes from the cook stove; by the time she was through, she was covered with the black slag and looked for all the world like an itinerant chimney sweep. Windows were scoured and curtains washed and draperies cleaned. Bette proved to be an excellent laundress, but there was so much ironing to be done, Martha had to help her, spending hours using the heavy flat irons that were heated on the stove.

Chelsea elected herself overseer for the two handymen Harlow assigned to the house. The back steps were fixed, and the veranda floors were sanded and stained and finally given a fresh coat of polish. The shutters were revitalized with fresh paint, as were the walls of the drawing room. The whole downstairs took on a freshness that made Chelsea glow with pride. Later, after vintage, they could begin work on the upstairs bedrooms.

Always at the end of the day Mrs. Russell rewarded them with an excellently prepared dinner. And always Chelsea would suffer through the meal listening to one of Martha's unending monologues. "My mother had that chifforobe brought from France, that table came all the way from Italy, and the carpet is from Turkey. The china and crystal were handed down from Aunt So-and-So, and the service plates were imported by Uncle What's-his-name, and the wallpaper in the hall was Chinese, and the dining room table is English." Chelsea knew the sour-faced Martha was trying to impress her with the Kane family background, and although she absorbed and memorized each morsel of information, it was difficult not to resent Martha's attitude of superiority.

A month after her arrival Chelsea felt the house was in near perfect order. All the bed linens, so patiently and expertly embroidered by her predecessor, Irmaline, were mended and laundered and stored among packets of fragrant sachet. Jenny had worked a miracle in the dairy, and fresh milk and butter were in plentiful supply. Mrs. Russell, a magician in the kitchen and an avid admirer of Chelsea, supervised Bette and Jenny and the house on Bellefleur.

During the busy month Harlow had not pressed himself on Chelsea, although she noticed that his eyes always seemed to be following her, hot and yearning. Maybe he was remembering her words on the night he'd attacked her, that waiting only sweetened the inevitable. He knew she would be his soon. Not once had he referred to that night, nor had she; now, it was almost as though it had never happened. Only in the darkness of the little garden house did she remember. Actually, he was the perfect gentleman with her, and right now she couldn't ask for more. The house was beginning to run with clockwork precision. Harlow was filled with compliments that brought color to Chelsea's cheeks. And Martha and Emma did their share of the work, albeit grudgingly.

Only Franklin remained aloof and unapproachable. All of Chelsea's attempts at friendship with the young man had been futile. She remembered Emma's revelation that Martha was convinced Chelsea was only after Harlow's money, that the marriage would only cheat the rest of them. Did Franklin really believe his sister's accusation? "He's such a mean boy," Emma had said, clicking her tongue in disapproval. "So ungrateful for anything Father has done for him. He was sent to the best schools, and the summer he was eighteen he was allowed to explore the western territories with a group of his classmates. He hates Bellefleur, too. He wanted to read the law and become a barrister, but Father wouldn't hear of it. As the only son, Franklin has to stay on Bellefleur, and now he says it's draining the life out of him. Mother used to say that Franklin was a sensitive child. I remember the way she cried when Father wouldn't allow him to continue school. He'd been accepted to Oxford, you know, but Father refused to pay for his education, saying he would get all the schooling he'd ever need right here growing grapes and becoming a vigneron. Franklin always says that when Father dies we're going to sell Bellefleur and go to England. Now, Martha keeps telling him that once Father marries you, there won't be anything left for us."

Chelsea had taken this information under advisement. Martha, it seemed, was not about to wait for Harlow to close his eyes. His oldest daughter had made it stingingly clear that the only way Chelsea could exist at Bellefleur without constant mutiny from her was to convince Harlow to send her to England, now! Chelsea decided that if Martha proved to be a constant bone of contention, then sending her to England was the best thing for all concerned.

Chelsea believed she had a little influence with Harlow, whom she now realized was something of a slave driver where Bellefleur was concerned. Whenever in his presence, she held herself aloof, plying her best manners and keeping him at a reserved, ladylike distance. She entertained him at dinner, saw to his creature comforts through Mrs. Russell, and always reaffirmed the notion that, above all things, Bellefleur came first and foremost. This last alone endeared her to Harlow, and he now believed himself to be getting a veritable treasure, thanks to Chelsea's keen acting ability. He repaid her in kind with compliments and praise and never overstepped the bounds she'd established. But Chelsea was well aware of the effect she had on him and knew that he was growing impatient to lay claim to

Chelsea herself. The prospect of becoming his wife sometimes struck her with a wild desperation. She had only to witness his treatment of his children and to remember his attack on her to know how insensitive and cold he could be. There was every possibility that once the marriage took place, she, too, would fall prey to his ruthlessness.

When Chelsea's thoughts took her as far as actual marriage to Harlow, she quickly occupied herself with other things. It was as difficult to see a life for herself at Bellefleur as it was to picture herself out on her own again, without the sort of life Bellefleur promised. She told herself that this was just another role she was playing, all the while biding her time to find a way to get to Quaid. There was only one man in her heart, and she dreamed of him each night after allowing Harlow a modest kiss on her cheek.

Somehow, some way, Quaid would come to her rescue and save her from her duplicities. How could she have ever thought him a common farmer? How could she have been so blind as to let ambition stand in the way of her having the only man she'd ever known who could set her pulse racing and accept her for herself? That he hadn't actually offered marriage when he'd asked her to come to Clonmerra with him . . . well, that was a simple detail time would correct. It worked in her favor that Quaid and Harlow were fervent enemies. After all, if Quaid had any feelings for her at all, and she knew he did, he wouldn't want Harlow to have her. All she had to do was arrange a meeting, preferably by chance, and then allow things to take their natural course.

It never occurred to Chelsea that the games she was playing could see her the loser. In her mind she and Quaid were meant to be together. He just didn't know it. Yet.

Harlow Kane entered the house through the kitchen carrying a small packet of mail. He placed it on the kitchen table, and a feeling of apprehension quivered through Chelsea as she strained to note the origin of the letters. When the *Southern Cross* had docked in Cape Town, South Africa, she had written diligently to Honoria's family, informing them of the sad fact of her death. Now she worried that Harlow would receive a letter of commiseration from Jason Munsey, until she counted on her fingers and realized that it was much too soon for a letter to arrive from England. In fact, her own letter to Honoria's family had probably only just arrived. And by the time Harlow discovered that the real Mrs. Harris had met with an untimely end, she would be safely with Quaid. If only she could arrange a way to see him without simply marching up to his doorstep.

"We've received an invitation to a party for the governor's wife in Sydney," Harlow told her beneficiently, leaning over to buss her cheek. "The timing is perfect, as I have business in the city, so we'll just extend our stay to include the party. It will be an opportune time to introduce you to my associates."

Chelsea's heart leaped. Party. Would Quaid be there? She didn't dare ask. "How wonderful. I'd very much like to meet your friends," she trilled. And your enemy, she thought darkly.

"Martha will accompany us and act as chaperone. Emma will stay here at Bellefleur with Franklin."

Even thoughts of being cooped up with Martha couldn't dull Chelsea's sense of excitement. "When do we leave?"

"Day after tomorrow. Does the idea of a party please you?"

"Of course." Chelsea beamed. "I can't wait to dress up in my pretty things. I do want you to be proud of me, Harlow," she said, lowering her eyes demurely, a gesture she knew Harlow liked.

"Good. Emma will probably kick up a fuss, but she's

really too immature to take with us. She'd most likely fall head over heels in love with the first young man who asked her to dance, and then there would be the same unpleasantness I experienced with Martha, who fancied herself in love with a man who only had his eye on the fortunes of Bellefleur."

How smug he was when he deprecated Martha, Chelsea thought, as though no man in the world could possibly find her attractive and lovable, as though all that existed were his precious Bellefleur.

"What will you do with the rest of your day?" Harlow asked casually. "If I had more time, I'd take you down to see the lake before the dry season, when we use the water for irrigation and hardly leave a puddle behind."

"Can't I go see it myself? Is it within walking distance?"

He frowned. "I'm afraid not. It's on the other side of the hills. Have you ever driven a buggy?"

"Oh, yes," Chelsea said eagerly.

"Then take it. I'll have one of the men hitch up the bay mare; she's placid enough, especially in this heat. Just watch the time and be back before dinner. I don't want you getting lost in the dark."

"You're so considerate, Harlow. I promise." Inside she was practically dancing. She knew Harlow was selfish with his possessions, and offering her the buggy was a major concession.

The minute Harlow left, Chelsea ran across the backyard to the garden house. She didn't want to explain to Martha or Emma where she was going or, worse, have to fend off pleas to go with her. Picking through her wardrobe, she decided upon a cool, light blue muslin embroidered in snowy-white rosebuds. Along with a flat-crowned, wide-brimmed straw hat, it would lend her a certain air of innocence and femininity. Quaid would love it.

Stripping down to her pantaloons and chemise, she

sponged herself with cool water from the pitcher and applied a light dusting of powder. The Australian summer heat was becoming abominable; she didn't want to look like a damp rag when she saw Quaid. She wondered if he would be home; she hoped so. What if he was in Sydney? Suppose he was visiting friends or doing business? No, she told herself firmly, he would be at Clonmerra, and he would be happy to see her. He would!

Suddenly, in spite of her high spirits and racing pulse, Chelsea sank down onto the edge of her bed. She had no reason to believe Quaid would want to see her. If he had, he would have made some excuse to inquire after her by now; he would have braved Harlow and stopped by Bellefleur on some pretense to see for himself. She remembered the last time she'd seen him in Captain Winfield's cabin, glass shattered on the floor, sherry stain spreading on the carpet, and black rage in his eyes. Suppose he hated her? He should, she admitted to herself. He had stood by her while on the *Southern Cross* because he'd understood how her mistaken identity had come about. But there wouldn't be any sympathy for her now, not since she'd blatantly and purposely lied, allowing Harlow to believe she was Honoria. Quaid would have every reason now to believe she was a fortune hunter. And worse, he would be right. A sick feeling settled in the pit of her stomach. One little lie had brought her to this sorry state of affairs. Mrs. Crain's words rang in her head. "There are only two kinds of women in New South Wales," the woman had declared, "those who serve and those who are served."

She'd had no other choice than to do what she'd done— and it was all Quaid's fault, after all. He'd added insult to injury by inviting her to Clonmerra without a word about marriage. And what would have become of her then? Her reputation would have been ruined; no decent man would have looked at her—not even the poorest of the poor.

Well, she'd give Quaid one last chance, and if he didn't ask her to marry him this time, she'd go through with her marriage to Harlow. She would be mistress of Bellefleur, lady of the manor. She would have servants, beautiful clothes, and wealth. She felt ill.

If she could go back in time, would she have done things differently? She had to be honest with herself. Under the same circumstances she would have done exactly the same things. What other choices had been open to her? Her life in Australia would have been no different than it had been in London, and most likely worse, if Honoria hadn't been so generous.

As much as Chelsea hated to admit it, she needed a man in her life. Besides the fact that she had had a taste of love and now craved it, any fool knew that a woman alone in a wild and unknown place, was at the mercy of the world. So many good things in life; happiness—even identity came to a woman through a man, and there was no use in pretending otherwise. Whether or not the man in her life was going to be Quaid was something she must face. There was little she could do except her best and hope that fate smiled favorably upon her. Either way, with Harlow or the man she loved, she must go on in this life, and it was easier to do it in luxury than in poverty. If she must be without the man she wanted, then at least she would be comfortable.

Once dressed, she brushed her chestnut-sable hair to a sheen, then added a dab of lip rouge and powder and a touch of cologne to make her feel beautiful. Feeling beautiful gave a woman confidence.

The buggy stood waiting outside the front door of the house. Lifting the hems of her skirts, she stepped into the driver's seat. As she reached for the reins, she saw the drawing room curtains slit open. Martha was watching her. Well, let her watch! Chelsea found herself laughing with delight as she picked up the traces and sent the buggy rattling down the drive.

An infantry of old man gum trees lined her path as she headed in the direction of the lake. Cockatoos and kookaburras spiraled in the air, catching wind currents beneath their wings and bringing a palette of colors to the scrubbed blue sky. The fragrance of eucalyptus perfumed the air as the sun baked the spiny leaves and the wind carried the scent across the countryside. How different from green, lush England was this aged place! The outcroppings of rust-red boulders seemed thousands of years old, and the brush climbing the shallow hills looked dry and lifeless, yet continued to exist on sparse water and too much sun. A sudden shower earlier that day now helped to reduce the flurries of red silt that the wind caught and blew with abandon. Yet there was life here: birds and animals, species of trees that had yet to be cataloged, vast areas of this land that had yet to be explored. Against all the reds and oranges of the landscape and cooling to the eye was the distant range of the Blue Mountains. Chelsea hungered for what she imagined were tall, deep green trees and lush, ripe undergrowth. Someday, she promised herself, she would go the Blue Mountains and walk beneath the trees, lie in a bed of fragrant grass, and fill her soul with the things she had not valued until they'd been lost to her.

As the buggy rounded a bend in the road, the vegetation became greener, lusher, and she caught a glimmer of sun sparkling on blue water. The lake was a large body of aqua separating Bellefleur from Clonmerra, three times longer than it was wide. Tall reeds hemmed the borders, and off in the distance upon the hills rolling down to the water was a sun-parched meadow specked by a herd of black-faced sheep, who lingered nearby for the sweet grasses fed by the lake and the abundance of water to quench their thirst. Chelsea drew on the reins and brought the buggy to a halt, her eyes feasting on the vista before her, which was the nearest thing to England she had seen since setting foot on the *Southern Cross.*

Following the road that led over the shallow hillocks, she came to a wide, inviting drive delineated by a graceful stone archway. Inscribed on a blacked brass plate set in one of the footings was the simple and beautiful name, Clonmerra. Leading the buggy up the drive, Chelsea stood, bracing the backs of her knees against the seat behind her, surveying this place that was home to Quaid. Like Bellefleur, the deep green and shadowed vineyards spilled across the terraced land to greet her.

Quaid Tanner sat on horseback at the top of the hill overlooking his vineyards, the russet-green leaves of his Malaga vines shading the sweet purple fruits from the harsh sun. If the weather held and there was just as ample an amount of rain in the next few days as there had been earlier that day, harvest this year would be bountiful—thanks to Jack Mundey, his overseer and assistant vintner who for many years had proven his faithfulness and diligence. Clonmerra had never promised more, and the new vine cuttings he'd brought from Bordeaux and Portugal were strong and doing well. If all he'd had to think about were the success of Clonmerra, he'd have been a happy man. But just over the hills on the other side of the lake was Bellefleur and Chelsea.

Out of the corner of his eye he caught a movement flying down the drive—a buggy, and in it a vision in pale blue standing on the driver's platform, whip raised above the haunches of a bay mare. One of Kane's horses. Chelsea. Here on Clonmerra, racing toward him.

Feeling as though he had conjured her from his dreams, Quaid dug his heels into his mount's flanks, spurring him onward, sprinting through the rows of Malaga vines shadowing the buggy's path and riding parallel with it. She was heading straight for the house. Cutting off to the left onto a cart path, Quaid lowered himself in the saddle, giving his roan full lead, covering twice the distance of the buggy in half the time. The drive wound leisurely through the gullies, the cart path crested the hillocks and led directly to the back of his house.

Dismounting, he slapped the roan's flanks to give him freedom to wander. Heart thumping madly, Quaid walked around to the front veranda. Four weeks. Four weeks of being so near her and yet unable to see her. His hands went immediately to his thick dark hair, fingers combing through the unruly curls. Hardly daring to breathe, wondering for a moment if his hunger to see her and be with her had triggered a mutinous mirage, he waited. When the buggy rounded the last curve, bringing her into view, he heard himself release his breath in a sigh of relief.

"In the neighborhood, I see." Quaid grinned insolently, unable to take his eyes from her, yet afraid to let her know how glad he was she had come.

"Since you didn't come to see me, I thought I'd come to see you." Chelsca laughed delightedly. How wonderful he looked, sun-bronzed and strapping. "Wipe that smug look off your face, Quaid. You're glad to see me, I know you are."

"I'm always glad to see a beautiful woman. Life at Bellefleur must agree with you."

Chelsea made a face and pouted, countering his insolence with her own. "It is rather trying to prepare for a wedding." Damn him! Why must they play these games? Why did everything he say border on the insulting? She would put an end to all this role-playing and devil take the hindmost.

"Quaid, you don't understand. I—"

"You thought you'd pay me a visit to renew our friendship," he said mockingly. Tell me, Chelsea, he demanded silently. Tell me how miserable you are at Bellefleur, how much you dislike Harlow Kane. Tell me you came because you can't be without me.

"You haven't changed a bit, I see. Still as insufferable as ever. Here, help me down and show me your house. After all, that's why I came, to see your precious Clonmerra."

"That's not why you came." He smiled, dark eyes dancing, white teeth gleaming against his tanned skin. "You came to have me make love to you. Admit it!"

"I'll admit no such thing!" But the conviction in her voice never reached her eyes. "I should get back in my buggy and spare myself your insolence."

"You should, but you won't." He raised his arms and lifted her down from the carriage, holding her for a moment against him, feeling her tremble in his embrace.

"Your . . . your flowers are beautiful," she faltered, feeling herself losing control of the situation. He was moving too fast, making her admit to things she didn't want to reveal.

"Not half as beautiful as you," he breathed against her ear. "You don't have to admit it, I know you, Chelsea. You need me, you want me. That's why you've come here." Say it, dammit! he wanted to cry. Tell me how you feel, tell me you want me, only me! Tell me you regret this game you're playing, that you have no intention of marrying Harlow Kane and never did. Tell me!

"You always did have a way with words, Quaid." Chelsea smiled sweetly, unaware of the turbulence raging within him. Why did he always have to be right? Mentally, she was already shedding her garments, and her naked body was melding into his. At the image, she had to turn her face away to hide the blush staining into her cheeks.

"I have more than a way with words, and you know it. How long can you stay?" His voice was too hoarse; something was beating against his chest, making it difficult for him to breathe. She was more beautiful than he remembered, and he wanted her more than ever. Just the thought of Harlow Kane having her was enough to drive him mad.

"Until dusk. I promised I'd be back before dark." Would he whisper all the right words when he crushed her to him? The right words, say them, say them! Marry me, Chelsea. Marry me, and stay here on Clonmerra with me. Leave Harlow Kane, let me be the man to make you happy. Marry me. Right words or wrong, they were the ones she wanted to hear.

Dusk. He had until dusk to make her love him, to make her want no one and nothing but him. He wanted to hear her say she would stay here with him forever. Four hours. Four hours till dusk. "Come with me." He took her hand. "I want to show you my house." His voice sounded even deeper than before, and he grimaced ruefully. She must think him a lovesick fool.

"I'll see your house later." Chelsea smiled. He wanted her; she could see the fever of desire in his eyes. "Right now I want you to make love to me."

"I always said I liked an honest woman."

"If I said I liked an honest man, what would you say?" Chelsea teased.

Quaid's eyes narrowed in the bright sunlight. "I'd have to say you were looking at one. Come along, love, I'm going to give you what you're looking for."

"That sounds like a promise."

"It is, love, it is. Let's put an end to these games, Chelsea. We both know why you're here, and it isn't to look at the flowers."

Chelsea drew back, her tawny eyes filled with sudden outrage. It was one thing to put games aside, but quite another for him to be so damn certain of himself. "On second thought, I think I'll just tell you your flowers are pretty and turn this buggy around and go back to Bellefleur."

Quaid's stomach flip-flopped. It would be just like her to come to Clonmerra just to tantalize and tease him. He reached out and seized her, preventing her from acting on her words. Lifting her into his arms, he carried her into the house.

The sound of the heavy wooden door closing behind Quaid as he slammed it shut with his foot was music to Chelsea's ears. At last she was alone with him, away from the prying eyes of the world. Alone to love him, to fall into his arms and hold on tightly while he transported them to paradise.

He carried her through the front hall and up the center stairs to his bedroom. The door swung shut behind him, and she raised her face to his, welcoming his lips, yielding beneath his kiss, parting to accept the gentle exploration of his tongue within the soft recesses of her mouth.

When he lay down beside her on his bed they were naked, their hands searching, caressing, arousing passions. He placed his lips on the pleasure spot at the base of her throat, worshiping her, adoring the abandon with which she expressed her desire for him. It was when he leaned over her, about to claim her lips again, that he looked into her face and her beautiful eyes locked boldly with his.

"I need you, Quaid. More than my next breath, I need you!" It was an admission he had been willing to die for, one that came from her heart and was born in her soul.

She reached for him, winding her arms around his neck, pulling him down to her fierce kiss, demanding more of him than she had ever asked before. Her soft lips were bruised with passion; she licked enticingly at his velvet-tipped tongue.

His lips parted, allowing her to dart within his mouth to tease and caress as her tongue dueled with his. Her breasts were crushed against his chest, her curves fit perfectly against the muscular planes and hollows of his body. Becoming the aggressor, he claimed her mouth with his and took possession of her body with his hands. The sound of her passion filled his head and throbbed through his loins.

Chelsea's eyes were glazed with desire and something more, something he hoped was love. He smiled down at her, drinking in the sight of her, knowing her to be the most sensual woman he had ever known, a woman in touch with her own needs and wants and able to communicate those same aching demands to him. She gave herself to him unequivocally, trusting him to gentle her, soothe her, find his own delight in her.

He murmured his praise of her. He whispered his wonder at how beautifully her body fit to his, how her skin was softer than satin, how she made him feel things he had never felt for another woman, how no other woman existed for him now that he had come to know her.

Chelsea responded to his love words, feeling them touch that secret core within her and fill her very being. Liquid fire bathed her in its heat; wave after wave of pleasure coursed through her veins. Being with him this way, bringing him pleasure, being pleasured, loving and being loved, was a woman's triumphant victory. When he placed himself between her thighs and she felt the weight of him pressing down upon her, she welcomed him, guiding him with her fingers, stroking him with the flat of her hands, urging him deeper and deeper into her velvet sheath. Her passions were ripe, her body so willing. His body moved upon her, filling her, the sweet friction between them rising, rising, carrying them upward. She strained toward him, opening herself to him, seeking and finding that certain touch, the delicious pressure that would transport her to a place beyond rapture.

He was watching her face, seeing the myriad emotions cross her lovely features with lightning quickness. First, the parting of her lips, the ragged gasps of her breathing, the furrows that formed between her winged brows as she drew deep within herself, and finally the victorious smile of rapture found. He took delight in her fulfillment; her satisfaction inspired his own, and finding his release, he buried his mouth against the hollow at the base of her throat and breathed her name. "Chelsea, my own little love."

They lay together for a very long time, holding, touching, caressing... but neither spoke a word. Chelsea couldn't trust her voice, afraid tears would choke her, more afraid that she would be unable to stop herself from begging him to keep her, to refuse to send her back to Harlow and a marriage that should never be.

The scent of her lustrous hair flooded Quaid's senses. How could he let her go? he wondered. He wanted this woman in his life, needed her. If only she would tell him this was where she belonged, say that Harlow Kane's fortunes meant nothing to her without love, that she would leave it all behind just to be with him. It was a bitter wine to swallow that Chelsea's ambitions could be satisfied by another man, more bitter still that he was less important to her than enjoying the benefits of Bellefleur. Most bitter that she could not say she loved him.

"It's almost time for me to go back," she whispered, her voice breaking the silence of the room.

"I want to tell you to stay here," he murmured, drawing her closer to him. "I want to say, 'Don't go back there, love. This is where you belong, here with me.'"

"Then why don't you?" She couldn't trust her voice. It seemed her next breath would never come. Silently, she waited.

"Because of Clonmerra," he said at last. "Because I can't offer you marriage and Harlow can. Remember, I said can't, not won't. Not yet, anyway, if ever. I want to ask you to trust me, Chelsea, but I don't think you ever will."

She lay very still, trying to digest his words, trying to find the trust he said he needed. But one question kept reverberating throughout her brain. Why couldn't he marry her? Why? It was a single word, spoken through a sob. "Why?"

"Because you're not the only one who keeps secrets, love. We all have them, even myself. I can't offer you marriage, Harlow can. And there are reasons I can't marry you, things in my past, the uncertainty of the future."

"I don't understand." She pulled away from him, propping herself up on her elbow and looking down into his face. "What things in your past? You ask me to trust you, and yet you won't trust me." She saw him turn his face away; she saw the misery in his eyes. And she also realized that he wasn't about to reveal whatever he was keeping from her. He was afraid she'd use it against him somehow. Chelsea was shattered. Slowly, she moved from the bed and went in search of her clothes. "I'll have to be getting back now." Her voice deadened at the thought of returning to Harlow and Bellefleur.

Quaid tumbled from the bed and took her into his arms, holding her fast against him, his lips buried in her silky hair. "I need time, Chelsea. Give me time to work things through. I don't want to lose you, yet I can't seem to keep you."

Chelsea leaned against him, her heart telling her to put her trust in him. But life had taught her never to trust anyone but herself. If she came here to Clonmerra, she'd be a kept woman, Quaid's whore. She'd never gain respectability and position after that, not even if Quaid married her a hundred times. Much as she wanted him, much as she loved him, there was just too much at stake—her future.

"Let's just leave it the way it is between us, Quaid," she

said softly. "It's never been a secret between us what I want out of life. Without marriage, you have nothing to offer, nothing." Only this, she thought, an agonizing pain clutching her heart as she tilted her face up to his and sought his lips with hers. A sound tore from his throat, a strangled sigh of torment that reverberated through Chelsea's soul.

The sun was a bright orange, low on the horizon, when Quaid silently walked Chelsea out to her buggy. Unwilling to part with her, he held her lovingly with his eyes and possessively with his hands, pulling her so tight against him that he could feel the elegant length of her thigh through her skirts. He was about to lift her into the buggy when a movement on the hill behind his house caught his eye: a woman's figure outlined by the sun. Squinting, he recognized the woman's posture, shoulders high and square, arms crossed over her chest. Martha.

He stared for a long moment, thinking he should mention it to Chelsea, but something perverse prevented him. Let her go home to Harlow, whispered a tiny voice inside him. Let Martha tell, and let Harlow throw Chelsea out. He would gladly pick up the pieces.

Chapter 11

The night crickets chirped their last song before dawn. Cockatoos and English sparrows received the melody and harmonized with the rainbow-colored parakeets who called to one another through the still morning air. Dawn, pink and mauve, spread over the low hills, painting the countryside from its artist's palette.

Chelsea slept fitfully in her garden house sanctuary, dreaming of promises broken and vague betrayals. When she finally tore herself from sleep, forcing her eyes to open, she was breathing laboriously as though running from her night terrors. For a moment she lay perfectly still, aware of a presence in her room. Her eyes widened, fingers reaching to draw the light sheet up to her neck, inching as far back against the bedstead as she could. "What do you want? Who . . . who are you?" Chelsea demanded through her panic. How long had this . . . this person been watching her as she'd slept? She had to be the largest woman Chelsea had ever seen, bigger even than Harlow or Quaid, awesome and frightening with her chocolate-brown skin and piercing black eyes. Chelsea's eyes dropped to the woman's hands—long, graceful hands, large, with long, long fingers and short, tapered nails that were stark white against her skin. One of those hands could cover Chelsea's face and wrap around her ears. The woman's well-shaped head was close-cropped, tight curls of burnt sienna hair, with a long, lovely neck. Shoulders wide and powerful, body lean and athletic. Chelsea didn't know whether she was more intrigued or frightened.

"I am Tingari." Her voice was husky, melodious, and she smiled as she spoke, showing larger, strong teeth.

"What are you doing here? Why were you watching me?"

"Tingari sleep. Mitjitji sleep, Tingari sleep."

Chelsea frowned; none of this was making sense. "Do you mean you often sleep here?"

The woman laughed, a deep, lusty sound. "Mitjitji needs a bed. I, Tingari, am woman of the desert, can sleep anywhere."

A sigh of relief escaped Chelsea. At least this black Amazon understood adequate English, and she seemed to speak it fluently enough. "Where do you belong? Do you have a home? What do you do?"

Tingari lifted her arm, long as a tree branch, and extended it toward the door. "Everywhere is home to a woman of the desert, whatever pleases. I work when there is work, if it pleases me."

"How do you live? How do you eat?" Chelsea's fascination grew, and without being aware of it, she crept slowly out from under the covers.

"People of the desert forage and hunt. It is called *yiwara*. People of the earth live from the earth. Now it pleases to work."

"You want to work for Mr. Kane, is that what you're saying?"

"I hear there is new white lady here, Mitjitji, you. You sleep outside Boss Kane's house."

To Chelsea this last sounded like a judgment. "It's a temporary state of affairs," she explained defensively.

"And this means?" Tingari asked, her black, deep-set eyes fixed on Chelsea, waiting for an answer.

"It means I'm going to marry Mr. Kane, but until then I stay out here to protect my good name."

"Tingari think Mitjitji not care for name and not care for Boss Kane."

Chelsea bristled. "I do care for him. I'm very fond of Boss . . . Mr. Kane. I will come to care even more as the days go by."

"A lie," Tingari said. It was a statement without challenge.

"I don't lie."

"Everyone lies," Tingari said offhandedly. "Boss Kane is not a lovable man, and he is hard on his women. I slept here when there was another Mitjitji."

Chelsea could not help herself. "Alone—or with Mr. Kane?" she asked.

Tingari shrugged and, without trying to defend herself, replied, "Both."

Disarmed by this tall, soft-spoken woman with the gleaming dark skin, Chelsea relaxed her hold on the bedcovers and smiled. "You could have lied to spare my feelings. You're quite the most beautiful woman I've ever seen." It was an honest statement, and it seemed to spill from her lips unconsciously.

Tingari clucked her tongue and accepted Chelsea's compliment. She'd heard comments on her unique beauty before, but always from men, never from a woman, especially a white woman.

"As far as I know Mr. Kane has no Aboriginals working here. Where are your people?"

A wave of her arm, an elegant gesture of her hand, spoke more than words. Her people were far, far away, and the expression of unspeakable sadness in those fathomless black eyes gave evidence of Tingari's pain.

"Boss Kane will have Tingari. I will sleep with the Mitjitji."

Chelsea became alarmed. "It might get a little crowded. I plan to stay here until I marry," she said.

"Mitjitji will not bother Tingari, she is very small."

At that, Chelsea laughed aloud. "No concern for me, eh? All right, you can stay."

Sunlight streamed through the open window as Chelsea leaped out of bed. If she dressed quickly, she could join Harlow for breakfast and break the news that she had found a new servant. She was tying a ribbon in her hair as she crossed the backyard and went straight to the dining room. Breathless, she took her place at the table.

"Harlow, the most wonderful and amazing thing has happened!" Quickly she related her meeting with Tingari. "She fascinates me, she must be the most unique creature I've ever known." Harlow's frown warned her he was going to balk. "I want this woman, Harlow. She can be my personal servant. I've asked very little of you, and you must admit I've worked wonders with the house. I insist," she said dramatically, sensing that to whine and cry would not work with this man.

"My dear Chelsea, it simply isn't done!" Harlow seemed more amused than annoyed. "Aboriginals are not personal servants, and decent people wouldn't allow them in the house. They're shiftless, lazy, and can steal the shoes off your feet. You say her name is Tingari?" Not waiting for a reply, he continued, "There was a woman here who worked for a while on the grounds. We fed her. Aborigines have no use for money. One morning she was gone, simply gone. No, Chelsea, ask anything of me but this."

Determinedly, she shook her head. "I want this woman. She can sleep in the garden house with me."

"Absolutely not!" All trace of amusement was gone now, and the annoyance she had first perceived was taking its place. "I've never heard of such a thing; it simply isn't done." He turned back to his breakfast, dismissing the subject.

Chelsea's back stiffened. "You never heard of such a thing? But you slept with her. She told me so."

Harlow flinched. "And didn't she tell you that everyone lies?"

"Do *you*, Harlow?" she questioned acidly. "Please, spare me the details. I'm perfectly willing to pretend I never heard a word. There are some women who would pack their bags and run if they were in my position. Are you refusing on the basis of not wanting an Aboriginal on Bellefleur, or is it this particular Aboriginal?"

"That's ridiculous. These people expect no better treatment."

"That may be the way you see it, Harlow, but not me. I want this woman to stay, and I won't take no for an answer."

Harlow knew when he was defeated. If Chelsea left after knowing him for little more than a month, how would it look to his friends? Besides, he didn't want to lose her. He was already thinking of her as one of Bellefleur's more valuable assets. "Very well, Chelsea, but don't say I didn't warn you when you wake up one morning and she's gone. She can work in the kitchen for her food, and you'll find her useful in the garden. See that she's dressed decently at least."

"Thank you, Harlow," Chelsea said sweetly. For a moment she'd believed Harlow wouldn't have backed down. Suddenly she remembered how utterly confident Tingari had been that Harlow would allow her to work at Bellefleur. Long after Harlow had left for the vineyards, Chelsea sat and sipped her coffee, telling Mrs. Russell, who had come in from the kitchen, that Tingari had been hired for her keep. Mrs. Russell, an Australian by birth, seemed to have no objection to having an Aboriginal underfoot.

"I've heard of this woman, Mrs. Harris," Mrs. Russell said with a frown. "There's those who say she's a mystic or something. With Aboriginals you never know. Their race goes back centuries before ours, and they keep to the ancient ways. If you say she works here, then that's that."

"I received the impression from Mr. Kane that Australians don't favor the Aboriginals," said Chelsea.

Mrs. Russell shrugged. "I don't bother them and they don't bother me. I'll fix her a plate and bring it out to her."

"Fix the plate, but I'll bring it out," Chelsea offered.

The day was already becoming hot when Chelsea went in search of Tingari, whom she found resting in the shade of a tree. The Aboriginal accepted the plate Chelsea offered but refused the spoon, preferring to eat with her fingers. Her actions as she picked up each morsel of fried potatoes were delicate, her long, tapered fingers bent and held with drawing room fastidiousness.

"Aren't you going to eat your ham and eggs?" Chelsea asked.

"Tingari does not eat what is dead. Cricket, lizard, termite, these have living *mamu*—spirit—and impart life."

Chelsea wrinkled her nose. She could just imagine Tingari's long, long fingers stretching out, white palms showing, to trap a moth drawn to the light and pop it, wings still fluttering, into her capacious mouth. "Just don't eat those things where I can see, or I won't need Boss Kane to send you packing—I mean, Mr. Kane. You're allowed to stay if you prove—"

"That Tingari is honest, that she does not steal or lie. I will stay. Until I am ready to leave."

Shaking her head as though to clear it, Chelsea considered the woman's words. What had she said? That she would stay until *she* was ready to leave? Again she had the impression that this situation—all of it—had been engineered by Tingari, and neither Harlow's reluctance nor her determined insistence had affected the outcome one bit. How strange. "When you finish eating, come to the garden house and I'll show you how to make my bed and handle my clothes."

"Boss Kane say I was to do this?"

"No. I said you are to do this. You do what I say, do you understand, Tingari?"

"Yes. If I like what you say."

"If you don't, then you'll have to leave."

"There are other places if Mitjitji does not want me."

"If you were to leave here, where would you go?" Chelsea asked curiously.

"To the other place, to the man who owns the opals. I have been there before." Tingari turned her head, a slow, eloquent gesture, and looked in the direction of Clonmerra.

"Tanner's vineyard?"

"This troubles Mitjitji? You know this man?"

"Yes, I know him," Chelsea said through clenched teeth.

"He works hard and loves the land. He is an honest man."

"I wouldn't go quite that far. You sound as though you know him rather well." She felt jealous and she knew she looked it. Harlow could have slept with Tingari for a hundred nights and she would not have batted an eye, but Quaid was another matter entirely. She could almost see how Tingari's unique beauty would stir him, and the vision heated her blood.

"Tingari worked in Tanner's kitchen and with his sheep. When I slept there last, he was gone."

"I don't understand. Do you just pick up and leave and sleep wherever you want? Don't you want to have a home and stay in one place?"

"Why?"

"Because it isn't right to go from place to place and from man to man."

Tingari's eyes fell on Chelsea, and her tone was that of a purring cat. "Does Mitjitji always do right?"

This brought vivid color to Chelsea's face, but there was no accusation in Tingari's glance. Nor did it seem she expected an answer to her pointed question.

Tingari hefted Chelsea's trunk into the buggy as though it were weightless, then added hatboxes, shoe bags, and parasols to the crowded baggage rack. It was a day-long journey into Sydney and not one Chelsea relished. A full day cooped up with Martha and Harlow was going to give her a raging headache, and she could already feel it coming on, squeezing into the soft depressions of her temples.

It wasn't long before Chelsea realized something was wrong with Martha. Hatred shone from her vapid blue eyes, and she made a great show of moving as close as possible to her father as though she couldn't bear dirtying her skirt hems by brushing against Chelsea. All attempts at conversation fell flat. Even Harlow, although he said nothing, was aware of his daughter's animosity. Hurt and embarrassed, Chelsea sat with her hands folded and her eyes straight ahead. Sharing a room with Martha, who was to act as chaperone, was not going to be enjoyable.

"You'll like Lucy and John Abernathy, Chelsea," Harlow said, and Chelsea thought she detected a note of desperation in his voice.

"I'm certain I will, Harlow."

"I especially want you to be nice to John Abernathy. He's my banker. Lucy is a shy woman who lives entirely in her husband's shadow. Spend time with her, try to draw her out. We must play politics at times in my business."

"Actually, Father, I'm surprised you're bringing Chelsea to this party. After the wedding would be soon enough."

How snide her tone was, how hateful, Chelsea thought. What had she done? Was it having Tingari come to work at Bellefleur?

"Chelsea is the reason and the *only* reason that I've brought you along, Martha, so I don't want to hear any more talk like that. Chelsea is to be my wife, and I want her to make friends. The sooner she does, the sooner she'll be accepted into our society."

Martha did not take her father's admonishment easily and spent the rest of the day with her lips clamped in silence.

They changed horses twice through the day during the ride to Sydney; the last exchange they made went lame and two hours out of the city had to be driven at an easy pace. Thus it was very late when they arrived at Harlow's townhouse, only time enough to be introduced to Mr. and Mrs. Lockey Druce, the housekeeper and butler, before retiring exhausted from the trip. The master bedroom was Harlow's, and the guest bedquarters were to be shared by Martha and Chelsea.

The bed looked inviting and cool. Wearily undressing and slipping into a nightdress, Chelsea fell into it gratefully. She was just drifting off to sleep when Martha's harsh whisper jolted her awake.

"I saw you. I know when you arrived and I saw you when you left."

Chelsea listened silently, brain spinning, speculating, devising excuses.

"Don't deny it," Martha continued. "What do you think my father would say? He hates Quaid Tanner."

Chelsea's throat went dry. "I'm not married to your father yet."

"If he finds out, he'll never marry you. My father would never take Quaid Tanner's leftovers."

"What a despicable thing to say!"

"What a despicable thing to do!" Martha hissed, a strange light burning in her usually vapid eyes.

Chelsea felt like a cornered rat in the back alleys of London. Denials would be futile, but that strange light in Martha's eyes told Chelsea she wanted something. "You were spying on me, Martha. That makes you a sneak."

"I'm protecting my interests. I have a bargain to make. In return for my silence I want you to see that I'm able to make it to England. The man I love was driven off by my father. I've had a letter from William, several letters. He wants me to come to him, but I can't go without money. You give it to me and I'll repay you with my silence. If you don't have it yourself, get it—I really don't care how. If you don't, I'll tell Father, and where will that leave you, Mrs. Honoria Chelsea Harris?"

Yes, Chelsea thought, where would it leave her? On the first boat to England, providing she could come up with the passage money, and then straight back to Cosmo Perragutt's theater company. "This is blackmail, Martha."

"If that's the word you choose to use, then so be it. I look upon it as protecting my—father."

Chelsea snorted. "How very noble of you. And how do you propose to protect your father if you're in England?"

"What I don't know then won't hurt me," she said childishly. Chelsea remembered that some children could be very mean.

"If you tell Harlow," she said reasonably, "he'll never allow you to go to England. I may be out on the street, but where will you be? Locked in that house doing chores for the rest of your life."

"That's true. But while I've already had a taste of that, you haven't. You don't want to be out on the street. Marriage to my father is fortune smiling on you. You can always *visit* Quaid for additional entertainment. If he wanted to marry you, he'd have done so already. He'd never let my father stand in his way. Quaid Tanner is a *man*. You're good enough to take to his bed but not good enough to marry."

The words hit home for Chelsea, and tears burned her eyes. Thinking the same thing and hearing someone else say it aloud were two different things entirely. She swallowed hard and spoke quietly. "Money seems to be your answer, then. You want me to get it for you. Do I understand you correctly? You will defy your father and leave Bellefleur if I can get it for you. How much?"

"One thousand pounds," Martha said, and smiled. She'd known it would work; Chelsea Harris was no fool. "Is it a bargain?"

"A bargain," Chelsea replied softly, "at twice the price."

For a long time after Martha had gone to her own bed, Chelsea lay awake, thinking. How did she always manage to get herself into such tight spots? Cosmo would throw up his hands in disgust. She understood Martha, that was the pitiful part. She could sympathize with the homely young woman. Hadn't she herself been locked into a similar situation in England? Who was she to sit in judgment? One way or another, everyone blackmailed someone sometime. She'd done it on a daily basis with Cosmo. But where in this world would she get one thousand pounds for Martha?

Chelsea bolted out of bed and stumbled about in the dark, fumbling in her baggage for her small velvet pouch. Her fingers probed Honoria's diamond ear studs and the opal ring Quaid had given her. She could never in all conscience part with the diamond studs; except for the wardrobe, they were all that was left of poor Honoria. The ring was a different matter entirely. It had been given to her; it was hers to do with as she pleased. Cosmo had a favorite expression, one she'd always detested; now, however, it seemed appropriate. "When push comes to shove," Cosmo was fond of saying, "you shove!"

She wondered if there was a pawnbroker in Sydney who could tell her how much the ring would be worth. Having no concept of the value of opals, and considering the way Quaid had so carelessly tossed it to her, she doubted it was worth much. In all fairness, she should first offer it back to Quaid. Martha wanted one thousand pounds, and that was what she would ask. No more, no less.

Chelsea glanced over at the rigid figure in the bed next to hers. She knew Martha wasn't sleeping; she could tell by her breathing. How desperate the woman must be to force such a showdown! Guilt stirred within Chelsea. Giving in to blackmail was one thing, but helping another human being was something else. Suddenly the pity she felt for Martha threatened to overwhelm her.

Without making a sound, she slid her legs over the side of the bed and padded over to Martha. She could almost feel the young woman's rigid body as she reached out and said softly, "Martha, we must talk. I don't mean blackmail talk, either. I mean woman talk. I know I'm of an age with you, so perhaps we could talk as sisters. I feel the need to talk to someone, and I can only imagine you feel the same. It isn't good to keep things bottled up inside, because the harder we try to hide them, the worse they get. They can even kill us in the end."

"What do you know of how I feel?" Martha said tightly. "How could you know? I don't believe for a moment that you love my father. Tell me the truth and maybe then we can talk."

Chelsea reached out for Martha's hand. "All right, we'll talk. You're right, I don't love your father. But I will make him a good wife. I was like you, Martha, at the end of my rope . . . until someone helped me. I have to try and do the same for you. It has nothing to do with the thousand pounds you asked for, either."

Chelsea spoke softly, gently, into the wee hours of the morning. She skipped nothing, left out no detail of her past. For the first time in her life she was as honest as she knew how to be. Once Martha squeezed her hand, and she knew there were tears on the girl's cheeks. When one dropped to her hand, she ignored it.

"Then you do know how I feel," Martha cried.

"Of course I know. I can feel your pain. In my own way I'm in exactly the same place you are—with one difference. There's a man waiting for you who loves you. I don't have that security. There's no one who loves me. To your father I am what he needs for society and someone in his bed to . . . to . . . relieve himself. To Quaid Tanner I'm an experienced woman who loves to make love, but isn't good enough to marry. If your father knew who I really was, do you think for one minute he'd want to marry me?"

Martha made a sound deep in her throat. Chelsea thought it was a chuckle. "My father is a cruel, hard man. He's very self-righteous. No, he wouldn't bestow his good name on you if he knew who you were. I don't envy you your marriage to him. But what makes you say you aren't good enough for Quaid Tanner to marry?" Martha asked curiously. "There must be a reason. Quaid is a fine man."

"Your father is a fine man, too, but you just answered your own question. Fine men don't want to marry actresses, now do they. Tell me something; would your young man want you if you were . . . tarnished?"

"Oh, yes," Martha breathed. "Nothing would make a difference to William. If I were to tell him about you, he'd say you had no other choice, that you did what you had to do and shouldn't be punished. He says everyone has a right to be happy. But neither of us can be happy with

Father controlling things. He's so hateful. He was never a kind or loving father, even when my mother was alive. After she died it was almost as though the three of us became his enemy. What other father do you know who would deprive his daughter of being happy? Not one, I'd wager."

"I know, Martha. I'll do my best for you. I want you to believe that."

"Then you really are going to go through with the wedding. You really are going to marry my father." There was awe in Martha's voice. There was despair in Chelsea's when she responded:

"I have no other choice."

"Have you tried talking it out with Quaid?"

"The one thing I want from him he cannot give me . . ." Chelsea paused; did she dare raise Martha's hopes? "But there is that ring I told you about—the opal—perhaps he'd buy it back and secure your passage."

Chelsea looked around the room at the shadows. Soon it would be dawn. They'd talked most of the night, and she wasn't sorry. She felt they were friends now, and Martha's tight hold on her hand confirmed her feeling. Martha wouldn't betray her, of that much she was certain. And she reaffirmed her intention to help get Martha to England any way she could.

"You'll look after Emma, won't you?" Martha asked tearfully. "Just until William and I can get enough money together for passage for her. You might have to help. Will you?"

Chelsea sighed deeply. How could she say no? She'd gone this far, she couldn't back out now. It would be the best thing for both girls to be together, in her opinion. Harlow would have to learn to live without his daughters just as other fathers did.

Martha turned and wept into her pillow. "You must think me a terrible daughter," she sobbed. Gently Chelsea smoothed back Martha's hair and spoke soothingly, hoping she was saying the right things.

Just as Martha dropped off to sleep, Chelsea found herself humming a lullaby. Why was it, she wondered wearily as she made her way back to bed, that there was no one to give her aid and comfort when she needed it? Honoria, poor thing, was the closest thing to a friend she'd ever had, and now she was dead. If circumstances were different, she could have been friends with Martha, but Martha was going away, too. She would be left alone with a new husband she knew she could never love. What bitter irony.

Harlow proved to be an entertaining, gay, and gallant escort. Each day he appeared in his best bib and tucker, discarding the faded utilitarian clothes he wore in the vineyards. He made quite a dashing figure with his suntanned skin and light gray eyes—a handsome man, dignified and sophisticated. In London he would have been called a "gent."

The townhouse in Sydney represented the more aesthetic side of Chelsea's intended. Three floors, red brick, and black iron ornamental railings, the house on Crescent Street displayed Harlow's fine taste in furnishings, even if they did lean to the masculine, and helped him present a picture of success to his associates. In fact, Chelsea had realized that Harlow had no close friends; his social inclinations leaned more toward business acquaintances. It also didn't take her very long to realize that he was viewed with respect and that as his wife, she would command the same.

There was an immediate camaraderie between Lucy Abernathy and Chelsea. Hour-long conversations concerning London, the latest fashions, and, of all things, the theater, pleased Chelsea immensely. Lucy spoke of the social season and the magnificent parties and soirees beginning in the month of July, Australia's winter season.

"It's an endless social whirl, Chelsea. I do hope you and Harlow will take part this year. Poor man, since he lost Irmaline we haven't seen much of him in the city. He claims Bellefleur takes every ounce of his energy and every moment of his time. If you think you'll be wanting dresses for the season, I can give you my lady's name. Have you given any thought to a wedding dress?"

"I have one, I brought it from England," Chelsea told her. "You will come to the wedding, won't you, Lucy? Harlow thinks the world of you and John, and I know he'd want you to be there." She wished she were speaking of her wedding to Quaid but knew she must let go of that dream. She was going to marry Harlow Kane, and no amount of fantasizing would change that simple fact.

"Of course we'll be there," Lucy was saying. "We wouldn't miss it for the world. We have so few chances to get out into the countryside. And if there's anything I can do to help, just call on me. I could even come out a few days early to help."

"You're very kind, Lucy."

"Not a bit; it would give me a chance to get away from boring banking conversation. Money, money, money, that's all these men ever talk about. Sometimes it makes me ill. Don't misunderstand, I love my husband and take an interest in his business—but there are other things in life."

What those things could be, Chelsea couldn't imagine. If it were Quaid she was marrying, she wouldn't care if they had to forage and hunt the way Tingari did, as long as he held her in his arms every night. Marrying Harlow, however, created a different set of priorities entirely.

"Chelsea," Lucy Abernathy confided, "you are the envy of every woman in this room, and Harlow has climbed a

few rungs in the eyes of the men here, I can assure you."
Lucy looked around the drawing room, surveying the
other begowned women who had come to her social.

"Have all your guests arrived?" Chelsea asked.

"Not all, but it's Quaid Tanner who's missed. He should
be arriving tomorrow. It wouldn't be a party without him.
Every foolish young girl has her cap set for him. He *was*
caught once, and it was the husband who was the worse
for wear." Lucy laughed. "Goodness, what's gotten into
me? I shouldn't be repeating such gossip; it must be Harlow's fine sauterne. John would certainly take me to task.
He's fond of Quaid, as we all are, and the men especially
overlook his little follies. Perhaps it's because they take
pity on him, being alone in Australia with his wife living in
Europe somewhere. Poor thing has a bad heart, and the
doctors forbade her to make such a long ocean voyage."

Chelsea felt as though the floor had dropped out from
under her. Quaid married? A wife in Europe? Then Quaid
had told the truth when he'd said he couldn't offer her
marriage. How could he, when he *already had a wife!* She
felt the color drain from her face; the room began to spin.

"Quaid is devoted to Clonmerra," Lucy chattered, obviously unaware of the shock she'd just delivered to Chelsea.
"He and Harlow have never been on good terms. Something to do with water rights from a natural spring lake.
Harlow keeps insisting Quaid should sell out to him, but I
don't believe that will ever happen," she confided. "For
one thing, Quaid doesn't need the money. He owns an
opal mine in the outback, and Clonmerra Wines are respected, if not widely distributed. Don't you be telling my
John I've discussed this with you, he'd positively have my
head. Now, where is that daughter of Harlow's?" Lucy
asked, abruptly changing the subject. "I wanted to see
about matching her up with the new minister from Cape
Town. It's difficult." She sighed. "Martha's no youngster

any longer, and she looks so lonely and out of place. I think she has a certain attractiveness, though, don't you? A certain character of face. Irmaline was hardly a beauty, and I suppose Martha takes after her side of the family. Irmaline was a good woman, don't misunderstand, but Harlow has the good looks in that family. Oh, I do rattle on, Chelsea, forgive me. I must be boring you to tears."

Chelsea managed to find her voice. "You're not, really. I'm interested in my new neighbor. Somehow I received the impression he was a farmer."

Lucy Abernathy laughed. "Quaid Tanner, a farmer! Oh, I suppose it's because he keeps sheep and provides pasture for them. Chelsea dear, Mr. Tanner's bank balance would be the envy of every man in this room. But remember now, not a word to anyone. Quaid is quite well off, extremely well off. He mines some magnificent opals, and I understand from my husband that he's commissioned his wines to a famous broker in Portugal. When Harlow discovers this, he's apt to throw a fit. He has personally courted this particular merchant for several years, and he thought he was close to success, but Quaid visited Portugal and secured the arrangement right out from under Harlow's nose. Dear heaven, I shouldn't be telling you this. You're going to marry Harlow. Well, it's best you heard it from me, this way you can prepare for it. Not that Harlow isn't a wealthy man in his own right; I'm certain you won't want for anything. It's just that he's not an overly generous man; sometimes he is even very, very frugal. But a young lady like yourself should know how to work around that. Men can be bought, Chelsea, if the price is right. Always remember that."

"I will, Lucy, I will." She wondered what Quaid's price was. She hadn't forgotten that she needed to get him to pay one thousand pounds for a ring he no longer wanted.

*   *   *

Chelsea spent the following day in a state of suppressed excitement edged with nervous trepidation. They had arrived early at Lucy Abernathy's under Chelsea's excuse of wanting to help Lucy with the refreshments. Chelsea looked beautiful, having taken extreme care with her toilette earlier that morning. It had taken her several hours to arrange her hair, meticulously curling it with the hot iron into exactly twenty-two curls that hung in different lengths down the back of her head. A fringe of wispy ringlets offset her high, intelligent brow and brought her marvelous tawny eyes into prominence. The hat she had chosen was a perfect match for her jewel-toned aquamarine afternoon dress of whisper-soft crepe de chine. As fashion dictated, it was styled with leg o' mutton sleeves and a modest neckline that only hinted at the smooth white skin of her breasts; from there it nipped down into a tiny waist exactly one and a half inches higher in the front than in the back, giving a long, graceful slope to her back. Bette had worked miracles with the fabric Chelsea had purchased from the Chinese trader in Madagascar and had arranged the new-fangled bustle in precise proportion to Chelsea's height. The gown had been carefully trimmed in grosgrain ribbon backed with ecru lace at the hemline and neck, and the overall effect was understated but classic. It was a style Chelsea had adopted, deliberately, wishing to portray her femininity without the overwhelming use of laces and bows some women favored.

Chelsea knew Quaid had arrived at the Abernathys' by the excited titters of several women. It was also obvious by Harlow's dark, disapproving glances. Suddenly nervous, Chelsea excused herself to step out into the garden. Harlow was about to accompany her when he was detained by an associate. "You go along, my dear," he told her. "I'll be out in a moment."

Martha followed Chelsea through the foyer, but just as

she was about to step outside into Lucy's attractive garden, Martha took a detour into the dining room. Curious, Chelsea followed.

"What are you doing?" she asked when Martha began fussing with the place cards.

"Seeing that you and Quaid are sitting beside each other. I want you to have every opportunity to speak to him about the money." Martha smiled. "Time is so important. Do you mind?"

Chelsea shook her head. "Do as you like. It's just that Mrs. Abernathy might object; she spent a great deal of time arranging the seating. Where is your father seated?"

"At the other end of the table. I'm seeing to all the loose ends, Chelsea. I meant everything I said, and I hope you meant everything you said. You hold up your end of our bargain and I'll hold up mine."

"Have you given any thought to the possibility that I might not have an opportunity to bring the subject up with Quaid—Mr. Tanner?"

"You will," Martha said confidently.

"Martha, I've been thinking about this all day. What will you do if you get to England and . . . and things don't go the way you expect them to? How will you survive? Any number of things could go wrong. At least you're safe here and will always have a home. You'd have me as a friend. It's important to have a home and family."

"For you, perhaps. It's not that I don't want your friendship. I want William and my own family. I thought you understood. We made an agreement, and I expect you to honor it." There was a note of challenge in Martha's voice that Chelsea recognized. The girl was desperate—and who could blame her?

"I'm not trying to get out of our agreement. I just have to be certain in my mind that you know what you're doing. You must understand that I can't force Quaid to give me the money."

Again Martha smiled. "I have the utmost faith in *all* of your abilities. I'm sure you'll manage."

"When we were talking the other night, why didn't you tell me Quaid had a wife in Europe?" Even now, after having had time to digest the information, Chelsea had difficulty saying it out loud.

"A wife?" Martha frowned. "But I thought that was only rumor; I never really believed it."

"Still, you didn't tell me. I had to hear it from Lucy."

Martha thought for a moment. "Chelsea, believe me, I thought it was only a rumor. When I heard it a few years ago, it was from a friend, a girl my own age. Remember, I haven't been about much in society, and a man's marital state is not a matter an older woman would discuss with a single girl; that's something for the girl's mother. But I guess my mother didn't think it was something I should know about."

Chelsea realized she'd been holding her breath. Some irrational part of her was hoping that Martha could discount what Lucy had told her. But now she'd heard it from two sources. Quaid had a wife.

"Chelsea, what difference does it make? You won't go back on your word, will you? You'll still help me?"

Chelsea looked at the anxious young woman for a moment, then smiled reassuringly. "Don't worry, Martha, I'll still ask Quaid for the money. And knowing Quaid has a wife has only made me more determined than ever to uphold my promise to marry your father." With that she turned, sweeping her skirts behind her as she walked through the garden doors. Martha looked after her, a puzzled expression on her sharp features.

Chapter 12

Dinner was being announced as Chelsea's eyes circled the room. Where was Quaid? He was to be house-guest to the Nelsons and they were here; she'd met them. Searching the room again, she noticed Harlow coming toward her, so she smiled and tried to look as though she wanted to be with him more than any other man in the world. It was a game, of sorts. Acting. Playing at acting, was more like it. If Quaid was staying with the Nelsons, where was he? Whom was he escorting to dinner?

"Did you enjoy meeting the other women?" Harlow asked jovially.

"Yes, I did. Did you enjoy talking to the men?" As if she cared. Damn you, Quaid, where are you?

"I think I enjoyed Masterby's wine more than his conversation. Still, it can't compare to my Chardonnay. I understand Tanner had the audacity to stop by here earlier today to leave some of his best wine. John assured me it would be served with dinner, and I can hardly wait to taste it. Now we'll see if he's half as good as his boasting," Harlow said.

"I didn't realize Mr. Tanner was here," Chelsea said. "I'll look forward to tasting his wine. I'm sure, Harlow, that it won't compare with yours. But the man has worked hard. We can all toast his endeavors."

"Here we are, my dear. I'm afraid I'm seated down at the end of the table." Harlow frowned. "Lucy must be addled. I never saw such an inconvenient arrangement. Look around you; everything seems mixed up."

"Perhaps one of the servants made a mistake."

"No, this is Lucy's doing. She likes to have her little amusements. My apologies, my dear. We'll all have to endure. I'm sure the guests on your right and left will entertain you. We'll meet after dinner and take a stroll in the gardens after the men have their cigars. Would you like that?"

Chelsea smiled. "I'll be waiting."

Harlow seated Chelsea and moved to his end of the table. In a moment, someone moved beside her. She raised her head, knowing whose eyes she would look into. Her pulse quickened as she withdrew her napkin from the ring and spread it on her lap. How intent his gaze was. He was being obvious. Suddenly Chelsea felt there was no one else at the table but the two of them. He was remembering their last hours together, just as she was. She fancied she could see his heart beating beneath his fine lawn shirt. Swoop me up and carry me off, she wanted to cry. I'll never look back. But now she understood why it could never be. To cover her confusion, she sipped at the wine in Lucy's fine crystal. "This is very good, Mr. Tanner," she said, turning to him with a pleasant smile. "I understand we have you to thank for tonight's dinner wine."

"It's my best wine," he told her, his eyes intent on hers. "I felt I should contribute something. I'm pleased you enjoy it. Tell me, Mrs. Harris, how do you like Australia?"

"I like it, Mr. Tanner. I plan to make my home here."

"That's what I've heard. I'm sure you'll come to love this country almost as much as you loved England."

"I didn't love England, Mr. Tanner. I couldn't wait to leave."

Quaid sipped his own wine appreciatively, hoping every palate at the table was as discerning as his. Who the hell did he have to thank for this seating arrangement? he wondered. He'd be damn lucky if he could swallow his food. All he wanted to do was drink in the sight of her. He knew if he lived to be a hundred, he would never get his fill of Chelsea. How was this ravishing creature able to torment him like this? He'd been with enough women to know the difference between lust and love. He loved her. And she loved him—he knew it. But she wouldn't come to him without marriage. And loving her as he did, he had no right to expect her to sacrifice the rewards and respectability marriage offered a woman.

"I much prefer Australia myself," he said desperately, trying to cover his lapse in conversation. "One day you'll have to drive over to Clonmerra to see my vineyards. I'd be most happy to show you around and offer you a glass of my finest champagne."

Martha, who was sitting on Quaid's right, spoke up eagerly. "What a marvelous idea, Chelsea! You could take the buggy when we get back. I'm sure you'll be able to find your way to Clonmerra."

"I couldn't do that, Martha," Chelsea demurred. "It wouldn't be proper. How would it look?"

"Emma and I can accompany you. What better chaperones than the daughters of your future husband? Do accept Mr. Tanner's invitation."

Quaid stared first at Chelsea and then at Martha. Why did he feel as though he'd been kicked in the stomach by a rambunctious mule? He waited to see what Chelsea would say, the wineglass poised halfway to his lips.

"If you really want to, Martha," Chelsea said hesitantly. If he had to, he would hog-tie the two girls out in the barn. But he didn't think it would be necessary. The one thing Chelsea Myles didn't need was a chaperone, and he knew she'd find a way to make the trip alone.

"My father is a lucky man, don't you think, Mr. Tanner?"

"Quite so, Miss Kane. Quite so."

"You will be coming to the wedding, won't you? And to the prenuptial party?"

By God, this was more than he could endure. A devilish twinkle sparked in his eyes. "But of course, Miss Kane. I wouldn't miss the wedding for the world. It will give me a chance to see you again, and your lovely sister." When he heard Chelsea's breath hiss between her teeth, he grinned and held his glass aloft. "To your happiness, Mrs. Harris."

Chelsea didn't know whether to laugh or cry. If ever there was a time for acting, it was now. Forcing a dazzling smile to her lips, she said softly, "May it last forever and a day."

It was Quaid's turn to seethe. What a bitch! No woman had ever tormented him like this, and by God, she *was* tormenting him. Sitting beside him, playing the seductress. A pity Harlow couldn't see her performance. Or was it a performance? He couldn't tell anymore. Either her acting had improved, or she meant the looks she was giving him. He brought his wineglass to his lips and drank. She knew what she was doing, damn her. But there was something new beneath her gaze, something closer to anger than seduction.

"Eternity is a very long time," he replied nonchalantly. At least he hoped his voice was nonchalant. "I have every intention of dancing at your wedding, and even kissing the bride." He turned to Martha. "Promise me the first dance at Chelsea's wedding."

Martha blushed but nodded her head in agreement. Her eyes, when she looked at Chelsea, were hopeful, yet there was a deep, warning look in them. Chelsea tipped her glass for the third time, then held it out to be refilled—and was immediately sorry. She could have toyed with an empty wineglass. When it was full she had to drink it. Her wits were slowing down and the room looked hazy. God, what if she drank too much and embarrassed everyone? Harlow would never forgive her. She would never forgive herself. Damn Quaid Tanner! He wanted her to get drunk.

Quaid watched as Chelsea attempted to pierce the fish on her plate with her fork and only succeeded in knocking the peas off her plate onto the spotless tablecloth. A gurgle of laughter rose in his throat, and he turned aside to Martha. "I think it might be a good idea if you were to excuse yourself and take Chelsea to her room before her condition becomes obvious to everyone," he whispered.

"Won't it look too obvious?" Martha asked anxiously.

Quaid shook his head, his dark eyes surveying the table. "If you do it now with the second course being served, you won't cause too much commotion. But hurry!"

Martha frowned and looked at Chelsea distastefully. "Very well, but I expect someone to bring dinner to my room. And that someone had better be you. Chelsea said she wanted to talk to you."

Quaid marveled at the way the slim woman next to him literally slid from her chair and walked behind the hovering waiters serving the next course. The other guests were busy talking and drinking; as far as he could tell, no one had noticed anything amiss. When Martha bent down next to Chelsea and whispered in her ear, Chelsea's bright gaze met Quaid's. He could see she was having difficulty focusing on him and suppressed a smile at the image of Mrs. Chelsea Harris drunk as the proverbial skunk.

A moment later Martha slid her skinny arm under Chelsea's and helped her from the chair. Her voice was low, whispery, as she led Chelsea from the room. Quaid heaved a sigh when the great double doors closed behind them. Their leavetaking had raised no eyebrows.

"The young lady appears to be indisposed," volunteered an elderly woman opposite Quaid.

"She's from England. I've heard that there are many people who can't tolerate the change in seasons. If you look at Mrs. Harris's plate, you'll see she barely touched her fish. I'm not saying that's the reason, but it is a possibility. I myself don't care much for fish. It leaves me . . ." Quaid searched for the word that would not offend the curious woman. "Rather full."

"You mean it gives you air. My husband suffered from the same thing. More's the pity. Fish is such a tasty dish. I certainly hope Mrs. Harris feels better. She's so charming and quite beautiful. Why, my husband was saying just yesterday that he can't even begin to imagine how Harlow managed to snare such a wonderful treasure."

"Harlow always was a lucky man," Quaid said generously.

"I don't mind telling you I look forward to the young lady's company in the future. There are just too many of us old fossils around here. We need young blood, young ideas, laughter in our lives. I do believe that you and Mrs. Harris are quite the youngest in our little social group. Of course, the children are young, but I'm talking about maturity."

"You're quite right, Mrs. Donner."

"For shame, Quaid. When are you going to call me Phyllis, the way everyone else does? Stop deferring to my age. You make me feel positively ancient, and I detest the feeling. Speaking of youth and old age, when do you think your wife will be able to withstand the rigors of a voyage to New South Wales?"

Quaid nearly choked. Phyllis's mention of his wife in the same breath with Chelsea threw him completely off stride, but he managed to bring himself under control. "I should think never. There doesn't seem to be any improvement, I'm sorry to say."

"Poor little thing. And poor you," she said sympathetically. "A man's wife can be his strength, you know. Just as I was to my Chester. This isn't the country for poor health and weak spirit. I've seen this land sap the life out of too many women. You should have been more careful when you made your choice," she scolded. "Clonmerra needs a woman's touch, it's been in the hands of men for too long. First your father and now you."

Phyllis Donner spoke bluntly, as the old often do, thinking their age and position had earned them the right. "I don't suppose I've ever told you how much I admire what you're doing here in New South Wales." She hesitated a moment and then scowled. "Australia," she corrected herself. "After a lifetime of knowing it as New South Wales, I can't quite get used to calling it by its proper name." She smiled at him with benign enthusiasm. "You've made Clonmerra into something, young man, and I'm not ashamed to say I never thought you'd be the one to do it. I expected you to have sold out to Harlow years ago. I don't mind telling you I was astounded to learn that you'd come back from England to take the reins. Personally, I'd have thought Luke was more the man for the job. How is that young man, by the way?"

"Well," Quaid managed, trying to keep his manner light and congenial, "I hardly ever hear from him. The slow mails, you know."

"Yes. As I said, a man needs a strong woman beside him in Australia," Phyllis replied, momentarily confusing Quaid with her nonsequitur. "You should have made a better choice. Not that you'd find someone suitable at one of these parties," she added. "There isn't a suitable young woman here with the exception of Mrs. Harris, and she's spoken for. These other little snippets don't count."

Quaid forced a laugh. "You better not let their mamas hear you say that. You could be tarred and feathered."

"Oh, posh! They all look like a good wind would blow them over. I'm telling you, not one of them is suitable for life anywhere but in the city. They belong in some fancy finishing school and then marrying some dandy with a lot of money so they can sit on a cushion and direct their households. Life here is hard. Now you take Mrs. Harris—Chelsea I believe she's called. Well, she'll do well on Harlow's spread. That young woman has grit. Reminds me of myself when I first came here. She'll make Harlow a good wife. Bear strong, healthy children. Good breeding always shows. Old Harlow still has some spit in him."

Quaid could feel his stomach turn over. Jesus, he'd given no thought to children. Of course Harlow would expect children from his union with Chelsea. The question was, did Chelsea's thoughts run in the same direction? Chelsea as a mother to Harlow's child! Quaid's blood ran cold at the thought. It should be his own child, their child, conceived in love and raised at Clonmerra. Sudden longings gripped him, longings he knew could never be satisfied. Here again was another reason Chelsea couldn't live with him on Clonmerra. Their children would be bastards, with no rightful claim to their birthright. Quaid suddenly felt sick.

It would be unforgivable to his hostess to leave the table now, he realized. He would simply have to wait out the rest of the meal and then disappear when the men went outside for a cigar. No one would miss him.

Dinner seemed to drag on forever. Course after course was served, and glass after glass of wine was poured. Finally, however, it was all over; Quaid excused himself politely and thanked Phyllis Donner for being such an engaging dinner companion.

The moment he was out of sight and earshot, he sprinted for the stairs, taking them two at a time. Christ, which was Chelsea's room? Was he supposed to bang on every door until Martha stuck her nose out to tell him he'd finally found the right one? But he soon realized there was little to worry about; all the doors stood open, save one. For some reason his knock sounded urgent to his ears.

Martha opened the door and smiled. "Mr. Tanner, how nice of you to call."

"Where's Chelsea?" he demanded.

"Indisposed. Sleeping off her wine." Martha gave him a weighing look. "I don't know if my father will be pleased or angry at your intervention."

"What is it you want, Martha? Why do I have this feeling that you're up to something?"

"Don't you think it's the other way around, Mr. Tanner? I was sitting at the table eating my dinner when you implored me to bring Chelsea up to her room. I did as you asked, and then you turn around and ask me what *I'm* up to. I don't understand."

"The hell you don't. I saw you that day on the hilltop, watching when Chelsea came to visit. You wanted me to see you, so you needn't deny it. You couldn't wait to tell your father, could you?"

"If I had told my father, you wouldn't be standing here haranguing me the way you are."

Quaid had to acknowledge the truth of her statement. Harlow would have come after him. There was no question in his mind who would have been the winner, but that was beside the point. "Are you sure Chelsea is all right?"

"She's all right inasmuch as she's sleeping off the wine."

"I'll take your word for it. Did . . . did she say anything?"

"Such as?"

"Any response to your comments at dinner. About coming to my house when you return to Bellefleur."

"As a matter of fact, she did. She said she would be there around noon on the second day after we get home. And you needn't worry, Mr. Tanner, neither my sister nor myself will be with her."

"I hate to ask this, but what's in it for you?"

"All in good time," she whispered. "You'd better leave now before someone sees you. I've my reputation to think of, and I'm also protecting Chelsea."

"Then I'll say good night—and good-bye. I'm returning to Clonmerra tomorrow. Give Chelsea my regards and have a safe trip back to Bellefleur."

Martha laughed. "We'll do that, Mr. Tanner."

Now why had he said that? Quaid could feel his shoulders slump as he walked down the stairs.

He'd had no intention of leaving Sydney until the moment the words were out of his mouth. It was Phyllis Donner's interrogation that was prompting his hasty return to Clonmerra. So rarely was there ever any mention of his wife that she was often quite easily forgotten. He felt no attachment to her, she was a stranger. But he never forgot his brother. That was a part of the past he would always remember.

Two people who could threaten everything he held dear. Two faces that stood between himself and everything he wanted, all that he lived for: Chelsea and Clonmerra.

In the garden house, Chelsea tried to ignore Tingari's watchful eyes as she primped and fussed with dressing. The Aboriginal's glance was all too knowing; there didn't seem to be any curiosity, only a kind of sad knowing.

Tingari filled the small garden house with her towering presence, her long arms reaching easily to the top shelf of the chifforobe, her enormous feet with their long toes remaining flat on the carpet.

"I'll be back late, Tingari," Chelsea told her, "but before dusk. I wouldn't want to get lost on the road or travel by dark. Mrs. Russell packed me a small lunch."

"Mitjitji will not eat lunch. There are other things on her mind."

Chelsea looked at the woman blankly. "How do you know so much?"

"Tingari not know *too* much. Enough to know your insides flutter like the wings of a moth."

It was too true. Her insides were quivering like a bowl of jelly. Anytime she knew she was going to see Quaid, she was a mass of nerves. And today she was going for Martha instead of herself. Before she forgot, she found the ring and placed it on her index finger, setting it firmly against her knuckle.

"The ring is very beautiful, Mitjitji."

"It's an opal," Chelsea said.

"Yes. I know that ring. It is very rare, the black opal." Tingari's eyes held Chelsea's. "It is Tanner's ring."

"No, Tingari," Chelsea replied defensively, "it is my ring. He gave it to me."

Tingari shrugged, reaching out to grasp Chelsea's hand, her fingers covering the stone. For a moment she stood motionless, as though listening. "It is Tanner's ring," she said simply.

Positively unnerved, Chelsea stumbled out of the garden house. Usually Tingari's quiet strength was comforting, but at times like this, when the woman seemed to reach beyond reality into the all-knowing, it frightened her.

Quaid Tanner waited all morning for Chelsea. He'd awakened at the crack of dawn, as was his habit, but instead of going out for a day's work beside his men in the vineyard, he had bathed and shaved and dressed. When he finally observed the ball of red dust two miles down the road, it was midmorning. Only Chelsea would run a horse in this heat, he knew, and he waited for her.

When the buggy flew up his drive, he stepped off his veranda to meet her. She was a vision that reflected the sun itself in her pale yellow dress. "Couldn't stay away, eh?" he asked, grinning devilishly.

"Don't flatter yourself, Quaid Tanner. This is strictly business."

"Now what kind of business could you and I have except . . ."

"Say it, and I will take this buggy whip to you," Chelsea threatened.

"Don't tell me Harlow sent you here to buy some of my cuttings."

"Harlow doesn't even know I'm here, and you know it. Don't bait me, I'm not in the mood." She stood and waited for him to help her down from the buggy.

"What are you in the mood for, little love?" he asked softly as he held her against him for an instant before she struggled to the ground. He had to be satisfied with the soft pink flush staining her fair English complexion.

Chelsea found her balance and walked away a few steps, making him follow.

"All right," he said impatiently, "Harlow doesn't know you're here, but Martha does. Both of you have managed to whet my curiosity. By the way, I never had the chance to tell you how lovely you looked at the Abernathys' party."

"Before or after I disgraced myself?" she demanded bitterly. "Damn you and your wine."

"Couldn't do without either, could you, love. Of course, I've no respect for a woman who can't hold her wine," he teased. "You were practically swimming in it, and I don't think it was because the flavor was so pleasing. What were you running away from, love?"

"Nothing! You . . . you simply make me nervous. You and Martha. I've been under a great deal of stress, thanks to both of you. What would you expect me to do?"

"Does what I expect really make a difference? You have a mind of your own, and you pretty much do as you damn well please. You're here now, you've come before, you're still betrothed, and still you come to me. What am I supposed to think?"

"Whatever you damn well please."

"I was hoping you'd come to your senses after your trip to Sydney and decided to leave Harlow. He'll never make you happy, Chelsea. There's more to life than position and security."

"Nothing that interests me," she retorted. "Someone told me you have a wife in Europe. Is it true, Quaid?" Her words were blunt, not so much a challenge as an accepted statement of fact. She turned to face him, searching his eyes for the answer. When he said nothing, when he didn't make the denial she so desperately wanted to hear, but looked silently down at her, holding her with those raven-black eyes she turned away again, this time to hide her emotions. "I told you I came on business. Invite me into your house; the sun is brutal today."

Quaid wanted to explain; Chelsea deserved that much, at the very least. But where to find the words? It was all catching up with him, standing between him and the woman he loved, and there wasn't a damn thing he could do about it.

"My house is yours, anytime," he told her, and meant it. Couldn't she see that he meant it? "Go along into the kitchen, there's cool tea and fresh scones. You'll have to help yourself, my housekeeper is off buying supplies and visiting her family. After the way you whipped this horse, he needs water and shade. I won't be long."

Chelsea climbed the five steps onto the wide, railless veranda and walked into the cool depths of Quaid's house. She loved this place; it was so like the man. It wasn't over-crowded with unnecessary furniture, and fresh flowers, placed in little bouquets on nearly every polished table, filled the air with a delicate scent. This she knew wasn't Quaid's doing, but he had to approve or his housekeeper wouldn't continue the practice.

The kitchen, fragrant now with the aroma of freshly baked scones, was a nice place to be. Anywhere that con-cerned Quaid was a nice place to be, she thought wistfully. This would probably be the last time she would come to this house, come to Quaid. She wouldn't visit him after she married Harlow.

"I see you found everything," Quaid said, accepting the glass of tea she poured for him.

"Quaid, I have to talk to you about something very im-portant. I need one thousand pounds, and I need it as soon as possible. It's not a loan, I have something I can sell you."

Quaid's brain reeled. Of all the things that had raced through his mind, this wasn't one of them. "I have the money," he replied cautiously, "but I think I deserve to know why you want it and what it is you're so willing to sell me. Can you tell me that?"

Chelsea's heart pounded. He couldn't refuse her, he couldn't. "I could tell you, but I'd rather not. Will you give it to me?"

"Chelsea, a thousand pounds is a great deal of money. I work long and hard to earn that much from the vineyard. Tell me what the problem is. I want to help you, but I need to know more."

"I knew you were going to be difficult! What is it you want in exchange?"

Quaid slammed his glass down onto the table. "Get your mind out of the gutter, Chelsea. I wouldn't demean you by paying for your lovemaking, and I won't have you doing it, either. That was a low blow."

She couldn't deny that's what she'd been thinking, and the knowledge shamed her. "It's just that I'm desperate."

"I can see that. What is it you want to sell?"

"This." Chelsea opened her clenched hand.

Quaid's eyes widened. "That's my opal. You want to sell me my opal?"

"It's not yours, it's mine. You gave it to me. I thought I'd do you the courtesy of first refusal. If you don't want it, perhaps you can sell it for me and bring me the money, if you think you can get a thousand pounds for it. I'll take whatever it will bring."

"I gave you that opal." Quaid growled, angrier than she had ever seen him, angrier even than he'd been in Captain Winfield's cabin when he'd learned she was going to marry Harlow. "You'd get a thousand pounds for it; you'd get ten thousand! That stone is priceless. I wanted you to have it."

Chelsea hesitated. "This isn't easy for me, you know—"

"The hell it isn't! You rattled off this whole deal as if you'd rehearsed it."

"It's my acting ability."

"Acting ability, my ass." He took a deep breath. "All right, all right, I'll give you the damn money. But you're going to tell me why you want it." There was murder in his eyes, and Chelsea backed away in sudden apprehension.

"All right, but you're going to be sorry you asked me," she told him. "It's for Martha. She wants to go to England, but Harlow refuses to allow it. She followed me the last time I was here, and she knows that we . . . that I . . . She threatened to tell Harlow. She's desperate, Quaid. I have to help her; I have no choice."

"How do you know she won't take the money and tell her father, anyway?"

"She gave me her word. I trust her."

Quaid raked his fingers through his hair. Christ! He couldn't believe he was doing this, actually paying to keep Chelsea at Bellefleur with Harlow. He looked into her eyes and then looked away again in defeat. He would give her the money. It was the only thing he had to offer; he had nothing else to give. His gut told him it was a mistake. It would be better if Harlow discovered their secret—then he would consider Chelsea unsuitable to marry. He knew from experience that Harlow was a hard man, unloving and even dangerous. How much better off Chelsea would be if she left Australia and went somewhere else to find a life for herself. But then she would be gone from his own life as well, he told himself. And what comfort was there to be gained in knowing that she lived just over the hill at Bellefleur? asked a small voice deep inside him. It didn't matter, came the answer. However small it might be, he was ready to reach out and grab it, regardless of the price.

"Say you'll help me, Quaid," she said, praying he would tell her to forget about Martha, forget about Harlow, and come to him at Clonmerra to be his wife.

"The money is yours, Chelsea," he told her, but she was so steeped in her own misery that she failed to hear the anguish in his voice.

Chelsea knew her eyes were going to be red and swollen when she got back to Bellefleur. As she drove the buggy, she kept wiping her eyes and blowing her nose.

He hadn't denied having a wife. Somewhere there was a woman who carried his name. She wanted to hate that woman, hate Quaid, but instead she hated herself. She still loved him, would always love him, even though all hope was dead. He'd given her the money, and it was the same as telling her to go through with her marriage to Harlow.

The tears turned to sobs and the sobs to hiccups as Chelsea rounded onto Bellefleur's drive. Tingari materialized from nowhere, her flat black gaze taking in the Mitjitji's appearance; but she said nothing. Together they walked to the garden house.

"Lie down, Mitjitji," Tingari suggested, finally breaking their silence. "You will sleep, and when you awake, your eyes will be cloudless. The man who brought these tears, he was worth it?"

A sob of self-pity caught in Chelsea's throat. "I don't know, Tingari. I'm so tired, I can't seem to think straight anymore. I never should have left England."

Tingari's hands were gentle as they placed a cool cloth on Chelsea's brow. She was a woman, she understood. "Leave such thoughts behind, come into the world of Dreaming," she crooned.

Sitting at the foot of the bed, she removed Chelsea's shoes and began to rub her feet, all the while humming a strange, tuneless melody. Chelsea felt herself drifting, drifting, floating, following the sound of Tingari's voice to a place known as Dreaming, where all was as it should be.

When Chelsea woke hours later, she felt better than she had all day. Whatever it was that Tingari had fashioned in the way of a poultice had worked wonders. The mirror never lied. Now all she had to do was dress for dinner.

"You must hurry, Mitjitji," Tingari told her. "The dinner hour is near. Miss Martha was here several times. I would not allow her to wake you."

"Tingari, she didn't . . . you didn't allow her to . . ."

"It is safe, Mitjitji. Your money pouch is safe. There is no cause for worry. Miss Martha was quite angry."

"I'm sure she was. Thank you."

"It is not wise, what you have done," Tingari said solemnly.

Chelsea didn't bother to ask what the woman was talking about. She'd given up trying to figure out how the Aboriginal knew the things she knew. "I had no other choice. I don't want to discuss it, Tingari. What you know stays between us."

"Yes, Mitjitji. Hurry or there will be questions. Questions you will be unable to answer."

"I'm ready. I'll speak to Martha myself."

Dinner was a dismal affair. Harlow and Franklin talked of nothing but the coming vintage. Emma picked at her food and twice had to be reminded to eat by a sharp-tongued Martha. Once, when Martha's eyes met Chelsea's bright gaze, she nodded imperceptibly. The sparkle that flew into Martha's eyes made Chelsea wince.

At one point Harlow turned and looked directly at Chelsea while he was still talking to Franklin. How beautiful she looked presiding over his table, he thought. She was going to make an excellent showpiece. Already his friends were talking about what a lucky devil he was, and some of them openly said they envied him. And rightly so. She was an asset, a prize. But if he didn't watch things, she could also be a handful of trouble. He was going to have to find a way to temper her tongue. A hot rush coursed through him as he wondered if she felt any desire for him. She was so cool and regal sitting at his table. It was unlikely that a lady such as Chelsea would allow herself to think of bedroom activities at the dinner table.

"What are your plans for tomorrow, my dear?" he asked casually.

"I'm serving luncheon to several ladies of the Horticulture Society. They're trying to entice me into becoming a member. Do you think I should join?"

"By all means. Bellefleur needs a woman's touch in the garden. Water is no problem."

This was new, this domestic questioning by Harlow. Chelsea's eyes flew to meet Martha's intense stare, and the slight answering shake of the young woman's head meant she had kept her end of the bargain. Whether Harlow was fishing or just making polite conversation was up to Chelsea to decide.

"I think that will pretty much take the entire afternoon," Chelsea continued after a slight pause. "There will be eight ladies for luncheon. Afterward, they're going to present me with a diagram showing where certain flowers, bushes, and bulbs should be planted. I think after a late-afternoon refreshment there will be little time until dinner. My day is well planned. Was there something you wanted me to do?"

"No, my dear. I'm happy that you're socializing and getting to know our neighbors. It's important out here in the country that we all stick together. Our social life at Bellefleur has declined over the past years and it's been my fault. Now that you're here, things will perk up. The girls need company, and Franklin could use a little entertaining himself. Perhaps a pretty young girl will set her cap for him."

It was said half in jest. But Chelsea was watching Franklin as his father spoke, and the angry light in the young man's eyes upset her. It was the same light that shone in Martha's eyes, a feral glow to which she would never become accustomed. On occasion she had even seen a similar flicker in Emma's vague, blank gaze. More and more she was convinced that there was no love between Harlow and his children. What in the name of God was he going to do when Martha informed him she was leaving? Her churning stomach told her there would be a bloody battle.

"I noticed quite a few young ladies in Sydney, Franklin,"

Chelsea said, trying for a little light conversation. "Their mothers are most anxious to find suitable husbands for them. After vintage we'll have a grand party, if your father approves, and invite some of the beauties. You'll be able to pick and choose."

"Pick of the litter, so to speak, Franklin," Harlow said jovially.

"If you don't mind, Father, Chelsea, I much prefer to do my own picking and choosing—when I want." The words were quiet, yet intense. Evidently, this was a sore topic of conversation between father and son. Franklin's eyes were smoldering now as he excused himself from the table. Martha averted her eyes, and Emma let her own blank gaze follow her brother from the room.

Emma's words startled Chelsea and brought a frown to her father's face. "Franklin doesn't like any of us. He doesn't like you, either, Chelsea. Ask Father. Franklin doesn't like anyone. He hates the vineyards and the grapes, and he hates Bellefleur."

"That's enough, Emma!" Harlow barked. "Leave the table. Immediately. I must apologize for my daughter's lack of manners, Chelsea. There are times, and this is one of them, when she gets carried away with her erratic notions. Martha, I thought you had this witless creature under control."

"I have no control over what comes out of Emma's mouth," Martha protested. "I never know what she's going to say until she says it. I'm sure Chelsea understands that what Emma says is not to be considered the gospel truth."

"One of these days she's going to embarrass the lot of us, and then what will we do? Tongues will wag and we'll be a laughingstock." Harlow's face, normally ruddy, was a bright crimson. How mean his eyes looked, Chelsea thought uneasily, and how sharply he spoke.

"Then lock her up somewhere if you're afraid of what she's going to say," Martha said callously.

"I don't need any advice from you, Martha. Mind your manners. What is Chelsea going to think of us?"

"Not what is she *going* to think, Father. It's what she *already* thinks. Isn't that so, Chelsea? We're a houseful of mindless idiots run by a tyrant of a father."

"Martha!" Harlow thundered. "That's enough!"

"You're absolutely right. Enough is enough! Excuse me, Chelsea, Father." She was up from the table, her plate of food barely touched, and out of the room before Harlow could get out of his chair.

Harlow's face was black with rage. First Franklin, then Emma, and now Martha. He hated the confused, frightened look on Chelsea's face. When a man couldn't control his children, he was a poor man indeed. After all, he was a father, a parent, and he demanded respect. Things had really gone to hell as far as the children were concerned since Irmaline had died. Well, they would do as he said when he said it, or they could leave.

Chelsea rose from the table, her face a mixture of confused emotions. She felt frightened and knew it showed on her face. She was trembling from head to foot. She'd never really known what the expression "the fear of God" meant, but now she knew. The man sitting across from her could turn his emotions off with the blink of an eye. He was smiling now, a devilish light in his eyes, as he apologized once again and suggested a short after-dinner stroll.

"I have a raging headache, Harlow. Perhaps tomorrow. Yes, yes, after dinner tomorrow, and we can talk about the ladies from the Horticulture Society. Good night, Harlow." She literally raced from the room through the kitchen and out to the garden house, slamming the door shut behind her.

Once safely inside her own private space, Chelsea took

a deep breath and sat down on the only chair in the small room. He had the devil in him, this man she was going to marry. She sat for a long time, long after Tingari came and lighted the lamp and turned down the coverlet and laid out her nightdress. She was still sitting in the same chair with her hands folded the same way when Martha rapped lightly and entered the room, a furtive look on her face.

"Give it to me," she cried in excitement.

"After the wedding. Not one second before."

"Oh, no, you don't. No tricks, Chelsea. We made an agreement. Don't force me to renege and tell my father."

"I gave you my word and I'll keep it, but after the wedding. If you want to persist in your threat and tell your father, I'll simply take the money and leave myself."

Martha's jaw quivered as she digested Chelsea's brave words. "What do you think of my father now that you've seen what he's capable of? You did notice his famous uncontrolled rage, didn't you? One day it will be directed at you, the way it so often was at my mother. Why do you think Emma acts so witless? It's the way she copes. She wasn't always as she is now."

"Martha . . . I—"

"I know, you don't know what to think or do. You wanted all of this," Martha said, waving her arms about. "But you're beginning to realize that you're getting more than you bargained for."

"That sounds like a warning," Chelsea said nervously.

Martha laughed, an eerie sound that made Chelsea clench her teeth. "It is. Don't think for one minute that you fooled me about Tingari. I know why you have her here. You're nervous, admit it. She's your protector. But when you move into the house, who's going to watch over you? Who'll save you from your own husband?"

"Tingari is a servant, that's all. You don't know what you're talking about."

"Don't I? I overheard you telling father, not asking him, that you wanted Tingari for yourself. The Aboriginals never come into the house. He told you that, and you said you didn't care, that you wanted her for yourself. And he finally gave in. That's when Franklin and I knew we didn't stand a chance here anymore." Martha's voice rose shrilly. "It isn't fair that you should come here out of nowhere and take what is rightfully ours. For myself, I no longer care because I'm leaving. But I do care about Franklin and Emma."

"Martha, you are all your father's children. He will always provide for you. Surely you know that."

"Until such time as you have children of your own. What about them, what's going to happen to them? When will they have lives of their own? When do you think my father would ever allow me to marry? Never! Forget about Emma. Franklin, do you think Father will allow Franklin to take a wife and share his life and money with someone else? My father keeps what is his, and he does not share. Only on his death will anyone—and that includes you and whatever children you may have—get a penny. You sit here now and think about all that has gone on this evening. Well, think hard, Mrs. Chelsea Harris!" Her words were bitter but not unkind.

Much later, when Chelsea got up from the chair and changed into her nightclothes, she felt stiff and sore. Exhausted, she crept into bed and pulled the covers up to her chin. She wished Quaid were here to take her in his arms and say everything would be all right. But she wasn't going to see Quaid again. She would never be his wife. She knew the loss would stay with her the rest of her life.

Tingari entered the room, spread her mat, and lay down to sleep. The moon rode the heavens majestically while Chelsea lay awake remembering everything there was to

remember about Quaid. Memories could be such a comfort when you had nothing else, she reflected. She would
grow old on her memories. Gray would creep into her
hair, her bones would become rickety, and her eyes would
get like Emma's. But the memories would be bright and
fresh because she would never let a day go by when she
didn't bring them to the surface.

Chelsea was snuggled deep in the cocoon of sleep,
dreaming she was in Quaid's arms, as the first light of day
crept over the huge gum trees. Her subconscious registered
that Tingari was up and folding her mat. She slept on.

The following Sunday, after a late breakfast, Harlow
sought out Chelsea, gallantly taking her arm to lead her
out to the garden. "It's time, my dear, that we set our wedding date," he told her. "Two weeks from today, I think. I
cannot wait any longer. I've heard whispers, and I don't
like it. Everyone is curious, and that's something else I
don't like. Too much time has gone by. I was mortified this
morning when the minister chastised me. I do believe he
thinks we're living in sin. Two weeks from today," Harlow
repeated firmly.

Chelsea nodded weakly. Two weeks. Fourteen days.
Later when she was alone she would calculate the hours
and the minutes. Not long enough. She knew she was expected to say something. "Have you told your children?"
was the best she could manage.

"I will over luncheon. I'm sure they've been wondering
why it's taken so long. I've been patient, but that patience
is wearing thin."

"Yes, I know, and I do thank you for allowing me this
time to become accustomed to Bellefleur. I was . . . I was
frightened, Harlow. Everything was so strange . . . I was
anxious. I tried too hard to make things right for everyone, to earn my place here."

"And you did a wonderful job of it," Harlow said sincerely. "Now it's time to take your rightful place and let others do for both of us."

"Of course you're right. I'll have to see about getting . . ." What, she couldn't think. Her clothes, proper clothes, Honoria's clothes. What? Dear God, two weeks was barely any time at all. Invitations! "Harlow, surely we won't have time to get the invitations out and make arrangements for everybody," she said anxiously.

"Don't worry, my dear. It's all taken care of. The minister will announce our marriage next Sunday. All you have to do is think about yourself and do whatever it is women do before marrying."

As he leered at her, Chelsea could feel her nails biting into the palms of her hands. She wished she knew someone to ask what it was she was supposed to do to be ready. She felt ill. "It's very considerate of you," she said, smiling weakly.

"What kind of man would I be if I worked my woman to the bone before her wedding and have her all tired out? That's not what I want. I want this to be a new beginning for both of us. We'll forget your dead husband and my dead wife and pretend we've never been married. It will be exciting, don't you agree?"

Dead. Why couldn't he at least have said "deceased?" For a moment she had to think whom he was talking about. Honoria's husband, of course. "Absolutely," she gushed. Her head was pounding now. Two weeks. She could still leave; Tingari would help her. All she had to do was pick up her feet and go . . . but she knew she wouldn't. She didn't ever want to be homeless and have to scavenge for food. Quaid didn't want her. Harlow wanted her so badly it oozed out his pores. Cosmo had always said to go for the sure thing—and Harlow was about as sure as she was going to get. Harlow was going to be her life from now on.

"Now that it's all settled, I think I should confer with Mrs. Russell," Chelsea said, and excused herself, eager to be away from him.

"Of course, my dear. You run along and speak with her. Make whatever decisions you want. After we're married, though, I'll be making the decisions in this household. Remember that."

"I will, Harlow. I will," she said, feeling as though her fate was sealed.

Chelsea got as far as the dining room. Then she had to sit down and get her thoughts in order. She poured tea and sipped it, but it did nothing to calm her heaving stomach. Mrs. Harlow Kane. Mrs. Harlow Kane, compliments of Honoria Harris.

At the thought of Honoria, her eyes widened in alarm. Until this very second she'd forgotten the few lines Honoria had insisted she write in her own hand. Honoria had thought of everything. Where was the damn letter? She'd have to root through everything to find it. God, maybe she'd thrown it away. How naive she'd been to think she'd be safe with Quaid should Jason ever inquire after his sister-in-law. Another dusty dream.

Chelsea returned to the garden house to search through all her belongings. Finally she came up with the letter Honoria had written. Now all she had to do was go back to the house, get an envelope from Harlow's study, and post it. She made a mental note to remind herself to mention it to Harlow in case he took it into his head to write on his own. Once it was done, all her loose ends would be neatly tied in a bow.

Chapter 13

The following two weeks were hectic for Chelsea. Wedding gifts arrived by wagon from Sydney and the other vineyards in Hunter Valley. Each one was unwrapped and appreciated, each was placed on several long, gleaming tables in the front hall, the name of the giver written in Emma's careful hand on a card placed beside each gift.

Late breakfasts, midday luncheons, and full dinners were served at Bellefleur as the guests began to arrive later in the week. It was a happy time for the bride-to-be, and Chelsea enjoyed every minute of attention and generosity. For the first time she felt as though she belonged, that she was really a part of Bellefleur.

The great house had been cleaned and polished. Freshly laundered and ironed sheets were placed on the beds, window seats, and anyplace a body could rest for the night. Even the bunkhouse had been scoured and aired, the gentlemen guests moving there to make room for the ladies at the big house. If Harlow had been on better terms with Quaid, his neighbor, wedding guests would have been invited to stay at Clonmerra.

Fresh flowers, brought by the armful, adorned every corner of the house. Dishes and silver platters gleamed, and the multipaned windows sparkled. Bellefleur was a reflection of Chelsea, of her caring and sense of order, and she was proud of it.

Most of all, it was the acceptance of people like Lucy Abernathy and the easy friendship of groups like the Horticulture Society that Chelsea valued. They liked her, they believed she was one of them, and she wanted to be. Marrying Harlow would give her that—respectability. Chelsea knew what it was not to be able to hold up her head in polite society. Actresses did not enjoy such benefits. Harlow was offering her what Quaid couldn't—marriage. Perhaps marrying Harlow wasn't a dream made in heaven, but it was the closest thing she was ever going to get.

Quaid Tanner paced his house from one end to the other. Nothing satisfied him this day. There was no chair that could hold him, no food that would stay in his stomach. In less than twenty-four hours Chelsea would marry Harlow Kane.

He uncorked another bottle of his vin ordinaire, making a pretentious ceremony of pouring the dark, shimmering liquid into a glass before gulping it. He ached, he hurt. He longed and he loved. He supposed he'd always known that somehow the past would catch up with him, but he'd always believed that it would take Clonmerra away from him. Instead, the past had insidiously separated him from the one woman in the world he wanted. To come forward with the truth would be to lose everything—Chelsea and Clonmerra, and probably his own neck in the bargain.

He loved her. God, how he loved her. And yet he could offer her nothing. To set things straight in order to marry her, questions would be asked, confessions would be made, and in the end Chelsea would be alone and without anything. He'd probably swing from the end of a rope, and Clonmerra would be relegated to decades of litigation; the land would never be developed, and it would never come into its prime in the hands of English lawyers, thousands of miles away.

Quaid brooded, trying to drown himself in Clonmerra's nectar. Misery was his only companion, heartache his only friend. And as he immersed himself in his thoughts of Chelsea, a strangeness overcame him: it was almost as though he were watching himself from outside his body. It must be the table wine, he decided. It was more potent than he remembered.

Chelsea escaped the din of her prenuptial party, sighing in relief as she walked across the backyard through the shrubbery to the garden house. It had been impossible to pretend a gaiety she did not feel. The laughter, the drinking, music and dancing, all the things she had once thought so important had given her nothing but a headache. If it had been in celebration of her marriage to Quaid, she would have danced the night through, joyously celebrating the first step of a lifelong journey with the man she loved.

"Ghosts walk in Mitjitji's eyes," Tingari said as Chelsea closed the garden house door behind her.

Chelsea was very close to tears. "This isn't what I want, Tingari. Not this marriage to Harlow. I want Quaid, so much there's an ache in my soul."

"A woman knows, Mitjitji," Tingari commiserated, gathering Chelsea into her long-armed embrace, allowing her to cry unchastened tears.

"Tingari can fix for Mitjitji. Come to bed." Gently, like a mother leading her child, Tingari helped Chelsea undress, slipping her silken nightdress over her head and loosening the pins from her hair. "Stay here, Mitjitji. Rest."

Quickly Tingari left the garden house, leaving Chelsea with unanswered questions. What was Tingari going to do? Did the Aboriginal think a simple herb cloth could chase away these demons that haunted her?

Tingari returned holding a dun-colored cloth in which

several items rattled. "Mitjitji watch. I will bring Tanner to you."

"On a flying carpet?" Chelsea asked, clearly skeptical. Then hope rose in her breast. "Oh, can you, Tingari, can you?"

"This night," Tingari stated.

Chelsea leaned over the side of the bed, watching Tingari sit tailor fashion on the floor, the fine hairs on the back of her neck prickling as the Aboriginal began to chant in her deep, musical voice. The dun-colored parcel opened under Tingari's long, elegant fingers, a sorcerer's kit of small objects. In the glow from the lamp each object seemed to burn with a life of its own as Tingari touched it. Pearl shells, a smooth piece of quartz, a round orb of glass, glittering and sparkling as she laid them side by side, rearranging the objects to suit her. A narrow piece of wood painted with concentric circles; a carving, half man, half beast; finely ground powder from a scrap of parchment; all were added to the objects Tingari placed before her. And always the even cadence of the chant she intoned in her deep, melodious voice.

Tingari picked up the small white shells and tossed them into the center of the floor. She seemed to be counting them, marking their positions. Once, she moved a shell closer to another. Again she scooped them into her hand. Again, she tossed them. After the third time she smiled broadly, large white teeth gleaming. "Tanner comes, Mitjitji." The shells and objects were quickly gathered and replaced into the dun cloth. She added a pinch of the mysterious powder to a glass near Chelsea's bedside. "Drink this, Mitjitji. Drink without fear."

"Is this what you call Dreaming?" Chelsea asked, swallowing the water in which the almost tasteless powder had dissolved.

"My people say *tjukurpa*, Dreamtime, when yesterday

is today and today is forever. All things have *mamu,* all *mamu* is Dreamtime."

Chelsea knew *mamu* meant spirit. Was Dreamtime then a kind of timelessness, a sacred knowledge of that which lived before and still brought influence upon the present?

"Mitjitji's lover comes," Tingari announced, and Chelsea had no doubts. None at all.

She lay in her bed, waiting, the lamp wick turned down to a mere flicker, the ruby-red shade creating a soft, ethereal glow. The powder Tingari had administered seemed to relax her, and she had no awareness of the passage of time or of the sounds of revelry from the big house. Her thoughts were on Quaid, only Quaid, and her dreams must have conjured him from the thin air—or was he actually standing beside her bed, looking down at her with tender eyes.

"You came," she whispered, stretching her arms up to welcome him into her embrace.

"I don't know why or how, but I'm here. I must be dreaming." Then he was in her arms, nuzzling the soft skin of her throat. "Perhaps it was the wine," he murmured. "God bless the wine!"

The wind outside the garden house lifted, stirring the branches of the twisted mulga tree, making it sway in an endless rhythm. The black night sky touched with stars was like a coverlet drawn over the tiny garden house when Quaid extinguished the lamp. They were alone, two souls wandering in the wilderness, finding each other, knowing each other.

Boldly her fingers found the fastenings of his clothes. If there was only tonight and tonight would be the last, she would have him and sate herself with his love. Naked together, they clung, kissing, murmuring, lips moving softly against lips. Her flesh came alive under his touch, her excitement and passion communicating with and stirring his own.

She was his love. He had held her this way before, worshipped at her breasts and taken possession of her inner-most core, yet she excited and stirred him as if it were the first time. There was so much more to Chelsea than fair skin and alluring curves; there was the woman within, the woman he could not live without. He pulled her on top of him, wanting her to master their desire.

Wild blood coursed through her veins, her aching need for him cried within her soul. This was the man she loved. She would marry another, but always her heart would be-long to Quaid. Only he could chase away the demons and bring this overwhelming sense of security. Only with him could she know the joys between a man and a woman, the tender words and gentle emotions they shared.

Her fingers traced the lines of his face, committing him to memory. Her lips tasted his, a kiss bittersweet, filled with the knowledge that tonight would be the last. She could offer him her body and stir his passions and give her heart, but she could never have him for her own. Not even Tingari's magic could make him free to marry her. If tonight was all she could have, then she would make it a night to remember.

Slowly he filled her with himself, and she opened to him, moving with him, imprisoning him in love's tender sheath. Chelsea whimpered softly, loving the feel of his body, responding to the sound of his tender whispers when he told her of her beauty and the way he loved the scent that was only hers.

He savored her lips, tasting the ambrosia of passion's fruit, tantalizingly withdrawing from her and entering again with slow, sensuous strokes and the caressing roll of his hips beneath her haunches. He inspired her to ride him, to take him deep within, helping her find the sweet fulfill-ment at the center of her being. His loving hands possessed her breasts, cupping their firmness, following their lovely slope to tease the rosily pouting crests.

Fire sparked where their flesh joined, but it was only kindling to the raging conflagration of their souls. And when their lips met again, they tasted the salt of tears and each thought it was their own.

Together they slept in one another's arms, but when Chelsea awakened she was alone. Had she only dreamed Quaid had come to her? Were the tears that had dried on her cheeks the result of a night terror? She turned her face, dreading the first light of day. Was she just imagining it, or could she smell the scent of him on her pillow?

Chelsea's knuckles were rigid and white when she uttered the words that would make her Harlow Kane's wife. "Till death do us part." That meant forever. Oh, Quaid, where are you? Chelsea thought wildly. It should be you standing here beside me making these vows.

"You may kiss the bride." The Reverend Archer smiled.

Harlow lifted Chelsea's short veil and kissed her soundly. The wedding guests smiled their good wishes. The narrow gold band on Chelsea's finger felt like a brand. It was done. She was now Mrs. Harlow Kane. Like it or not, she had accepted a new life. Cosmo would have said she'd made her bed and now had to lie in it. Well, she would. She wouldn't like it, but she would.

Proudly Harlow led his bride to the receiving line. Smiles, handshakes, light breathless kisses, all wishing her happiness. But happiness, she knew, was on a place called Clonmerra.

Musicians struck their opening chords; the guests began to gravitate toward the elegantly ornamented tables laden with food and fresh flowers. It was all for her, this lavish display, and in her heart she wanted none of it. Today she must give the performance of her life, smiling, pretending a happiness she did not feel. Only this was a role that would play on forever. Cursed by a woman's need for security, for respectability, Chelsea wept, the glistening tears running in rivulets down her cheeks to be quickly dried with the edge of her lacy handkerchief and to be excused as sweet sentimentality.

Later, Chelsea found herself standing beside Franklin. What to say to this surly, angry young man?

He should have congratulated her, kissed her lightly on the cheek. Something. But no, he had to sulk. People were watching. Again, Chelsea forced a wide, warm smile and touched Franklin on the arm. "People are staring at us, Franklin. Your father is watching. Smile as though you mean it. Welcome me to the family, and then I'll walk away. Do it quickly, your father is making his way toward us. Don't shame him, Franklin."

A grimace stretched tightly across Franklin's lips. "The second sorriest day of my life was when you arrived here. The first sorriest day, in case you're interested, was the day I was born. Bellefleur has another prisoner today. You'll grow old here, Chelsea. You'll learn to hate it as I do. But first you'll come to hate my father and the sacrifices he'll demand of you, all for the sake of Bellefleur. You'll give your youth to that parched land and your beauty to each hard-earned harvest. And then you'll die for Bellefleur, just the way my mother died. And in the end you'll know it was my father who killed you, just like he's killing me."

Chelsea hated herself for asking, but she had to. "Franklin, if Bellefleur were yours, what would you do with it? How would you change it; what would you do differently?"

"I'd sell it to Quaid Tanner or to the highest bidder within an hour of acquiring the property," Franklin said coldly. "I see your new husband is about to descend on us. I'll take my leave." Another grimace whipped across Franklin's face, and then he melted into the crowd.

Harlow placed his arm familiarly around Chelsea's shoul-

ders. She wanted to shrug it off but knew she couldn't. Instead she smiled at her husband.

"What did Franklin have to say?" he asked.

"He wished us well and said I made a beautiful bride,"
Chelsea said.

"I find that hard to believe, but I'll take your word for
it. You'd never lie to your husband, would you, Chelsea?"
There was an undeniable threat beneath the simple words.

The party seemed to go on forever before the musicians
wound down and the last lingering guests retired for the
night. In the morning, after breakfast, all of them would
be gone. Franklin was helping Harlow up the stairs. She
hadn't seen the young man take a drink, and she'd watched
him when the toast was made. He'd brought the glass to
his lips but hadn't swallowed. Harlow, on the other hand,
had consumed great quantities of the grape.

"Hadn't you better be getting upstairs to my father?"
Martha asked quietly.

"Don't worry about me," Chelsea replied. "I know what's
expected of me, and I was never one to shirk my duty."

"I want the money, Chelsea. My ship leaves Sydney in a
week. I'm packed, and the arrangements have been made.
Don't disappoint me."

"I wouldn't dream of it. We made a bargain, and I'll
hold to my end. You'll have your money when it's time to
leave. I promise."

"I haven't congratulated you, have I?" Martha raised an
imaginary glass. "To you, Chelsea. May your life here be
as happy as mine. I wish you longevity and the patience to
endure. Go upstairs to *him* and try to pretend it's Quaid
Tanner instead of a hateful old man," she said scornfully.
"Tomorrow's another day; you can run off to see your
lover then."

The sharp crack of the slap echoed in the still room, and
even Chelsea flinched. The red mark on Martha's cheek

and the tears that sprang to her eyes made Chelsea want to cry, too. It had been a long day, and she was tired and dreading what lay ahead of her. "I'm sorry, Martha. I shouldn't have done that. Forgive me."

Martha's narrow shoulders slumped. "No, I was hateful. I deserved that. My nerves are getting the better of me."

"Don't explain. I understand. Please go to bed, now. And sleep well. Dream about your prince in England and how you'll soon be with him. I envy you. What you're doing takes courage, more than I have."

"Will you take care of Emma?"

"Of course. She'll miss you terribly. Trust me, Martha."

When Martha turned to face Chelsea, her smile was warm and genuine. "I do. Somehow, I do. I even feel sorry for you, Chelsea."

"Don't waste your tears on me. This journey began a long time ago with one little lie. I'll learn to live with it."

Upstairs, Chelsea closed the bedroom door behind her. She was alone. Alone, to wait for her husband to come to her. There was no urgency to shed her clothes, no anticipation to climb into the big bed. Someone, probably Bette, had laid her pale blue nightdress across the bed. The covers were already turned down.

Methodically, Chelsea undressed, leaving her wedding dress in a careless heap on the floor at the foot of the bed. She bathed her face in cool water and quickly sponged her body. Cologne was patted behind her ears and between her breasts, a dab of scent on a linen handkerchief placed beneath her pillow.

Wanting to do anything to delay getting into the double bed, Chelsea crossed the room to open the door a crack. She still had her hand on the knob when Harlow appeared.

"I do like an eager woman," he leered as he closed the door behind him.

Unceremoniously, he stripped out of his clothes, then

walked jerkily to the bed and almost fell into it. His breath reeked of wine, and Chelsea could smell the ripe odor of sweat emanating from under his arms. She tried to smile; this was, after all, her wedding night.

The bed creaked and groaned with Harlow's weight as he struggled to stretch his perspiring body over Chelsea. She tried to ease her own position, but Harlow's hands and mouth were all over her. She felt herself pinned beneath him as his mouth sought hers. Then the sour taste of wine invaded her mouth and she cried out, thrashing beneath him. She didn't know if her cry excited him or angered him, for suddenly he was biting her, her shoulders, her neck, her breasts. She cried out again in pain.

Spittle dripped onto her chest; she could feel the sliminess of it. She swallowed hard, willing it all to be over. She felt her knees brutally jerked apart, and again she cried out as he stabbed into her, ruthlessly invading her unwilling flesh.

An eternity later, he rolled off her. She struggled to bring her legs together, the ache in her thighs as real as the pain in her back. She knew she was covered with bruises and teeth marks. Shame pierced through her. She had been degraded, abused, and humiliated.

Long into the night Chelsea lay beside Harlow, listening to his breathing, her eyes staring at the ceiling. At one point a sob caught in her throat, and tears ran silently down her cheeks. Once again Harlow had proven how ugly the sex act could be without love.

When Chelsea awakened the next morning, she was surprised to find she'd slept at all. Harlow was gone. The day on Bellefleur had already begun. Gingerly, aware of each bruise her husband had inflicted upon her, she crept out of bed. She didn't want to stay in this room a moment longer than necessary. She washed, wishing she could linger in a long, hot bath.

From her window she could see work progressing in the

garden. A good reason to dress and escape the house for the outdoors, where she hoped the air and sunshine would chase away last night's ugliness.

Chelsea walked outside to observe the gardeners as they dug and spaded the hard-packed earth. Great barrels of water stood ready to moisten the flowers and shrubbery. It kept her mind occupied as she referred to the diagram showing what was to be planted where. From time to time she made a suggestion and was pleased to see that the workmen did her bidding without argument. She wouldn't think about Quaid, and she wouldn't think about Harlow. She was also going to try not to think about dinner this evening, when Martha planned to announce that she was sailing for England at the end of the week. Still musing over the probable effect of Martha's announcement, Chelsea stepped onto the veranda, which was slightly cooler than the yard. It was pleasant, she decided, the white wicker furniture an effective contrast to the highly polished floor with the woven mats.

"Emma, what are you doing here?"

Emma smiled. "Thinking."

"About what?"

"About Martha and how I'm going to feel when she leaves. She plans to tell Father tonight at dinner, you know. Her trunks and bags are all packed. I said she could take a lot of things that were my mother's. I won't have any use for them, and if Martha is going to marry, she'll need them. Wasn't that nice of me, Chelsea?"

"It was very nice. Of course you're going to miss Martha. She's going to miss you, too. But she'll write and send presents to you. You'll like that. And I'll be here for you to talk to. We can really get to know one another."

"Martha said I'll miss her at first and then I'll forget her. That's not true."

"No, it isn't, but Martha didn't want you to feel bad."

"Father isn't going to let her go. I wanted to tell Martha that, but I didn't."

"Emma, Martha has the money for the passage. Your father won't stop her. There's nothing for her here."

"He won't like it. She wanted to go before. She cried for weeks, and he still wouldn't let her go."

An uneasy feeling settled over Chelsea. "Emma, you didn't say anything to your father or to Franklin, did you?"

"Gracious, no! Martha made me promise not to. Chelsea, do you think a man will ever want to marry me? I don't know if I would like living with a strange man and taking off my clothes so he could look at me. I don't like babies, either. They cry too much."

"Where is Martha? I haven't seen her all day."

"Hiding in her room. She does that sometimes. She's reading William's letters. Then she answers them but doesn't mail her answers. Father won't allow it. The only reason she has mail from William is because Mr. Tanner brings it from town. Father doesn't know." Emma chortled.

"Mr. Tanner does that for Martha?" Chelsea asked in surprise.

"Yes, I just found out myself. Martha told me before the wedding. That's why she used to walk to Mr. Tanner's house. If Father ever found out he'd be very angry."

"I thought you said that Martha was smitten with Mr. Tanner."

"I did think that, and I told her so, but she set me straight. Do you like me, Chelsea?" Emma asked suddenly.

Emma, as Chelsea had found out, could never stay on any one subject for very long. Her mind constantly wandered to different things, particularly to her romantic notions. "Of course I like you."

"Do you think a man will ever kiss me? Not just any man, but a man like Mr. Tanner."

"One day when it's time for you to be kissed, some man

will come along and sweep you off your feet," Chelsea said, and hoped she sounded convincing.

"No, they won't. I'm different. I'm not like Martha and you. Father says I take after Mama's side of the family. I have three witless aunts, he told me. Am I witless, Chelsea?"

"No ... of course not." Chelsea faltered. "You're a very sweet young lady, and I like you a lot. We're going to be good friends."

Emma picked herself up, gathered together her books and her satchel of needlework, waved airily in Chelsea's direction, and left without another word. A sinking feeling settled in Chelsea's stomach, and she swallowed hard. What would Harlow say when Martha told him she was leaving?

Suddenly Tingari appeared on the veranda. "Mitjitji, Miss Martha calls you."

"That's fine, Tingari. Tell Miss Martha that I'll be there in a moment—and will you bring me a glass of lemonade, and one for Martha, too?"

"The wind is bad today," Tingari said.

"What does that mean'?" Chelsea asked anxiously. Ever since Quaid had appeared at the garden house, Chelsea paid rapt attention to anything Tingari said.

"It means trouble, Mitjitji. The scent is in the air. Before the day is over there will be much trouble."

Chelsea snorted. She didn't need Tingari to tell her that. The minute Martha told her father she was leaving, there was going to be an explosion.

"Tingari, I'm new here, I don't know all of my husband's ways yet, but Martha is his daughter and he will be fair. I think. I hope."

"It will not be," was Tingari's stolid prediction.

"Come in," Martha called when Chelsea rapped on the door.

"You look very busy," Chelsea said, eyeing the array of clothing and the open trunks strewn about the room. There was no sign of Emma.

"I am. Chelsea, when are you going to give me the money?" Martha said anxiously. "I have to pay for my passage ticket."

"In plenty of time. You can purchase your ticket an hour before sailing. You aren't going to have a problem. There's no way you can get into Sydney before the weekend. I won't fail you."

"No, I don't think you will," Martha said thoughtfully. "You look different somehow. Isn't married life agreeing with you?"

Chelsea chose to ignore the hateful question, and it was hateful—she could tell by the gleam in Martha's eyes. How quickly she could change! One minute she acted as if she cared and would show concern, and the next it was almost as if given the chance, Martha would throw her to the dogs. "I'm fine. I think I'm worried about you. Tingari expressed concern. Those people seem to have a sixth sense at times. She also claims to know your father rather well."

"Do you find that hard to believe? Men, especially men around here, take their loving where they find it. I think Franklin is following in Father's footsteps with Tingari."

Chelsea gasped. "Martha!"

"Why are you surprised? Franklin has no time to go into Sydney, and there are no young women close by. You know it's early to bed and early to rise around here, especially during vintage. A man needs to have a woman from time to time."

"But he's so young compared—"

"And aren't *you* young compared to my father?"

"That's different."

"I didn't say Franklin was going to marry Tingari, I just said I thought he was sleeping with her."

Chelsea had seen no sign of it from Tingari. Her face was inscrutable. "Martha, I hesitate to mention this, but I could ask Tingari to make you a potion."

Martha's shrill laughter circled the room and seemed to settle directly over Chelsea's head. "A potion! Why would I need a potion? I don't believe in Tingari's black magic. I find all of this highly amusing. You're supposed to be so educated, Chelsea."

"I know it works. I—I experienced one of her spells."

Martha tossed a stack of petticoats into the trunk, an uneasy look on her face. "What kind of potion? What will it do?" she found herself asking.

"Whatever you want it to do. I think Tingari is worried about what your father is going to do when you tell him this evening. He certainly isn't going to take it lightly. You know that. I myself am concerned. You are his eldest daughter, and he isn't going to want you to go so far away."

"Oh, pooh, is that all? Tell Tingari to keep her potion. I'm going, and that's all there is to it. I'm all packed except for this trunk. I wasn't sure if I could count on Franklin to take me to the ship, so I asked Helen Bakus if her husband would drive me. Everything is settled. Father can't stop me."

Chelsea wished she felt as confident as Martha sounded. "Well, the decision is up to you, of course. Now, I'll leave you to finish your packing. I'll see you at dinner."

Martha took a deep breath and exhaled slowly when the door closed behind Chelsea. She was frightened, almost out of her wits. In the end, what could her father do, except beat her or forbid her to leave? In either case she would still leave. A potion might alleviate some of the pain of the beating, but she would still carry the scars of it in her heart. Whatever was to be, would be.

It was time to attend to some of her wifely duties, Chelsea thought as she made her way down the stairs. Dinner was progressing nicely. Fresh-baked bread was cooling on a long wooden table. Garden-picked greens were being pared and chopped. Whatever was in the pot was fragrant and simmering, sending its aroma throughout the house. A huge pan containing a cherry cobbler sat next to the cooling bread. Chelsea picked at the flaky crust and smiled her approval at the cook.

From her inspection of the kitchen, Chelsea made her way to the back porch, where Bette was wringing wet clothes to hang on lines that ran from the porch to the trees. Bed sheets, pillow slips, and towels sat in a sodden mound waiting to be hung.

If she had the buggy prepared, she could drive to Quaid's house in minutes. Her tawny eyes looked down the road.

"It does no good to dream, Mitjitji," Tingari said softly, coming up behind her.

"I know," Chelsea replied just as softly. "I'm trying, but sometimes I can't help myself."

"Mr. Tanner was a fine man."

Chelsea's eyes widened. "You make it sound as though he's dead."

"To you, Mitjitji. You are Boss Kane's woman now."

Tears burned her eyes. "Yes, I know. It must get better as the days go on. Tingari, this is none of my business, but are you and Franklin . . ."

"If it not Mitjitji's business, do not ask. There is work."

Chelsea grimaced. How like Tingari to put her in her place. Shaking her head, she entered the house. Maybe a nap before dinner. If she did that, she wouldn't be able to sleep tonight. With nothing else to do, Chelsea lay down on the bed and closed her eyes. She wouldn't sleep; she'd just rest.

Emma rapped on Chelsea's door shortly before the dinner hour. "Are you sleeping, Chelsea? It's almost time for dinner," she said, poking her head in the doorway.

"I guess I did doze off. Thank you for waking me. I'll be down in a few minutes. Go along, Emma, you don't have to wait for me."

Chelsea picked through her dinner. Emma stirred her food with her fork and looked constantly at her sister. Martha's eyes were unusually bright, and there was a flush on her cheeks. She was eating her dinner slowly and methodically. Harlow stared at her several times, and Chelsea could sense the tension building at the table. Franklin watched his father and had little to say. Conversation for the most part had been limited, as always, to talk of the grapes, the bottling, and the huge new oaken barrels. It was all so boring, Chelsea thought she could fall asleep and not miss a thing. She took a large gulp of the vin ordinaire when she saw the rest of her life stretch before her. Thousands of dinners, just like this one. Good God, what had she done?

The moment Martha laid her fork down and folded her napkin, Chelsea's back stiffened. Emma slid down in her chair, trying to make herself invisible. Franklin's eyebrows rose, as did Harlow's. "Father, I'd like to speak with you," Martha said nervously.

"I'm listening. What is it, daughter?"

"I wanted to tell you that I'm leaving. On Saturday. I should have told you sooner, but I—"

Harlow was half out of his chair. "Leaving? For where? I don't remember giving you permission to go anywhere. Sydney is no place for a woman alone. You aren't going anywhere, Martha, so get that notion out of your head. You just came back from Sydney."

"I'm going to England."

Harlow threw back his head and roared with laughter. But it didn't sound funny to Chelsea, and Martha wasn't smiling. Franklin's face looked as if it were carved from stone. Emma giggled as she slid farther down on her chair.

After a moment Harlow sobered. "England? Do you plan to swim? Where would you get the money to go to England?"

"William sent me the passage money," Martha said. "I'm going, Father."

"You aren't going anywhere, you're staying right here. I'll not have some scoundrel putting in claims on my lands. I told you he was no good! I ran him off and I'd do it again! You just get all these notions out of your head."

Father and daughter were both standing now; their chairs pushed back behind them. "I said I'm leaving," Martha said firmly. "My trunks are packed, and Mr. Bakus is driving me to the ship. Everything has been taken care of."

Chelsea cowered in her chair. She saw the blow coming, but Martha had turned her back on Harlow. It caught her on the left side of the head. She staggered and screamed for Franklin to help her. Harlow's hands pulled and yanked at Martha's hair, spinning her around to face him. He slapped her and beat at her face with his closed fists. Martha screamed again for Franklin and then for Emma, who was hiding beneath the table.

The sound of Martha's gown ripping sent Chelsea into a tizzy. She knew she would hear Martha's screams for days, just as she would see her bruised and battered face for the rest of her life. She was about to get up from her chair and intervene when she felt Tingari's strong hands on her shoulders, pinning her to her chair.

"Now tell me you're going to that low life you call a man," Harlow thundered.

Martha's mouth would swell to twice its size. Her nose was bleeding, and one eye was nearly closed. A long scratch ran down the length of her narrow cheekbone, but still she managed to stare defiantly at her father. "I'm going!"

Chelsea later swore she had felt the blow that Harlow dealt his daughter. Tingari's strong hands dug deeper into her shoulders.

"Tell me again, daughter, what you're going to do," Harlow raged.

Martha was on her knees as her father kicked at her with his knee, sending her sprawling across the room. And when she tried to get to her knees, he kicked her again. "We'll just see how far you'll get," he said, and scooped her up like a lifeless kitten. He carried her to the front door and kicked at it until Franklin scurried to his side to open it.

"Boss Kane throws his child into the dirt," Tingari said emotionlessly. "His *mamu* will suffer."

"I don't believe what I just saw. I can't believe it. No man, no father acts like that. Why didn't Franklin help her?"

"Boss Kane is hard on women. He would be harder on his son. Believe this, Mitjitji, you must not interfere."

"Go to her, Tingari. Help her. Do something. Please," Chelsea pleaded. "Take her to Mr. Tanner's house. Tell him I—"

"Tingari knows. Listen well, do not interfere."

As if she would. For the rest of her life the scene she had just witnessed would stay with her. What was she supposed to do? Ignore the entire incident? Confess her part in it? Did she dare to openly despise Harlow's brutality?

"Emma, get out from under the table. Sit here next to me," Chelsea said urgently. But Emma refused to budge, and in the end Chelsea got up from the table and made her way to the foyer and the stairway. She refused to look at Harlow when she walked past him. There was more than one way to show contempt.

Chapter 14

Chelsea lay awake the entire night, listening for Harlow's footsteps, waiting for him to come to their room and dreading that he would. When the new day crept over the hills, Tingari opened the door and came into her room. She searched the Aboriginal's eyes for knowledge of Martha. "Tell me," she asked hoarsely, wanting to know, fearing the answer.

"She is with Tanner. She is in his good hands."

"What did Mr. Tanner say?"

"It is what he did not say," Tingari whispered. "Martha will go to the sailing ship. Tanner does this for you, Mitjitji. Tingari has been sent to bring Martha's trunks."

"How can we do this?"

"When Boss Kane go to wine house. I will carry the trunks to the road to meet Tanner. Do nothing, Mitjitji. Tingari and Tanner do all."

Quaid was coming here, as near as the road? If only she could touch him, see him. There was nothing she could do but remain in the house and keep watch. "Harlow will kill you, Tingari, if he learns you helped Martha."

"No, Mitjitji. Boss Kane will not touch me. I fear for you." She opened her hand, and there on the startling white palm lay a string of small dark beads no larger than apple seeds. "Mitjitji wear this, it is good *mamu* and keep you safe."

Chelsea remembered the potion Martha had refused and gladly took the beads.

"The others wait to eat," Tingari told her.

"No. I don't want to see Harlow—or Franklin, either. Let them have breakfast without me," Chelsea said adamantly.

"Yes, you eat," Tingari insisted.

"I'm not going to sit across from those two men and try to make polite conversation. They disgust me, both of them! And there's something I want to know. Are you sleeping with Franklin, Tingari?"

"It is not important for Mitjitji. I do what I must. My reasons are my own."

"I think you should make a potion to get rid of both of them. What Harlow did to Martha last night was horrible, and Franklin never lifted a finger to help his sister."

Tingari frowned in disapproval. "Potions and *mamu* are for good, Mitjitji. Evil potions, evil Boss Kane, it is the same."

Chelsea realized her mistake. The magic Tingari practiced was only to protect, never to harm; by telling the Aboriginal to do so, she had put her in the same class as Harlow. "Tingari, I never meant to insult you or to take your magic lightly."

"Tingari knows," she replied, having already forgiven Chelsea. "Food will come to you, Tingari will bring it. Mitjitji must be strong."

A while later there was a soft tapping at the door, and Harlow entered dressed in his work clothes. He wished her a good morning and asked how she felt. Then, "Chelsea, I noticed last evening that you avoided me, and I thought I would give you a chance to calm yourself before we talked. I sense you disapprove of the way I handled Martha's ridiculous outburst last evening. She is my daughter, and she will do as I say. A dutiful daughter obeys her father or suffers the consequences. Martha will come crawling back when she sees the error of her ways. She has no clothing, no money. She can't go far. Understand, Chelsea, I am not apologizing for my rightful authority as her father."

Chelsea sank deeper into the pillows. She forgot Tingari's warnings and blurted, "You were so brutal! She's a woman, how could you beat her with your fists? Would you do that to me if I displeased you? And your son, what kind of man is he to allow his sister to be beaten? I could never respect a man like that. I will never forget that scene, ever. Poor Emma hid under the table."

"My family is my business, as is how I deal with them. I will not tolerate interference from you or anyone." Harlow shoved his hands into his pockets. How dare she criticize him! His eyes narrowed with suspicion. "Did you have anything to do with what happened last night? Did you fill Martha's head with ideas of England and love and other foolishness?"

"Of course not. Martha has a mind of her own. I don't see anything wrong with her wanting to go to England. She said she has family there and the young man she loves. There doesn't seem to be much here except living the life of a spinster, pitied by the other women, with only Emma for company. Surely you don't want that for her, do you?"

The answer was in his eyes. He wanted to be in total control of everyone and everything. "I knew you were a domineering man, Harlow." Chelsea said at last. "I just didn't know until last evening to what lengths you would go to remain in control. She's a woman, with a woman's needs; why can't you allow her a little happiness?"

"Be careful how you speak to me, Chelsea. I told you

my children are my concern, not yours. When Martha comes back with her tail between her legs, she'll understand the way she is to live her life."

The beads beneath Chelsea's nightdress gave her the courage to speak out boldly. "You don't know your daughter, Harlow. If you did, you'd know she will never come back here. And I don't blame her. First of all, she's in love, and you've no right to deny her that happiness. Secondly, she could never live here after what you did to her. She must hate you and Franklin." Chelsea was breathless by the time she'd finished, but her hands never left the beads at her throat.

Harlow's face was purple with rage. "You'd better hope you're wrong, otherwise I'll be forced to think you had something to do with all of this." He moved a menacing step closer to the bed and stared intensely at Chelsea. "Pray my daughter comes back to this house."

Chelsea managed to meet Harlow's gaze and hold it. "She won't be back, know it now. But before you begin placing blame, look to yourself and your own relationship with your children. It wouldn't surprise me if Franklin wasn't contemplating the same move as Martha." There, that would give him something to think about. His son leaving, his right hand abandoning Bellefleur.

She was gasping for breath when the door closed behind her husband. For a moment she'd believed he was going to strike her.

When Tingari returned with Chelsea's breakfast, she found her mistress in a state of distress. "Tingari, Harlow won't be able to stop Martha, will he?"

"Tanner is smart, Mitjitji."

"What if Harlow decides to go to Sydney and force Martha to come home?"

"Boss Kane's pride will not allow him to think so far.

He rules with a strong hand. He threw his child in the dirt with nothing," Tingari said. "He does not believe she can go without a dress and money."

"What about when he sees her trunks are gone?" Chelsea wondered nervously. "Listen, Tingari, I have an idea. We'll send Martha my trunks. They're stored in the garden house. We'll simply transfer her clothes and hope to buy her time. We could fill Martha's trunks with bedding and lay some nightclothes on top. I don't think Harlow will go through them; just seeing them will be enough. We'll have to get Emma out of the way. Where is she?"

"She trims corks for her brother in the wine house."

"Then we've got to move fast."

Two hours later, all of Martha's clothing and some of her own were nestled in Honoria Harris's trunks. Thank God she would never have to look at them again.

Chelsea watched in wonder as Tingari bent down and picked up one of the heavy trunks. She did a balancing act for a second or two until she had the trunk on her shoulder. Chelsea knew that it would have taken Franklin and another man to carry the trunk out to the road. Tingari made three more trips, then returned to the garden house for the pouch of money.

Chelsea raced back to Martha's room to make sure her hurried job of stuffing Martha's trunks would pass muster. Satisfied with the disarray she had created, she made her way back downstairs to the dining room. "Fetch me two cups of coffee," she told a startled servant. She would sit here until Tingari returned. Childishly, she crossed her fingers. It would all work out.

Saturday, the day Martha's ship sailed, was hot and airless. Emma was at her worst, whining fretfully, refusing to go to the winery with her father. Chelsea sat through lunch with her teeth clenched. As usual, Franklin glowered at her the whole time. Chelsea knew she wouldn't draw a free breath until after sundown when the ship sailed. Was Quaid still in Sydney waiting to see Martha off? She hoped so. How much did Emma know or suspect? As far as she could tell, Martha's trunks were still the way she'd left them. Bette had told her that Mr. Kane had gone once to Martha's room to see if things were intact. Then, satisfied his daughter's fate was still in his hands, he had closed the door and, as far as anyone knew, had not entered it again.

Chelsea did not like what was happening to Harlow, and she felt as though she were walking on eggshells. He took pleasure in goading poor Emma and enjoying her misery. She missed Martha terribly and at meals the empty chair was a constant reminder. Harlow's suspicions were aroused as to Chelsea's part in Martha's mutiny, and he treated her with contemptuous politeness.

"I miss Martha," Emma cried suddenly as they ate lunch. "She's not coming back, is she? Today is the day her ship leaves for England! I want to go with her!"

Startled at Emma's outburst, Chelsea dropped her fork and it clattered onto her plate.

"That's enough, Emma," Harlow commanded. "Martha isn't going anywhere. When she's had enough of scavenging the hills, she'll be back. She has nothing, everything she owns is here; she has no money, no clothes, and no way of obtaining any."

"I want her here now. I'm tired of cutting corks in the winery. I miss Martha," Emma continued to whine defiantly. "Martha has money, she has lots of money. She can buy new clothes. She isn't coming back. I know she isn't."

"Emma! Martha has nothing I didn't give her. She will return. You, meanwhile, are to go back to the winery and help Franklin. It's your duty!"

Franklin stood abruptly, the expression of rampant disgust unmistakable. Chelsea believed she had fallen into a snake pit.

Emma began to cry, great heaving sobs. If she'd hoped for comfort from Harlow, she was disappointed. Disgusted with her, he stomped out of the house, leaving Chelsea to comfort her and take her to her room. "She isn't coming back, is she, Chelsea?" Emma sobbed.

"No, she isn't. You'll have to get used to not having Martha around. When she's settled she'll send for you. Martha won't break her promise."

"I wish you'd never given her the money. I know where she is, I watched Tingari."

Emma's words unnerved Chelsea. This girl could destroy everything, all of them. When she spoke, her voice betrayed her by quivering. "What are you talking about, Emma? What money? I thought Martha's young man sent her the money."

"Martha told me, it was a secret. She said you got it from Mr. Tanner for her. Martha couldn't keep the secret from me. I can keep a secret; I didn't tell Father."

"And you won't, will you!" It was a command.

"Not if you..." Emma lifted her eyes to look at Chelsea and seemed to change her mind. "I just told you I can keep a secret, I'm tired, I want to sleep," she said as she lay back on her bed, curling herself into a ball and pulling the edge of the coverlet under her chin.

Chelsea watched helplessly as Emma drifted off to sleep. With Emma, there were no guarantees. She might pick up her thoughts immediately when she woke, or she might not mention anything about it for days. How was she to cajole this fey girl into keeping quiet? Right now, all she needed were hours of quiet until Martha's ship set sail. She would stay right here with Emma until she awoke and then keep her busy.

The room was quiet and dim with the curtains drawn. Chelsea sat with a book open on her lap. Her thoughts, however, were on Quaid. When tears gathered in her eyes and her heart skipped beats, she forced her thoughts to Emma and what her damaging words could do to life at Bellefleur. From now on she was going to have to be Emma's constant companion. Her shadow. Hopefully, it would keep the young woman under control.

When Emma woke shortly before dusk, Chelsea was aware, even in the dimness of the room, that the girl's eyes were feverish. She leaned over and felt her forehead. "Are you feeling all right, Emma?"

"I don't feel very good," Emma said in her best little-girl voice. "I don't think I can go down to dinner."

"I'll have a tray sent up, something light. Bette will stay with you." How relieved she sounded to her own ears. A reprieve. Now all she had to do was keep Emma away from Harlow a little while longer, and Martha would be safe. That *she* would suffer the consequences was something she couldn't think of right now. She sat with Emma a while longer to see if the girl would mention Martha. Harlow, she knew, would never bother to check on his daughter, leaving such things to her and the servants.

Chelsea dressed for dinner that evening with extra care. She felt jittery and out of sorts as she made her way down to the dining room for dinner. She didn't know why. Perhaps it was Tingari's dark gaze or the implacable look on her face.

There was only Harlow and herself at dinner. Chelsea went on at great lengths about Emma and how feverish she was. Harlow nodded and commended her solicitude in regard to his daughter. Chelsea forced smile after smile to her lips as she spoke of one thing and another. The dinner plates were being carried out to the kitchen to make way for the rich dessert Harlow favored when Chelsea saw Bette walk past the dining room door to return Emma's tray to the kitchen.

Chelsea's stomach started to churn. She shouldn't have left the girl alone. Suddenly Emma appeared in her nightdress, her face shiny clean. The long braid hanging down her back made her look winsome and woebegone. Chelsea sucked in her breath, eyes wide with apprehension. It was coming—her moment of reckoning spurred on by this witless woman-child. She could feel it in every bone in her body. Martha was safely out to sea now, and there was nothing Harlow could do to bring her back. The thought only made her more uneasy. She was going to pay for the help she had given Harlow's daughter.

"Father, you must come with me. I have something I want you to see. You lied to me," she accused. "You said Martha was coming back. Come, Father."

Harlow's eyes narrowed. Chelsea sat rooted to her chair. Tingari stood outside the dining room door, her large arms folded across her ample breast, watching, waiting. Chelsea listened to Harlow's booted steps going up the stairs and down the corridor to Martha's room. Minutes later the thunderclap of the slamming door shuddered through her.

"Why?" Harlow bellowed as he entered the dining room. "What you have done is unforgivable. Why did you interfere?"

The black rage on Harlow's face was directed at her and more awesome than his attack on Martha. Chelsea trembled with fear as Harlow towered over her. "It was best for Martha," she managed to reply.

"Who are you to decide what is best for my daughter? I'm the only one to decide that. How dare you interfere with my orders?"

"I didn't decide, Harlow," Chelsea said, rising to face

him. "Your daughter decided. Yes, it's true that I helped
her. She asked for my help. I couldn't refuse her."

"And where did you get the money to give her?" Harlow demanded murderously.

"You know very well where I got the money. Emma told
you. Martha's gone now, sailing to England. It's done
with. History. We can't dwell on it now. We should both
drink a toast with your finest wine to your daughter's happiness," she said defiantly.

"A toast with vinegar to that slut would be asking too
much. You've made me a laughingstock. You betrayed me
to my enemy. I'll never be able to hold my head up again.
My wife, going to that man. What exactly did you do for
Tanner to get the money for Martha? . . . Answer me,
damn you!"

Chelsea backed up a step and then another as Harlow
advanced upon her. "I sold him a ring. A ring that meant a
great deal to me and that was given to me out of . . . out of
love. I also sold it at a great loss. It was very valuable, but
I thought that . . . Martha was so unhappy." There was no
need for Harlow to know that the whole episode had
started out as a blackmailing scheme and ended up with
her wanting desperately to help the unhappy young woman.

"A likely story. This sordid little escapade will be all
over Sydney by now." Harlow cut short his scathing
words and glowered murderously at Chelsea. It was what
he wasn't saying that made Chelsea back closer to the
door where Tingari stood.

"Boss Kane wants vengeance," Tingari hissed in
Chelsea's ear.

Chelsea heard the words, but her eyes were on Harlow
as he thundered from the room. She turned and fell into
Tingari's arms. "What will he do to me?"

"I do not know, Mitjitji. You have taken his control,
and he will not forgive. He is shamed."

"What if he does to me what he did to Martha?"

"Boss Kane is hard on women. His *mamu*, his spirit, is cruel and mean. Men of this *mamu* do not enjoy old age." Tingari's fathomless black eyes, rife with mystical knowledge, pierced Chelsea.

"Where will I go?" she cried. "What would I do? The friends I met here are Harlow's; they won't take me into their homes against his will. . . . No, I'm being silly. I'm his wife; what I've done really isn't terrible. He wouldn't treat me as he did Martha." Even to her own ears her words lacked conviction.

"Mitjitji, there is Tanner."

"No. Never. I can't ask for his charity, I can't go to him like a whipped dog. Harlow simply would not throw me out of this house. He wouldn't."

"Mitjitji forgets young boss."

"Franklin? What does that mean?"

"Young boss is angry and filled with hate. He would like Mitjitji to be gone. Always a son can talk to his father."

Chelsea fumed. "You're being ridiculous. I know Franklin is jealous and angry that I've come to Bellefleur. He feels he's working to support me, and his share of Bellefleur will be less. But he would never . . ." Her words trailed away as she stared at the tall Aboriginal. "How do you know how angry Franklin is?"

"Tingari knows."

"Tingari knows because she sleeps with him." Chelsea seethed. "You don't like him, why do you do it? He's using you!"

The Aboriginal shook her head. "No. Tingari used him. I carry a child."

"Oh, no!" Chelsea sputtered, already contemplating the consequences. Harlow and Franklin would throw Tingari off Bellefleur as soon as they found out. Sleeping with an

Aboriginal was one thing, having a mixed-breed bastard running around the place was another entirely. "Why didn't you make one of your potions? Why didn't you do something?"

"Tingari never hoped to have a child, " she replied, placing one of her huge hands on her belly. "This is my joy!" She beamed. "Mitjitji should make a child. You would always have a home on Bellefleur."

There was truth in what Tingari was saying, but the idea was abhorrent to her. "No. Not if it can be helped. Do you think I would want a child of Harlow's after I see what kind of man he is and what his seed spawns? Another witless Emma; a surly, unloving Franklin; another scheming Martha? No, Tingari, I couldn't."

Tingari turned Chelsea to face her, her large, slender hands cupping her mistress's face. "Mitjitji, a child is a child," she said slowly, meaningfully. "A child would protect you. Any man can plant his seed; a child belongs to its mother."

Chelsea's eyes widened. "Are you suggesting I find any man to give me a child?" she gasped. There was no reply from Tingari. "I couldn't," she bleated. "No, I couldn't."

"Mitjitji will have a child. It is better she chooses the father."

"It's too cold, too callous."

"Tingari thinks Mitjitji chooses Tanner."

"Men have ethics, too," Chelsea said. "Doing that to Quaid would be unthinkable."

"Think how you would feel birthing Boss Kane's seed. A man does not know what becomes of his seed once it is spent. Mitjitji, I stay here when another woman sleep in your bed. Again, I remind you Boss Kane is hard on women. That other woman was old before her time, her *mamu* died and then her body."

Chelsea thought of the nights when Harlow came to her

room, of the ugly, loveless couplings and his forceful taking of her even when her body was not ready or receptive.
Never a tender kiss or a fond caress, nothing to stir her to
anything even resembling passion. He was methodical and
quick, not caring that she was stiff and unyielding and her
body dry and resistant. Her mirror told her what those
nights were doing to her. Circles beneath her eyes, a new
tightening around her mouth. Gasping like a fish out of
water, Chelsea struggled to speak. "How . . . how should I
do this? When?"

"Mitjitji knows how. Whatever is Mitjitji's moon cycle.
Nine days after."

Chelsea's brain clicked as she counted on her fingers.
The flush on her cheeks brought a smile to Tingari's generous mouth. "Three days, three more days."

Harlow Kane climbed out of the deep bowels of his
winery to stand at the small narrow window that had been
cut into the four-foot-thick masonry walls, watching his
wife as she strolled among the newly planted flower beds.
His eyes narrowed. She was beautiful, and she was his.
Her defense of Martha had come as a shock to him; more,
it was a personal betrayal. Everyone on Bellefleur had his
place, and Chelsea was no exception. She'd had no right to
defy him and to intervene for Martha. It was the fact that
she had elicited the help of Quaid Tanner that cut him to
the quick. She'd sold a ring to him. And what else? he
wondered spitefully. He could feel heat rushing through
him at the thought of Chelsea and Tanner together. But he
had no proof, and accusations were a waste of time. His
gut churned as his imagination played vividly. He hated—
a deep, searing hatred—the man who was his neighbor
and possibly his wife's lover.

Then Harlow did something foreign to him. He tossed
his smock onto a bench and left the winery before midday.

His step was firm and purposeful as he joined Chelsea in the garden. "Come with me," he demanded hoarsely.

"What's wrong, Harlow?"

"Nothing. I merely wish to exercise my conjugal rights."

"Now? It's mid—"

"Don't argue, you've done enough of that. Get into the house."

In the bright sunlight of her bedroom, Chelsea watched as Harlow stripped naked; then, at his stern urgings, she undid the buttons of her gown. She could feel the burning flush of shame color her flesh as Harlow's eyes licked at her nakedness.

Obscenities rolled off his tongue as he dragged her to the bed, and she squeezed her eyes shut and tensed for the onslaught. When it was over he stood beside the bed viewing her nakedness. His expression was cold and half-mocking as he watched the agony in her eyes turn to shame. Carelessly he tossed her the coverlet.

Tingari was sitting on the back porch, an odious-smelling cigar clamped between her teeth. Smoky spirals surrounded the Aboriginal's closely shorn head. "What did you mean yesterday when you said men of evil *mamu* did not enjoy old age?" Chelsea demanded, hatred for Harlow flooding her senses.

Tingari shrugged, but her expression told Chelsea she knew something.

"Tell me, dammit! I need to know! Did you mean he's going to die?" Chelsea was aghast to hear the hope in her tone, but honest enough to acknowledge it as such. "Tell me!"

"I have thrown his stones." She took another puff on the foul cigar, evidently taking great pleasure from it.

"And you've thrown my stones, too, haven't you? That's why you said I need a baby."

"Why does Mitjitji speak with Tingari? Things bad when Boss Kane takes you to your room?"

"They never go well, but today was beyond insult. What did my stones say?"

Tingari looked silently at her mistress. "They say you need a baby."

"Do you throw stones for yourself?"

Now there was a reaction in Tingari—anger. "No! Tingari never do that. I am a woman of magic and Dreamtime. It is forbidden to me to throw my stones." A tragic expression filled those ebony eyes, and Chelsea knew Tingari was lying. She had thrown her own stones and was frightened of what she had seen.

Chapter 15

Chelsea slapped the reins on the bay's broad rump as she steered the buggy down the road toward Clonmerra. Her heart pounded even louder than the hooves of the bay, and today the abominable red dust went unnoticed. She could think of nothing at this moment except Quaid's reaction to her arrival. Dear God, what would he think of her? Married less than a month and already beating a path to his door. A baby. Quaid's baby. Tingari had said it, and so it must be true. A baby to hold and to love; Quaid's baby.

Over the past days she had contemplated what an ugly thing she was planning to do to Quaid. She felt like a thief, stealing something from him, taking his seed to produce a child and depriving him of the knowledge and the pleasure of recognizing that child as his own.

Quaid Tanner walked hatless across the distance from the winery to the storage shed. He had given his instructions to Jack Mundey, his foreman, to run the sheep to pasture. For the thousandth time, he wished he could keep his mind on what he was doing. For some reason today, Chelsea was uppermost in his thoughts. Where was she? What was she doing? Was she happy now that she had what she wanted? Had Harlow ever discovered what had become of Martha and did he know about Quaid's part in the ploy? Harlow should have come to the realization that Martha wouldn't be back.

He remembered the expression of gratitude on Martha's poor battered face as she hurried up the gangplank of the ship that would take her to England. He suffered no misgivings; he would help Martha again if he had to, and Harlow Kane be damned. The Kane family was now history as far as he was concerned, and his relationship with Chelsea over. He must accept it and live with it.

In the view of the world he was a married man. He had no right to want Chelsea so desperately to expect her to sacrifice respectability and social acceptance to live as his mistress. This wasn't England or Europe; this was Australia, an isolated continent of sparse population, where social ethics and personal morals were mercilessly scrutinized.

Slinging a case of bottles onto his shoulder, Quaid eased the shed door shut behind him. As he shifted the case for a better grip, his foot rolled on a stone and made him do a crazy dance. The sound of laughter startled him. Chelsea! Damn, was he so lovesick he was imagining her here? When the trilling laugh erupted a second time, the case of bottles fell with a loud crash, shards of glass shooting in all directions.

"You're hell on anything breakable, Quaid," she teased, walking toward him. "I've missed you. You'll never know how much."

"I was just thinking about you. I suppose you came to find out if Martha reached the ship safely. Well, she left with a smile, if that's what you wanted to hear."

"It's what I wanted to hear. What were you thinking about me, Quaid? Tell me."

He felt foolish standing there in the hot sun surrounded by broken glass, but he knew this moment would never come again. "I was thinking how much I missed you," he told her, the expression in his eyes revealing more than words could ever say. "I was wishing I could have offered you marriage and respectability. Wishing I weren't so imprisoned by my past."

"We're all prisoners of our past, aren't we," Chelsea said softly. She lowered her face, unable to meet his gaze, misery washing over her in great beating waves. "I keep remembering everything, every word since I first met you. It's the only thing that keeps you alive for me when I can't be with you. I hated you when I thought you didn't love me, that I was just an amusing pastime for you. Then, when you warned me not to marry Harlow, I thought it was because you were jealous and just wanted to keep me dangling. I was haunted by my past. I thought you didn't believe I was good enough to marry. I hated you for that, but I loved you, too. And when I found out you already had a wife . . . only then did I realize I could believe those things I saw in your eyes and what you made me feel when you touched me. And I loved you, more than ever. Don't hate me for marrying Harlow. I saw a chance for life to be different for me, a chance to be accepted and have the security I've never had."

Quaid stepped closer to her, putting his hands on her shoulders, willing her to lift her face and look into his soul. "I don't hate you, Chelsea. Good God, it would be so much simpler if I could!" His voice was deep, choked with emotion.

When she lifted her face, she saw tears glistening. "I wanted to be married. It was my one chance to escape my past. In this world a woman needs a husband, or else she has nothing. Can you understand? Please, understand."

Quaid crushed her to him, burying his lips in the silk of her hair. "Oh, Chelsea, there's so much I can tell you, so much I've never told anyone. My back was to the wall. If I'd asked you to marry me, we would have had each other but little else. Clonmerra would be gone, everything would be gone. And perhaps I'd be forced to pay for a crime I didn't commit. So you see, love, I had nothing to offer you. There would always be the fear that any moment it could all be torn away. I love you too much to do that to you. Even if I had to lose you to Harlow Kane, I wanted more for you than I could offer."

Chelsea saw the raw emotions in Quaid's eyes, heard the grief in his voice, felt the rigidity of his shoulders beneath her fingers. Questions flew through her brain, but she knew without doubt that when he answered her, she would be hearing the truth.

He took her up to the house, sitting her down on the porch steps, seating himself on the step below her where he could watch her face. A soft breeze was blowing, cool and dry, a portent of the coming winter. It wasn't until she placed her hand tenderly on his shoulder that he found the courage to tell her.

"We were two brothers, born and raised here on Clonmerra. We attended school at the academy in the outskirts of Sydney. Two boys, Luke and Quaid. Our father was already up in years when we were born, and after Mother died he thought of nothing but returning to Ireland and his family's estate. We were eighteen when we left Australia, and we finished our education in England. When we came down from Oxford I took a position with a wine importer; my brother, who had a head for numbers, was offered a seat at the bank. Our father believed young men should earn their keep with gainful employment. Most everything he owned was far away in Australia, and Clonmerra was lying fallow. So you see, he had little to offer us. It was my uncle who had inherited the Tanner family fortune. Father was a younger brother."

He was silent for a long time, looking into his past, gathering his thoughts. It was Chelsea's pressure against his shoulder that prompted him to begin again.

"I don't think I ever had any illusions about my brother. He'd always preferred scheming to working, and he had a taste for high living. He was married by then, to a beautiful but ambitious woman. He and Madeline were having marital problems, and my brother was finding consolation in the arms of a little doxie who lived down by the wharf. I'm still uncertain of the details, but one night he sent a message for me to meet him in a rooming house on the East End. From that moment, my life has never been the same."

There was grief and anguish in his eyes when he looked up into Chelsea's face. For an instant she thought he'd be unable to continue, but she also realized his desperate need to unburden himself, to have her understand. She waited, tenderly brushing back the thick dark hair from his tanned brow. When he began again, his voice was softer, hardly more than a murmur.

"I went to the rooming house and found my brother nearly out of his mind. He'd been with his mistress that night, and he'd had a good deal to drink. For whatever reason, they'd argued and he'd knocked her around. He admitted to me that he'd beaten her in his drunken rage, but what happened next was something he'd never intended. Somehow, because of one of his blows, she hit her head. She was dead, and he'd killed her. Neighbors had heard the fighting, and so had the nightwatch walking the beat. He barely escaped."

Quaid was like a man putting down a heavy burden, slowly, carefully, still aching from carrying the load for such a long time. When he began talking again, his words came in quick bursts, as though he couldn't wait to be rid of his secret.

"When my brother sent the message to me, he'd also sent one to his wife. He planned to return here, to Australia, but he needed money, and he wanted Madeline to leave England with him. He knew the police would learn who had killed the woman; my brother was no stranger in the neighborhood, and it was well known that he visited her regularly. He even confessed that several people had seen him with her that night. He was a frightened man, Chelsea, afraid for his life. He needed money, and he needed it quickly; that was to be my part in it, to provide it. Christ, he was my brother! How could I refuse? How could I just stand by and watch justice take its course and live with myself while my brother rotted in jail or went to the gallows? I had to do it!"

Chelsea's touch calmed him. He buried his face in his hands. "What I tell you next will prove I'm as much of a coward as my brother ever was. Madeline arrived. I could see immediately that she'd never go to Australia with him. She was frightened for herself, for what being married to a criminal would do to her life. I'd returned by then with the money and had also booked passage for two on a freighter that was leaving port that very night. So help me God, Chelsea, and may He forgive me, all the while I was getting the money and booking passage, all I could think of was that if my brother didn't get away from the police, Clonmerra and everything else would be lost to the Tanner family forever. Since my brother had no legal heirs, Clonmerra and the abandoned opal mine would be returned to the Tanner estate, going directly to my uncle's heirs, who didn't give a damn about it. Clonmerra, the only place in the world where I felt I belonged. The only thing in the world that mattered to me."

He groaned then, an awful sound of remorse and agony. "When I returned to the rooming house, my brother was very agitated. He was crying, and he couldn't bear to look at me. Under the circumstances I didn't think it strange. Madeline, too, was nervous as a cat. I remember seeing her glancing at the door from time to time. It wasn't long before I knew why. I heard a commotion on the floor below—men's voices. Instinct told me it was the police. I only knew I had to get my brother out of there to safety. The window and a run across the rooftops was the only way out. Without even thinking, I pushed my brother out the window onto the ledge. He was yelling the whole time, resisting me, but I forced him. Then it was as if he had a change of heart—suddenly we were scrambling across the slippery tiles, trying to make our way to the next street. But it didn't work. I knew it wasn't going to work when I heard the bobbies blowing their whistles and the sound of footsteps on the pavement below. We took cover in the shadow of the chimneys, scared half out of our minds.

"Suddenly, my brother wanted to go back. I couldn't understand it; all we had to do was wait our chance. 'I have to go back,' he told me. 'I can't live with myself if I don't. I have to set things right!' When I still didn't understand, that's when he told me that Madeline had gone to the police while I went to get the money. She told them that I had contacted my brother and asked him to meet me at the rooming house, that I had confessed to him that I had killed the woman. It was *me* the police had come for, not my brother! They had blamed *me*!

"I wasn't thinking, nothing was making sense. Below, in the street, the police were shouting for us to come down. It was my name they were calling, Chelsea. My name! *Luke Tanner! Not Quaid, Luke!*"

Chelsea drew in her breath, afraid to hear what was to come next. The man she loved was telling her he wasn't who she thought he was—that when they made love the name she whispered wasn't his!

"I was mad—out of my mind. I couldn't accept what my brother was trying to do to me. He and his wife had tried to accuse me of a crime he'd committed. I attacked him, struggling with him on the ledge of the roof. He got away from me, and I ran after him to the other side. That was when . . . when he fell."

His shoulders shook with grief; he turned to bury his head in the comfort of Chelsea's lap. She stroked his head, soothing him, tears streaming down her own cheeks, knowing what this terrible confession was costing him.

"I vaulted down onto a neighboring roof and from there onto the top of a shed. I was able to get to my brother before the police had a chance to make it around the corner and come chasing up the alley. Chelsea, it was horrible. He must have fallen head down!" He pushed his face into his hands, struggling to wipe the vision of his brother from his mind. "There he lay, head bashed in, the oldest son, Quaid Tanner, heir to Clonmerra. He'd betrayed me, and now he was dead, leaving me to clear my name. And he'd taken with him any hope of my ever seeing Clonmerra again. That was when I did it. God help me, Chelsea, in some way I've paid for this action every day of my life since. I exchanged wallets and identification. Such a simple thing, taking no more than a second. By then, the bobbies were coming up the alley, and whatever I had done I'd have to live with it. That's how I inherited Clonmerra and my brother's wife to go along with it. Madeline's a greedy creature; she was more than willing to go along with the scheme since she knew a dead husband with outstanding debts could offer her nothing, but a man with a secret is only too willing to pay blood money on a quarterly basis. To all intents and purposes, I became Quaid Tanner. No one here in Australia ever realized the difference, since my brother and I were so much alike in appearance and so many years had passed.

"Now do you see? Now do you know why I couldn't have you for my own? I love you, Chelsea! I've loved you from the first moment I saw you. I'm a man haunted by his past; a man who doesn't even answer to his own name. A coward who lives a lie because he burned to make Clonmerra his own." He looked up into her face, saw the tears of compassion streaming from her eyes. His heart melted. "Don't cry for me, Chelsea, don't ever cry for me. I never wanted to make you unhappy, I only wanted to make you understand."

"I do understand," she whispered, her lips quivering, "and I love you. I loved you yesterday, I love you now, and I'll love you forever." She collapsed into his arms, falling into his lap, winding her arms around him, holding him close. She would keep his secret, protect him and Clonmerra. What was done was done, and nothing could erase the past. Luke, no *Quaid*—she must never think of him by his real name—had at last given her the real reason why he couldn't marry her. To all the world he was Quaid Tanner in order to save Clonmerra, and Quaid was a married man.

He held her, his arms hard around her, his dark head bent to hers. A great welling constricted his chest, and he knew it to be an overwhelming grief. "Dear God, Chelsea," he said, "what have we done?"

It was a poignant moment, the two of them holding each other in the bright sunshine; but night had fallen in their hearts. Lies and charades had come between them, endless shadows from their pasts, and now they would be paying the price for all eternity. "Tell me," he urged softly, "I want to hear you say it again."

Chelsea shook her head. "No, not here, love. Take me to your bed, that's where I'll show you my love."

Alone in the dim shadows of his room, they held each other tenderly, each realizing the fragility of the other, wanting to soothe away the pain. Always before they had tried to express their love through a touch, a kiss, a passion. Today it was not enough, and Chelsea reached up to hold her love's head between her hands, tilting his face until his eyes met hers. "I have loved you in many ways, my darling, and so often the words threatened to spill from my lips, but always I bit them back. No longer. I love you . . . Luke. With all my heart. I want you to touch me, make love to me. But most of all, I want you to tell me, too."

The sound of his own name spoken from her lips filled him with unspeakable joy. At least here, alone together, they could lay the dead to rest and open themselves to the light instead of hiding in the threatening shadows of the past.

"I do love you," he confessed, his eyes cloudy with emotion. "And this is our first love, our only love. Everything that came before this was between two other people. This is our first time."

His mouth descended upon hers, sealing his words, branding them upon her lips. She held herself against him, feeling her body slide full length beneath him, winding her arms about his neck to make him her loving captive. They had never kissed with such tenderness and longing. Passion was a thing apart from this moment between them. They were creating a warm, safe world for the two of them to share, a world where expressions of love were said like prayers. He took her gently, never taking his eyes from her lovely face, watching in wonder when at the moment of rapture she looked up at him, mouthing the words that blazed in her heart.

When he took his own release, the sound of her name tore from his throat, and there was such emotion and love in the sound, as though for him no other name existed.

Chelsea lay quietly in his bed. The pillow beside her still held his scent, the coverlet still held his warmth. He had left her while she pretended to doze, and she knew it was only to save her the pain of parting that he had taken himself away. How was she to live from this moment without him? His tortured, whispered "Good-bye, Chelsea, my love" would ring in her ears forever.

Eventually, she forced herself to stir. After she had dressed, she turned and looked at the tousled bed. Quickly she bent and straightened the covers, her hands burning with remembered feelings. Then she turned and strode from the room without looking back.

The sun was about to set when Chelsea reined the buggy into the yard at Bellefleur. The first thing she saw was Tingari, standing tall and silent beneath the shimmering leaves of the spinifex trees. Her stillness frightened Chelsea. Climbing from the buggy, she went to the woman. A single tear rolled down the Aboriginal's cheek.

It was Tingari who spoke first. Her wondrously large hand reached out and fell onto Chelsea's middle; her voice was low and solemn. "The seed is within you." Chelsea believed, and for the first time that day she remembered the reason for going to Clonmerra today. She placed her small white hand atop Tingari's and believed that within her she carried Quaid's child—and something that would have once brought her shame gave her great joy instead. She would have Quaid's child to love.

Suddenly Tingari loosed a sob, a great frightening sound. "What's wrong?" Chelsea cried. "Something's wrong!"

"Mitjitji was right. Tingari did throw her stones. My child will never be born. Tingari swears to you, I will give my life for this child you carry."

Chelsea was stricken with pity. "But you said it was bad magic to throw your own stones. I don't understand. Why?"

"A haunting came over Tingari. My child's *mamu* became weak, and I knew the life was seeping from my womb."

Chelsea followed Tingari's tortured gaze. A bright rivulet of blood striped Tingari's leg. Chelsea's hand flew to her mouth to stifle a cry of agony for her friend and protectress. Holding up her arm to stave off any interference from her mitjitji, Tingari turned and went to the garden house.

Chapter 16

Two Years Later

Chelsea made a pretty, if lonely, picture sitting on the veranda with her darling Gabrielle. Time and motherhood had changed her. Her skin was still the perfection of an English rose and her eyes still clear and dark, but time had stolen their sparkle and warmth, except when she looked upon her daughter. Her waist was still slim, her torso long and graceful, but there seemed to be a heaviness upon her shoulders, and her chin never seemed to lift as high and proudly as it once had. While still beautiful, her ripe womanhood seemed to have faded, and her spirit was as lusterless as her eyes. Bellefleur still afforded a kind of security, marriage to Harlow still provided social acceptance and respectability, but the shadows beneath her eyes and the hollows in her cheeks declared the price she paid too high. She was like the grapes dying upon the vine, and like the water they so desperately needed, Chelsea needed the man she loved.

Gabrielle watched her mother in rapt adoration as Chelsea read simple stories and pointed to the colorful pictures, saying some words very slowly so her tiny, dark-haired angel could repeat them after her. Gabrielle was just a year and a half old, with her father's dark eyes and determined chin. Her sable curls wound softly around the fingers just like Quaid's, and she shared the same twinkle that always lit his eyes from within. Gaby's skin was as fair as Chelsea's, and her little button nose and curving upper lip promised her mother's beauty.

Chelsea offered the baby a sip of cool water, encouraging her to drink with maternal cluckings and soft urgings. Tingari had warned that the little ones especially needed fluids in this heat, and Chelsea couldn't help wondering what they would all do if and when the precious water supply from the underground spring should run dry. The drought was hell on everyone and everything; people, animals, and especially Harlow's vines.

Tingari sat in the shade nearby. She had become Chelsea's constant companion and Gabrielle's vigilant protectress, just as she'd promised the day she'd miscarried her own child. As she glanced in Tingari's direction, Chelsea saw the woman sit bolt upright, her chin lifted as though she were sniffing the air, her back long and straight. One hand shielded her eyes as she looked into the distance, those incredibly long fingers stretched and poised.

"What is it, Tingari?" Hope sprang to Chelsea's heart. "Tell me. Is it rain?" She'd long ago learned to trust her Aboriginal friend. Somehow Tingari was always the first to know when rain—scant and rare—was coming.

"No. Not rain, Mitjitji. . . . Something."

Chelsea settled back with Gaby, shaking her head. She'd known Tingari to be mysteriously aware of an antelope crossing the far edge of Bellefleur, saying she had felt its *mamu* searching for water.

Water, thought Chelsea. In this god-forsaken land there either seemed to be too little or too much of it. The winter and spring when she'd been pregnant with Gaby had seen torrential downpours that had obliterated the landscape and churned the very earth into a sea of thick red mud. Even if it hadn't rained within miles of Bellefleur, the ever-present ridge of the Blue Mountains would cast its spilloffs from every rivulet and stream down to the valley and inundate the plains with water. And now this drought. When would it end? The gardens she had planned and planted were long dead; only the gum trees and other twisted specimens peculiar to this land seemed to survive. It had been a terrible year. She'd lived with Harlow's silent but terrible rage that Martha had gone to England despite him. She'd lived with her overpowering loneliness for Quaid. Chelsea reached out to touch Gaby's soft curls, as she so often did whenever she thought of the man she loved, still loved.

Quaid had been gone almost two years. Soon after the last time Chelsea had seen him, Tingari had told her that he was gone. His mysterious leave-taking was shrouded in rumor. Some had it that he'd gone to the hellhole of Coober Pedy in search of opals to weather the dissipation the floods had caused his vines. Others thought that he'd gone back to England. No one seemed certain. All Chelsea knew was that she missed him terribly and that he'd gone before she could tell him she was carrying his child.

"Mitjitji! Mitjitji!" Tingari cried suddenly. "There is something in the wind. Something."

"What?" Chelsea demanded, the expression in Tingari's eyes frightening her. "What is it?"

"There is bad *mamu* coming. Very bad."

Chelsea saw Tingari put her hand to her breast to feel the little pouch of stones she always carried beneath her thin cotton dress. "The wind carries the secret, Mitjitji, but it is too far to hear."

Harlow Kane inspected his vineyards and knew the nightmare for what it was. Bellefleur was ruined. The only hope for any of them was rain. In his soul he knew he was fighting a losing battle, but it was a conclusion he refused to accept. Eighty percent of the vines were dead; the rest wouldn't last the week, even with the protection afforded against the relentless sun by hastily erected canopies. All the years of hard work, all the dreams, were gone.

Everything seemed to be falling apart around him. His marriage to Chelsea was a sham, an abomination in the eyes of God. Chelsea had never loved him, he'd known that from the beginning; but he'd thought she had respected him and would be a worthy mistress for Bellefleur. Love was only another form of infatuation, entirely unnecessary to a man like himself. Respect, authority, and dedication, those were important to a man, not the vacillating emotions of a woman. Yet when he looked into Chelsea's eyes he saw none of these things, only a form of contempt. Where had it all gone wrong? Things had soured after the business with Martha. He'd been shamed, defied, challenged, and he'd lost. A man was only as good as his family. If he couldn't control his own daughter, how could he control anything else in his life?

Martha was gone. He refused to allow anyone in the house to correspond with her, but he suspected Franklin disobeyed him. Martha had exposed him as weak and ineffectual, and now none of the rest of his family gave him the respect he deserved. Even Emma, who had pined and wept for her lifelong companion, was able to ignore his demands by willfully retreating into her world of melancholy. Even that half-wit had challenged him and won. Franklin, Harlow's one hope for the continuance of Bellefleur, was lazy and shiftless and cared only for the time he spent in Sydney away from the needs of the estate. What was it all for if a man couldn't leave a lifetime of work in the hands of his own son? Even the child Chelsea had birthed was a daughter, another mouth to feed with no return on the investment. He was the only one who cared for

Bellefleur; it was his life, and now it was dying before his eyes, and his own helplessness was devouring him from within. He was consumed by his love for the vineyards, and nothing else existed for him: only Bellefleur and the drought.

Harlow had driven himself like a madman, working from sunup to sundown carrying water to the vines. He'd also done something he wasn't especially proud of, but he'd had no other choice. He'd run a clay pipe from Quaid Tanner's lake to irrigate the most important vines on Bellefleur. Tanner was gone, mining in the outback some said, solid proof that the man didn't give a damn about Clonmerra. Tanner wasn't a vintner; he was only playing at the role when the mood suited him. Why else did he keep sheep at Clonmerra? Why else would he leave to mine useless opals in Coober Pedy? If a man loved the land, he never left it. Never.

Suddenly Harlow sat down right where he was, weary to the bone. Too little sleep, not enough food, too much work, all had taken their toll. He knew he presented a frightening appearance—gaunt, stooped, a mere shadow of his former self. But a man had to fight for his life, and that was exactly what Bellefleur represented. No one understood—not Chelsea, not Franklin. Neither of them cared that it was Bellefleur that put food into their mouths and clothes on their backs.

Harlow's sun-blackened hand wiped his eyes. He was always alone, so alone. He was fighting for something no one but he cared about—and he was tortured by regrets, knowing that when Bellefleur died, everything he had died with it. Other men had their families, their wives, their children. He had nothing.

As Franklin rode up to the potting shed, the first thing he saw was Harlow. In his entire life he'd never seen his father sleep anywhere but in his own bed and at night. His heart started to pound madly. Was it possible his father was dead? He looked so still. Something pricked at Franklin's eyes, and he rubbed whatever it was away with the back of his hand. He wasn't surprised to see the red dust on his hands smear. Tears. He blinked.

He should get off his horse and check on his father, but he didn't move. If his father was dead, there was nothing to be done. If he wasn't, he could sit here and watch him. He'd never had the opportunity to observe his father at such close range. He looked like a tired old warrior. No, he corrected himself—a *defeated* old warrior.

Something stirred in him as he watched his father. In sleep he looked kind and gentle. For years he'd worked himself raw for this man with never so much as a thank-you. He knew he would have continued to do so from morning till night just in the hope that one day his father would slap him on the back, call him son, and say, "Well done." Now he knew that day would never come.

A fat black fly buzzed around Harlow's face. Franklin watched with interest as his father's nose twitched in response. He was alive.

There must have been a time when he'd loved his father. Perhaps when he was little. He wished he could remember. Everyone needed someone to love. At first he'd been secretly glad when his father had said he was remarrying. How naive he'd been! He'd hoped that marriage would soften his father, make him more aware of his own son. But it hadn't worked. And then he'd grown angry at the realization that he was half killing himself for some young woman he barely knew. He'd vented his hatred in every direction after the wedding. He'd even been stupid, going into town and gambling. He hated cards, but he liked the companionship of older, fatherly looking men. He even liked Quaid Tanner, but he'd never tell his father. Quaid had never pressed him for the money he owed from several long-standing gambling debts, and Franklin had been too embarrassed to explain why he couldn't pay up; reluctant to reveal too much about what went on at Bellefleur. But there was talk about him, and he was aware of it. He'd had to give that up, too. It seemed all his life he'd been giving up things.

The thing that ate at him the most, that positively chewed at his guts, was that he'd not had the nerve to stand up to his father when he'd attacked Martha. Instead it had been Chelsea who'd helped. Tingari had told him that Chelsea was a good woman, and he believed her. Chelsea and Quaid Tanner had helped his sister, who was now a mother herself in England and happy with her life there.

Happy. If anyone deserved to be happy, it was Martha. At least she had something—and someone—to love. Getting away from Bellefleur had been Martha's salvation. And now she wanted to help Emma get away. Secret letters, sent and received in Sydney, because Harlow adamantly refused to allow any communication with Martha. Another restriction imposed by Harlow, another sacrifice for Bellefleur. If Harlow thought their life's blood would nurture the vines, he would take it. Franklin almost wept. It wasn't his blood he was losing to Bellefleur, it was his life. Shut away here, alone, so terribly alone. He'd never known what it was to be young and carefree. His life had been an endless sacrifice to Harlow and Bellefleur, a hopeless, endless future without reward. So often he wished for the courage to leave. Something within him cried to see the world, to become a part of it, to experience it. He damned himself for being unable to defy his father and shirk his duty. In reality, he was more Harlow's son than he cared to admit.

Harlow stirred slightly, and Franklin continued to watch him, all kinds of thoughts running through his head. He wished he could feel something. He wished he could understand his father's obsession with the vineyards.

Franklin looked down at his father's hands, then held out his own to inspect. His were just as callused. He knew his back ached just as much as his father's. And he was just as tired.

They'd lost, and yet his father insisted on fighting. "Goddamn the vines to hell," Franklin muttered. "Goddamn Bellefleur! Goddamn you, Father!"

Quaid Tanner rode from Sydney to Clonmerra, taking in the devastation the drought had caused. The seasons had not been kind to this southeastern part of Australia known as New South Wales. Rains had been too sparse, and from what he had heard, none had fallen during the past eight months. White clouds, heavy with moisture, would pass over the land, casting their shadows as they passed before the brutal sun, but drifting far out to sea before depositing their burden of precious rain. Jack Mundey had written that he was finding it difficult to save root cuttings to begin the vineyards again once the dry spell ended, if it ever did. That was why he was returning to Clonmerra now, after more than two years away. He had a responsibility to Clonmerra, to the land and the men who worked for him.

In the fields of Coober Pedy, living underground to escape the savage heat and burrowing even farther into the bowels of the earth to mine the precious opals had toughened him. He was thinner, stronger, and there was a raw intensity in the quickness of his glance.

John Abernathy had mentioned it to him when he had returned to Sydney to find financial chaos. "You're lucky, Quaid," John had told him. "Most of the vignerons in the valley have gone under long before this, as have the farmers. Sheep ranchers are finding it hard to survive. They're losing their herds by the thousands. Men are ruined, and countless families have returned to England and Europe.

Clonmerra will be rebuilt because of the wealth of opals you've uncovered. Other men are not as lucky as you."

"Lucky," John had called him. Was he fortune's child when he'd run from his home to escape the daily reminder that the only woman he could ever love was the wife of another man? And during the months spent in the devastating solitude of Coober Pedy, where men lived like lizards beneath the rocks, had he been so lucky to dream of nothing but Chelsea every night? To see her lovely face always before him until, on the brink of madness, even death had seemed preferable to the intolerable loneliness?

As he kneed his mount up the drive of Clonmerra, he was welcomed by the sound of gunshots and assumed the men were hunting for their supper. A wide smile split the features of young Tooley Joe as he raced from the stable to take the reins from Quaid's dust-covered gloves. Quaid clapped the boy on the shoulder. "It's good to be back."

"It's good to see you, Mr. Tanner. Things ain't been the same since you went. There won't be no grapes to harvest. Last year the same. Blasted drought."

"I know, Tooley, but none of us can control the weather, didn't your old mum tell you that?"

"Aye, she did. But it's still a shame, it is."

"There's no shame in what can't be helped." He was sorry to see Clonmerra come to this, but it wasn't the end of the world. There were other priorities in life, he had learned. And it had been a difficult lesson: he was not the same man who had left Clonmerra two years ago. A little older, a little wiser . . . but still aching from his last encounter with Chelsea. He would always ache for the love of his heart.

His house—the house that should have been theirs, his and Chelsea's—stood empty, a sad, vacant, lifeless shape on this dry, forbidding landscape. All the flowers were gone now, water being too precious for trivialities. Without realizing it, he was climbing the stairs to his bedroom. It was the same, except for a thin layer of dust. On impulse he threw back the coverlet. Would her scent still be there? No. The linens were fresh, wrinkle free. It was as if she'd never been there at all, and suddenly the weight he felt he had been carrying these past two years seemed to shift and make him almost physically ill. A moment later he shook his head grimly, his lips a taut, forbidding line. He had to be strong and put such foolishness behind him. He had to go on.

Another burst of gunshot took him to the window. The sound seemed to be coming from the lake, too close for the men to be hunting. He strode from the room and closed the door behind him, wishing he could close off the part of his life that was Chelsea just as easily.

Tooley Joe was banging on the front door. "Mr. Tanner! Mr. Tanner!"

"Come in!" Quaid shouted as he bounded down the stairs. "What the hell is going on out there?"

It's Mr. Kane from Bellefleur. He's shooting at the sheep to keep them from what's left of the lake water. He wants the water for his vines."

"What vines?" Quaid demanded. "He can't have a leaf left in this drought, much less vines."

Tooley Joe shrugged. "He's been making big trouble for the past two weeks. Jack Mundey gave up on your vines months ago, saving the water for the poor blasted sheep. Kane's giving us a hard time of it."

Quaid's eyes narrowed. "Has anyone been hurt?"

"Just a few sheep killed, four or five. Kane shoots over their heads, driving them back to pasture."

"Get the men, Tooley Joe, and ride out behind me. I'll put a stop to this right now."

Quaid rode the shoreline, his rifle clutched in one hand. The lake that bordered between Clonmerra and Bellefleur was not very large and had always been shallow. Now it was little more than a glorified mud puddle, the last green vegetation trying desperately for survival around the shrinking waterline. His horse reared at a sudden blast of shots, the poor docile sheep, sick-looking and thin, bleating their fear as they were driven back by the rain of bullets zinging amidst them.

"One more shot in this direction will be your last," Quaid shouted to be heard across the narrowest part of the lake.

"Sez you and what army?" came the reply.

"This is my shoreline and my sheep. You go back and tell Kane that Quaid Tanner is home, and he won't be killing any more of my sheep or driving them back from what water is left." For emphasis, he raised the rifle butt and fired three shots in rapid succession.

The water was dangerously low, and if it didn't rain soon, his animals would die. Kane was wasting it on his shriveled, lifeless vines. The man must be mad! It was then he spotted the clay pipe running from the water's edge across the flat land. When Jack Mundey and his men arrived, Quaid ordered them to remove the pipes and haul them over to Clonmerra land. "Take every one of those damned pipes and haul them. Two more days of his futile irrigation and my sheep will die. Move fast, men, I don't want war breaking out with you on his land. Tooley Joe, you herd the sheep back here and let them drink their fill."

"We heard there was rain to the north in Queensland," Tooley Joe volunteered hopefully.

"Not soon enough to do us any good. By the time it trickles down here, all the sheep will be dead, poor bastards. I've seen droughts before. Kane's harvest is ruined and has been for months, but he's a stubborn man. He'll pump the last drop if we let him have his way. He was always too proud to raise sheep to offset the bad years, and now he'll pay for it."

The irrigation pipes were stored in Quaid's barns. By sundown he knew Harlow would be riding onto Clonmerra with his rifle in tow. As it turned out, he didn't have to wait that long. Just before noon Harlow Kane appeared from the brush on Quaid's side of the lake.

"You removed my pipes. Who the hell do you think you are, Tanner? Turn over those pipes before I set the law on you."

"Don't talk to me about the law, Kane. Tooley Joe tells me you've been killing off my sheep. I won't stand for it, so don't push me."

"I know nothing about your sheep. There's water in that lake, and I want it for my vines."

"Your vines are dead, and all the water in Australia isn't going to help them. You've lived through droughts before, and you're not a stupid man; you want to ruin me because I helped Martha. I'm sorry for the way she left, but I'd do it again."

"Didn't you leave something out of that little statement?" Harlow snarled.

Quaid's rifle was rock steady, but his trigger finger itched. His gaze was direct and dangerous, but the tone he used was insolent and goading. "You mean your son's gambling debts? He does owe me a hefty chunk of money. Now that I think of it, it is time some member of the Kane clan began to pay off. When can I expect the first payment?"

"I don't know what trick you've got up your sleeve, Tanner, but my son does not gamble."

"Next you'll tell me he doesn't have anything to do with women, either. Franklin owes me over three thousand pounds; that's sterling," he added menacingly. "He's had a two-year grace to repay it. Now that I'm back, this is the day of reckoning."

"You're lying! Do you take me for a fool?"

"Only if you're fool enough to think I lie. Talk to John Abernathy. Franklin has a hefty debt to settle with your friend as well."

Harlow gasped, and his face became a rich shade of purple. "Stay away from my family, Tanner. Especially my wife! I know all about that little exchange you made, giving her money for Martha. A man doesn't give a woman money for nothing, not a man like you, at any rate. I'm warning you: stay away from Chelsea and our daughter."

Quaid shifted in the saddle, the rifle coming up slowly, its muzzle pointed directly at Harlow's heart. "There's no reason for me to have anything to do with your family except perhaps to extend Mrs. Kane and Emma my good wishes."

"I wasn't referring to Emma but to my youngest daughter, Gabrielle. My wife gave me a child last year," Harlow told him, smirking.

Quaid's last defense crumbled. The rifle lowered to rest on his thigh. A child. Chelsea shared a child with this man. Harlow was watching him closely, baiting him, goading him, a superior smile cracking his face. "Give your wife my congratulations," he said at last. "Now get off my land, Kane, and don't come back, because I'd like nothing better than to put a bullet through your heart. As far as the lake, you can use the water but not with pipes. You want it, you'll have to carry it. Shoot at my sheep and you're dead. Now, get out of here!"

The infernal red dust arrived at the house on Bellefleur before Harlow. Something was wrong, Chelsea thought. Tingari was right. It wasn't even midday and Harlow never came back to the house until noon. She caressed Gaby's soft, dark curls. It was so hot and the baby was suffering as much as anyone else from the heat. When Harlow went back to the fields she would give Gaby a bath, letting her play in the sacred water Harlow hoarded so stingily. Every drop had to go for the vines; he had issued the edict. Even Gabrielle's bathwater had to be used several times before being carried out to vines that were already withered and dead. Even the cow had been replaced with a goat, which required much less water, and Gaby's requirement for milk was thus filled with less digestible offerings. Always the vines, the damn vines. Lord, how she hated wine and anything to do with it, almost as much as she hated her husband.

The servants were gone, sent away last year when the first harvest had failed. Chelsea was workworn and weary, doing what it had taken three women to do to keep Bellefleur running. Tingari, thank God, had stayed, and Chelsea knew it was the Aboriginal's devotion to Gaby that had quelled her wanderlust. It seemed every ounce of her own energy went into maintaining Bellefleur, the wonderful dream that was to have given her security and luxury. Now she was even less than the servant she had once feared becoming. A servant at least had a choice of employer; Chelsea was married to her life.

"Where's Franklin?" Harlow demanded as he came up the steps to the veranda.

"In the house. I heard him tell Emma there was nothing to do in the vineyards and he was leaving for Sydney. Is something wrong?"

Harlow ignored her question and burst into the house. Chelsea picked Gaby up in her arms and took her to Tingari in the kitchen. She was coming through the dining room to follow Harlow when she heard his bellow of rage. "Franklin!" Chelsea's hands went to her throat, a gesture of fear.

Franklin's expression was belligerent as he bounded down the stairs in response to his father's summons. Chelsea watched in horror as Harlow's fist shot out, knocking Franklin to the floor.

"You're no better than that harlot sister of yours. You dare to betray me and jeopardize Bellefleur! Gamble with Tanner, will you!" Chelsea screamed as Harlow's booted foot kicked directly into Franklin's chest. "How much do you owe the bastard? And John Abernathy—making a fool of me in front of my friends, my own son!"

The trickle of blood oozing from Franklin's petulant mouth smeared when he tried to wipe it. He slid backward, afraid his father would kick him again. "I don't remember. It wasn't that much."

"I don't want excuses. I want to know who you think you are to gamble with Bellefleur money. A debt is a debt. I'm not paying it, Franklin."

The young man turned belligerent. "I have no money. I have nothing but another day's work in your vineyards. I'm sick of your penny-pinching, sick of everything going back into a dying vineyard. All you ever think of are the vines; none of us mean a damn thing to you. I'm not sorry," he added defiantly. "I was trying to win enough to get myself out of this stinking hellhole."

"One more word out of you and I'll whip you to within an inch of your life. I thought you were a man. You're nothing but a sniveling coward!"

This last exchange seemed to make Franklin wild. He scrambled to his feet, his eyes blazing hatred. "A man. I'm not a man! What do you call yourself? You let another man take your wife to bed and father her child. Does that make you a man, Father?" he asked contemptuously. "There's no Kane in that child. Look at those flashing eyes and her coloring. She's a Tanner—through and through. The only *man* around here *is* Quaid Tanner, if you want the truth. I'm getting the hell out of here. Take your spite and hatred out on someone else."

Chelsea ran back into the kitchen, not staying to watch Harlow's attack on Franklin.

"He knows, Tingari, he knows!"

There was no need for an explanation; Tingari had also heard. She rose from the chair, put Gabrielle in Chelsea's arms, and placed herself protectively in front of them.

"Mitjitji not be scared. His ears are closed, his head is mixed." She circled her forefinger at the side of her head. "Come to garden house, you will be safe. Trust Tingari."

Chelsea shivered in the hot sun as she hurried across the yard, little Gaby clinging tightly to her neck. "It was terrible, Tingari. Poor Franklin. He said he was leaving. Only Emma and Harlow are in the house now. How did Franklin know, Tingari? How?"

"Eyes see what they want to see. Boss Kane did not want to see. Hatred for Boss Kane made Franklin want to look."

Gaby cried in her mother's arms, and Chelsea soothed her by rubbing her cheek against the little girl's head. Gaby was indeed undeniably Quaid's child. Throughout her pregnancy Chelsea had feared Tingari was wrong and that the child would be Harlow's after all. But no one who cared to look could deny the baby's father; otherwise it was possible to believe Gaby's dark hair came from Chelsea and her sparkling black eyes were only a few shades darker than her mother's. Gaby was a perfect blending of her parentage.

"Quaid is home," Chelsea said tonelessly.

"Tingari knows. He will help."

"Not this time," Chelsea replied adamantly. "I won't go to Quaid. I won't make him answer for what I've done."

"It is time Tanner knows."

"No! No! I've brought him enough heartache. Swear to me, Tingari!"

"To swear is to offend the *mamu*. But I understand."

It was less than a promise, but Chelsea knew it was the most she could extract from the Aboriginal.

"Mitjitji's heart speaks to Tanner," Tingari intoned sadly.
"Just the mention of his name and I fall to pieces inside.
I yearn to see him, even if from a distance. I ache to touch
him, if only in passing. My heart bleeds that he cannot
know his daughter. He is a noble man, Tingari, and I cannot compromise him. I love him too much to enter his life
again."

"If Tanner comes to Mitjitji?"

"No magic, Tingari. We both have different lives now. If
you interfere," Chelsea warned sternly, "I will banish you
from Bellefleur and from Gaby."

Tingari looked deeply into her mistress's eyes and saw
the truth.

Chelsea deposited Gaby into Tingari's arms. The child
adored this black woman who so tenderly cared for her,
and she went willingly. "Keep her in the garden house with
you, Tingari. I'll return to the main house. I have to face
Harlow sooner or later, and the waiting and not knowing
will kill me."

Tingari's elegant hand fluttered over her head in a kind
of blessing as Chelsea left for the house. She would go into
the kitchen and prepare lunch as though nothing had happened. It would give her something to do while she waited.
She set about her tasks, struggling to keep her mind on the
work at hand, but her thoughts kept returning to Quaid.
Where had he been these last two years? Had he come
back now because of the drought? No, she mustn't entertain these thoughts. Quaid was lost to her forever. Only
Gaby remained now, a flesh-and-blood memory of her lost
love.

Gaby was such a joy, a treasure. The pregnancy and
birth, however, were something Chelsea didn't like to remember. Harlow had been as demanding as ever, coming
into her room almost nightly, taking his release upon her
forcefully, almost brutally at times. And then, after the

baby was born, all social engagements had been curtailed, not that Chelsea had minded. The drought had taken its toll financially on most of the vineyards, and parties and soirees were luxuries of better times. With the servants dismissed and a baby, Chelsea had been busy from morning till night. Emma was no help to her; since Martha had gone, she'd become even more witless. She hardly ever stirred from her bed before noon, and her days were spent whining for her sister. She was useless about the house, and Chelsea had little patience for standing over her, directing the smallest chore, which she herself could have accomplished in one-quarter the time. Chelsea had long ago discarded any hope of becoming a friend to her. No, everything in Chelsea's life was Gaby. The child *was* her life, for she had no other.

Harlow was less than nothing to Chelsea. He equated his manhood with the success of his vineyard, and from the time of Gaby's birth he had become impotent. Perhaps he suspected or had known all along that Gaby was not his own. Whatever the reason, he blamed Chelsea for the loss of his manhood, and she knew that in some bizarre way he also blamed her for the decline of his Bellefleur.

Chelsea had learned to be honest with herself over the past two years. She hadn't been the best wife in the world, but she had tried. She'd done as she was told, been considerate and as caring as she could be, and her efforts had gone unrewarded. There was no doubt that she came third in Harlow's life: first was Bellefleur and second, the damn vines. She had tried to care for him, tried to be a decent wife, and she had failed. But she was not going to stop trying. It was her penance, and Bellefleur was her hell.

Harlow stormed into the house just as Chelsea placed a napkin near his plate. His face was a ruddy-brown color, carefully controlled hatred spewed from his pale gray eyes; it was a look with which she'd become all too familiar. He glanced at the carefully set table with the bright yellow napkins and snowy-white cloth. The bread was fresh, soft and golden. The cold mutton had been cut into bite-sized pieces with all the fat trimmed off, just the way he liked it. There was cheese made from goat's milk and a crystal glass of the claret he preferred. It took Chelsea only an instant to realize her efforts had been in vain. The glass was upset, cherry-colored wine spoiling the cloth, the mutton sailed across the room, and the soft cheese became a smear on the nearest wall. Fear gripped her as she clutched the back of the chair.

"It's all your fault! All of it! You sent my daughter away, and now you've driven my son from my house! I wish to God I'd never laid eyes on you." This last was said with deadly calm.

"Harlow," Chelsea said quietly, trying to reason with him, "Martha would have found a way to get to England even if I hadn't helped her. She deserved a chance at life; I gave her that chance, and I'm not sorry. You've a grandchild in England! William was as good as his word—he married Martha."

"It was the way you did it, Chelsea." Harlow held tightly to his control.

"Because I sold a ring to Quaid Tanner? I owe the man nothing. Emma is terribly miserable here; she wants to go to Martha. You've denied her this. Why, Harlow? Why do you deny your own children happiness? And it was you who drove Franklin away, not I."

"I should have killed him. None of this would have happened were it not for you."

"I didn't incur Franklin's debts. I pity him. I heard him say he gambled in hopes of winning his way out of Bellefleur. What has he ever known except work? You never took him into partnership with you, you never promised him a future. I think Franklin saw his life being wasted, working his father's land, feeding his father's family, scraping and bowing to his father's demands. I know he asked you for a portion of the land to work himself, but you wouldn't allow it. He wanted to build a home, a place where he could bring a wife and raise children of his own, but you were so greedy for every inch of Bellefleur land you wouldn't give it to him. You're obsessed with Bellefleur to the point that you can't see what you've done to your own children."

Shadows lurked within the depths of Harlow's glowering eyes. Chelsea knew he hadn't heard a word she'd said. He was building up to something, she could feel it in the close air around her. She drew in a deep breath, her knuckles whitening on the back of the chair. Gaby was next. Gaby was the crux of what was to come.

Instead, Harlow lowered his head, his voice low and grieving. "The vines are dead."

Fearful for her mistress's safety, Tingari stood beneath the open dining room window, listening to every word, ready to take action if needed. Franklin's insightful declaration concerning little Gaby had come as a sudden shock. Instinctively, Tingari hugged Gaby tighter to her breast. Boss Kane was a dangerous man. All that belonged to Bellefleur was Bellefleur; Gabrielle did not belong. Boss Kane tolerated no intruders—not even a rabbit or a galah bird touched foot on Bellefleur and lived, because they took from the land and did not belong. Tingari moved her long black fingers over the baby's head in a protective blessing. Like the rains that awaited the pattern of their time, Boss Kane would swallow what Franklin had told him . . . and then the storm would come.

Chapter 17

Quaid Tanner leaned against the porch railing of his house on Clonmerra. He was exhausted, sickened and exhausted. He'd been back from his trip to England to settle his past for nearly two weeks and the work was endless, despite the drought or because of it. The water from the lake was almost completely gone. The deep well out in back of the house was already muddy and nearly depleted. He'd had to resort to handing out bottles of wine for the men's daily rations, and there was no joy in drinking the fine burgundy or clarets that were the fruit of Clonmerra vines. Wine could not substitute for the most basic necessity of life—water.

Harlow Kane and his men had taken him at his word. They spent the days hand-carrying the precious water from the lake to the already dead vines. Some of it was preserved for the cuttings that were carefully stored away in the winehouse; just enough moisture to keep the roots from drying out, not enough light to encourage growth. If properly tended, Kane's cuttings as well as his own held the future harvests at Bellefleur and Clonmerra.

The lake water Harlow was taking could have been put to better use watering the sheep, but even that was a lost cause, Quaid knew. What possible difference could another week or two make to the dumb animals? Instead, Tooley Joe was overseeing the slaughter of the animals, and in this intolerably dry heat, the stench from the slaughterhouse was overpowering. Another irrevocable duty spurred by the drought.

The marketplace in Sydney was overrun with sheep, and the price of lamb on the hoof had dipped to a ridiculous new low. He'd heard that many outback ranchers were undertaking long drives to cart their poor beasts farther west, hoping to weather the drought. Quaid held little hope for them. As for himself, his herd had dwindled and trying to save it was hardly worth the effort. Instead, he'd ordered the animals slaughtered. At least the cooked meat would help to replenish the body's daily need for water. Under Quaid's orders, Jack Mundey had organized a small drive to herd the doomed animals farther north, where several Aboriginal tribes were finding it hard going. The Aboriginals could live on next to nothing, but this drought had put them to the test. And if ever there were a people who fully utilized every offering of nature, it was these dignified and mysterious blacks. At least this way the animals wouldn't go to waste by being allowed to die in their tracks.

Quaid leaned his head back and closed his eyes against the burning sun. In the dismal wasteland of Coober Pedy, he'd learned to spend endless days alone. Why was it then that here on Clonmerra he was overwhelmed with loneliness? And after Coober Pedy, when he'd gone back to England and had been surrounded by a sea of humanity, he'd dealt with a feeling of separation—but never the devastating aloneness that he carried with him now, on Clonmerra. He squinted in the direction of Bellefleur. Chelsea. His eyes were hungry for the sight of her. His arms ached to hold her. But she was as far from him as life could take her. She had borne a child, Harlow's child, and he knew instinctively that nothing he could offer would ever separate

Chelsea from that child. It had all been for nothing. The opals, the money, Clonmerra, the time spent away from here in England. It all amounted to nothing without Chelsea.

He felt the brutal sun burning his face and turned his head away. There was a restlessness within him, a feeling that predicted change. "Something in the wind," Tingari would have said, a world of understanding and meaning behind those simple words.

"Something," Quaid said quietly to himself. And then, in futile anguish, "Anything!" Anything to ease this yearning, this hopelessness that was consuming him.

Madeline Tanner smiled winningly at the captain of the *Tudor Rose,* appreciating his courtly bow. She knew she made a pretty picture as she stood at the rail to watch their entrance into the magnificent Sydney harbor. One tiny gloved hand poised on the rail, the other held the sweetest ruffled parasol to protect her flawless complexion from the sun. She'd chosen to wear a gay afternoon dress of cobalt-blue silk, the color offsetting her upswept flaxen curls. Complementing her costume and dramatically highlighting her coiffure was the most minuscule of hats, which allowed a froth of blue veiling to kiss the tip of her delicately upturned nose.

"If you could guarantee such wonderful weather for every crossing, Captain, I might be tempted to make the voyage again."

The captain tipped his hat. "It would be my pleasure," he assured her. "The *Tudor Rose* and myself are your servants, madam." The captain knew he was grinning like a silly schoolboy. He was years older than she and not ordinarily smitten with women, but Miss Tanner was the most charming young woman it had been his pleasure to meet in a very long time. Fifteen years younger and fifty pounds lighter, and he would have given any man aboard a run for his money with respect to the delightful Madeline Tanner.

She lifted a delicate hand to hold her hat against the off-shore breezes. It was a gesture that delineated the slimness of her torso, the alluring swell of her breasts, the graceful turn of her arm. And she knew it. Madeline tried to hide her smile. There wasn't a man aboard who wouldn't fall a willing victim to her charms. Not a man she couldn't have just by crooking her little finger.

The captain, no inexperienced bumpkin, was well aware of Madeline's seductive powers, and in spite of himself, he wished his numerous duties hadn't prevented him from pursuing her. Every free moment of the voyage had been spent seeking her company or watching her charm the buttons off the shirt of every eligible man. She was a popular companion—too popular, if one paid any attention to the catty remarks of the female passengers. To their relief, Madeline's attention had focused upon Mitchell Severson ever since he'd boarded ship in Cape Town. Even now, the captain knew she was waiting at the rail for Severson to join her. But he also knew Madeline Tanner was going to be quite disappointed if she ever decided to look into Severson's actual assets. He'd seen men like Severson before—well-dressed, perfect manners, suavely handsome . . . and not a penny in the bank. His fortune was his smile; his ambition was to make a profitable marriage.

"Ah, Mitchell, there you are," Madeline cried happily. "You did say you'd help me once we disembarked. I'm going to hold you to that promise."

Severson smiled, and Madeline thought it the loveliest smile she'd ever seen on a man. "I'm true to my word. Just put yourself in my hands, and I'll have a dray for you in no time at all. But first I think you should book a room at an inn in case things go awry when you get to . . . where was that place you're going?"

"Clonmerra," Madeline said. "And you're absolutely

right. I'll take a room at the same hotel where you're staying. You're very kind, Mr. Severson."

"Why this sudden formality, Madeline?" he asked.

"Because I wouldn't want anyone to arrive at the wrong conclusion concerning our relationship," she murmured. "A woman traveling alone must take great pains with her reputation; surely you understand." She lifted her striking blue eyes to his and squeezed his arm conspiratorially.

Captain Zachary was amused by this exchange between his passengers. Obviously they were unaware that the wind carried their words directly to his ear.

"You're as safe with me as you'd be with a husband." Mitchell laughed quietly. Madeline squeezed his arm again, this time possessively.

Captain Zachary rolled his eyes and turned to take his position on the bridge. He admired the couple's penchant for propriety, but anyone who'd been aboard ship with them these past weeks would have had to be deaf and blind not to acknowledge the relationship between them. Madeline fluttered like a butterfly whenever she was in Severson's company. Such an outrageous flirt. Severson was getting more than he bargained for, and sooner or later he would discover that his sweet little butterfly had the talons of a hawk. The captain laughed aloud, a booming sound that made his first mate turn to stare. Ah, yes, the captain found himself thinking, there was a God in His heaven. Never was a pair more suited to each other than Miss Tanner and Mr. Severson. And whatever Miss Tanner was up to, he wished her well.

On the quay in Sydney, people stopped to stare at the elegant couple who had just disembarked from the *Tudor Rose*. The bright midday sun seemed to pale in comparison with their handsome golden-blond looks. Their clothes were finely tailored in the latest fashion. She was a painting by Manet, a tiny, petite, angel-faced vision in blue silk and lace, her parasol tilted at a perky angle. He was tall, a striking figure of a man in gray serge, his tanned skin and golden hair perfectly complementing hers. And they were so attentive to one another, laughing and smiling and speaking in hushed whispers. Anyone could see that he was completely beguiled by her; anyone could see that she was a sweet-tempered, virtuous young lady.

At Mitchell's insistence, Madeline decided to spend her first night in Sydney at the inn. There they would inquire for a dray and a driver to take her to Clonmerra.

After settling themselves at the Gateway Inn, which had been recommended by several other passengers, Madeline and Mitchell discreetly joined a party of diners from the ship for their first meal in Australia. Soon afterward, Madeline retired for the night, pretending not to notice Mitchell's disappointment. She even made a point of remarking that her room was next door to Mrs. Watson's, a dour-faced matron whose character and sense of decorum were above reproach. Giving him an enchanting move, Madeline declared that she was totally exhausted from the day and only hoped she didn't toss and turn the night through because the walls were "paper thin" and Mrs. Watson's sleep would be disturbed. Mitchell received the message.

The next morning, after an early breakfast, Mitchell helped Madeline into the rented dray, warning the driver that he was to take exceptional care of his passenger.

"Are you certain you want to make this trip alone, Madeline? The innkeep warned that you'll find conditions quite primitive tonight at the wayside accommodations. Promise you won't try to make Clonmerra in one day."

"I promise, Mitchell. And yes, I must go alone, otherwise I'd be happy for your company."

"I don't understand what business you have at this place. And to arrive so unexpectedly; don't you think you should messenger ah—"

Madeline squelched Mitchell with one scathing look. Then she smiled—so quickly and so sweetly that he thought he'd only imagined the first. "I'll be fine. I have business, and I am expected. I should be back before the week is out. Really, Mitchell," she said, pouting, "if you don't let me get on my way, it will be long past dark before we make the wayside inn."

"I'll be waiting for you." Mitchell pressed her hand.

Madeline could feel his gaze boring into her back as the dray pulled away. She didn't turn around but settled herself as comfortably as she could. It was nice to know that whatever happened, someone like Mitchell was waiting for her. But of course everything would go as she wanted. She was holding the high card, and there was nothing else for her "dear husband" to do except pay up.

Quaid had worked that morning alongside Tooley Joe in the blacksmith's shed. Shoeing the horses, hard work that it was, had been therapeutic. There had been no time to think about Chelsea as he worked at the anvil, no time to miss her or anguish over her. His muscles were tight, and his hands burned from pounding the hammer. The heat from the forge had been intolerable, and Tooley Joe had pleaded with him to continue the work in the morning, when the weather would be cooler.

He didn't recognize the dray stationed outside the front gate to his house. It came as a complete surprise, since visitors during a drought were rare; everyone tried to conserve their animals. This dray was rented, he could tell by the shabby animal, and he didn't recognize the driver, who had fallen asleep beneath the wagon in the shade after watering the horse from the supply in the trough.

His gut churned as he washed his hands in the basin outside, smoothed down his hair, and tucked his shirt into his trousers. He stomped his boots outside the kitchen door to rid them of the red dust. The screen door creaked, a sound he normally found welcoming; today, it had an ominous sound. He could feel his teeth grinding together as he prepared to meet whoever had come to Clonmerra unannounced. The business he had gone to England to settle loomed before him. His past reared up like an angry, rushing river, and he felt as though he were stretching his neck to keep above water. When he'd returned to Australia, things had not been settled adequately. There were still questions to be answered, judgments to be made. He'd stuck his neck out, and his head might easily be sliced off as a result, and Clonmerra torn out from under him. But he'd done it for Chelsea, because of Chelsea—only to come home and find her eternally bound to Harlow through her child.

Shrugging off his thoughts, he prepared to meet his unknown visitor. But nothing could have prepared him to meet the woman who sat in his parlor delicately sipping wine from a crystal glass.

"What the hell are you doing here?" he demanded. The words were a hiss escaping from between clenched teeth. He was almost afraid to hear her answer; he wanted to turn and run. Instead, he poured himself a snifter of cognac and took a long, deep swallow.

"Darling husband, it's been more than a year since I've heard from you," she said sweetly. "I've come to assure myself that you're alive and well." She allowed sarcasm to creep into her words. "After all, I do depend upon you for my living. Do you expect your loving wife to fend for herself in this big, bad world?"

"If you squandered what I sent you, Madeline, that's not my problem."

"Oh, but it is, darling. What a charming place Clonmerra is. Your brother would have been proud of the home you've made here."

"No, he wouldn't. We both know he never gave a damn

about Clonmerra. What do you want? Whatever it is, you aren't going to get it."

"Don't be so sure." Gone was the sweetness, the mild sarcasm. Now her tone was abrasive, threatening. "I've had enough of these games, Luke." She used his true name, her tone issuing a veiled threat. "I want my share now, up front, and I expect you to sell Clonmerra if it's the only way I can get it."

"You have no share. Don't try to force your will here. Clonmerra is mine."

"Darling Luke, you have a very short memory. We made a bargain, remember? I'd stay out of your life provided you were prompt with the bank drafts. That hasn't been the case, has it?"

He stared at her, the fury in his eyes pinning her to the back of her chair.

"Don't do anything foolish," she warned. "Too many people know I've come to Clonmerra. I'm expected back in Sydney day after tomorrow." She laughed when she saw his reaction. "Oh, you didn't think I'd come to stay, did you? No, poor darling, living in this isolation isn't to my liking, I'm afraid. I much prefer polite society and parties and travel. I love to travel. Did I tell you I'd spent the winter in the south of France? So you see, I'm quite dependent upon your generosity. Travel expenses mount, and my dressmaker's bill is exorbitant! When you switched identities with Quaid, I automatically became your wife. Unless you want the entire world to know what you've done, I suggest we come to terms. After all, you have no real claim to Clonmerra, have you?"

He flinched. She was hitting too near the truth. Had Madeline's eyes always been so hard and cold, her mouth so thin and greedy? When her lips pulled back in a smile, he knew he was looking into the mouth of a vulture ready to pick his bones. "How much?" he demanded after taking another swallow of cognac.

"I want it all. It's really so simple—all, everything. I've had enough games, Luke. I was a fool to go along with your charade. It's mine, all mine, and I want it."

"And just how, do you figure? I'm not forgetting you and my brother tried to blame me for a crime I didn't commit. And I know damn well who put that idea into his head."

Madeline shrank back against her chair. "It was Quaid's idea. He was always a coward. I had nothing to do with it."

"But you went to get the police. I'd have been left to prove my innocence while Quaid slipped out of England using the passage I'd booked for him. *If* I'd ever been able to prove my innocence."

"That's all history," Madeline said uneasily. "I'm more interested in the present. I really don't see that you've much choice. As Quaid's widow, I naturally inherit his estate, and that means Clonmerra and everything else that goes with it. And of course, you are still wanted for murder. There is that little nuisance, isn't there?"

He found himself laughing, head thrown back, the sound erupting and filling the room. Madeline was startled, then frightened, afraid he'd gone mad. "There's quite a bit more to the story than you think, Madeline darling. A few facts of which you are obviously unaware. First, let me tell you that I have just returned from England. At great expense and a good deal of trouble, I might add, I've managed to prove myself innocent of killing my brother's mistress. Second, it's my pleasure to inform you that my brother died a bankrupt. The two of you had squandered everything."

"Not everything—there's still Clonmerra!"

"That, darling, is where you are totally mistaken. My brother died without issue; do you know what that means? A child, Madeline. I suppose it never really made much difference to him because he never placed any value on

Clonmerra and his Australian holdings. When Quaid died, Clonmerra reverted to my uncle. Happily, I was able to purchase Clonmerra and the other holdings, and the deeds now carry my name, my real name, Luke Tanner! In short, Madeline, you are entitled to nothing."

"That's impossible!" she gasped. "I don't believe you! You wouldn't have dared return to England. You couldn't have cleared yourself."

"But I did. When I returned to England this last time, I was determined to clear my name, and I had enough money to oil the wheels of justice. I suffered the most unspeakable conditions to mine opals in Coober Pedy in order to purchase Clonmerra from my uncle, something I'd never have been able to do if I hadn't assumed my brother's identity. All I'm waiting for now, Madeline darling, is the final decree from the courts that will finally free me of you."

"Aha! Then it's not settled, is it? You could still lose everything, couldn't you?"

"Yes, I suppose I could," he answered with more courage than he felt. "My petition to the courts could be denied, and I might still be forced to stand trial for my brother's crime. There's a little charge of obstructing justice that rests against me, and of course if I'm imprisoned, I could still lose Clonmerra. My uncle's terms were conditional at the time of the sale. But in any case, I'd rather take my chances with English law than with you."

"I don't believe you; I don't believe a word of it. Everyone still thinks you're Quaid. You haven't told anyone who you really are. You wouldn't take that chance."

"But I did. You see, there was something I wanted more than Clonmerra, more than anything, and the lies and deceit were standing in my way. If you'd like to see the deeds and the other papers from the courts, I'll be glad to show them to you. I'm even beginning to think of myself as Luke again."

She looked up into his face and saw he was telling the truth. "But what about me?" she cried. "I stood by you; I lied for you. You'd never have gotten Clonmerra if I'd told the truth that night, if I'd told them you weren't my husband. You said yourself you'd never have been able to buy Clonmerra from your uncle if you hadn't come here to earn the money."

He thought for a long moment. "You're a greedy woman, Madeline, and I should throw you out, but there's truth in what you say. I said I wasn't going to give you another cent, but I will give you this." He crossed the room and unlocked a desk drawer, withdrawing a little velvet pouch. He poured the contents into Madeline's outstretched hand; her palm glittered with blue and green fire.

"Opals, Madeline. There's more than enough to give you a new start if you're careful."

"How careful?" she asked, her fingers closing over the gems possessively.

Luke Tanner laughed, this time with relief. Madeline would no longer be a problem; she was accepting his offer.

The afternoon was brutally hot and airless. Not the slightest breeze grazed the land. It was too hot to cook, nearly too hot to breathe, and the air was so dry it parched the throat. Insects had descended. Flies by the hundreds had invaded the house, despite Chelsea and Tingari's efforts to keep them out. Outdoors it was even worse, the filthy black creatures pestering man and beast, hovering about the face to take the most meager drop of moisture from the eyes, nose, or mouth. Gaby was plagued with their bites; red, swollen patches bruised her exposed skin. Chelsea was frantic to keep them off her baby, and Tingari, knowing they carried disease, had rubbed the baby with oil of bay; but the hungry, thirsty things persisted.

"Harlow, won't you come in and have something to

eat?" Chelsea asked softly through the screen door. He'd been sitting on the porch most of the day, even through the worst of the heat, his gaze fixed on the sky. White rain clouds had drifted over the distant ridges of the Blue Mountains earlier that day. But they seemed to hang like cobwebs, never coming nearer to Bellefleur. "You haven't eaten all day, you know. Please come in. Tingari has cooled some tea, at least have a cup."

But he wasn't listening; she was wasting her breath. A posture of utter defeat had descended upon Harlow, and Chelsea felt her heart swell with pity. She should hate him, but she couldn't, not really. She was afraid of him, but she couldn't hate him. She'd used him, betrayed him, and she was sorry for it, terribly sorry. But since the last time she'd been with Quaid, the afternoon Gaby had been conceived, she had tried to be the wife Harlow needed. She'd tried to make it all up to him, somehow.

Harlow picked himself up slowly, like a man bearing the weight of the world. When he turned to face her, there was an emptiness in his eyes that frightened her almost as much as his rage. "It's got to be done, you know," he said quietly, his voice drifting off at the end.

"What must be done?"

"Someone must pay. I'm a cursed man, and until I avenge myself, nothing will save Bellefleur." He turned his head, meeting her eyes directly. "It's all your fault, Chelsea. Yours and Tanner's. You've brought a scourge upon my land, you and your betrayals and scheming. Martha is gone and Emma is mad and my son has left me. *My* children, Chelsea, not like that brat of yours. They were *my* children!" His voice rose, and as the volume increased, his tone grew deadly. "That brat of yours isn't mine. She's Tanner's. The both of you have brought this curse down upon me, and it won't be lifted until I avenge myself!"

Terror gripped Chelsea's throat, choking off the words

she tried to utter. She clutched the porch railing, trying desperately to steady herself. Tingari had warned this would come, but she'd refused to listen. "Harlow, please, listen to me. This drought has nothing to do with a curse, that's foolishness. Listen to yourself, you're talking crazy."

"Not as crazy as you wish! Not nearly as crazy! I've been a fool not to know if a child is my own or not. Franklin put it into words, but I'd been thinking it a long time. Ask that black servant of yours. She'll tell you I've been cursed, and she'll tell you there's only one way to cure it." He loomed over her for a minute, a large and powerful threat, and then turned and entered the house.

"Harlow!" Chelsea called after him anxiously. "What are you going to do? Where are you going?"

He ignored her frenzied questions and took his rifle down off the wall, murder in his eyes. "Get out of my way, woman. I'll deal with you and your brat later. Get out of my way!" He knocked her aside, sending her careening into the newel post at the bottom of the stairs. Then he paused for a moment, as if to gather his energy before stepping out the door. Determination set in the carriage of his shoulders, his feet marched a steady course.

Chelsea turned and ran through the house out the back door to the garden house. Her breath exploded in a cry of relief when she saw Tingari offering goat's milk to Gaby from a little tin cup. "Tingari, I tried, but he didn't hear a word I said. He took his gun. He was rambling on about avenging himself of the curse. What curse?"

"Boss Kane's vines are dead. He knows nothing else. Now he must place the blame."

"Tingari!" Chelsea cried. "He took his gun and left the house! He said he'd take care of me and Gaby later. He knows, Tingari, he knows!"

"Mitjitji stay here, I will come back."

"Where are you going? No, don't leave me, don't leave Gaby!"

"I will go and come back. Tanner must be told."

"Harlow is crazy, as crazy as Emma."

"Tingari has spoken of his *mamu*. It is almost time. His vines die, and he will die. I tell Tanner."

"No!" Chelsea shrieked. "I don't want Quaid to kill him. He couldn't live with that. He'd never be certain he didn't do it for me. He mustn't," she cried, "he mustn't!"

Chelsea was rocking Gaby to sleep in the comparative cool of the garden house, hoping to put her down for a nap, when Emma appeared.

"Where is everyone?" she asked. "I can't find anything. I want to eat. I'm hungry!" She rubbed her eyes, and Chelsea noticed the crusting at the edge of her lashes. Emma, for one, appeared to have taken the water rationing seriously. Her pink gown was smudged and dirty, and Chelsea could almost swear she'd been wearing it for an entire week.

"Would you like me to fix your hair, Emma?" Chelsea asked with more patience than she felt. Combing out the tangles and snarls would be a thankless chore, but it was one way to get Emma to leave the little house.

"Not now. I think I'll walk down to the lake. Do you still go to the lake, Chelsea?"

"Not anymore. It's too hot, and there's hardly any water there now."

"Martha is sending me passage money to go to England. Franklin brought the letter yesterday."

Chelsea knew that Martha's letter had arrived six months ago. Like a fool, Emma had ignored Chelsea's advice and run to tell her father, who had exploded with rage. Emma had cried and stayed in her room for more than a week. She would never get to England as long as her father was alive.

Straightening her dirty pink gown at the neckline and patting her tangled hair, Emma chirped, "If I see Mr. Tanner at the lake, do you want me to say hello for you? He's back at Clonmerra. But you already know that, don't you?"

"Yes, I know. Emma, don't go by the lake," Chelsea urged. "Why don't you go to the winery? At least it's cool in there. I'm going to put Gaby down for her nap." Chelsea's thoughts were whirling at a frantic pace, but she knew from experience that Emma mustn't be unduly upset. One wrong word, and she'd have a crying, unmanageable woman on her hands. And right now, she needed to think.

"You didn't fix lunch," Emma complained.

"There's some tea that's cooling and a tin of biscuits. Run along, Emma. I'll fix you something to eat as soon as Gaby is asleep."

Chelsea turned her attention to Gaby, rocking her smoothly, encouraging sleep. "My poor little one," she whispered. But her tears were for all of them, even for Harlow.

Luke Tanner watched Tingari for a moment as she stood on the hill behind his house. He would have recognized the tall, graceful form anywhere. Chelsea's protector, the keeper of his love. The Aboriginal stood for a moment, her dress billowing out behind her, and he was reminded of the day he had seen Martha there, outlined by the setting sun. There had been trouble then, and he knew there was trouble now.

Tingari towered above him. After the long walk over the hills in the hot sun, she should have been breathless and sweaty, but she wasn't. Tingari, woman of the desert, could stride along at a horse's pace for days, taking neither water nor food. Hers was a race older than antiquity, and the Aboriginal kept close to the ancient ways.

"Tingari comes to tell Tanner Boss Kane comes with a rifle."

Luke could feel the fine hairs on the back of his neck as they danced in the hot breeze. He wanted to plunder her with questions, but he was wise enough to realize Tingari would tell him only what she wanted him to know.

"Boss Kane was shamed by his son," Tingari said.

"Because of the gambling debts?"

Tingari shrugged her proud shoulders. "Franklin is gone."

Luke had to ask. "Chelsea? Did Mitjitji send you for my help?"

"No. Only to warn. Boss Kane comes for one reason only—murder."

Luke's fear for Chelsea prompted him to question. "If Kane is hell bent on murder, how can your mistress manage with a baby?" Something was wrong here, and he didn't like it.

"Mitjitji is a mother now," Tingari said as if that explained everything and anything.

"What did she name her child? Does she look like Chelsea?" He hadn't wanted to ask or even to know, but the words came tumbling out of his mouth.

"Mitjitji calls her Gabrielle, Gaby. The child"—Tingari's fathomless gaze held him—"looks like Tanner." And with that she left as purposefully as she'd come, picking her way among the rocks and dry bush that littered the path.

"Tingari, wait!" Luke shouted. "I don't understand. Come back here! You can't tell me something like that and walk away." Shaken to the core, he chased after her only to skid to a stop. She had said what she'd come to say. He knew she would ignore his pleadings, and he also knew that if he tried to detain her against her will, she would turn and snap him in two like a dry twig.

The shout, when he heard it, came from his left, followed by a zinging bullet penetrating a gum tree. Luke ducked, covering himself behind the brush. He'd left his rifle back in the house.

"I won't kill you, Tanner, not yet," called Harlow Kane. "This is a warning. You've made a fool of me for the last time!"

A second volley of shots was fired, and Quaid held his breath, crouching low. At the sound of Kane's horse pounding the dry-packed earth, he drew a sigh of relief. The man was a lunatic.

For the rest of the day shots were fired intermittently at Clonmerra, breaking several windows in the big house and peppering the winery. Luke clenched his teeth and stalked his property like a hunter in search of big game. He would have liked to go after Harlow, but as long as the madman concentrated the destruction on himself and Clonmerra, Chelsea would be safe.

Several hours before dawn the next day, Luke awakened to quiet, his heart pounding with dread anticipation. Earlier that evening he had made his presence known in the house, attracting Harlow's attention away fiom Jack Mundey and his men. The gunfire had been relentless, periodic, volleys being fired approximately each half hour, almost like clockwork. Sometime during the night Luke had fallen into an exhausted sleep, and now he realized it must be nearly six hours since he'd heard the last of Harlow's shots.

Threading his fingers through his hair, he pondered the situation. That Chelsea was in danger there was no doubt, and all he had been doing was bargaining for time. Leaping to his feet, his decision made, Luke left the house, bellowing for his horse to be saddled. He was going to Bellefleur to get Chelsea and the baby. He'd had enough.

Chelsea awakened with a pounding headache. A premonition of something dark and deadly seemed to hover over her. The sky was just growing light when she crept down the stairs to check on Tingari and Gaby, who were staying in the garden house. Her hand flew to her mouth to stifle a cry when she saw Harlow standing in the dim kitchen. At first he didn't seem to notice her, but at her muffled sound he turned. She'd been dreading this moment, knowing it was to come sooner or later. Harlow's eyes were hard and staring, glittering with a dangerous light.

"Can I get you something, Harlow?" Chelsea asked hesitantly.

Harlow ignored her question, but the hatred in his eyes made Chelsea fly past him out the back door, straight to the garden house. Tingari was up and dressing Gabrielle.

"Tingari! Something's wrong. Gabrielle isn't safe here. I saw what Harlow did to his own children, his own flesh and blood. God only knows what he would do to another man's child. Take her. Go to the Blue Mountains. Hurry, there's no time to lose."

"Mitjitji come, too," Tingari ordered.

"I will. Don't waste time, take Gaby and go!"

Tingari hesitated, looking at Chelsea with great concern.

"I'm going, but not with you. I'll lead Harlow away from you. You stand a better chance with Gaby than I. You can provide for her and survive better without me. Damn you, Tingari, go!"

"Mitjitji come with Tingari. Now!" Incredibly long and forceful fingers closed over Chelsea's arm. Tingari would have it her own way—Chelsea would come with her.

Emma stood in the kitchen, a frown on her face. Everyone was going away. First it was Martha, then Franklin, and now Chelsea and the baby. She was the only one left. She had to be good, or her father would throw her in the dirt as he had Martha and Franklin. Maybe she wouldn't go to Martha. Maybe she would stay here with her father. Nobody cared what she did or didn't do. Maybe she should go back to sleep. She could curl up on a chair and doze for a while until her father came back. No, no one was ever going to come back for her. She would be all alone in this pretty house, by herself.

Emma was standing on the veranda in her nightdress. Goodness, she'd been wrong; someone *was* coming to Bellefleur. She should have worn her blue gown and prepared for visitors.

"Mr. Tanner! How nice of you to come calling. Can you stay for luncheon?"

"Luncheon! It isn't even breakfast. Emma, where is Chelsea?"

"You needn't be so sharp with me, Mr. Tanner. Chelsea isn't here."

"It's barely dawn. What do you mean she isn't here?" Quaid said sharply.

"Sakes alive, Mr. Tanner. Calm yourself. My father went out before it was light. With his rifle. I think he went to your house. Tingari took the baby and Chelsea and left for the mountains. You must fetch them back, Mr. Tanner. I'm all alone here. Will you fetch them back? Or should I wait and tell my father to fetch them?"

"Emma, listen to me. I'll go and fetch them. Now, look at me. In the eye, Emma. Ah, that's good. I'll bring them back. There is no need for you to worry your father about this. He has enough on his mind. Do you understand what I'm saying?"

"Of course I do. But Father will be angry with me if I don't tell him Chelsea and the baby left. I tell Father everything. I don't want him to throw me in the dirt the way he did Martha and Franklin."

Sweet Jesus, the girl was as balmy as a loon, Quaid realized, frowning. He was just wasting his time here. As he turned away he heard Emma call, "Are you sure you don't want me to set another place for luncheon?" Waving a hand vaguely in reply, he spurred his horse out to the road.

Which way to go? On foot or horseback? The Blue Mountains? Why hadn't Chelsea come to him for his help? Harlow must have threatened her, she'd had to make a run for it. Nothing else made any sense. Thank God Tingari was with her. Well, this time, Chelsea old girl, you're going to get my help whether you want it or not.

The strange look in her father's eyes frightened Emma, who was busily setting the table for lunch. "I knew you'd come back," she said happily. "I told Mr. Tanner you would come back. He went to fetch Chelsea and Tingari. But Chelsea took food with her. Do you think they're going to have a picnic, Father?"

Harlow Kane's eyes glittered angrily. "Picnic?"

"Everyone is gone, Father. Mr. Tanner went to fetch them back so you wouldn't have to leave me alone."

"Don't talk foolishness, girl. Where's my wife?"

Emma shrank back in fear, whimpering as she brought the hem of her skirt up to her mouth.

"I won't ask you again, girl. Where's my wife?"

Emma minced her way to the kitchen window, never taking the hem of her dress from her mouth. "Mr. Tanner doesn't want me to tell you they went to the Blue Mountains. I told him I tell you everything, Father. I'm a good girl, not like Mother."

"The mountains?" Emma nodded. "Did you tell Tanner that's where they went?" Emma nodded a second time.

Harlow paused, frowning as he calculated the odds of overtaking his wife—and her lover. Chelsea and the Aboriginal had a two-hour head start, with Tanner following closely behind. Providing he went in the right direction, he had three hours of hard riding ahead before he'd sight his quarry. Harlow nodded in satisfaction. He could make it. Without another word to Emma, he left the house.

Mounting his horse he slapped the reins and dug his heels hard into the animal's flanks. The horse responded by rearing back his huge head and driving forward. The sound of Harlow's whip cracking the satiny hide was loud in the still, mid-morning air.

There was only one thought in Harlow's mind as he drove the animal beneath him: kill Tanner and Chelsea. His life had been fine until they'd conspired together to ruin him. He'd been an upstanding member of the WGA— he'd had wealth, position, power. All that was gone now. Gone with the hot winds, lost to him forever. And it was Tanner's fault. He'd lost his oldest daughter, thanks to Tanner's and Chelsea's intervention. His son—flesh of his flesh, who was one day to have run his beloved vine-yards—was now lost to him, too. In debt to Tanner and a like amount to Abernathy. He was wiped out now; how could he ever hope to pay his son's gambling debts—to save face? Once he killed Tanner and Chelsea, Franklin would come back and run the vineyards. There would be no debt . . . and no reminder of his wife's infidelity.

When he heard a horse wickering softly in the brush, he reined in to investigate, a crafty look on his face. Tanner's horse, and from the looks of things quite lame. So, Tanner was on foot. He'd catch up to him soon. And wherever Tanner was, Chelsea and the brat wouldn't be far behind. He smiled, an evil grimace of pleasure at what he was going to do. He thought he could almost smell Tanner's body scent. With a diabolical gleam in his eyes, he looked down at the trail and the broken branch. It was a sign from above. God in His infinite wisdom was showing him the way to the sinners.

Chapter 18

Tingari walked tall and strong, little Gaby slung safely over her shoulder. The Aboriginal's rhythmic strides rocked the baby, lulling her to sleep. Behind her, Chelsea trudged along, already too weary to consider another step. They had been walking since early that morning, taking a northwestern path where Tingari had said they would find safety. The heat was overwhelming and thirst a moment-to-moment agony. The afternoon sun beat down upon them relentlessly, and finally Chelsea begged Tingari to take a rest.

"Mitjitji will follow. She will not think of heat or thirst. Mitjitji will think of safety." Tingari raised her arm, pointing off into the distance. "To stay here is to die. There is water. There is food."

She spoke with such certainty that Chelsea was forced to follow, the reward of food and drink pressing her onward. The shadows were already long and the angry sun a deep crimson on the horizon when Tingari motioned that they would soon make camp. Gaby was crying miserably, her little voice hoarse with thirst.

Throughout the day Chelsea had noticed the change in the landscape as they covered the distance to the Blue Mountains. Tall, dry grasses that had been green before the drought had given way to a shorter, stubby growth that tore at the hem of her skirt. The earth, parched and cracked, had spit upcroppings of rubble and rock that dug into the soles of her shoes and threatened an unwary ankle. Tingari, barefoot as always, covered the land as though it were carpeted with cashmere. Her huge feet were tough-soled and her long legs carried her steadily. In the heat of the afternoon, Tingari had removed her simple cotton dress and made a sling to carry Gaby. Chelsea was awed both by the Aboriginal's beautiful body and her lack of embarrassment at her nudity. This was her proper setting—out here under the sky, walking proudly over the harsh land—not the formality of a house encumbered with unnecessary furnishings. This was Tingari's place, her world; and she embraced it with an inward faith, born of thousands of years in race memory, that it would always nurture and keep her safe. It was that knowledge of the land, that unnerving instinct for survival, upon which Chelsea was counting. If anyone could find safety for herself and Gaby, it was Tingari.

"Soon now, Mitjitji." Tingari had grasped her arm and was pulling her along. She'd been heading in this westerly direction since late afternoon as though she had a particular destination in mind.

"How soon?" Chelsea gasped. Life about the house on Bellefleur had not prepared her for such an expenditure of energy. She sucked on the smooth round stone Tingari had put in her mouth to tease the saliva glands and keep her mouth moist.

"Soon. There we will camp." The Aboriginal pointed into the distance, where Chelsea could almost see a ridge amid the foothills. It looked so far away, too terribly far.

Evening had fallen when Tingari quickened her pace. Chelsea forced herself to keep close, fearing the Aboriginal would leave her behind in the darkness. In a few minutes they skidded down the slope that led to the foot of the ridge.

"No more, Tingari, I can't go another step." Gaby was crying, a fretful, hollow sound. Even Tingari couldn't comfort her. "The baby is hungry and thirsty," Chelsea said breathlessly.

"First water, then food." Tingari motioned for Chelsea to rest at the base of the ridge, putting Gaby into her arms. "First water, then food," she repeated.

Chelsea peered dully into the darkness. Not even Tingari could provide the basics of life in this wilderness. Ancient trees peppered the landscape, their twisted, ghostly arms reaching for rain that had never come. The brush underfoot was kindling dry, the earth itself parched to a powder that clung to the skin and invaded the eyes. Chelsea collapsed against the stone ridge, trying weakly to comfort the baby, wondering how quickly death would come in this godforsaken place. Not even the stars glittering in a velvet-black sky seemed to speak to her of a presence of God. She wanted to cry but was too weary, and too sick. Nightmarish illusions of herself burying her dead child made her shiver. Between death and her child stood one lone woman, black of skin and wise in the ways of the ancients. One woman, proud and determined to see them through this nightmare. Upon Tingari rested their safety, and it seemed too immense a burden even for her.

Off in the distance, Chelsea heard Tingari working among the trees. Pounding, chopping sounds echoed in the night. In a while Tingari returned, carrying a large twisted limb and several pieces of kindling. "Come, Mitjitji, there is water."

"Water? Where?" Chelsea struggled to her feet while Tingari took Gaby into her arms.

Wordlessly, Tingari led her into a thicket. "It is there, in the tree." Working diligently, she began chopping with the sharp edge of a stone into a bulging knot just beneath the bark. Chelsea heard the wood split and saw Tingari lift Gaby to hold her against the tree, directing the baby's mouth toward a miraculous trickle of moisture that dripped from the knot. Patiently Tingari worked with Gaby, encouraging her to drink, wetting the child's mouth and cheeks with the precious water. She murmured in her strange tongue, cooing, urging, teaching Gaby to take her water from God's own reservoir.

After Gaby and Chelsea, Tingari drank as well, swallowing the precious liquid in thirsty gulps. Then she offered the trickle a second time to Gaby, who, experienced now, drank quickly and efficiently. Finally, placing the baby once again in Chelsea's arms, Tingari knelt at the base of the tree and chanted, giving her thanks to the tree's *mamu* for sharing the water of life with them.

Back at the ridge, Chelsea was able to rest more comfortably. Water for Gaby had been her primary concern. Food was a secondary and less urgent necessity.

Tingari had gathered more kindling and was working quickly with stone and stick to start a fire. Slowly the embers caught, consuming one blade of grass at a time until Tingari had fed enough fuel to give them light.

"Mitjitji will place stones around fire. *Mamu* of fire is greedy, eating all in its way."

Chelsea knew Tingari was warning of a brush fire and she worked as instructed to surround the campfire with stones and clear away the vulnerable brush grasses just beyond the circle's perimeter.

It seemed a very long time until Tingari returned. The dress in which she'd slung Gaby was now bundled under her arm and seemed to be alive with squirming creatures. Startled, Chelsea grabbed Gaby and pressed herself against the stone ridge. "What have you got there? What is it?"

"Food. Life," Tingari answered simply.

Instinct told Chelsea she didn't want to know what was captured in the dress, so she turned her face away, hoping not to hear the sound of the rock or the last futile cry as Tingari took its life. Soon the stench of burning pelt smoked in the fire, and as Tingari worked, Chelsea believed she saw the long smooth tail of a rodent. Squeezing her eyes shut, she turned away once again.

Surprisingly, the meat was palatable. Chelsea took the bits offered by Tingari and chewed them lightly before putting them into Gaby's mouth. Somewhere, Tingari had found the hollow burl of a tree, which she'd brought back to camp filled with water from another tree knot. Her thirst quenched and her tummy full, Gaby yawned sleepily and curled into Chelsea's lap to be rocked to sleep.

"You haven't eaten, Tingari."

"This one does not eat of living things," Tingari reminded her. "Many of my race eat, but not Tingari. It is my belief. When the sun rises, it will show the way to carnaba root and coolibah. Then Tingari will eat."

"Did you know we'd find water in the trees?" Chelsea asked.

Tingari nodded. "The signs were shown. It is a place I know. All the people of the land know many places like this one. This place has great *mamu* from many who have passed and from many who are dead. It is to a place such as this that Tingari will come to rest her bones."

"You already know where your grave will be?"

Tingari nodded. "There is no child of Tingari's loins to lay me there. So Tingari must choose the time to set her *mamu* free."

Chelsea heard the abysmal sadness in the woman's voice. Tingari had told her of the duties an Aboriginal must perform for his ancestors, and setting their bodies in a predestined place was one of them. Without a child to bury her, Tingari must choose the time of her own death in that secret place where she believed her *mamu* would be set free to dwell again in some other life form.

"Tingari, is this a graveyard for your people?"

"No, Mitjitji. It is a place of Dreaming. It is where Dreamtime begins. Come, I will show."

Placing Gaby in Tingari's arms, Chelsea picked up a burning branch and followed the woman to the face of the ridge, then up a steep path and into a shallow cave. There, Tingari indicated with a wave of her arm that Chelsea was to hold the torch closer to the rock face. Ocher and crimson caught the light and reflected dimly off the smooth rock.

"Tingari's people before this life," she explained, pointing to an owl-like drawing. It was crudely yet beautifully drawn, simple straight lines indicating a plumage of feathers, and just above it a handprint, ancient as time itself, outlined in deep red ocher. Farther down the rock face were other drawings, stick-line interpretations of hunters, their spears held above their heads; and obviously female figures, large, pendulous breasts and fuzzy-haired, all of them with dilly bags slung over their shoulders like peddlers' sacks.

"It is Namarakain, the spirit who dances from sickbed to sickbed. See her long teeth that eat the souls of the dying." Tingari shivered unexpectedly, sending chills up Chelsea's spine. "There is Thunder-man. He holds the lightning in his hand. Here are more hunters. See, barbed spears and skin throwers. This is where Tingari comes from. These are her people."

Tingari's voice resonated off the stone cliff as she explained her people's history. In the beginning of Dreamtime, the beginnings of life, the Aboriginals had decorated stone cliffs with pulverized rock mixed with water. They were nomads, living together in small family groups, often spending their entire lives without seeing or knowing a stranger. Yet they knew others walked the land, and in that basic need to communicate—or perhaps to leave their mark upon the earth—they began to draw on rockfaces near watering holes. Each painting was a story, a narrative of their life. Tingari said she had seen rock paintings of the evil spirits upon which the people's misfortunes were blamed. In painting their likenesses upon the rock, the people had hoped to drain the spirits of their power. Other pictures chronicled great hunts or depicted a natural catastrophe such as fire or flood.

Some paintings held mystical charms, Tingari explained. Spiny anteaters, egg-laying mammals that were hunted as a delicacy, were often painted in the hope of magically increasing their numbers. Often a panorama of fish was drawn in the hope of bolstering the supply in nearby ponds and rivers. But no portrait was ever drawn of a living person for fear of entrapping that person's *mamu* in the rock. All the dancers, hunters, and stick figures were faceless. Neither did Tingari's people ever develop a written alphabet. The only signature of an artist to be found was the handprint stamped above the paintings. All over the land there were caves and rockfaces such as these, Tingari explained proudly. Her people had walked where none others had gone; not even the white man and his modern ways could conquer the land and live from it like Tingari's people.

At the campfire once again, Tingari chanted a song as she fed more kindling into the fire. She had shared some of herself with her friend, Mitjitji, and with that sharing had come a peace of her soul.

"Tingari, where will we walk tomorrow?"

"Not walk. Here Mitjitji and Gaby stay with Tingari. This a good place, good *mamu*. We not stay long. Soon he will come for us."

"Who? Who will come?" Chelsea cried, frightened. But

Tingari was chanting and praying, and nothing could extract an answer from her as she rubbed warm ashes over her arms and legs and prepared herself for another day protected by her ancient spirits.

For two more days Chelsea and Gaby stayed with Tingari at the cliff rock. By day they searched for water, storing quantities of it in burled tree knots Tingari had fashioned crudely with her sharp-edged stones. While Chelsea sought the area for the carnaba and coolibah roots Tingari preferred, the Aboriginal was busy trapping the evening meal. Wisely, Chelsea never asked what she was eating and feeding Gaby. Just the shape of the tiny bones she picked and the furry pelts Tingari buried along with the entrails told her more than she wanted to know.

On the third morning Chelsea awakened to find Tingari searching the horizon. "What is it? What do you see?"

"There is nothing to see. There is to feel. Soon. Soon."

Before she could question further, Tingari loped off into the thicket to begin the day's chores. Gaby played nearby with several smooth stones Tingari had provided. The sun danced off the baby's gleaming dark curls and had burnished her skin to a golden brown. At that moment Gaby's resemblance to her father was astonishing, especially in the teasing little grin that lit her eyes when she held out one of the stones to show her mother how clever she was.

In the torpid heat of the day, they rested in the shade of the cliff rock. Waves of heat vaporized and shimmered in the air, creating a huge mirage of a cool blue sea. But Chelsea knew there was no sea, only the vast expanse of wilderness, cruel and beautiful and unforgiving.

Beside her, Tingari became alert, peering off into the distance, searching the horizon. "Soon. Soon," Chelsea heard her murmur.

That afternoon Tingari approached Chelsea and spoke

quietly. "Mitjitji will take baby and walk that way," she said. "Tingari will walk there." She pointed in the opposite direction. "There is where Boss Kane looks for his wife."

At the mere mention of Harlow, Chelsea's heart began to pound with fear. "I can't. We'll stay together. You can take us deeper into the outback. You know how to hide from him."

"There is no place to hide, Mitjitji. Nowhere is safe. Thunder-man throws his light, the land will burn. Take baby, go."

All the fragile security Chelsea had felt since coming to Tingari's Dreaming place evaporated like the chimera of a mirage. Nowhere safe. Harlow looking for her and the baby. The baby!

"Tingari, show me where to walk. You take the baby, she'll be safer with you. Tell me what to do."

Tingari shook her head. "No. Mitjitji will be safe. Tingari leaves a trail for Boss Kane to follow."

"Don't you see?" Chelsea anguished. "I can't take care of Gaby out here. Only you can do that. I don't know how to find water or food. Only you can do that! You swore to me, Tingari. You swore you'd always protect my child. You swore it on the *mamu* of your own dead child! You've got to save Gaby!"

Tingari shook her head, sadness filling her eyes. "Tingari's heart is here." She touched Chelsea's breast with the flat of her hand.

"And my heart and my thanks are here." Chelsea's slim white hand reached out to touch Tingari. "But the child comes first; before anything, Gaby comes first! Show me where to walk. Tell me how to leave a trail."

Hours later, Chelsea ran a path through the brush as Tingari had told her. She was intent on leaving a clear trail for Harlow to follow; Gaby's life might depend on it. Rivulets of perspiration rolled down her face as she stumbled over the hard, dry ground. The front of her dress was soaking wet, making the thin material cleave to her body. She knew what the loss of that precious moisture could do to her unless she could replenish it. Already she was dizzy with fatigue, but she drove herself onward, praying that Tingari would carry Gaby to safety. Bless Tingari.

A broken branch here, her handkerchief there, a shred of her dress somewhere else—all clues for Harlow to follow, all leading away from Tingari and Gaby.

Onward. Forward. Don't look back. Never look back. The devil was back there, a devil who wanted to kill her and her child. Faster. Forward. Don't look back—a sound! What was it? A bird in the brush, some small mountain animal. What kind of animal? Chelsea wondered fearfully. A snake! Please God, no snakes. Faster, Faster.

Her breath was coming in ragged gasps as she pushed higher and higher up the steep incline. Her hands were raw and bleeding, but she took no notice; in fact, she almost welcomed the pain. *She* deserved the pain, not Tingari or Gaby.

Again she heard the sound, this time closer. Trapped like a wild rabbit in a snare, she dove headlong into a patch of thick brush, then clapped a hand over her mouth to still her harsh breathing. It was someone on foot, someone walking fast. Harlow? Dear God, how had he found her so quickly? Where was his horse? What would he do when he saw that Gaby wasn't with her? Tingari, she prayed silently, keep my baby safe.

Bitter tears of frustration mingled with the perspiration coursing down Chelsea's cheeks. It was hopeless. She should have known that from the beginning. Her shoulders drooped, and she huddled into herself, holding her breath. *He* was closer. Brush was rustling, leaf mold sailing upward in thin spirals in his wake. Another minute and he would be almost upon her. How intent would his gaze be? Would he think to look down? When was the last time she had left a broken twig, a clue? It seemed hours and hours ago. Time had no meaning to her now.

Childishly, she clapped her free hand over her eyes. She wouldn't look at him until she had to. Then, unable to do what she wanted, she peeked between her fingers. He was almost abreast of her. Her hand fell away. Harlow didn't wear kidskin boots—he wore heavy work shoes with copper tips!

"Luke!" she cried, crawling out from the brush. "Luke!" She was being helped to her feet; strong arms, familiar arms, were crushing her in a powerful embrace. The breath was being driven from her body, but she didn't care. Luke. Dear God. "How did you find me?"

The lump in Luke's throat made it impossible for him to respond. He had to swallow twice before he could manage to croak a few words. "You left a trail that any fool could follow."

"You were never a fool—I was the fool. My God, can you ever forgive me?"

He placed a finger on her lips. "Shhh, there's no need for blame. I'm as guilty as you."

"Harlow wants to kill me and my baby. Luke, he's mad! I tried, my God, how I tried. It wasn't enough. You can't let him kill my baby."

"Our baby," Luke said hoarsely. "Tingari told me. Where is she, Chelsea?"

"I'm not sure. I lost my bearings, and I don't even know how long I've been out here. I sent her out first with Gaby in a different direction. She knows how to survive."

"You're exhausted," Luke said gently.

"Not anymore. I could go on forever."

Luke took stock of his surroundings. He thought of Tingari, who knew the mountains. Which way would she go—up or down to the ravine? It was hard to second guess the Aboriginal, who had his daughter's fate in her hands. Then, of course, there was Harlow.

"Chelsea, listen to me. I want you to climb down, go into the ravine. I'm going to climb; I'll leave a trail, and then I'll double back and follow you. Be careful. Don't worry about me, I'll find you. Harlow won't think we'd go into the ravine because technically we'd be trapped there. This is the only way out. Trust me, Chelsea."

"I do. You know I do. Tingari—"

"Neither of us needs to worry about Tingari. She knows these mountains. We have to trust her." He leaned over and kissed Chelsea lightly on the lips.

Chelsea sighed. "I think, Luke Tanner, that your soul just touched mine. Is that possible?"

"Tingari would say it is. Go now. I'll join you as soon as I can."

All weariness gone now, Luke climbed the mountain at a vigorous pace, his breathing harsh but even. His life had purpose now; he could do whatever had to be done. He climbed steadily for over an hour, leaving little clues the way Chelsea had done. How clever of her, how brave of her, to offer her life in place of their child. But she was no match for Harlow Kane. He didn't think his heart had ever been so full. With a devilish gleam in his eye, he stooped down and squatted on his heels to view the trail he had just climbed. If he was any judge, Kane would be sitting in this same spot a few hours from now.

Panting with exhaustion, Chelsea dropped to the ground. She couldn't go one step farther—she needed water. A tree sapling seemed to reach out to her, offering her comfort. She reached for the feathery, leaf-covered branch, swaying for a moment. No, she couldn't go on. The branch left her

bloody hands with a swish. She would rest for just a moment. A moment wasn't very long. She wouldn't even close
her eyes; she'd just lean back against the tree and wait for
Luke. . . .

Just the thought of his name made her crawl to her feet.
He would be so disappointed in her if she gave in now.
He'd said to go on, that he would find her. She foraged
ahead, unmindful of the branches and brambles that attacked her already tattered dress. It was cooler here, she
thought vaguely. The smell was different, too—a smell she
hadn't been aware of for months. Dampness. Dampness
meant water. The river—of course! She must be close.

Luke found her sitting along the river bank, and an expression of amusement settled briefly over his features.
From the back, she looked as though she were on a summer outing. The only things missing were the blanket and
the picnic basket.

Chelsea whirled about when he called to her and fell
into his arms, crying his name over and over to make sure
he was real and not some figment of her imagination.

"We'll rest for a little while, then try to move north. Not
long, Chelsea," Luke said gently.

"I know. I just needed some water. I'm fine now, really I
am."

"It will be dark soon."

"Did you see any sign of Harlow or Tingari?"

"None. But then I didn't expect any. I'm going to take
off my boots and soak myself. You do the same. Tooley
Joe said there was rain north of us, in Queensland. The
river here is fairly high. A pity it hasn't trickled down to
the riverbed. We could have used this water months ago."

Chelsea slipped off her shoes and a moment later was
floating in the water with Luke holding on to her shoulders. Their bodies were buoyant in the swirling river
water, and each strained toward the other. It was enough

for Chelsea to be with Luke. For now nothing else mattered. There would always be later.

Harlow stood on the edge of the ravine and watched Tanner as he slid down the steep, rocky incline. A grim smile stretched across his face. Tanner was doing it the hard way. If he'd gone just a little farther, he could have followed the track that led to the river. He'd been up here not too long ago trying to figure out ways to get the water to his vineyard, but the river was as low as it was at Bellefleur.

It was good, they were all together now. Did that fool really think he was going to go up the mountain and follow his little trail of clues? He'd simply sat back on his horse, sipping from his flask as he waited and watched. He'd known that Tanner was trying to throw him off the trail. That had been his first mistake. His second mistake was going down into the ravine. There was only one way out from there.

Harlow sat for a long time, getting a feel for the wind. When he was satisfied, he prodded his horse to the trail that would take him to the foot of the ravine. He waited till he was almost at the bottom, then reined in the horse, slipped effortlessly from the saddle, and dug around in his saddlebags. He withdrew a flint and in moments had a long, dry branch in his hands. A sound to his left made him jerk around. A wild animal of some kind. But he'd been diverted from his actions, which had given him enough time to contemplate what he was about to do.

Murder. He was going to kill his wife and her lover. He turned, disoriented for a moment, wondering if he could really light the dry branch and kill two people in cold blood—possibly four, if Tingari and the brat were anywhere near.

Harlow argued with himself, bringing the flint to within

an inch of the dry branch, only to take it away. Murder. It would be on his conscience. He wouldn't have to hide out at Bellefleur in shame if there remained no reminders of what had happened. He'd start over; he was strong and healthy—and he knew the thought was a lie.

His shoulders slumped. He'd never understood why he was driven the way he was. Irmaline had tried to tell him, to help him be the man she'd said she wanted, but he'd ignored her the way he'd ignored Chelsea. No one, not even the reverend, had ever been able to explain to him why he loved the land and the vines more than his family. He'd wanted to love Chelsea, but he didn't know how, just as he hadn't known how to love Irmaline and his children.

He was so tired, and the horse was weary. He smoothed down the sweaty hide of the animal's head. His touch was gentle, tender for the animal that had been carrying him and his guilt. He laid his own sweaty cheek next to the animal and was rewarded with a soft wicker. Animals were loyal and never betrayed their masters.

In the end all a man had left was pride. When others judged him, he had to be able to stand proud. If his vineyards died out, so would hundreds of others. Their owners would be in the same position he was . . . only they would have wives and family at their side to make a new beginning. They would all know that his wife had betrayed him, had given birth to another man's child. If Chelsea and Tanner died, no one would blame him . . . especially if they were found locked in each other's arms; an adulteress and her lover. He would grieve and be the recipient of everyone's sympathy.

Yes, it was the only way. Harlow struck the flint, and the branch flared. He held it aloft as he climbed into the saddle, then spurred his horse forward slowly as he bent over, dragging the burning branch behind him. His eyes gleamed triumphantly as flames shot up in the rear. The horse whinnied and reared at the smell of smoke. Harlow kept his seat as he watched the wind carry sparks and set other fires. The whole ravine would soon go up in flames, and he was guarding the only way out. He felt calm, his face betraying no emotion as the flames licked upward. There would be no survivors.

Chelsea and Luke slept peacefully as the fire crept closer, spewing smoke and ash in all directions, destroying everything it touched. Chelsea stirred first, coughing and sputtering. "Luke! Luke, wake up! I smell smoke."

Startled, Luke opened his eyes, took in the scene, felt Chelsea's horror, and was immediately on his feet. "The son of a bitch is trying to burn us out of here! Run, Chelsea, to the river. Hurry!" he shouted to be heard above the crackling flames. "If you lose me in the smoke, just head for the river. It's the only place we'll be safe. Straight, Chelsea— don't waver to the right or left, or you'll get lost. Run!"

"What about you?" Chelsea cried over her shoulder. "I can't go without you."

"Just do as I tell you. Now go!"

The fear in Luke's voice spurred her forward. She ran as though the hounds of hell were at her heels. Twice she had to stop to beat at the flames that licked at her dirty dress, which now hung in tatters about her knees. She smelled the river before she saw it and splashed headlong into the water, floundering wildly. Gasping and coughing, she tried to stay afloat as Luke had shown her. Panic engulfed her as she slipped beneath the black water, only to struggle to the surface seconds later. Always she emerged with Luke's name on her lips, as if it were a prayer. And when she felt her hair being pulled, she realized her prayer had been answered.

"Don't fight the water, Chelsea, or you'll go under again. Lean on me. I'll hold you up."

"Luke, Tingari and Gaby . . . is the fire just here in the ravine or in the foothills, too?" Chelsea asked fearfully.

"I don't know," Luke replied. "My guess would be that Harlow set this fire. This is just a guess, mind you, but I do believe he thinks we're all together. If that's true, Tingari and Gaby are safe. Tingari will smell the smoke and simply move to higher ground. We're too low, the fire will be contained here."

"We can't get out, can we?"

"No, Chelsea, we can't. If the wind changes, we might have a chance, but that seems unlikely. We've had an east wind for days now. I'd wager Clonmerra that Kane is sitting at the top of the ravine waiting for us to try and get out. We're staying right here, here in the river."

"How long?" Chelsea managed to whisper.

"I'm not going to lie to you, Chelsea. For as long as it takes. It could be days, it could be a week. The whole ravine is going to have to burn itself out. This is the only place we're safe."

"I don't understand. If the river is this high, there must have been rain. The trees and brush must be wet. Wet wood doesn't burn."

"This river runs hundreds of miles north. I told you it rained in Queensland. This river is now almost full, and ours will be, too, when this manages to run down to our land. Everything here is dry. I know it feels damp and wet, but that's just around and near the river's edge. The trees and brush are bone dry. Listen to the crackling of the flames as the trees burn."

Chelsea tried to pierce the orange light, but all she could see were hungry flames dancing upward, driving the hot air through the burning trees. The air was scalding hot, and periodically Luke pulled her beneath the water. The sky was one wall of black smoke, and against that darkness, along the crest of the ridge by the ravine, flickered an angry phalanx of red. Smoke swirled toward them, so thick it made them choke and cough. Luke reached down and brought up Chelsea's wet skirt to cover her mouth and nose.

The strong wind roared over the ridges like a cascading waterfall and created a powerful wheel of racing downdrafts above the river itself. Smoke and sparks and burning fragments flew high into the air, spit out by the force of the conflagration. A tall tree near the river's edge suddenly flared like a torch as the fire crossed the river to the other side. Thickening smoke flowed up the deep channel of the ravine.

Chelsea pulled her skirt away—it was dry now from the hot air—and wetted it again, securing it over her mouth and nose. Luke squinted against the cinders and soot, stunned that the fire had come upon them so quickly. The strong wind was responsible—he could almost envision Harlow waiting for just the right moment before he'd set the fire that was to kill them.

"Over the ridges, to the south, look!" Luke shouted above the roar. Heavy smoke, propelled by a vicious downdraft, rolled toward them. If the fire didn't kill them, he thought, the smoke would. Again and again they slid beneath the water, only to emerge to flames and an impenetrable, noxious pall of smoke.

It seemed such a long time, perhaps hours, during which Chelsea realized she could barely open her eyes. Her shoulders and face were seared from the intense heat. Fire was everywhere, above them, surrounding them, feeding itself on young saplings and brush. The oils within the eucalyptus trees burned a white-hot blue and seemed to flare forever before their hollow shanks were also consumed by the greedy flames. Insatiable, it raged on and on, exploding trees and running through brush until it seemed the earth itself would burn. But they endured passively, for there was no other choice. They remained in the watery fortress, their only hope for survival. Only their heads broke the water's surface; they crouched in the warm depths like animals, waiting for the fire to burn itself out. Time lost all meaning; day seemed the same as night. Except for the orange-red glare of the flames, there was no reality.

Suddenly Chelsea tightened her grip on Luke's shoulder. He turned to see the entire face of the hill they had climbed down turn into a towering wall of flames, which licked at the sky like sharp-tongued serpents. For the space of one wild moment, Luke felt as though the burning wall were going to topple down upon them; then the smoke closed in again, and the massive blaze was lost to the sky.

Time moved on, and the roaring, thundering flames filled their world with fear. The fire was a stampeding herd of buffalo, and they were in the path of the pounding hooves. The branches that landed upright in the water with their ends burning reminded Chelsea of the sacred candles Tingari burned in the dark of night.

They choked and coughed, and the only air they could breathe safely was the draft directly on top of the water. Invariably, Chelsea would get her nose full of gaseous vapor and Luke would have to slap her on the back. But they endured, and somehow the day passed once more into night.

During the long midnight hours, while Chelsea dozed on Luke's shoulder, the fire seemed to Luke to be reborn in the darkness all about them. It burned fiercely and, like an angry dog, snapped and snarled at everything in its path. Eventually, however, Luke thought he heard a new tempo in the fire's song. Was it beginning to burn itself out? He could only hope. He was too weary to think now; all he could do was try to keep Chelsea's head above water and his as well. At times it was a losing battle, as his eyes would close and he'd begin to slip beneath the water. Then Chelsea's cries of fright would awaken him, and again he would watch the fire like the sentinel he was.

It wasn't his imagination: the light in the sky was a new dawn. He could see the new day, he thought jubilantly. But only the thought was jubilant; his body was too weary to respond. Still, they were alive, and that was all that mattered.

Harlow Kane sat on his horse at the edge of the ravine for two straight days, watching with an eerie calm as the ravine below him burned to cinders. Nothing, no one, could live through that inferno. Now it was time to go down and see for himself the results of his handiwork.

Midway down the trail, the horse threw a shoe and stumbled, and Harlow landed in a pile of smoldering ashes. He paid no heed as he got to his feet and started the climb down to the foot of the ravine. The dying embers of isolated lowbrush fires were stomped on with hardly a glance. He was coming down here for a reason; he just had to remember what it was. He'd gone too long without sleep. Watching the vines night and day always took its toll on him. No one seemed to care. No, that wasn't true; Chelsea cared. She was always pampering him with cool cloths for his brow, asking if he was tired and could she fetch him this or that. Cooking meals and putting flowers on the table. He liked that. Chelsea preferred his wine to Tanner's. She'd said so on more than one occasion.

He was at the bottom of the ravine now and stopped for a moment to get his bearings. His eyes narrowed in the smoke-filled air . . . and he remembered. His rifle hung loosely from its strap on his shoulder, and his hand sought the barrel. How comforting it felt.

Gabrielle chattered to herself in the backpack Tingari had fashioned for her. There was no smile on the Aboriginal's face as she began her climb down from the mountain. As soon as she'd smelled the smoke, she had known what had happened. And the moment the wind had shifted, carrying the billowing black smoke in a southerly direction, Tingari had started her trek back—praying she wasn't too late. The surrounding calm soothed her as she spoke to the child who had been entrusted to her care. It wouldn't be long now. Searching for a path known only to herself would save her many hours. When she found it, she quickened her step as though she heard some urgent message. Her stride was long, purposeful, and Gaby jostled happily in her backpack.

The Aboriginal arrived at the river's edge directly on Harlow Kane's heels. Her dark eyes sought out the footprints in the ash along the river bank. Unmindful of the heat searing her bare feet, Tingari ran in search of her Mitjitji.

It was the sound of Gaby's gurgling that forced Harlow Kane to turn, from his quarry—the lovers sleeping in each other's arms on the river bank.

"Tingari!" Chelsea cried, suddenly awake. "Give me my baby."

"Don't move. That goes for you, too, Tingari, you black witch," Harlow said menacingly as he backed off a step. "Give me the child."

"Tingari, no! Harlow, please, she's just a baby!" Chelsea pleaded. "Don't hurt her. I'll do anything you want! Please, Harlow, don't hurt my baby."

Luke Tanner had eyes only for the laughing baby on Tingari's back. His daughter. His and Chelsea's. God, the reality was so awesome he could almost forget about Harlow and the gun he was pointing at them.

"No, Boss Kane. The child belongs with her mother. Come back with me to Bellefleur. I will show you the way. Boss Kane, listen to my words."

"Why should I listen to a crazy old woman like you? Give me that brat and get out of my way."

"No, Boss Kane."

Chelsea had inched over beyond Luke and was almost to where Tingari stood. She was ready when Tingari slipped her arms from the vines that had been fashioned as straps for the makeshift backpack. She caught Gaby as the child slid to the ground. Later, she could never say how it happened, nor could Luke, who was busy trying to take his child from the confining backpack. But they were both dead, Harlow Kane with a broken neck and Tingari with a bullet through her heart.

Chelsea sat in the shade on the veranda at Clonmerra. Beneath the spinifex tree on the side yard, Gaby played, serving little cakes to her tea party of dolls. The air was clear, the sky bluer than blue. At Chelsea's side was a cradle, and she rocked their son gently. Young Luke, three weeks old, slept peacefully. Soon the young seedlings she had planted to replace those destroyed by the drought would be in bloom. Clonmerra had survived, and now it flourished. Vine cuttings that Jack Mundey had saved would grow into new harvest. The winery would be filled with the heady scent of clarets and ports and a new vintage laid.

Even Bellefleur was enjoying a new prosperity. Franklin had returned to take his place as rightful owner, and there was a young woman who, it seemed, would soon be the new mistress of Bellefleur. And Emma had had her wish granted; she'd joined Martha in England.

If happiness could be harvested and pressed into wine, Chelsea thought to herself, she would be drunk with it.

Her eyes caught a movement along the drive, a whirlwind of red dust as it spewed out from behind Luke's horse. He was coming home, coming to her, and as always, her heart beat for joy. Hatless, the sunlight dancing in his dark hair, he dismounted and walked toward her, his arms already opened and welcoming to receive her.

This would be theirs forever, this life they shared. They would laugh through the good days and suffer the bad, but they would have each other. Life was like wine, Luke had told her once. It could be bitter or sweet. Chelsea's smile was as bright as the light of a thousand candles as she lifted her face for his kiss. All of life was a lesson, she reflected, but one thing she knew: However bitter the wine, so sweet the rapture.

If you enjoyed *To Taste the Wine*, you won't want to miss
Fern Michaels's brand-new stand-alone novel,

SOUTHERN COMFORT

Turn the page for a special preview.

A Kensington Hardcover, on sale in May 2011

Prologue

Atlanta, Georgia
March 2002

Detective Patrick Kelly—Tick, to his friends—signed out of his precinct and headed to his car, an eight-year-old Saturn with 120,000 miles on it. It purred like a baby when he turned the key. Then it sputtered and died. He'd given it too much gas and flooded the engine. He knew the drill—wait five minutes, try again, and if he was lucky, Lulu would get him home.

Sally, his wife, had named his car Lulu but never told him why. She'd just giggle and say it was a lulu of a car. Sally drove a ten-year-old Honda Civic. The only good thing about owning two old cars was not having to make car payments. Everything was about cutting corners, saving for college for the kids and doing without.

Tick sighed, leaned back against the headrest, but didn't close his eyes because, if he did, he'd go to sleep. He'd worked a double shift because Joe Rollins had a ruptured appendix, and he'd filled in for him. He couldn't wait to get home to Sally and the kids, take a shower, maybe eat something Sally had kept warm for him, and go to sleep with her spooning into his back. When he felt his eyelids start to droop, he turned the key, and, miracle of miracles, Lulu turned over. He was on his way to his family, whom he loved more than anything on earth. He loved them more than he loved his job, and he dearly loved his job. There were days when he hated the job, but the love always won out. He truly believed he made a difference. Where his family was concerned, there was no doubt, he loved them 24/7, unconditionally.

When he worked the late shift, he always let his thoughts go to his wonderful little family as a way of unwinding on his way home. He'd met Sally in the seventh grade, when she transferred from out of state. He fell in love with her that day when she stood in front of the class and said, "My name is Sally, and I'm new today." He'd seen the sparkle of tears in her eyes and knew instinctively that she was afraid. Afraid the kids wouldn't like her, afraid she'd make a mistake, and they'd laugh. He never did figure out where or how he'd known that, he'd just known it. Then, when he found out she had moved one street over from his own street, and they'd be walking to school at the same time, he'd almost done cartwheels. Later, Sally said she didn't fall in love with him till they were in the eighth grade. He'd been heartbroken at that news but had covered it up well. She loved him, and that was all that mattered.

Married for fifteen years now, and he loved her as much as he did that day in the seventh grade when she introduced herself. He hoped and prayed nightly that his two children would find mates as wonderful as their mother when it was their time.

Sally Pritchard Kelly was the wind beneath his wings. She was the reason he got up in the morning, the reason he was still sane considering the fact that he was a homicide detective. Because of Sally and the kids, he didn't carry his work home with him. When he walked in the front door of his mortgaged-to-the-hilt house, he was in another world. Worn, comfortable furniture waited for him. Sally always waited at the door for him, a smile on her face and smelling of a summer day. Always. He couldn't remember a single day in all the years they were married that she hadn't greeted him with a smile and a kiss on the lips. A real kiss that said she loved him, missed him, and now things were the way they should be because he was home. There would always be a warm meal in the oven if he was late. Didn't matter how late he was. Sally would curl up on the couch and wait. Sally was the constant in his life.

Prettier than a picture, he always said. He loved the freckles that danced across her nose, loved the crooked eyetooth she refused to have straightened. There wasn't one thing he didn't love about his wife, because in his eyes, she was perfect. At this point in his reverie, even if he was so tired he couldn't think straight, his eyes always misted up. He'd just curl up and die if anything ever happened to his beloved Sally. Well, that wasn't going to happen anytime soon; they had at least another fifty years to look forward to. Both he and Sally came from families where longevity was the rule.

Tick could feel his eyes start to droop again, so he pressed the stereo unit and turned up the volume. His and Sally's favorite song was burned on every inch of the CD so he could play it over and over. "Mustang Sally." He started to sing along with Wilson Pickett at the top of his lungs, *"Ride, Sally, ride!"*

He was two streets away from where he lived on David Court when he saw the strobe lights shooting upward to the sky. Blue, red, white—just like it was the Fourth of July. But it wasn't the Fourth of July. He knew what the lights meant. Good cop that he was, he knew he was going to have to stop to offer any assistance if needed. Sally, the kids, and sleep would have to wait just a bit longer. He turned off the CD player and turned the corner, and his world came to a screeching halt. He saw the barricade, the yellow tape, the crazy arcing lights, the crowds of people, and too many police cars to count.

All parked in front of *his house,* in the driveway, on the lawn and sidewalk. He slammed on the brakes, threw open the door, and lunged forward. He heard his name being called from all directions, arms trying to reach him, someone trying to tackle him. He plowed ahead, driven by an energy he didn't know he possessed. And then he was in a vise grip, unable to move. The more he fought and struggled, the tighter the hold became. He looked up to see the face of the man holding him and was stunned to see his captain, tears rolling down his cheeks. "Easy, Tick, easy."

Tick ground his teeth together. He had to show respect to the captain. "Did someone rob my house? Where are Sally and the kids? Captain, I asked you a question."

"Tick . . . I . . ."

Rising onto his toes, Tick reared upward, loosening the hold his captain had on his arm. He sprinted forward as fellow officers rushed to prevent him from entering the house. He evaded all of them.

The house was deathly silent. The crime-scene personnel took that moment to stop what they were doing and stare at the man who looked like the wrath of God. "Where are they?"

Someone, he didn't know who it was, pointed to the second floor. Tick took the steps two at a time. It looked to him like there were a hundred people in his small upstairs. He bolted down the short hall to his bedroom. In his life he'd never seen so much blood. He saw her then, his beloved Sally, lying in the doorway leading to the bathroom. He knew it was her because of her nightgown and robe. And her wedding ring. There was little left to her face. How could that be gone? Those beautiful freckles dancing across her pert little nose were gone. Her throat was a gaping hole. Tick's knees buckled. Strong hands held him upright. "Ride, Sally, ride," he blubbered.

"Get him out of here. Have the ME look at him."

"Where are the kids?"

"Not now, Tick. Please," his captain said.

"Where are my kids?" Tick roared.

"In their rooms. Tick, please, let us handle this. I'm begging you, don't go there."

"Get the hell away from me. . . ."

Tick found them huddled together in the closet, which was full of toys and balls. There was blood everywhere. Too much blood for two tiny little creatures who once carried his life's blood. Now it was a river on a hopscotch-patterned carpet. He wanted to bend down, to scoop up his children, to hold them close, but they wouldn't let him. He wanted to run his hands through his daughter's curly hair, which was just like her mother's but was matted with blood, and he couldn't see the curls. He looked at his son and fainted dead away. He felt himself being carried someplace, heard voices he couldn't identify, then he felt something prick his arm. Ride, Sally, rideeee.

The Governor's Mansion
Tallahassee, Florida
August 2009

Thurman Lawrence Tyler checked himself in the mirror one last time. He adjusted his Hermès tie, examined the crease on the French cuffs of his custom-made shirt, brushed an imaginary piece of lint from his imported Italian suit, inspected the shine on his shoes, and smoothed a thick white errant hair in place before stepping into the foyer, where Elizabeth waited. At six foot one, he had an athletic build, and sharp blue eyes that rarely missed a beat, and she thought her husband still as handsome as the day she had met him. Maybe even more so.

"Thurman, dear, you look as handsome as you did the day of our wedding." Elizabeth Tyler, his wife of forty-six years and right hand of Governor Thurman Lawrence Tyler, looked every bit the elegant wife of a dignitary. Perfectly coiffed blond hair, her grandmother's pearl earrings and necklace glowing next to her porcelain skin. A pale blue Chanel suit brought out the cornflower blue of her eyes. Both were tall, slim, and in excellent physical condition, and they appeared almost perfect as they scrutinized each other.

"And you, my dear, look like the innocent that you were." Thurman studied his wife for a moment longer. She'd aged extremely well, unlike many of her friends. Elizabeth was always careful to protect herself from Florida's punishing sun, never smoked, and rarely drank anything more than an occasional glass of white wine. She played tennis three times a week, had a facial once a week, and her hair touched up every third Thursday of the month. Of course he wasn't supposed to know this, so he pretended her blond locks were as natural as those of a newborn.

"You're too kind," she replied.

"Nonsense," he responded.

Without another word, he escorted her to the elaborate dining room, where they had their breakfast. Each consumed two cups of coffee, his with skim milk and hers black. Both had one half of a Florida ruby red grapefruit with one slice of homemade dry wheat toast. After they'd consumed their meal, they took their daily doses of vitamins with a bottle of mineral water imported from Switzerland.

Their morning routine was like clockwork and had been ever since Thurman was elected governor of the fine state of Florida almost eight years ago. With his second term coming to an end, both were preparing for the next step of their career: president of the United States. Yes, it was *their* career because Thurman never made a decision without first consulting his dear wife.

When they finished their meal, the governor went to his office and Elizabeth went to hers, where she spent the morning going over the menu for an upcoming gala they were hosting. With nothing more on her agenda, she went to the personal living area that connected their offices. Knowing her husband would be occupied for the rest of the day with his lieutenant governor, she placed a phone call to her son, Lawrence. Hanging up after several rings that went unanswered, Elizabeth called an old high school friend. They made plans to have lunch soon. Free time was rare, and she decided to take advantage of it and relax with a book. She'd spent her life promoting literacy and was very involved with the public library system, but never once in all her years of reading had she told anyone of her love of horror novels. Today she planned to read Stephen King's latest.

Settling into a Queen Anne chair next to the window overlooking the garden, Elizabeth spent the next two hours immersed in her novel. Later, when she heard Thurman shouting on the phone to Carlton, she hid her book beneath the chair's cushion and hurried to the door, where she stood silently, listening to her husband's private conversation.

She and Thurman had done everything in their power to see that Lawrence never found out. It would ruin him and his father if the public got wind of this. Elizabeth thought she had done the right thing by keeping him. No, she *had* done the right thing. He was her son, the only child she would ever have. Whatever it took to ensure that he wasn't ruined by her and Thurman's past mistakes, Elizabeth would do it. After all, she was his mother, and if he couldn't count on her, then poor Lawrence had no one.

Every hope and dream they had ever imagined was about to be destroyed. They had worked too long and hard for this moment. Elizabeth refused to allow anyone to ruin the future that was just now within their reach.

She'd made numerous sacrifices throughout her life in order for Thurman and Lawrence to be successful. Now that someone threatened her life's work, she wanted to fight back in anger; but that had never been her way, and she would not start now.

She went to her private office and sat down. She removed a sheet of creamy personalized paper from her desk. Lawrence would have to know this someday. If neither she nor Thurman were around to tell him, then a letter would suffice.

My Dearest Son,
If you're reading this letter, you must know
that your father and I are no longer of this
earth. There is something I have wanted to tell
you since you were a little boy, but the time was
never right. Then as you got older I thought it
would be a disservice not to tell you, yet I could
never find the right time. If you hate me or your
father after reading this, know that I will under-
stand and love you in spite of it. The first time I
laid eyes on your father, I fell madly in love . . .

Chapter 1

The 1,203 residents of Mango Key never knew what to call *it* or how to refer to it. For the most part, in the beginning, they called it a castle, then they switched and called it a fortress. As it neared completion, they became puzzled at the high brick wall and the massive iron gates that sparked if they were touched and simply referred to it as *that place* at the end of the island.

The residents didn't know who lived in *that place,* but they speculated that maybe it was some aging film star who didn't want anyone to see his or her lost looks. Or perhaps, since the only activity seen or heard came late at night, it was some drug lord trying to hide out from the law.

The residents of Mango Key were simple folks and earned their living selling their mangoes, oranges, and grapefruit to the boats that came into the Key once a week, and they didn't really care about the phantom people who maybe lived or maybe didn't live in *that place.* They had never seen a soul in the light of day since *that place* had been completed five years ago. For the most part, they forgot that it was even there because it didn't affect them in any way.

In truth, there were 1,204 residents of Mango Key, but the additional resident wasn't a native, so the residents more or less ignored Patrick Kelly the same way they ignored *that place*. But that hadn't been the case when he had first arrived on Mango Key.

Even Patrick Kelly, known to old friends as Tick, although those friends were long gone, ignored the place, which was three miles down the beach from where he lived.

The reason he'd ignored the construction was because he had been in a drunken stupor for the two years it had taken to build it, and the third year, he was just more or less coming out of his stupor. And the least of his worries was someone building a house, a castle, a fortress, or *that place*. It simply held no interest for him; it was all he could do to get through one day so that he could go to sleep, wake, and struggle through the next. Today, seven years after the fact, he still had no interest in what he considered an abandoned structure he happened to see when he walked the beach, swam, or fished.

It was a beautiful August day on Mango Key. But then most days were beautiful except during hurricane season, and those exceptions usually lasted only a day or so. The sun was startlingly bright, warming Tick's body as he walked out of the ocean. He had his dinner in a net—a fish he couldn't name. Nor did he care if it had a name. He called all fish dinner. A few wild radishes, some equally wild onions, a few mangoes and maybe an orange, and dinner was ready. A great diet. He'd dropped twenty-five pounds since arriving at Mango Key. He weighed 170 pounds, the same weight he'd carried when he was twenty-eight and in top form. Now pushing the big four-oh, at six foot two inches, he still carried the weight easily. He was brown as a nut, living in cutoffs and sandals. He couldn't remember the last time he'd worn a shirt. Maybe hurricane season last year, when the temperature dropped to sixty-five degrees.

Patrick Kelly, hobo, derelict, beach bum, drunk, former homicide detective, ex-father, widower, rich best-selling author, and recovering alcoholic.

Tick stopped two hundred feet from the place he'd called home for almost seven years. His abode, that was how he thought of it, had been little more than a lean-to with iffy rusty plumbing and an even rustier generator when he arrived. It had stayed that way for close to three years, until he woke up one day and knew that his drinking days had to come to an end or he would die, which had been his purpose all along. But that particular morning, with the sun warming his bloated body, he'd taken his best friend, his only friend, Jack Daniel's, and dumped him in the ocean.

He wasn't sure now, but he thought he'd had the shakes, the crawlies, the hallucinations for a full week before he had shed all the bad toxins from his system. Then he'd reared up like a gladiator and taken a few steps into the land of the living. After which he took a few more steps and headed for the mainland, where he ordered all the lumber and nails he would need to redo his house, which he worked on from sunup to sundown. He'd made two more trips to order furniture, generators, appliances, a new laptop, a printer, scanner, cell phone, and anything else he thought he might need to make his life easier. The renovation took eleven months. He now had a skimpy front porch, with a swing and a chair. He'd christened the finished product with a bottle of apple cider. He'd even given his new abode a name. He called it Tick's Tree House because he'd rebuilt the structure on stilts. He loved it as much as he could love anything these days.

Tick started up the steps that led to his porch and started to laugh when the parrot who came with the house started to squawk. At least he thought it had come with the house, but with his foggy memory, he couldn't be sure. He couldn't remember if the bird was in residence when he had arrived or if it came later. He marveled at the bird's vocabulary and couldn't remember if he'd taught it to talk or if it had learned from somewhere else. He called it Bird and had no way of knowing if it was male or female. Bird ruffled his feathers, and said, "You're late."

"Am not."

"Five o'clock."

Tick looked down at his watch. It was four thirty. "It's four thirty. Four thirty means I'm not late." Bird rustled his feathers, then swooped down and perched on Tick's shoulder.

"Five o'clock, time to eat. Five o'clock, time to eat!"

"No, Bird, it is not time to eat. We eat at six o'clock. I tell you that every day."

"Bullshit!"

In spite of himself, Tick burst out laughing. He wondered then for the millionth time who the bird had once belonged to. Obviously someone with a salty tongue. "Go on, Bird, I'll call you when it's time to eat." If anyone from his other life could see him dining with a parrot, they'd lock him up and throw away the key. He even set a place for Bird at the table.

Tick was sucking on a mango, the rich juice dribbling down his chin, when Bird's head tilted to the side. His feathers rustled as he flew out of the mini kitchen straight for the front door. The hair on the back of Tick's neck went straight up when the parrot screamed, "Intruder! Intruder!"

Tick slipped off his stool, his bare feet making no sound as he backed up to the small cabinet where he kept his gun. Because he was a cop, he kept the Glock locked and loaded. It felt comforting in his hand. He never got company. *Never.* If one of the Key residents came around, they always rang the bell out by the oversize palmetto.

Bird was literally bouncing off the walls as he circled the small living room, whose door opened onto the little front porch. "Hey, anyone home besides that crazy bird?"

Tick blinked. He'd know that voice anywhere. It belonged to his twin brother, Pete. He jammed the Glock into the back of his shorts. "Enough, Bird. It's not an intruder!" The green bird squawked one more time as he settled himself on the back of Tick's favorite chair. Bird's eyes were bright as he watched his roommate walk over to the door.

They were the same height, the same muscular build, but there the resemblance ended. Tick was dark-haired, dark-eyed, thanks to his mother's Italian heritage. Pete was a redhead with blue eyes, thanks to his father's Irish heritage. "I was in the neighborhood," Pete said quietly.

"Bullshit!" Bird squawked.

"That's my line, Bird. C'mon in, Pete. How'd you find me?" They should be hugging each other, at the very least shaking hands or just doing brotherly things. Instead, they eyed each other warily.

"Nice place," Pete said, looking around. "That's a joke, Tick. What, eight hundred square feet?"

"More or less. How'd you find me?" Tick asked a second time. "It's been, what, almost seven, maybe eight years, and suddenly here you are."

Pete shuffled his feet. For the first time, Tick saw he was carrying his loafers and was in his bare feet. Maybe that was why they hadn't shaken hands. Yeah, yeah, that was probably the reason.

"I just got back two weeks ago. Yeah, I know I was supposed to write. You know me."

Tick motioned to one of the two chairs in the small room. He noticed that Pete favored one leg over the other. "What happened?"

"I got a little busted up on the rodeo circuit. Got a new hip and knee. Met up with this guy from Argentina and he asked me to go with him to take care of his polo ponies. Seemed like a good idea at the time. Hell, I still think it was the best thing I could have done at the time. The guy paid me ten times what I was worth, gave me incredible bonuses. Everything was free, great lodgings, free food, my own Jeep. I banked every cent of my money.

"Listen, Tick, I didn't know about Sally and the kids. If I had known, I would have hopped on the first plane I could find. I went to see Andy, and he told me. Jesus, I walked around in a daze for almost a week. He wouldn't tell me where you were. Good old Andy wouldn't tell me. I couldn't believe it. He wouldn't tell *me*. I threatened him with everything in the book, and I gotta tell you, he's a hell of a friend and one hell of an attorney; he didn't give you up, Tick."

"You're here!"

Pete squirmed in his chair. He looked down at his shoes as though he wondered why he was still holding them. He bent over, winced, and set them on the floor. "Yeah, I did a little breaking and entering. Jeez, his office is a house on Peachtree. A ten-year-old could pick that lock. I looked in your file and found out you were here. So, here I am, a little late, Tick, but I'm here now. What can I do?"

Tick smiled. "I wish there was something you could do, but there isn't. I'm okay. You can go back to Argentina knowing I'm okay and don't need you or anyone else."

Pete leaned forward. "That's not quite true, now is it? You need Andy. I know he takes care of all your finances, I saw it in the files. Seems like you're doing pretty well for an ex-cop-turned-author. I'm okay with you not needing

me, but don't start handing me bullshit, Tick. Jesus, I'm
bleeding for Sally and the kids. I know the story, so you
don't have to tell me anything you don't want to tell me. I
can't go back to Argentina. My boss fell off one of his
ponies and got stomped to death. I came back with enough
money to go into business for myself. I even brought you a
check for that five grand I borrowed from you." He
reached into his pocket and pulled out a crumpled check.
He laid it on the small table next to his chair.

"Keep it."

"Nah, it doesn't work like that. I always pay my debts.
I found a bar and grill on Peachtree. Pop would have loved
it. Andy's checking it out to make sure it's as good as it
sounds. I have enough to pay cash and will have quite a bit
left over. I have a Realtor looking for some digs for me in
the area. And, I'm getting married in six months. I want
you to be my best man the way I was yours when . . . you
know."

Tick couldn't keep the surprise out of his voice. "You're
getting married! You?"

"Hard to believe, huh? Yeah, I met her in Argentina.
She was there on vacation with a few friends. She works
for the State Department. Right now she's in England and
will be back in six months, then she's quitting. She loves to
cook, so we're going to buy the bar and grill together.
She's willing to put in half the asking price. So, will you be
my best man?"

A burst of panic flooded Tick's whole being. Standing
up for his brother would mean he'd have to leave his nest.
He had to say something to wipe the awful look off his
brother's face. He shrugged. "Six months is a long time
down the road." He hated the way his voice sounded, all
shaky and squeaky.

Pete nodded as though he understood. "You might not
want to hear this, but I'm going to tell you, anyway. I went

out to the cemetery. I took flowers. Said some prayers,
talked to . . . Christ, that was the hardest thing I ever did
in my whole life. I sat there on the ground and picked the
flowers apart. So I went back and bought some more.
They were pretty, Tick. I remembered how Sally had all
those rosebushes in the yard. I left a standing order for the
flower shop to deliver them every Saturday. I wanted to do
so much more, but, Tick, there wasn't anything else to do.
If there's more I can do, tell me and I'll do it."

Tick bit down on his lower lip. He should have done
what Pete did. All those years and no flowers on his family's graves. He should have made arrangements to do
what Pete did. Oh, no, it had been more important to put
his snoot in a bottle and hide out. All he could think of to
say was, "Thanks."

"You gonna talk to me, Tick? Do I have to drag it out of
you?"

Tick finally found his tongue. "I'm sure Andy told you
all the nitty-gritty details. After the funeral, which I really
don't remember, I got in my car and started to drive. I honest to God do not know how I got here. I do know that I
was in a stupor for about two and a half years. It's all one
big blank. I woke up one morning and knew I was going
to die. At first I didn't care. Then I did care. I thought
about what Pop told us as kids when we did something
wrong. He'd say, it's time to straighten up and fly right.
The village people must have taken care of me. I have
vague memories of people standing over me. There always
seemed to be food for me to eat. A boat comes once a
week with supplies, so I have to assume I somehow made
arrangements to get liquor delivered.

"I write books these days. Do you believe that? And,
they've made movies out of them. Who knew I could do
that? Certainly not me."

Pete waved his arms about. "So, this is it? The end of

the road for you? There's a lot to be said for peace and quiet and tranquillity, but to withdraw so totally, I can't believe that's a good thing. Don't you miss Atlanta and all the action? You had a lot of friends back there on the force. Everyone just said you fell off the face of the earth."

"I'm content. For now. Things might have turned out differently if they hadn't caught the punk who killed my family. They gunned him down right outside my house. I would have hunted him down and killed him myself. There's nothing back there for me now." His voice was defiant when he said, "I like it here."

"Yeah, I can see that. Kind of small, though. How about I stay around long enough to help you build another room onto this . . . stilt house? Remember when we helped Pop build a sunroom for Mom? I'm free as the breeze for the next six months. Let me help, Tick. I *need* to do something for you. If you're writing another book and need to concentrate on that, I can do it on my own. I was always better at the hammer-and-nails thing than you were. Even Pop said so. A nice big room with wall-to-wall windows so you can see the ocean. Maybe a big, fancy bathroom. By the way, do you own this place?"

"Yeah. I bought it a few years ago from the village. It's kind of complicated. Everyone in the village is related. Indian heritage. This Key is the result of some kind of land grant. One of the elders came out here one day and he had this big stick. He asked me to follow him and he kept dragging the stick; and then he said everything within the lines was mine. He held out his hand, we shook, and I paid him two thousand dollars. That's all he wanted. He signed his name on a piece of paper, and I signed mine. End of story."

All Pete could think of to say was, "Uh-huh."

Tick remembered that he was a host. "Want a beer?"

Pete's eyebrows shot up to his hairline. "You drink?"

"A beer now and then. I learned my lesson, I know my limitations. I don't crave it, if that's your next question. It's nice to see you, Pete. I mean that. I guess I wasn't very hospitable when you showed up. I didn't quite know what to do. I've been running from the past, then, suddenly, there you were, front and center."

Pete nodded. "No social life, eh?" Tick laughed. "I guess what you're asking me is, do I miss sex? He laughed again. "I go into Miami every so often. I bought a cigarette boat. I see a lady there at times. She's one of those people who knows everything there is to know about computers. It is what it is. So, do you want that beer or not?"

"Yeah. Yeah, Tick, I do. Having a beer with my brother . . . it doesn't get any better than that."

Tick looked at his twin for a long minute. "You're right, Pete. And yeah, you can stay, and yeah, we can build the room. It will be like old times."

Pete let his breath out in a loud *swoosh*. "I didn't bring anything with me. I'll have to go back to the Keys to get my stuff. You got some old shorts or old clothes. I'm sweating like a Trojan."

"I'll run you down there tomorrow," Tick said, tossing him a pair of khaki shorts and a threadbare T-shirt. "Bathroom is in there," he added, pointing to his left. "I'll get the beer, and we can sit on the porch. It sits two."

Pete guffawed. "I noticed."

And then it was like old times, two brothers who actually liked each other, talking about world affairs, women, work, and the weather as they shared a beer.

Then they were on the little porch, Pete on the swing, Tick on the chair, his feet propped up on the banister. "Tell me about the lady you're going to marry."

"She's great, Tick. You're going to like her. She's grounded. I know she works for the State Department, but that's all I know. She doesn't talk about what she does. I don't know if she just isn't comfortable talking about her job. She must be well paid, because she has enough money to invest in our business. Her name is Sadie. Her real name is Serafina. She's Italian. Mom would have loved her. We call and e-mail. But there are times where she's offline for weeks. She never gives me an explanation other than to say, 'It's job related.' I learned to accept it. I've known her for three years. She's thirty-seven."

"I'm happy for you, Pete. I mean that."

"Do you want to talk about *it?*"

"No. It's not time yet. Maybe that time will never come. What color were the roses you took to the cemetery?"

"Yellow, and some pink ones for Emma. Daisies for Ricky. The monument is nice. Andy took care of that. A mother angel and two little ones." His voice broke, and tears flooded his eyes. He swiped at them with the back of his hand.

Tick cringed. Everyone was doing what he should have done.

"Hey, let's take a walk on the beach. Show me how much of this glorious paradise is yours." Pete hopped off the swing and yanked at Tick's arm, jerking him to his feet. Then they were in each other's arms, hugging each other and pounding each other on the back.

"Sometimes life out and out sucks. It doesn't mean it won't ever get better, it just means you have to work harder at making it right. Hey, what about the bird? Do you have to put it in a cage?" Pete asked, hoping to drive the stricken look off his brother's face.

"When did you get so smart? The bird is a free spirit. He just moved in one day and decided to stay. I don't even remember what day or year it was. Suddenly, he was just there. We get along just fine, but he's a tad salty."

"When I was lying in a hospital doped to the eyeballs for my pain, I had a lot of time to reflect. A lot of time.

Hey, I can tell when it's going to rain within three hours. If my bar and grill goes belly-up, I can probably get a job as a weatherman. You always gotta look at the positive. You got a bed for me, or do I have to sleep on the floor?"

Tick doubled over laughing. "That is an accomplishment. Not to worry, I have one of those blow-up beds that come in a sack, and the only reason I have it is Andy keeps saying he's coming down here. Since he hates to fly, I don't see that happening anytime soon."

Tick looked up at the star-filled night in time to see a shooting star flash across the sky. He wondered if it was an omen of things to come. A light breeze ruffled his hair as he strode along. The ocean's warm water lapped at his feet and ankles. It was so soothing, he knew that if he ever left here, he would miss this nightly ritual.

A long time later, Pete said, "What the hell is *that?*" pointing to *that place.* "It looks like something you might see at the gates of hell."

Tick frowned. He hadn't realized they'd walked so far. A full moon rode high in the sky, outlining the enormous building that stood like a dark avenging something or other. "I have no idea. The village people refer to it as *that place* at the end of the beach. As far as I know, it's uninhabited. I never come this far on my nightly walks and usually I go the other way. I've never seen anyone around the place or on the beach, at least I haven't during the day. I thought I heard someone there crying once, though I'm sure it was an animal. At night I think someone comes and goes. I'm not sure why, never really cared to find out. It was being completed when I was just coming out of my drunken stupor. I never really cared enough to inquire and, besides, who would I ask? I can tell you one thing, it cost a bundle to build. That's for sure."

"Are you sure it's empty?"

"No, but I never see anyone. I hear voices late at night

sometimes if I'm out walking. No boats coming in. I've heard a motorboat. The coast guard rips by five or six times a day. Usually the same boat. I can tell by the sound of the engine. And when they start to approach that thing, they throttle back, so it's my guess they're keeping their eye on it. In order to get there on foot, you have to go past my place. I never see any lights, so I just assume it was built by some drug lord who got caught, and the place just sits there now because everyone is afraid to go near it. No one wants to get caught up in anything drug-related or whatever goes on there during the night."

"What do *you* think, Tick?"

"You know what, Pete, I try not to think about it. I have enough of my own problems without worrying about an empty building and the coast guard keeping an eye on it."

"Does anyone check on it?" Pete asked.

"You mean aside from the coast guard? Maybe the DEA, the DOJ, hell maybe ICE has an eye on that thing. Aside from all the drive-bys I've heard, no one else has been poking around, at least to my knowledge. Why are you so curious about an empty building?"

"You live just down the beach from it, Tick. Those drug people shoot first and ask questions later. I would think with your background, you'd be a bit more curious."

"You trying to spook me, Pete?"

"Hell, yes, I'm trying to spook you. You need to keep your wits about you. Jesus, there's not a soul to be seen except for you and me. If no one checks on you, you could be shot dead and no one would know but that damn parrot, and I doubt you've taught him how to call 911."

Tick turned around and started back the way they'd come. "I think we're both tired, and it's time to go to bed. If you like, we can check it out tomorrow in daylight."

"Yeah, let's do that. You're right: It's been a long day."